PAWN

KAREN LYNCH

For my sisters

Frances, Elizabeth, Peggy, Christina,
and Anne-Marie

ACKNOWLEDGMENTS

Thank you to my family and friends for your support and encouragement. Thank you to my readers for coming on this new journey with me. And thank you to Amber for being my sounding board and for helping to keep me sane when things get crazy.

1

"Sorry, kid. I wish I could help you, but you know how it is."

I gave the manager of the coffee shop a weary smile. "I appreciate you taking time to talk to me."

"I heard one of the hotels in Hoboken is looking for maids," she said as I turned to leave.

"Thanks." I didn't bother to ask which hotel because there was no way I was getting a job across the river. My parents would never allow it. I hadn't told them I was extending my job search into lower Manhattan. I figured I'd wait until I found a job before I brought it up. If Dad had his way, I wouldn't leave Brooklyn until I went to college.

I left the warm shop and stepped out into the brisk November air. Pulling up the collar of my coat, I leaned against the building while I contemplated my next move. It was late afternoon and I'd been out here all day, but I wasn't ready to give up yet.

I pushed off from the building, and a poster tacked to the wall of the newsstand next door caught my eye. It was an Agency recruitment poster, featuring a male and a female agent, both sharp and attractive in their crisp black suits. "THE FAE ENFORCEMENT AGENCY NEEDS YOU," it read in big bold letters.

Beneath the poster was a rack of celebrity gossip magazines. My eyes skimmed the covers, and I wasn't surprised to see the front-page story on every one of them was about the new Seelie prince and his upcoming introduction to society. There weren't any pictures of him, so no one knew yet what he looked like, but the entertainment world had been abuzz with speculation for months. The closer we got to his big debut, the more the excitement built.

I didn't get what all the fuss was about. Sure, we hadn't had a new Fae prince since before I was born, but it wasn't as if there weren't already a ton of royals for people to gawk at. What was one more? There were more important things to obsess over, such as the shortage of jobs.

"Come back here, you little freak!" yelled a man's voice.

I looked up the crowded sidewalk and caught sight of a tiny figure weaving between the pedestrians, with a large angry man in hot pursuit. The kid, who couldn't be more than eight or nine, was a dozen feet from me when I saw pointed ears protruding from his white-blond hair, and luminous green eyes. His face and clothes were filthy, and he looked scared out of his wits.

As he came abreast of me, my hand shot out and snagged his thin arm. In one move, I yanked him forward and shoved him behind me into the narrow gap between the newsstand and the coffee shop. I backed up, hiding his small body with mine and ignoring the tiny hands pushing ineffectually at my backside.

The man slowed to a stop, his mean face mottled and sweaty as he furiously scanned the area. When he didn't spot his quarry, he let loose a loud string of profanities that earned him looks of censure from the people around him.

Behind me, the elf boy whimpered, and I put a hand on his shoulder. "Shhh."

The man stomped away, halting at the intersection to look around again. I didn't know what beef he had with the elf, and I didn't care. There was no good reason to chase down a child like he was an animal.

Feeling eyes on me, I looked across the busy street and caught sight of a tall, dark-haired man watching me. He was in his early twenties, handsome and well-dressed in dark pants and a gray shirt that did nothing to hide his powerful physique. I was pretty sure he was a faerie, but he was too far away to say for certain.

He continued to watch me, probably wondering why I would go out of my way to protect an elf street urchin. I stared back in a silent challenge, while praying he didn't tip off the other guy.

I let out a breath when a silver SUV pulled up beside him and he looked away from me. He and a blond male, who also looked Fae, got into the back of the car without another glance in my direction.

"Hey! Let me go," wailed a muffled voice behind me, dragging my attention from the departing SUV. I glanced around to make sure the elf's pursuer had moved on, and then I stepped aside to free the little guy.

His pale face was pinched in indignation. "What did you do that for?"

"Do what? Save you from that brute?"

He drew up to his full height, which was all of four feet to my five-seven. "I don't need no saving. I can take care of myself."

"Yes, I can see that," I retorted, taking in his gaunt face and brittle eyes that had probably witnessed more than any child should ever have to see. Life on the street was rough, but it had to be twice as hard for children, especially faeries.

I opened my mouth to ask him if he was alone out here, but he bolted before I could speak. I watched him dart away through the passersby, who paid him no heed. It was a sad statement about our society that the sight of a homeless child didn't make people bat an eye.

No longer in the mood to wear a polite smile, I decided to call it a day and resume my job search tomorrow. I stuffed my hands into my coat pockets and headed to the subway station half a block away. Passing storefronts with festive holiday decorations in the windows, I was reminded I still hadn't started my Christmas shopping. Knowing Mom, she already had our presents wrapped and hidden in her closet. I smiled to myself. There was no one as organized as my mother.

It wasn't until I was at the subway turnstile and reaching into my back pocket for my MetroCard that I realized my day had taken another downward turn. I felt around in my pocket a few times to be sure, and then checked my other pockets, before my shoulders sagged. That little bugger had picked my pocket and made off with my card and the ten dollars I'd had there.

Way to go, Jesse. I patted my coat pocket, relieved to find my phone still there. At least he hadn't gotten that.

Heaving a sigh, I turned away from the booth. I cast one last longing glance at the train before I climbed the stairs to the street. I had a long walk ahead of me, and if I wanted to make it home before dark, I needed to get moving.

A bus passed me as I neared the bridge, and my lip curled at the video ad playing on the side of the bus. It was for one of those entertainment shows, promoting their upcoming exclusive interview with the as-yet-unseen Seelie prince. We had faerie kids living in the gutter and stealing change to survive, and the country was obsessed with some royal faerie who hadn't known a day of suffering in his pampered life.

Thirty years ago, when the Great Rift happened, my parents had been kids. A tear had formed between our world and the faerie realm, forcing the faeries to reveal their existence to us. At first, there had been widespread panic, but once people got over their shock, they embraced the Fae with open arms.

Well, some of the Fae. The beautiful, immortal Court faeries, who looked like genetically-perfect humans, were accepted immediately. Among them were the Royal Fae, who became instant celebrities and moved in the upper circles of society. Lower Fae races such as dwarves, elves, trolls, and many others, lived among us, but their lives weren't as easy as the upper Fae. They had to deal with bigotry and hardships that their beautiful upper class didn't need to worry about.

Mom and Dad loved to tell me stories about what life was like before the Great Rift. I found it hard to imagine a world where faeries and magic existed only in books. The old movies we watched that were made before the Rift didn't feel real to me.

What *did* feel real was the cold drizzle that started just as I reached the halfway point of the bridge. "Great," I muttered, increasing my pace. Not that it made any difference. By the time I reached the Brooklyn side, the drizzle had become a steady rain, and I could barely see through my glasses.

I was soaked through and chilled to the bone by the time our three-story brick building finally came into view. I spotted a tall, dark-haired figure getting out of a blue Jeep Cherokee farther down the street. My father looked up, and his smile became a frown when he took in my appearance. I didn't need a mirror to know I resembled a drowned rat.

"Don't ask," I grumbled when he met me at the steps. One thing I didn't do well was lie to my parents, and I really didn't want to tell Dad I'd gone to Manhattan *and* gotten my money stolen.

He chuckled and followed me into the building. "That good, huh?"

I glowered at him as Mrs. Russo came out of her apartment the moment we entered the small lobby.

"Patrick, the pipes in my bathroom are making that noise again," said the eighty-year-old widow, her messy updo at least five shades redder than my ginger curls.

Dad rubbed the back of his neck. "I'm sorry, Mrs. Russo. I'll look at them tomorrow if you can wait until then."

"That'll be fine." She smiled warmly at him, and then her gaze narrowed on me. "Child, are you trying to catch your death, running around like that?"

I was saved from answering by the arrival of a stocky, gray-skinned dwarf with scruffy black hair, who came through the front door behind us, pushing a bicycle. He stopped when he saw the three of us and lifted a hand in greeting. "Evening," he mumbled in a guttural voice.

"Hey, Gorn," I said as he propped his bike against the wall beneath the mailboxes and opened his box.

He grunted and flipped through his mail. With a curt nod in our direction, he grabbed his bike and wheeled it to his door, which was directly across from Mrs. Russo's.

If he were human, Gorn's behavior would seem standoffish and rude. But as far as dwarves went, he was downright sociable.

"Such a nice boy." Mrs. Russo gave an approving nod. "Never has much to say, but he always takes out my garbage for me." She patted my father's arm. "You're a good man, Patrick, for letting his kind live here."

Mrs. Russo spoke with the candor of someone who had lived a long life and felt they had earned the right to say whatever they wanted. But we knew she didn't have a racist bone in her body. When she said "his kind," she meant lower faeries, not just dwarves. Many landlords refused to rent apartments to lower faeries, and they were not required by law to do so. That meant most faeries, like Gorn and the quiet elf couple on the second floor, were forced to live in slums and pay exorbitant rents.

I was proud to say my parents were nothing like those landlords. Our building might be a little dated, and something usually needed repairs, but anyone was welcome as long as they weren't criminals. Not that the criminal element was stupid enough to come around here.

Dad and I stayed for another minute to chat with Mrs. Russo before we climbed the stairs to our apartment on the third floor. The unit across from us was home to Dad's best friend, Maurice, when he was in town. He traveled a lot for work, so his place was empty at least nine months out of the year. That meant we mostly had the floor to ourselves.

The mouthwatering smell of meat loaf greeted us as soon as I opened the apartment door. Mom's meat loaf and mashed potatoes was one of my favorite meals and the perfect way to make up for my crappy day.

Mom was in the kitchen when we entered the apartment. Her hair, the exact same shade as mine, was pulled back in a ponytail, and her glasses were in their usual spot on top of her head. If I wanted to know what I'd look like in twenty years, I only had to look at her. Except for the blue eyes I'd inherited from Dad, I was a carbon copy of Mom, right down to the dusting of freckles across my nose.

"Great timing. Dinner's almost ready," Mom said before her eyes landed on me. "Jesse, you're soaking wet."

I grimaced as I kicked off my Chucks. "I'm fine. Nothing a hot shower and your meat loaf won't fix."

She laughed. "Call your brother when you're done."

My wet socks left a trail behind me as I walked to my bedroom, which overlooked the street I'd lived on my entire life. My room was small, but I made the most of the space. The walls were a cream color, and my twin bed was covered in a pretty patchwork quilt that brightened up the room. On one side of the window was my desk, and on the other side was a stuffed chair that had seen better days. Next to the chair, my old acoustic guitar was propped against the wall.

Grabbing a change of clothes, I went down the short hallway to the bathroom. Three people sharing one bathroom wasn't the most convenient arrangement, but we made it work. And my parents were great about giving me privacy.

As chilled as I was, I would have loved a prolonged stay under the hot water, but hunger had me rushing through my shower. I left my room twenty minutes later, dressed in a long-sleeved T-shirt and warm fleece pants.

In the living room, I went over to the small tree house in one corner of the room. A narrow ladder ran from the floor to the house, which was nearly hidden behind the flowering vines that covered it.

"Finch, it's dinnertime," I said to the tree house.

The vines moved, and a round, blue face framed by bright blue hair appeared. Large lilac eyes blinked at me, and a devious smile was the only warning I got before he leaped at me.

"Gah!" I yelled, even though I should have expected the attack. I tripped over my feet and fell backward onto the couch, making sure not to crush the little monster in the fall. My reward? An evil, twelve-inch-tall sprite tickling the crap out of me until I begged for mercy.

"Finch, stop torturing your sister," Dad called from the dining room. "Mm-mmm these fresh blackberries sure are tasty."

Finch was off me and out of the room before I could blink.

Grinning, I got to my feet. I followed him into the dining room where he was already sitting on the table beside his plate, stuffing a fat blackberry into his tiny mouth. Juice dribbled down his chin, but he was blissfully unaware as he devoured his favorite food.

"How did it go today?" Mom asked Dad as he helped her set the meat loaf and potatoes in the center of the table.

"Phil and I caught that banshee he's been after, so we'll get half the bounty for that one."

"That's great!" She sat across from me, looking pleased. "I spoke to Levi earlier, and he said he might have another level Four for us this week. He'll know in a day or two."

"November might be our best month this year," Dad said with a smile.

I dug into my food while my parents talked shop. Most kids listened to their parents discuss their office jobs or something else equally mundane at dinner. I'd grown up hearing about bounty hunting.

The Fae presence in our world hadn't come without complications. Suddenly introducing faeries and magic into the human realm caused a whole slew of problems. Crime increased, and our police force was not equipped to handle the nonhuman cases. The Fae Enforcement Agency was established to police and protect the Fae, and to regulate the use of magic. But even the Agency couldn't keep up with it all.

That's where my parents came in.

The Agency contracted out the overflow of their cases to bond agents, who, in turn, gave the jobs to bounty hunters. I didn't know all the ins and outs of the business, but I'd heard enough from my parents to know that bounties were classified by threat level, and the higher the threat, the bigger the payout. There were five levels that I was aware of, and a level Four job carried a nice fat bounty.

Mom and Dad were two of the best hunters on the eastern seaboard, and widely respected by their peers. That was why Levi, one of the bond agents they worked for, always gave them a heads up when a choice job was coming down the wire. Bounty hunting was a competitive business, and everyone wanted the top jobs.

Our neighbor, Maurice, was also in the business. He'd started out working with my parents, but now he traveled all over the country, taking on the really big jobs. Dad always said if there was someone better than Maurice Begnaud at bounty hunting, he had never heard of them.

"Any luck today, Jesse?" Mom asked.

Yeah, bad luck. "I think I have better odds of marrying a Fae prince than finding another job in this city."

She chuckled. "You'll find something. Nancy gave you a great reference."

Nancy owned the coffee shop where I'd worked part-time for the last two years. After I'd graduated in May, I'd gone full-time at the Magic Bean, the plan being to take every shift I could and bank all my earnings for college. It had been going well until a freak drought wiped out entire coffee bean crops in South America.

Overnight, the price of coffee beans skyrocketed, and most people could no longer pay for their daily cup of joe. Smaller coffee shops, like the Magic Bean, hung on as long as they could before they were forced to close their doors. Even some of the chain stores were struggling now that only people with money – like the patrons at that Manhattan coffee shop – could afford to drink coffee.

I toyed with my food. "Unfortunately, there are too many people like me with good references."

"The economy will turn around," Dad said cheerily, even though we both knew that wasn't going to happen anytime soon with the country in its second year of a recession. The only business booming these days was bounty hunting.

"I guess I could always join the family business," I joked, earning disapproving looks from both of my parents.

Dad laid down his fork. "As proud as I would be to have you working with us, you are going to college. You still want that, don't you?"

"More than anything."

"Good." He nodded and picked up his fork again to dig into his mashed potatoes.

Something cold touched the back of my hand, and I looked down to see Finch standing beside my plate, holding out a blackberry. His pretty eyes were sad, like they always got when he saw I was down.

"Thanks." I took the offered blackberry and popped it into my mouth. "You're the best brother a girl could ask for. You know that?"

His face lit up, and he scampered back to his own plate. I couldn't help but smile as I watched him attack a piece of mango. All it took to make Finch happy was to see his family happy. That and lots and lots of fruit.

Realizing my parents had gone quiet, I glanced up to see sadness flit across Mom's face before she hid it behind a smile. As I replayed my words to Finch in my head, I berated myself for my thoughtlessness.

Finch must have seen it, too, because he walked over to bring her one of his precious blackberries. She smiled and leaned down to let him put it in her mouth. Sprite children liked to feed their parents as a sign of affection, and Mom loved it when he did it. He was close to both of our parents, but there'd always been a special bond between him and Mom.

Her phone rang in the kitchen, and she jumped up to answer it. She was back a minute later, wearing a serious expression I knew well. It was her work face.

"That was Tennin," she said to Dad. "He's in town, but he's leaving again tomorrow. If we want to talk to him, we need to go now."

Dad was already standing by the time she finished speaking. The two of them looked at me, and I waved them off.

"Go on. I'll clean up."

I finished my dinner while they hurriedly changed into work clothes, which consisted of combat boots and dark jeans and T-shirts. Though I couldn't see weapons, I was sure they both carried them. My parents never went anywhere unprepared.

"We shouldn't be too late," Mom told me as she tucked her phone into her back pocket.

"Be back by curfew, or you're both grounded."

Finch whistled in agreement and wagged a finger at them.

Mom laughed, and Dad winked at us as they rushed out the door.

I put the leftovers in the fridge and made short work of the dishes. Leaving Finch to finish his meal, I went to my room and spent the next hour scouring the classifieds and job sites. It was a depressing task, but one I did every night. I *was* going to college, even if it took me years to save enough to get there.

I looked at the envelope bearing the official seal for Cornell University that was pinned to the bulletin board above my desk. Beneath that envelope was one from Stanford and another from Harvard.

I had been over the moon when I got acceptance letters from three of my top picks, until I saw how much it would cost. Tuition had almost doubled in the last decade and colleges didn't give full-ride scholarships anymore unless you were an athlete. Mom and Dad had some money put away for college, but it wasn't enough to pay for tuition, books, and years of living expenses. I'd thought I could work my way through college, but I would need a full-time job with great pay just to cover tuition.

Last spring, the Agency had tried to recruit me into their intelligence program after graduation. It was normal for them to recruit from the top five percentile of high school graduates, and I'd been in the top one percent. In addition to training, the program included a free college education at the school of your choice, as long as the degree was in an area that could be utilized by the Agency. The lure of a free college education was strong, but I'd also be obligated to work for the Agency for five years afterward.

My phone vibrated on the desk, and I read the text from my best friend, Violet. **How goes the job hunt?**

Guess, I wrote back.

A sad emoji appeared. **Mom or Dad would give you a job.**

Violet's father owned a big accounting firm, and her mother was a high-powered defense attorney. Even if one of their firms had an open position, it would be nothing that an out of work barista with a high school diploma was qualified for. If Violet asked them, they might create an intern position for me, but that felt too much like charity. I wasn't at that point yet.

Ask me again in a few weeks, I said.

Will do.

The twang of a guitar string interrupted my texting. I looked over my shoulder at Finch, who stood beside my guitar, watching me hopefully.

"Maybe later."

He plucked another string with a little more force, and I knew he wasn't going to leave until he got what he'd come for.

Shooting him a playful scowl, I picked up the guitar and went to sit on the bed. "I just learned a new song. You want to hear?"

Finch signed, *Annie's Song.*

I scrunched up my nose. "Aren't you sick of that one yet?"

He shook his head and climbed up to sit on my pillow.

"You're such a dork." I started to play. Ever since Mom had come home with an old *John Denver* album last year, Finch had been obsessed with that one song. It was a good guitar song, so I'd learned to play it for him, but now he wanted to hear it all the time.

Sing, he signed.

I shot him the stink eye and started over, singing the words I knew by heart. My voice was passable, but Finch fell into a trancelike state every time I sang to him. It didn't happen when Mom or Dad sang, and I'd read that something like one in a million people could entrance lower faeries with song. I'd tried it once on Gorn, and he'd looked at me like I was nuts. That was when I'd learned it didn't work on all faeries.

I'd used singing against Finch a few times to get my own way when we were younger – until Mom and Dad found out and grounded me for a whole month. I'd also endured a lecture about taking advantage of my brother, who had already suffered too much in his young life.

When I was nine, my parents rescued Finch after they busted a ring of traffickers. Because of their size and exotic beauty, sprites were often illegally sold as pets on the black market. Finch's parents had been sold off already, leaving the one-year-old sprite orphaned and traumatized. The traffickers had clipped his gossamer wings to prevent him from flying away, and there was no way he would survive on his own or be accepted by other sprites in Faerie. So, Mom and Dad brought him home to live with us.

In the beginning, Finch was so terrified and grief-stricken he wouldn't eat or let anyone near him. For the first week, we'd all feared he would die. But with time and a lot of TLC, he recovered and warmed up to us. Sprites lived in trees in Faerie, so Dad built him his own tree house in our living room, complete with a ladder because Finch could no longer fly.

Sprites couldn't vocalize human words, so they were often thought to be of lesser intelligence. But I knew from firsthand experience that they were extremely smart. Finch understood our language just fine, and it had been easy for him to learn sign language. He'd actually picked it up faster than we had. Now, he communicated with us using ASL and a series of whistles. He might not be human, but he was as much a part of this family as any of us.

I played five more songs before I laid down the guitar, and we went to the living room to watch a movie. He picked out the one he wanted, and we lay on the couch together.

I didn't remember falling asleep. Hours later, I sat upright on the couch, looking around in confusion. A familiar song filled the room, and I reached for my phone, which was on the coffee table. It was Mom's ringtone – *Bad to the Bone* – and I blearily wondered why on earth she was calling me at this ungodly hour.

"Hello?" I rasped.

Instead of a reply, I got an earful of garbled sounds. I thought I could hear voices in the background, but they were too indistinct to make out the words.

"Mom?" I said, but there was no response.

I yawned and rubbed my eyes. "You have to stop butt dialing me. This is bordering on child abuse."

I pressed the button to end the call at the same time that a muffled scream came from the phone. My fingers froze on the screen.

What the hell was that?

My first reaction was to call her back, but I stopped myself before I hit the button. Bounty hunting could be messy and dangerous. Mom had probably dialed me by accident in the middle of a capture, and calling her would only distract her, especially if she saw it was me.

They're fine, I told myself. We'd have a good laugh about this tomorrow.

I turned off the lights and made my way to bed. Rolling onto my side, I closed my eyes and willed my body to relax, despite the unease that had stolen over me. Eventually, my mind calmed, and I slipped back into sleep.

2

They didn't come home.

I'd woken up at seven, expecting Mom and Dad to be here, but the apartment was quiet and their bed hadn't been slept in. I'd showered, made breakfast for Finch and me, and cleaned up. Still, there was no sign of our parents.

It wasn't unusual for them to stay out overnight on a job, but they always called to let me know they wouldn't be home. Always. No exception.

The clock on the mantle chimed noon. I should have heard from them by now.

I tried Dad's phone first, then Mom's, and both went straight to voice mail. I swallowed dryly. There was no one more capable of taking care of themselves than my parents. Maybe I was overreacting, but I couldn't wait any longer.

My parents' office was nothing more than a small bedroom that served as a work space and a storage area for all the weapons and tools of their trade. On one side of the room was the desk, bookcase, and filing cabinets, everything neat and in its place. This was Mom's domain. She managed all the finances and administrative side of the business. Dad was the tactical and information expert, and he managed everything in those areas. He knew more about weapons, combat, and the Fae than anyone else I knew.

I went to the desk and sat in the chair. Ignoring the computer, I opened the top drawer and pulled out the address book Mom kept all their contacts in. She had them on the computer, but she often said you should never put all your trust in technology that could fail on you at any time.

She was right. A few years back, a hobgoblin went on a rampage in Manhattan, and his magic took out every computer in a city block before a group of hunters, led by my parents, caught him. We had iron grounding rods on the roof to protect our building against that, but Mom wasn't taking any chances.

Finch jumped up onto the desk, startling me. I almost scolded him until I saw the worry in his eyes. He whistled and signed, *Mom and Dad?*

"They'll be home soon," I told him, wishing I knew that were true. "I'm just going to call around to some of their friends."

By *friends*, I meant their fellow bounty hunters in the area. Most hunters worked in pairs, but they sometimes teamed up to help each other out on difficult jobs. And they watched each other's backs. Thankfully, Mom had them all clearly marked in her address book.

I spent the next hour calling every one of Mom's contacts. I couldn't reach a few of them, but no one I spoke to had seen either of my parents in the last two days, except for Phil Griffin. He was the one Dad had helped on that banshee job yesterday. Phil didn't sound too worried when I told him they hadn't come home. I had to bite back a retort when he said I shouldn't concern myself with these matters and that my parents knew what they were doing.

After I'd exhausted all their local contacts, I dialed Maurice's number. Last I'd heard, he was somewhere in the Everglades on a big job, but he would want me to call him. I wasn't surprised when I got his voice mail, and I left him a message detailing everything that had happened since yesterday. He'd call me back as soon as he got my message, whenever that was.

The last person I called was Levi Solomon. I didn't know what job Mom and Dad were working on, but it had to be one of Levi's. If anyone knew where my parents were, it was their bond agent.

Feeling hopeful, I dialed his number.

"Hello?" rumbled a gravelly voice that sounded like its owner smoked two packs of cigarettes a day.

"Hi, Mr. Solomon," I replied, all businesslike. "I'm Jesse James. Patrick and Caroline James are my parents."

That's right. My name is Jesse James. I could thank my dad and his obsession with old westerns for that.

There was a short pause before Levi Solomon cautiously asked, "What can I do for you?"

KAREN LYNCH

I cleared my throat. "Well, um...I was wondering if you know where my parents are. They went out on a job last night and didn't come home."

"Sometimes bounty hunters stay out all night," he said with a note of impatience. "It's part of the job."

"Yes, but they always let me know if they won't be home." Dread coiled in my stomach as I told him about the strange call I'd gotten from Mom last night.

"They were probably making a capture," he replied casually.

"If you could tell me what job they were –"

"Sorry, kid. I can't discuss Agency jobs with just anyone."

I gripped the phone tighter. "But they're my parents, and they're missing."

He coughed loudly and wheezed. "Listen. I have no idea if you are who you say you are. And a person has to be gone longer than a few hours to be declared missing. If you are Patrick and Caroline's kid, you should know they can take care of themselves. I'm sure they'll turn up soon."

"But –"

The line went dead.

I stared at the phone in disbelief. Did he really just hang up on me?

Finch waved a hand to get my attention. *They never stay out this long,* he signed fearfully.

My chest squeezed. I picked him up and gently hugged him to comfort me as much as him. "Don't worry. I'll find them."

I chewed my lip and pondered what to do next. My fingers automatically went to the braided black leather bracelet Mom had given me when I was twelve. I rarely removed it, and I took comfort in its familiar texture.

I picked up the address book. The longer I stared at Levi Solomon's name, the more my jaw tightened until it hurt. He was my only lead to finding Mom and Dad, and I'd be damned if he was going to brush me off that easily. If he wanted proof I was Patrick and Caroline James's daughter, I'd give it to him.

Setting Finch on the desk, I pushed back the chair and stood. In my room, I changed into jeans and a thermal top and pulled on a coat. I stuffed my phone, a credit card, and some cash into my coat pocket and picked up my keys.

Finch was waiting for me in the living room. *Where are you going?* he signed.

"To talk to that bond agent. I'll be home as soon as I can."

Waving goodbye to Finch, I left the apartment and locked the door behind me. I hated to leave him alone when he was worried about Mom and Dad, but I wasn't going to get any answers sitting at home. All that would do was drive me crazy.

It took me over an hour to reach the four-story brick building in Queens that housed Levi Solomon's agency. The Plaza, as it was called, was home to over half a dozen bond agencies, and it was like walking into a bounty hunter convention when I entered the main lobby. Four armed hunters conversed off to my left, while five others talked to my right. Two more waited by the elevator with a bound ogre supported between them. The yellow-skinned ogre growled something around the gag in his mouth, and then he tried to butt one of the hunters with his bald head.

The elevator dinged, and the doors opened. I watched the three get on and decided I'd better wait for the next one. Ogres were unpleasant on a good day. No way I was getting in a little metal box with that one.

I felt eyes on me as I waited, and I met the curious stares of several hunters. I didn't know any of them, but I was aware of how out of place I was here. Bounty hunters were like a club that everyone knew about, but only members got to see what went on inside. Except for Agency operatives, outsiders didn't come to their place of work.

"You lost, kid?" a woman called a second before the elevator doors opened.

"Nope." I stepped inside, and the doors closed behind me.

I got off on the fourth floor and immediately spotted a door to my right with *The Solomon Agency* painted on it. The door was unlocked, and a bell tinkled when I entered.

I wasn't sure what I had been expecting a bond agency to look like, but it wasn't this one-room windowless office that reeked of stale cigarette smoke. There was a metal desk in the corner and a row of tall filing cabinets along one wall. The other walls were covered with wanted posters featuring just about every race of faerie you could think of – except Court Fae, of course. It was extremely rare that a bounty was issued for one of the Fae ruling class.

At the back of the room was a door I hadn't noticed when I came in. I had no idea if it led to a bathroom or to another office. There was no one sitting at the desk, and I stood uncertainly for a minute before I took a seat on one of the rickety visitor chairs. Levi must have stepped out briefly, or he wouldn't have left the door unlocked. I would just wait here for him to return.

Five minutes passed before the door at the back of the office opened, and a very overweight man came out. His dark hair was peppered with gray, and he had so many chins I couldn't see his neck. Wheezing, he lumbered over to his desk, without looking in my direction, and eased his body down onto his chair. Metal groaned ominously, and I held my breath as I waited for the chair to give out under his weight. Miraculously, it held, and I couldn't help but wonder if he was using some kind of Fae spell to support it.

It wasn't until the man was seated that he finally noticed me. Surprise flitted across his face, but it was quickly replaced by suspicion. His hand went under the desk, no doubt to grip a weapon he kept there. With that in mind, I decided it would be prudent to stay seated and not make any sudden moves.

"Mr. Solomon, my name is Jesse James," I said before he could speak. "I spoke to you earlier on the phone."

It took a few seconds before I saw recognition dawn on his face. No one who knew my mother could miss my resemblance to her.

His posture relaxed a bit, but he kept his hand under the desk. What did he think I was going to do? "Miss James, you're a long way from home, and I'm sure your parents would not be pleased to find you here."

I had to bite back a snarky reply. If he'd been helpful when I called him, I wouldn't have had to come here to see him in person.

I pasted on a smile instead. "You told me you had no way of knowing I was who I claimed to be. I came here to give you proof of my identity and to ask for your help."

He pursed his lips. "I'm sorry you came all the way down here, but like I told you on the phone, your parents are more than capable of taking care of themselves. They haven't even been gone twenty-four hours."

"And I told you they wouldn't stay out this long without calling me." My stomach clenched painfully. "Something's wrong."

"You don't know that." He pulled his hand from beneath the desk and waved it dismissively.

I fought to keep my anger in check, knowing it wouldn't help me. "Can you at least tell me what job they're working on?"

"Your parents normally have three or four active cases, and they could have been working on any one of them last night." He put up a hand. "Don't ask me what those jobs are because we don't discuss Agency business with outsiders."

"Outsiders?" I shot to my feet. "I'm their daughter, not some total stranger. I can call up a dozen bounty hunters who will vouch for me."

Levi's expression changed to one of annoyance as he rested his thick forearms on the desk. "It wouldn't matter if the Pope himself came in here on your behalf. If you aren't in the business, no one is going to tell you anything. That's just the way it is. You ask anyone in this building and they'll tell you the same thing."

I paced in front of his desk. "So, that's it? People you've worked with for years disappear, and you won't do anything?"

"Listen here, kid. I've been doing this since before you were born, and I think I know a bit more about this business than you." His multiple chins wobbled. "I'm not going to raise alarms for two of the top bounty hunters in the state just because they forgot to call home. If we don't hear from them in another thirty-six hours, I'll report them missing to the Agency and they will send someone to investigate."

"That's all you'll do?" Frustration and fear welled inside me. Mom and Dad could be hurt and unable to call for help, and no one would even start to look for them for another day and a half.

He tapped a finger impatiently on the desk. "That's all I can do. We have rules I have to follow. Go home, and let us take care of things here. This is no place for a young girl like you."

My anger flared again. "I'm eighteen, old enough to be a bounty hunter."

"That may be, but you're not one, which means you have no business here."

I stalked to the door and threw it open. "As long as my parents are missing, this is my business. I'll be back in thirty-six hours, Mr. Solomon."

He grumbled something that turned into a hacking smoker's cough. I'd be lucky if the guy didn't keel over before he had a chance to send someone to look for Mom and Dad.

In the elevator, I tapped my foot impatiently as I waited for the car to reach the first floor. I couldn't believe I had wasted half my afternoon on coming to see a man who couldn't care less about my parents. I should have known better after he'd hung up on me. The jerk.

The elevator doors slid open, and I hurried out, almost running into the two sandy-haired men waiting to get on. I jumped back and let out a silent breath of relief when I recognized Bruce Fowler. He and Dad had gone to high school together, and like most of my parents' friends, he was a bounty hunter. He was a nice man, and his family lived only two streets over from us.

"Jesse!" exclaimed the younger man with Bruce.

I suppressed a groan when my eyes met the brown ones of Bruce's son, Trey. You might think that with our parents being friends, Trey and I would be good friends, too. You would be wrong.

Two years older than me, Trey had been one of those cocky, good-looking boys who loved being the center of attention and having a cute girl on his arm. That would have been fine if he hadn't spent his time between hookups trying to get into my pants. Like that would *ever* happen. I knew he'd only wanted me because I had been one of the few girls from school he couldn't have.

He'd only gotten more full of himself since he'd started bounty hunting with his father last year. You'd think he was some kind of superhero with the way he bragged about his job. I knew better.

"Hi," I said tightly, although the smile I gave Bruce was genuine.

Bruce's brows drew together in concern. "Jesse, what are you doing here? Are you with your parents?"

I shook my head and swallowed past the lump that suddenly formed in my throat. "I don't know where Mom and Dad are. They went out last night and never came home." I told him about the weird call from my mother and that Levi had refused to help me find them.

Trey puffed out his chest. "It's an Agency policy to wait two days. There are a lot of rules we bounty hunters have to live by."

If I hadn't been so worried about my parents, I would have rolled my eyes. Trey was harmless, but he could be a pompous idiot at times.

"I'll talk to Levi and see what I can do. But the Plaza is no place for you. Go on home, and I'll call you if I hear anything." Bruce laid a comforting hand on my shoulder. "I'm sure your parents will be home soon."

"Thanks." I didn't want to go home and sit around waiting to hear something, but I wasn't going to learn anything else here. And if Bruce said he'd try to help, I knew he would. I just hoped he had more luck getting information out of Levi than I had.

I said goodbye and exited the building, having to step to one side at the door to allow three hunters to enter, carrying a shackled, thrashing female between them. The woman's black hair was wild and matted, and her dress was little more than rags. A muzzle covering the lower half of her face did not completely mute her screeching, and my ears ached from the sound. It was my first time seeing a banshee up close, and I hoped I never ran into one that wasn't gagged.

Outside the building, I descended the steps to the street and paused while I checked the subway schedule on my phone. I silently cursed my stupidity when I saw Trey had followed me.

"Come on. I'll give you a lift home," he said with a saccharine smile. "You don't need to be riding the subway alone."

My hackles went up at his insinuation that I couldn't take care of myself. "I've taken the subway plenty of times. I think I can handle it."

He was a little taken aback by my tone but quickly recovered and tried another tactic. "Your father would want to know someone was watching out for you while he's gone. Dad agrees with me that you shouldn't be all alone in the apartment either. I'd be happy to sleep on your couch until your parents come home."

I bet you would. "Thanks, but that won't be necessary."

"I'm serious, Jesse," he pressed. "This city can be a dangerous place for a girl on her –"

"Do not finish that sentence, Trey Fowler, if you value your life." I planted a hand against his chest and shoved him backward. "This girl is more than capable of taking care of herself, thank you very much. And if you don't mind, I'll be leaving now to catch my train."

I spun away and stomped off down the street toward the subway station. The gall of him to suggest I was helpless because I was a female. I should go back there and kick his ass, just to show him how well I could defend myself. I wasn't as good a fighter as either of my parents, but thanks to Dad's rigorous self-defense training, I could hold my own.

My temper had cooled by the time I reached the station. I paid my fare, thinking I should probably buy a MetroCard if I was going to be taking the subway a lot. My old job had been within walking distance of home, so I hadn't needed to take the subway to work.

I was waiting for my train when I got the eerie sensation of being watched. My gaze scanned the station and landed on a tall man in a long, dark coat leaning against one of the support columns about twenty feet away. A hood shadowed all but his lower face, so the only thing I could make out was that he was white. But I could feel his eyes on me. I stared back, hoping to make him look away, but his gaze stayed locked on me.

A cold tingle ran across the back of my neck as my creep alarm went off. I edged closer to the other people waiting for the train and out of his sight. When the train arrived, I got on with everyone else and made sure I sat with a group of passengers.

Daring a glance out the window as the train departed the station, I nearly sagged in relief when I saw the man standing in the same spot. He looked up when my car passed him, and all it took was one glimpse of his beautiful face to know he was a faerie. Our eyes met for the briefest moment, and the cold scrutiny on his face sent a shiver through me. It was a good ten minutes until I felt warm again.

By the time I got home, I had convinced myself that I'd overreacted to a stranger's harmless stare. I was under a lot of stress today, and it was making me imagine things.

Finch was standing on the back of the couch waiting for me when I opened the door. The relief on his small face made guilt prick me. They were his parents, too, and he'd been here alone for hours with no idea of when I'd come home.

"Hey." I tossed my coat over the back of a chair and faced him with my hands on my hips. "What? No dinner?"

I was rewarded when he made a face. Finch hated cooked food, especially any kind of meat. If it wasn't fresh fruit or vegetables, he refused to touch it.

Mom and Dad? he signed, watching me closely.

I let out a long breath. "Sorry, buddy. No one will do anything until they've been missing for two days. But don't you worry. I'm going to find them, with or without anyone's help."

How?

"I don't know yet. I'll think better after I get some food in me."

I entered the kitchen and took last night's leftovers from the fridge. Putting a large portion of meat loaf and mashed potatoes on a plate, I stuck it in the microwave to heat while I made up a small fruit plate for Finch.

When both of our meals were ready, I carried our plates over and laid them on the coffee table. Mom didn't like us eating in the living room, but there was no way I could sit at the table and look at her and Dad's empty chairs.

After I'd washed up our plates, I headed for the only place that could give me a clue to my parents' whereabouts. Mom was meticulous about record keeping. If there was anything to find, it would be on her computer or somewhere in her desk.

Luckily, Mom had given me her password ages ago. "Just in case," she'd said. At the time, I couldn't imagine ever having a reason to go into their work computer. I think, at the back of my mind, I'd always known there was a chance one of them could get hurt or worse on a job. But I had never let myself consider the possibility of something happening to both of them, and at the same time.

I logged in and thanked Mom for her amazing organizational skills when I easily located the main folder for the business. Inside was a directory of subfolders, all titled by year, and in the folder for the current year, I found a spreadsheet containing every job my parents had worked on since January. Each job was color coded by level, with links to other tabs that contained more detailed notes.

I scrolled through the spreadsheet, amazed by how many jobs my parents had done this year. And not level One jobs either. All of these were Threes and Fours.

All bounties were categorized by threat level, according to Agency guidelines. Level One was the easiest, and the bounty for that one was a thousand dollars. Level Two carried a bounty of two thousand. Level Three jumped up a bit with a bounty of five thousand. A level Four was a whopping ten thousand dollars. There was a level Five, but I had no idea what the bounty was for that one. If my parents had ever brought in a level Five, they hadn't told me about it.

Experienced bounty hunters competed for the Threes and Fours because they were the most lucrative. Beginners and junior hunters took most of the Ones and Twos until they were ready to move up to the next level.

According to the spreadsheet, Mom and Dad had two open jobs, a level Three and a level Four. The Three was for a goblin that had been burglarizing houses in several Brooklyn neighborhoods for the last month. The Four was for a dealer peddling a highly addictive drug called goren.

Goren was made from a Fae plant of the same name that had been banned in our realm. Faeries ate it as a garnish on their food, and it was harmless to them. For humans, it created a state of intense euphoria. It didn't harm them physically, but once they tried it, all they cared about was getting more of it. They would sell everything they had just to get more of the drug.

"Aha!" I almost shouted when I spotted a name I'd heard before in the contact list for the second job. Tennin. Mom had mentioned him yesterday at dinner. I rubbed my chin as I tried to remember what she'd said. Tennin was in town for a day, and they had to talk to him before he left again. *He* was the one they'd gone to see last night.

According to Mom's notes, Tennin was a photographer, and she'd flagged him as a trusted confidential informant. Wondering what was so special about a photographer, I did an internet search for photographers named Tennin in New York City. It didn't take long to find out that he was a paparazzo, and a damn good one, if his website was any indication.

I sat back in the chair and stared at the monitor as I contemplated what to do with this new information. I could call Bruce and Levi and ask them to talk to Tennin, but there was no guarantee either man would take me seriously and actually reach out to the photographer. Or that Tennin would confide in them about why my parents had gone to see him. He was listed as a confidential informant, so he might not take too kindly to being outed to others.

And then there was the fact that Mom had said Tennin was only in town for a day. I only had today to talk to him before he was gone again, for God knew how long.

I was standing before I realized I'd made a decision. I would go talk to Tennin myself. If I explained the situation, he might open up to me because of who I was. It was worth a try, and it was all I had right now.

Taking a piece of paper, I jotted down Tennin's address and logged off the computer. I called goodbye to Finch, and I was about to leave the apartment when a set of car keys hanging beside the door caught my eye. Dad's keys. I hadn't noticed them earlier, but their presence meant Mom and Dad had taken her car last night instead of his Jeep. They always used the SUV when they expected to do a capture, which told me they hadn't planned on anything big going down last night.

I hesitated only a second before I grabbed the keys from their hook. Then I hurried from the apartment for the second time that day.

3

I stared at the tall, blond male who opened the door of the Williamsburg apartment. My gaze took in his stunning blue eyes, full mouth, and perfectly symmetrical face, and I knew immediately that Tennin wasn't human. No human gene pool or plastic surgeon could produce such flawless beauty. He certainly looked nothing like those scruffy, unkempt paparazzi I'd seen glimpses of on TV.

"Hello, gorgeous," he drawled appreciatively as he looked me up and down. "When you buzzed up and said who you were, I was dubious. I guess I don't need to see your ID to confirm your identity. Has anyone ever told you that you could be a clone of your mother?"

"I might have heard that before."

Tennin smiled and waved me inside his sparsely furnished apartment. In the living room, there was a white leather couch with a matching chair and some small glass tables. The walls were mostly bare, and the place hardly looked lived in. It was a nice apartment, but a lot less grand than I would have expected for the home of a Court faerie. Not that I'd ever been in one of their homes before, but I'd imagined they lived more luxuriously than this.

"What brings you to my home, Miss James? I'm delighted to have such alluring company, but I am reasonably certain your parents don't know you are here since Patrick isn't beating down my door."

I turned to face the faerie. "I'm here because my parents came to see you last night, and now, they're missing."

The playful smile fell from his face. "Missing?"

"They never came home, and I haven't heard from them. And before you say something about them being able to take care of themselves, I know that. But they would never be gone this long without calling me." My words came out sounding defensive, so I softened my tone. "I just want to know what you told them, and if you know where they might have gone when they left here."

He pressed his lips together, his gaze flitting impatiently from me to a door off of the living room. "You caught me in the middle of something very important. Not that your parents aren't important," he rushed to add. "But this is time-sensitive. I need to take care of it and then we'll talk."

"Okay." What else could I say? I needed his help.

I followed him into an office and stopped short at the sight of the room that was such a contrast to the rest of the apartment. Where the living room looked like it was barely used, the office was bursting with color and personality. Magazine covers and celebrity photographs covered almost every inch of wall space, and the large bookcase was full of camera equipment instead of books. The L-shaped desk was cluttered with more cameras and piles of photos, along with a bowl of questionable food I suspected was Fae in origin.

Tennin sat at the desk in front of two large monitors and typed something on his keyboard. Since there were no other chairs in the room, I stood near the door, waiting for him to speak. He surprised me by calling me over beside him so I could see what was on his monitors. On one was an open folder of digital photos, and on the other was photo editing software.

"I need to get these uploaded ASAP," he said as he selected a few dozen pictures and opened them in the software. He clicked around too quickly for me to follow him and ran some kind of batch program. In seconds, all the pictures had a watermark of his name across the faces. Opening a browser, he uploaded the edited pictures to a gallery on his website. The whole process took less than five minutes.

"How do you sell the pictures?" I asked, fascinated by this glimpse into his work.

He started to work on another group of photos. "Most I sell to agencies, who sell them to magazines. The hotter ones I auction from my website. When I upload new pictures, an alert is sent out to interested parties, and they can log in to bid on the pictures they want." He tapped the monitor. "This lot is going to make me a fortune."

"Who is he?" I leaned in for a closer look. Most of the pictures were of a blond faerie, probably royal if the pictures were as hot as Tennin said. Only royal Fae got people really excited these days.

Tennin smiled smugly. "That is Prince Rhys."

"Who?" I furrowed my brow, trying to place the name. "Oh, the new prince, right?"

He spun in his chair to narrow his eyes at me. "Are you serious?"

I shrugged. "I'm not really into celebrity stuff, but I do know he's a big deal."

"A big deal?" he sputtered, shaking his head. "He's *only* the crown prince of Seelie, whose debut the *entire* world has been going crazy about. Well, everyone but you apparently."

"I know this will come as a shock to you, but some of us have lives that don't revolve around your royalty." I pointed at the monitor. "If no one has seen the prince, how did you get pictures of him?"

Tennin smiled deviously. "I have my ways. I found out he was going to be at the Ralston yesterday for a secret exclusive interview that will be aired with his official intro into society. People will pay seven figures for these photos of him."

"That's obscene." Seven figures for pictures of some faerie prince whose face would be everywhere in a few weeks anyway?

"I know." Tennin rubbed his hands together. "It's all about supply and demand. I have a product everyone wants, and they are willing to pay big for it."

I narrowed my eyes at him. "Wait. Aren't you Court faeries already rich? Why do you do this?"

"Because I'm exceptionally good at it and I enjoy the game."

I shook my head at his total lack of humility and studied the prince's face again. "Why are you letting me see the pictures? Aren't you afraid I'll tell someone about the prince?"

Tennin laughed as if I'd said something hilarious. "My dear girl, by the time you walk out of here, these pictures will already be in the hands of my buyers, and in the process of being uploaded to their websites. By the time you reach the street, millions of ravenous fans will be feasting their eyes on the new prince."

"Oh," I said, feeling foolish.

"Even if you did run out and tell the world before I'd uploaded the pictures, you'd only be able to say that he's blond and handsome, like half of the faeries in existence. No one has been able to get shots of him because this is the first time he's left Faerie, so I doubt anyone would take you seriously." He turned back to the monitors and uploaded the last batch of photos. "And now we wait."

Guilt suddenly pricked me. I was supposed to be looking for my parents, and instead, I was chatting away as if this were a social call. "Can we talk about my parents now? I know they came to see you about a job they're working on. Can you tell me what you told them and where they might have gone after?"

Tennin hesitated as if he was deciding how much to share with me. "I told them one of my contacts said the goren dealer is an elf, and they might find out more about him at Teg's."

"What is that?"

His brows drew together. "If you have to ask, it's no place for you."

I was getting tired of men trying to tell me what my place was today. "I can look it up when I leave here, or you can save me the trouble and tell me."

Tennin huffed. "It's a place where humans and faeries go to socialize and hook up."

"I've heard of those. My friend Violet has been to a few Fae clubs." Violet was a little Fae-crazy, like half the population. She'd started going to their clubs the moment she turned eighteen, because that was the legal age to enter a Fae establishment.

"Teg's is not one of those upscale night clubs. It's a bar, and it can get wild there at times." Tennin looked like he regretted mentioning it. "That place will eat you alive."

"What's that supposed to mean?"

He scowled. "Look at you. You might as well walk in there and ring a dinner bell."

I looked down at my outfit of jeans, red top, and short puffer jacket. "What's wrong with what I'm wearing?"

"It's not the clothes, silly girl. It's you." He waved a hand at me as if I should know what he meant. "And you don't even know who's who in Fae royalty. The moment you open your mouth, they'll know you don't belong there."

I crossed my arms. "I can be tough if I need to."

His arched eyebrow said he didn't believe that for one second.

Tennin's computer dinged, and a new email notification appeared on the screen. He rubbed his hands together. "And so it begins. If you don't mind, I need to take care of a little business."

"Sure." I walked around to the other side of the desk to give him some privacy.

Tennin didn't waste time. He hit a few keys and settled back in his chair, wearing a broad smile. "Two point five. I'd call that a good night's work. Wouldn't you?"

"Two point five *million*?" I nearly choked out the last word, unable to imagine having that much money. A tenth of that would pay for all the college I wanted.

"Like I said, it's all about supply and demand." He stood and began packing camera equipment into a bag. "I hate to cut our visit short, but I have to be in LA in two hours for Princess Titania's birthday bash." He stopped what he was doing to shoot me a quizzical look. "You *do* know who she is."

I scoffed lightly. "Of course." Just because I didn't keep up with current celebrity news did not mean I didn't know Fae history. Princess Titania was the first faerie to address the world after the Great Rift, and she was the most loved and celebrated among the royal Fae.

Tennin resumed packing, and I wondered what it was like to be able to travel across the country or the world in a matter of minutes. Faeries were able to do it by creating portals between our two realms. They passed through the portal into their world and then created a second portal to arrive at their destination here in our world.

There had been much debate and speculation over the years about when and if this technology would ever be available to humans. But humans could not enter Faerie, so I couldn't see how the portals could work for us.

Tennin zipped up his bag. "Something tells me it's no use asking you to stay away from Teg's. If you insist on going there, don't go alone. Take someone you trust with you, preferably someone who knows more about us than you do."

"I will." I already had the perfect person in mind.

"Good. Come on. I'll walk out with you."

"You can't wear that."

"Why not?" I frowned at the petite Chinese girl standing in the doorway of my apartment.

Violet Lee shook her head of long, blue-and-black hair and walked past me into the apartment. She wore artfully ripped jeans, a white V-neck camisole, and a gray suede jacket that probably cost more than I'd made in a month at my old job. She'd paired the outfit with knee-length boots that brought her within an inch of my height.

"The jeans and combat boots are great, but that sweater and coat..." She wrinkled her nose. "You're going there as the daughter of two of the most badass bounty hunters this city has ever seen. You need to channel Caroline James and dress like you mean business."

"You're right." I turned on my heel and went to my room to change into a plain black T-shirt. Then I walked down the hall to my parents' bedroom to borrow one of Mom's short leather jackets. I stood in front of her mirror, my chest tight as I donned the jacket that smelled of her favorite soap. With my hair tied back in a ponytail, I could pass for her from a distance.

I was about to turn away from the mirror when my gaze landed on a framed photo sitting on the dresser. I looked at the beaming faces of my much younger parents and a chubby, red-haired baby boy. My brother, Caleb.

I'd never known Caleb. He had been only two months old when he'd died from an undiagnosed heart defect two years before I was born. Because of that, I'd spent the first year of my life under the care of a pediatric cardiologist. Thankfully, I had been blessed with a strong, healthy heart.

We didn't speak of Caleb often because it hurt Mom to talk about him. Dad was better at hiding his emotions, but I could see a flash of pain in his eyes whenever Caleb's name was mentioned.

"That's more like it," Violet said from the doorway. "Do you need to wear those glasses?"

I frowned. "Yes, if I want to drive."

She tilted her head to study me. "I guess they do work on you."

"Thanks, I think." I rolled my eyes as I walked past her.

She followed me. "Ready to go?"

"Almost." I went to the office where I rooted through the supplies. I picked up a knife but decided against it. I'd had a lot of self-defense training, but I'd never practiced with a weapon. Placing it back on the shelf, I continued my search until I found a small leather pouch. I checked the contents and stuck the pouch into the inner pocket of my jacket.

"What's that?" asked Violet.

I patted down the front of my jacket to make sure there was no bulge. "Just a little protection in case we need it."

"Protection from what?"

"The boogeyman," I quipped dryly. "Protection from faeries, of course."

She chuckled. "You might be more like your parents than I gave you credit for."

"Just because I don't have your obsession with faeries doesn't mean I don't know much about them."

Sharing a home with two bounty hunters gave me access to information the average person didn't have. My parents had accumulated an impressive collection of reference books on everything Fae, and I'd read them all from cover to cover.

Mom and Dad didn't want me hunting with them, but they'd always encouraged me to learn everything I could about faeries. When I went to college, I planned to study law so I could be a legal advocate for lower faeries, like Finch and Gorn, who didn't have someone to fight for their rights.

We left the office, but I turned and went back. I searched the desk drawers until I located Mom's spare bounty hunter ID. It might come in handy, and the picture on the card was so small that I was counting on no one looking at it too closely.

Back in the living room, I found Violet and Finch watching an entertainment news show. Finch didn't like most outsiders, and he normally disappeared the second we had a visitor. Violet was the exception. She'd spent so much time here with me that he was used to her. Plus, she was the only one who would watch these shows with him. I think he secretly loved it when she came over.

"I still can't believe someone actually got those pictures of Prince Rhys," she said.

Tennin's photos of the prince were splashed across the TV screen. The internet had blown up last night the minute his pictures hit the first gossip site. You couldn't look at social media or television today without seeing the prince's face.

"It was bound to happen eventually," I said with a shrug.

Violet gave me the side-eye. "How can you not be the least interested in this? A new Fae prince is like *history* in the making."

I snorted. "A new world leader is history. This is pop culture." I didn't tell her I'd seen these pictures before they'd been released into cyberspace and taken on a life of their own.

"You're hopeless." She glanced at her phone screen. "We should probably get going."

I looked at Finch, who sat on the back of the couch. "I'm leaving now. I'll try to be back before midnight." I hated leaving him alone, but I didn't have a choice if I wanted to find our parents. He understood my reasons, and he wanted Mom and Dad to come home as much as I did.

"Later, Finch." Violet have him a finger wave as we left and he waved back.

She stopped me when we reached the lobby. "By the way, Mom wants you and Finch to come stay with us until your parents come home."

Warmth filled my chest. "If it were just me, I would. But I don't think Finch will want to leave here. He's pretty upset about Mom and Dad, and you know how he is with strangers."

"I figured as much, but she still wanted me to ask."

I gave her a one-armed hug. "You're the best."

She pushed open the main door. "I know."

Teg's was a graffitied, one-story brick building in the Bronx. It didn't look like much on the outside, but Violet said she'd heard it was a popular spot.

Music, laughter, and a wave of warm air hit me when I opened the heavy door and stepped inside. The place smelled like alcohol and an intoxicating scent I couldn't identify. It made me a little lightheaded and filled me with a sense of longing, but for what I didn't know.

Violet caught me sniffing at the air and leaned over to whisper in my ear. "It's the Court faeries. When you get a lot of them together, they can be a little overpowering. You'll get used to it."

"Oh." I felt stupid for not remembering that from the books I'd read. Everything about Court faeries made them attractive to humans: their beauty, their voices, and even their smell. It was forbidden for them to use their magic on humans, but it wasn't as if they needed help finding willing bed partners.

The interior of the bar was bigger and much less dingy than it appeared from the outside. To my right was a cluster of tables where I recognized trolls, elves, ogres, and a few humans, sitting and drinking together in small groups. Past them was a raised section where all I could see were Court faeries and humans.

On my left was a long bar manned by three bartenders, who were busy serving up drinks to the human and faerie patrons lining the bar. Violet was right. Teg's was a busy place. Tennin had been full of it, though, when he'd said this place was too wild for me. It looked pretty tame.

"Do you see him?" Violet asked, coming to stand beside me.

"Not yet." I scanned the room for the bar's owner. I'd done a little research on Orend Teg last night. There wasn't much to read about him, but I'd found a picture of him on his bar's website. Not that it was much help. Teg looked like half the male faerie population: young, blond, and beautiful. The other half was young, brunette, and you guessed it – beautiful.

We walked over to the bar and squeezed between two men in their mid-twenties, who looked like they'd spent more time getting ready tonight than I had. The man next to Violet looked me up and down before his gaze slid to her.

"Whatever you're drinking, I'm buying," he said to her, earning a scowl from the pretty blonde on his other side.

Violet smiled politely. "No thanks."

"One drink," he pressed, and I thought I heard an angry harrumph from the blonde.

"Sorry, not interested." Violet leaned in to direct a saucy wink at the other girl. "But I just might steal this beautiful girl if you don't treat her better."

30

The girl blushed and averted her gaze, but her little smile told me she wouldn't mind being stolen by my best friend.

A bartender approached me. "What can I get for you?"

"I'm looking for Orend Teg. Can you tell me where to find him?"

He studied me for a moment, and his brow furrowed. "Are you sure? You don't look like his usual female visitors."

I swallowed a scoff, having a pretty good idea of the kind of visitors he was referring to. Pulling out my mother's ID card, I flashed it at him, just long enough for him to see the official Agency seal. "I'm here on business."

The bartender nodded and pointed toward the rear of the room. "In that case, you'll find him in his office. Just follow the hallway in the back."

"Thanks." I tucked the card into my pocket and went to Violet, who was making eyes at someone on the dais.

"Teg is in his office," I said, pulling her attention to me. "Will you be okay out here alone while I go talk to him?"

She frowned. "You don't want me to go with you?"

"I think I can handle it. I'm just going to ask him if my parents came to see him the other night."

"Okay." She winked. "Don't worry about me. I can think of something to keep me occupied."

I shook my head. "Behave yourself while I'm gone."

Violet looked toward the dais again. "Take your time."

Leaving her to her fun, I strode with purpose to the back of the bar. A number of Court faeries looked my way with interest, but I ignored them. I was here for one reason only, and I had zero interest in hooking up with anyone.

I easily found Teg's office and knocked sharply on the closed door. I waited thirty seconds and was about to knock again when it swung open.

Orend Teg's pictures hadn't done him justice. Up close, he was even more handsome. When a slow smile spread across his face, he exuded that potent sensuality that Court faeries were known for. Tennin had it, too, but I had a suspicion he'd been holding back because of who I was.

"You're early, but I can't say I'm put out about it. Jesper outdid himself this time." He took my hand and lifted it to his lips to press a light kiss to the back of it.

A little thrill went through me at his touch. I tugged my hand out of his as I schooled my face into a polite expression. "I'm sorry. I think you've mistaken me for someone else. I'm here on Agency business."

Teg's eyes widened a fraction, and then he let out a delighted laugh. "The

Agency. I love it. The glasses are a nice touch, by the way. Where on earth did Jesper find you?"

"I don't know any Jesper," I said tightly, reaching for my mother's card. I held it up for him to see as I'd done for the bartender. Except Teg wasn't content with a brief glance. He caught my hand in his firm grip and studied the card – closely.

His whole countenance changed, and he dropped my hand to go sit behind his desk. Leaning back in his chair, he watched me with cool shrewdness that hadn't been there before. It felt like his eyes could see right through me, and I had to stop myself from squirming.

"It's a crime to impersonate an Agency employee, including bounty hunters," he said in a voice that had gone hard. "I admit you look the part. You could pass for Caroline James if you were a little older."

"You know my mother?" I blurted before I could stop myself. So much for being coolheaded.

"Your mother?" Teg stared at me, and recognition dawned in his eyes. "How did I not see it? You could be her –"

"Her clone. I know." I took a step toward the desk. "My name is Jesse James. You know my parents?"

Teg gave me an are-you-kidding-me look. "Everyone knows Patrick and Caroline James, but I had no idea they had a daughter. Seeing you now, it's clear why they kept you a secret."

I ignored his comments about me and got straight to the point of my visit. "Did my parents come to see you two nights ago?"

He thought about it for a moment. "I haven't seen them in at least a month. Why are you asking?"

Before I'd come here, I'd thought about how much to divulge to him. Even though I'd confided in Tennin, I didn't think it was smart to let the whole world know my parents were missing. Instead of the truth, I gave him a cover story I'd concocted. "They're testing me. I'm supposed to track them down while they work on a job."

"Testing you for what?"

I held his gaze. "To see if I can work with them."

At this, his eyebrows shot up. "*You're* training to be a bounty hunter? How old are you?"

"Old enough." My shoulders straightened.

His gaze swept over me again. "You don't look old enough."

"You didn't think I was that young when you opened your door," I retorted.

Teg smiled lazily. "What I have in mind is a lot less dangerous than hunting, and infinitely more pleasurable for both parties involved."

"I'm...uh...sure it is." Heat rose in my face.

He leaned forward to rest his arms on the desk. "Curious, Jesse?"

"No, I'm not, *Mr.* Teg."

His smile widened. "I think I like you, Jesse James."

I folded my arms across my chest. "You're still not getting into my pants."

He threw back his head and laughed. "Okay, *Miss* James. Tell me why you think your parents paid me a visit?"

Feeling like I was back on solid ground, I said, "They're hunting a goren dealer who has been seen here."

"Someone dealing in my bar? I think not."

"Do you know every person who comes into your bar?" I asked.

"I don't need to," he replied confidently. "My wards prevent anyone from entering with drugs or weapons."

"That's good to know." I was glad that I'd decided not to come here armed.

"By any chance, did your parents tell you the name of this dealer?"

"No, just that he's an elf. I don't think they know his name." I didn't really care about the dealer's identity. As much as I didn't want someone peddling Fae drugs to humans, all I cared about was finding my parents. "Is it possible my parents were here and didn't ask to see you?"

Teg shrugged. "It's possible, but I can't see them taking the time to come here without talking to me."

My shoulders slumped. He was right. My parents were thorough in their job, and they never did anything halfway. But if they hadn't come here after talking to Tennin, where had they gone? I'd hoped to find something at the bar to lead me to them, and I had no idea where to go from here.

A knock came at the door, and Teg called for them to come in.

The door opened, and a pretty, fuchsia-haired young woman entered. She wore jeans and a tight black T-shirt with the bar's name across her chest, and she had piercings in her nose and eyebrow. She stared at me with open curiosity before she addressed her boss. "You have visitors."

"Who is it?"

"Rand and his men."

"Tell Rand I'll see him in five minutes." Teg rubbed his jaw, his good humor gone.

"If he'll wait that long," the woman muttered and left.

Teg gave me a look of regret. "I hate to end our little visit, but Cynthia is right. Lukas Rand is not someone you keep waiting."

I nodded as if I knew who that was. "Thank you for taking the time to talk to me."

"Anytime, Miss James. Happy hunting, and try to stay out of trouble. Although, something tells me the world of bounty hunting will never be the same."

Dejected, I left his office and went to look for Violet. I had a feeling I'd find her on the dais, so I scanned that section as I walked toward the bar.

"Oof!" I uttered when I made contact with a hard body. I stumbled backward and might have fallen if a pair of hands hadn't grabbed my arms to steady me.

The man released me, and I backed up a step to see who I'd plowed into. My breath caught when I looked up into cold, midnight-blue eyes beneath brows that were drawn down in a scowl. The man's hard gaze held me like a deer in a car's headlights, until a deep chuckle to my left startled me back to my senses. My eyes roamed over the face before me, taking in its perfect masculine lines and sensual mouth, and I knew immediately that this was no man at all.

"I can't tell if she's mesmerized by your pretty face or scared witless," joked the male on my left.

Tearing my eyes from the faerie in front of me, I glared at his companion. The other faerie – also dark-haired and handsome but in a decidedly better mood – smirked at me in response.

My gaze swung back to the one I'd collided with. As with all Court faeries, he was well over six feet tall, but unlike most, he wore his hair short, and he had an air of power about him that made my stomach dip. It was dark and dangerous, and it told me this was one faerie I didn't want to mess with. There was also something vaguely familiar about him, but I couldn't put my finger on it.

I took another step back and saw three unsmiling blond faeries forming a semicircle behind him. Like him, they all had short hair, which made them stand out. The five of them made a formidable group, and I got the distinct impression they weren't here for a drink.

"Excuse me," I said, moving to go around them.

"Teg likes his girls young," one of the faeries said scornfully, bringing me up short.

I scowled at them, unsure who had spoken. "Just because I'm in his bar doesn't mean I'm one of his girls."

A blond faerie with a crew cut and the greenest eyes I'd ever seen, curled his lip in a sneer. "Whatever you say."

"You're here, too," I said sweetly and maybe a little recklessly. "I guess that makes you his boy."

The faerie stiffened, and I heard a few gasps from nearby. I glanced around to see the faeries within hearing distance watching us with shocked expressions. Some even looked a little scared.

The joker in the group let out a laugh. "Damn, Faolin, you got served." He slung an arm across my shoulders. "I think I'm in love."

"Hey, hands off." I ducked out from under his arm. Several strands had come loose from my ponytail, and I tucked them behind my ears, feeling disheveled and annoyed. I had too much on my mind to deal with a bunch of arrogant faeries lacking basic manners.

I looked up to find the faerie I'd run into watching me with cool curiosity. Even though he hadn't spoken, his position at the center of the group told me he was their leader. I would have bet he was Lukas Rand, the one Teg had said didn't like to be kept waiting.

"Well, this has been fun," I said in a cheerful voice that dripped sarcasm. "Have a nice night, *gentlemen*."

None of them spoke this time as I walked away. Putting them out of my mind, I searched the faces of the women on the dais, looking for Violet. I caught sight of her deep in conversation with two female faeries at a table toward the back, and I headed in her direction.

I reached the steps to the raised section, but before I could climb them, a blond Court faerie stepped in front of me, blocking my path. My first thought was that one of Lukas Rand's group had followed me. Then I realized this one had long hair. His flirtatious smile and the interested gleam in his eyes told me he had more pleasurable pursuits in mind.

"I haven't seen you around here before," he said in a low, husky voice.

I smiled politely. "That's because I've never been here before."

His eyes widened in delight. "Is that so? Then you must let me buy you a drink in honor of your first visit to Teg's."

"Thank you, but I'm just going to get my friend so we can leave." I craned my neck to look around him, but I couldn't see Violet from this location.

He made a pouty face. "But the night has barely begun. Surely, you and your friend don't want to leave so soon."

"Maybe she needs the right enticement to stay, Korre," said a male voice from behind me.

The faerie in front of me stared at someone over my head, his mouth tightening in displeasure.

I turned slightly to see a second blond faerie. The two of them looked so alike

35

that it made me wonder, not for the first time, how small the Fae gene pool was. They all had a similar physique and perfect facial features. Even Lukas Rand and his companions, as fierce as they looked, could be easily identified as faeries.

The newcomer smiled at me. "I'm Daoine. May I ask your name, beautiful one?"

"Jesse." I had to stifle a laugh because he was laying it on a little thick. But he seemed harmless enough, and everyone knew faeries were huge flirts.

Daoine took one of my hands and lifted it to his lips. "It's a pleasure. Please, allow me to accompany you to your friend's table. Perhaps I can convince you both to stay a little longer."

I tugged my hand from his, but I couldn't think of a way to refuse his request without seeming rude. What harm could it do to walk across the dais with him?

Korre raised an arm to block us when we turned to the steps. The glint of annoyance in his eyes conveyed his unhappiness with Daoine for moving in on his action. "Daoine, didn't I just see you with the lovely Nicole? You should return to her, and I'll take Jesse to her friend."

Daoine chuckled. "Nice try."

"I think Jesse can decide for herself who will accompany her," Korre said, his pretty eyes meeting mine.

I shook my head. "Listen, I'm flattered by your interest, but –"

Beside me, Daoine sucked in a sharp breath. "What are you doing? That is forbidden."

"What?" I jerked my head in his direction, but he wasn't looking at me. He was staring at Korre, a mix of shock and reproach on his face.

"What are you talking about?" Korre asked a little too innocently.

"You tried to glamour her."

Alarm shot through me. Glamouring a human violated at least three treaties and carried a punishment of banishment from our realm. The thought that he'd tried that on me made my hackles rise.

"Don't be ridiculous," Korre said insolently. "Does she look glamoured to you?"

My hand automatically went to the bracelet on my wrist. *Thank you, Mom.*

"I felt your magic," Daoine accused him before I could say anything.

Korre smirked. "Says you."

Daoine placed himself between Korre and me and spoke to me over his shoulder. "Go to your friend, Jesse. I am sorry for this."

I appreciated Daoine's chivalry, but I wasn't going to walk away from someone who had tried to glamour me against my will. I considered myself an easygoing person most of the time, but even I had my limits.

I pushed past Daoine and poked Korre in the chest. "You jerk. Are you that pathetic you have to use magic to get a woman?"

Korre laughed arrogantly. "Humans come to Teg's for one reason, and that is to hook up with my kind. You can't come in here looking like that and pretend to be offended when we take notice."

Looking like what? I peered down at my outfit, which was anything but sexy, and then glowered at him again. "How any woman looks doesn't give you the right to violate her. I'm sure the Agency will be more than happy to explain that to you."

Korre's humor fled, and he grabbed my arm. I reacted on instinct, hitting him with a palm strike beneath his chin. If he'd been a human, it would have hurt him, but Court faeries were stronger than we were, and all it did was make his hold tighter.

"Release her." Daoine shoved Korre hard just as I brought my knee up between Korre's legs. The dual attack knocked him off balance and forced him to let me go. Since I only wanted to get away from him, that was enough.

Until the ogres joined the fight.

4

In my defense, I hadn't meant to involve anyone else, especially a bunch of those bad-tempered brutes. But a girl can't be blamed for protecting herself, can she?

I watched as Korre stumbled backward and crashed into a table of ogres. Drinks went flying, and angry bellows filled the room amid the sounds of breaking glass.

An ogre reached for Korre, who lay across their table, and grabbed the front of the blond faerie's shirt in his large hand. In the next instant, Korre was sailing through the air into a group of trolls in the corner.

The trolls, who resembled hairy humans except for their fangs and huge underbites, jumped to their feet, snarling. One troll jumped on Korre, while his four buddies charged the ogres. In the middle of the melee, someone threw a chair that knocked out an elf, sending his companions into a rage. Before I knew it, every faerie in that section was embroiled in a huge brawl.

That would have been bad enough if Korre hadn't started screaming bloody murder. Court faeries from the dais ran past me and jumped into the fray. Soon, the fight spilled toward us, and I had to step aside to avoid being struck by a flying chair.

"Jesse!" Violet yelled from behind me.

I looked back to see her on the dais, gesturing frantically for me to join her. But before I could move, I was surrounded by dozens of angry faeries doing their best to throttle each other. Dodging the brawlers at every turn, I tried to make my way toward the safety of the bar on the other side of the room.

A boot glanced off my thigh, and I swerved away from it. I collided with a tall, thin elf, sending him crashing to the floor beside me. The troll he'd been fighting fell on top of him, and the two of them continued punching each other.

Something squealed, and a small, white, furry body ran between my feet, desperately trying to escape being trampled to death. It was a hama, a Fae creature about the size of a kitten that resembled an earless rabbit. Hamas were gentle animals and popular pets among faeries and humans.

I bent and grabbed for the hama, my fingertips barely touching him before he darted forward out of my reach. I cringed when he narrowly avoided being squashed under a large ogre boot. The little guy was going to get pancaked if I didn't help him.

I reached into my inner pocket and pulled out the pouch I'd put there before I left home. Loosening the string, I hurriedly poured a small amount of a fine gray powder onto my palm. It wouldn't take much for what I had in mind. I lifted my hand to my mouth and blew hard on the powder in the direction the hama had gone.

Every lower faerie in my path who inhaled the powder slowed their movements until it looked like they were fighting in slow motion. It would have been comical to watch if I'd had time. But the effects of the powder wouldn't last long.

The powder, called fey dust, was a blend of iron powder and some other secret elements. It could slow some faeries, but it didn't harm them. It was made by a witch in New Orleans, and it was extremely difficult to acquire. I was pretty sure my parents got their supply through Maurice's connections.

Hoping no one had witnessed my little stunt, I quickly tucked the pouch back into my pocket. I scanned the floor for the hama and spotted a bundle of white fur just beyond the feet of a slow-moving ogre.

I dived after the hama. My fingers closed around the tiny bundle of fur, and I landed on my stomach, clutching the creature in my outstretched hands. "Gotcha!"

I lifted my head and found myself eye to toe with a pair of black boots. My eyes followed the jean-clad legs to a gray shirt and stopped when they met a dark blue gaze.

Lukas Rand quirked an eyebrow at me, and from this vantage, I wasn't sure if he was amused or annoyed. Based on my previous encounter with him, I was putting my money on the latter.

"And she's back," crowed his jokester friend. "Why is it that the ladies only throw themselves at your feet, Lukas?"

The faerie in question gave his companion a small smile that made my stomach do funny things, even though the smile hadn't been directed at me. Damn faeries and their amped-up pheromones.

Rolling to my back, I sat up, still holding the frightened hama. I cradled it in one hand and used the other hand to fix my glasses, which had gone askew.

I let out a startled squeak when hands slipped beneath my arms and lifted me to my feet as if I weighed nothing. I spun to face Lukas Rand. His face was back to being impassive, but I thought I saw a gleam of amusement in his dark eyes.

"Thank –" My words ended in a squawk when he suddenly pulled me against his chest. Something brushed against my back, and there was a thud of a body hitting the floor where I'd been standing a moment before.

"Kerr, Iian, take care of this," said his authoritative voice above the shouts and crashing sounds from the fight. Though the words were clipped, the voice was like warm honey, and I could feel the vibrations in his chest when he spoke. That combined with his tantalizing male scent made me feel a little lightheaded and more aware of him than I'd ever been of another man.

He's not a man, I reminded myself. He was a faerie, and everything about him was alluring to humans. Apparently, I wasn't immune to it either, and that revelation was like a bucket of cold water in my face.

I pushed back from him, and the steely arm holding me fell away. Avoiding his eyes, I turned toward the fight and watched two of his blond companions, who looked so much alike they had to be brothers, wading through the brawlers and pulling them apart. Some yelled in protest, but their complaints were quickly silenced when they saw who was interrupting their fight. Whoever Lukas Rand and his men were, they were well-known among other faeries, and no one was willing to challenge them.

"Lukas," called Orend Teg. I glanced to my left to see the unhappy bar owner striding toward us. Teg took in the destruction, and his scowl turned almost scary.

"Thank you for stepping in," he said to Lukas when he reached us. "I haven't had a fight in here in ages. What set them off?"

"I think I have a good idea," Lukas replied dryly.

There was a brief silence, and then Teg spoke, a note of exasperation in his voice. "Miss James, why am I not surprised to find you in the middle of this?"

I raised my chin. "Hey, this is not my fault. I was about to leave when one of your *fine* patrons tried to glamour me. I was only defending myself."

"Who?" Lukas and Teg demanded at the same time. I wasn't sure which one of them looked more pissed off.

I looked around the bar for the other faerie. "His name is Korre, but I don't see him. He must have left. There was another faerie named Daoine who can back me up."

Teg's eyes were cold and flinty as he showed me a side of him I hadn't seen in his office. "I know of Korre. He started coming in a few months ago. Rest assured, he will be dealt with."

I shivered at the hardness in his tone. The fact that Teg didn't question whether or not my story was true spoke volumes. He must have a reason to believe Korre capable of such a thing. Something told me the bar owner would not be relying on the Agency to handle this.

"As for you, Miss James, I think it would be best if you left as well," Teg said.

"You're kicking me out?" I asked incredulously. "But I did nothing wrong."

The coldness left his eyes. "I know. If anyone is at fault, it's me for being too distracted to realize you would draw certain attention. With everyone worked up from the fight, it would be safer for you if you left."

I opened my mouth to ask what he meant by that, but someone collided with my back and threw their arms around my waist.

"Don't ever do that to me again," Violet shrilled. "My heart nearly stopped when you disappeared into that mess."

I patted her hands, which were clasped tightly at my midsection. "I'm okay. Or I will be when you stop squeezing the life out of me."

"Sorry!" She released me and came to stand beside me, where she let out a tiny gasp. I slanted a look at her to see her gaping at Lukas Rand and his friends with something akin to awe.

Kerr and Iian chose that moment to return to the group of faeries, which was getting far too crowded for my liking. I smiled at no one in particular as I grasped my friend's elbow. "We'll be leaving now. It's been real."

"But...but..." Violet sputtered as I started to pull her away.

I stopped suddenly and turned back to them. The closest one to me was Teg, and I thrust the hama into his hands. "Can you see that he gets back to his owner? Thanks." Ignoring his shocked expression, I left, pulling Violet after me.

"But I don't want to go," she wailed as we passed a couple of elves nursing their bruised jaws.

Her protests fell on deaf ears, and the closer we got to the exit, the less fuss she made. I pushed open the door and drew in a deep breath of cold air, glad to be away from this place. If I was lucky, I'd never have to come back.

We were a dozen steps from the building when the door opened behind us. I looked over my shoulder and saw a dark-haired faerie step outside. I didn't recognize him, but the intense way he looked at me made my skin crawl. I thought back to Teg's comment about me drawing the wrong attention, and my stomach knotted in apprehension.

"Come on," I said to Violet in a low voice, and we started toward the Jeep. The last thing we needed tonight was another unwanted faerie encounter.

I stifled a small scream when a tall figure suddenly appeared at my side. I relaxed slightly when I saw it was Lukas Rand's wisecracking friend.

"What are you doing?" I asked him.

"Making sure you get home safely."

"Yes, please," Violet said eagerly.

"That's not necessary. My car is parked just down the street." I pointed at the Jeep less than ten car lengths away.

He nodded. "Then I will walk you to your vehicle."

I eyed him suspiciously and resumed walking. "Why? What's it to you if I get home safely or not?"

"Are you this distrusting of everyone or just faeries?"

"Mostly of strangers who follow me from bars." I gave him a pointed look.

He laughed. "Fair enough. I'm Conlan, and to answer your question, I don't get many opportunities to be chivalrous. Plus, I like anyone who can go toe-to-toe with Faolin."

"I wouldn't exactly call tossing a few insults going toe-to-toe."

"Then you don't know Faolin," he said. "Men wet their pants when he gets that look in his eyes."

"Good thing I'm not a man then."

We stopped at the Jeep, and I unlocked the doors. Violet climbed in, but I paused with my hand on the handle and looked at Conlan. "Can I ask you something?"

He gave me a cocky little grin. "Is it my phone number?"

I couldn't help but smile at him. "Teg and Korre both said something about me drawing attention to myself. Do you know what they were talking about?"

Conlan surprised me by reaching out to touch my ponytail. I pulled back, and he let my hair slip through his fingers.

"It's your hair," he said almost wistfully. "That is a particularly lovely shade of red."

"Oh." I almost slapped my head, feeling like all kinds of an idiot. There were no redheads in Faerie, just blonds and brunettes, so natural red hair was a desirable trait in humans. For the less than two percent of the earth's population that were redheads, this was great news, and Scotland, for obvious reasons, boasted the largest faerie presence.

According to my mother, when humans found out this juicy bit, they flocked in droves to salons to get their hair dyed red. They soon discovered, to their dismay, that faeries preferred natural red hair and they could tell the difference.

I opened the driver's door. "Thanks for answering my question."

"It was my pleasure. A word of advice, though. Stay away from Teg's. They can get some unsavory people here, and I can tell you don't normally frequent such places."

"Ha!" Violet called from the passenger seat. "You can say that again."

Ignoring her, I climbed in and started the engine. I cracked the window to say goodbye to Conlan.

Violet leaned over the center console to bat her lashes at the handsome faerie. "Thanks for keeping us safe."

His smile turned sensual. "Anytime, beautiful."

"And we're out of here." I waved to Conlan and drove away.

Violet pouted. "But I like him."

I shot her a sideways look. "Um, are you forgetting that you like girls?"

"I said I like him, not that I'd do him." She sank back in her seat. "You're no fun."

"You always say that, yet you keep coming back."

"True."

Violet and I had met on our first day of kindergarten, and if there ever was a case for opposites attracting, it was us. I'd been the brainy, studious one, and she'd been outgoing and adventurous. In high school, I was the person other students had come to for tutoring, while Violet had run the drama club. I'd been class valedictorian; Violet had been prom queen. I dreamed of walking through an ivy-covered college campus with an armful of textbooks. Violet dreamed of a career on the big screen and walking the red carpet.

She opened the visor mirror and reapplied her lip gloss. "Tell me you at least got that hot faerie's number?"

"No, of course not." I pinned her with a hard stare. "You know that's not why I came here tonight."

She smiled sheepishly. "Sorry. Did you find out anything about your parents?"

"No." A weight settled on my chest at the mention of them. I knew nothing more than I had when I left the apartment. At least, before I'd come here, I had hope of finding something to lead me to them. Now, I had nothing. I was back to square one, waiting on Levi Solomon and the bounty hunters to get off their butts and do something.

Violet's soft voice broke the heavy silence. "It's only been two days. They'll come home."

I nodded mutely, and my fingers gripped the steering wheel. I couldn't bear to imagine what could have happened to keep them away this long, but I refused to believe the worst. Someone or something was preventing them from coming home, and I wouldn't stop searching until I found them.

"Thanks, Bruce. Please, let me know if you find anything."

I hung up the phone and looked at Finch, who sat on the desk, watching me with big sad eyes. He'd been depressed since I came home last night and told him I hadn't found any leads at Teg's. I desperately wanted to be able to give him some good news.

"Nothing yet," I said, keeping my voice light. "Bruce is asking around, and he's going to see Levi today."

It was all I could do not to spit Levi's name. My first call this morning had been to him, and he'd been delighted to tell me he had finally reported Mom and Dad missing to the Agency. Like I should be happy he'd done anything at all.

When I'd asked if he was going to look for them, he'd told me that wasn't his job. The Agency would handle it from here. Before he'd ended the call, he had made sure to remind me to leave this to the professionals.

Helplessness and frustration threatened to smother me, and I got up to pace the small office. If I were the one missing, my parents would tear this city apart until they found me, and no one would dare tell them to let someone else handle it.

Now that our roles were reversed, all I could do was sit at home and make phone calls. I didn't have their connections and knowledge of the city to go find them on my own, and none of their colleagues would tell me anything because I wasn't in the business. What did I have to do to get these people to take this seriously?

My gaze slid over Dad's neatly organized shelves of weapons and gear to the bookcase crammed with books on faeries and hunting. A frustrated sigh escaped my lips. I had everything a bounty hunter needed at my fingertips. If only I –

I spun and stared at the computer as if it held the secrets of the universe. It didn't, but it did have something equally valuable to me. It contained all of Mom's files and her detailed notes on every job she and Dad had done. It had city and state maps you wouldn't find in any bookstore, lists of the places where they bought supplies, and every connection and contact they had. It was basically an encyclopedia of bounty hunting that had been accumulated over many years in the business, the kind of knowledge that could make a good bounty hunter great – and an average girl into a bounty hunter.

I smiled for the first time that day as I sat and logged into the computer. My heart sped up, and a thrill of excitement went through me when the reality of what I was contemplating hit me.

A sharp whistle interrupted my thoughts, and I looked at Finch, who was watching me with a confused expression.

Why are you happy? he signed.

My smile grew into a grin. "I'm happy because I have a plan."

What? Hope lit his eyes.

"None of Mom and Dad's work colleagues will tell me anything because I'm not one of them. So, I'm going to join the family business."

Finch's eyes widened. *How?*

"I still need to work out the details." Such as how to get my first job. No bond agency was going to give a job to a novice hunter on her own, and you weren't considered a real bounty hunter until you got your first job on the books.

Can I help? he asked.

"Of course. I can't do it without my partner." I thought for a moment. "You'll manage home base while I'm out. And I'll need help preparing for jobs. That is the most important part."

Finch's thin chest puffed out. *I'm good at that. I helped Mom and Dad.*

"I know. We are going to be such a badass team." I put up a hand, and he gave me a high five – or a high four in his case since sprites had four digits on each hand.

I turned my attention back to the computer. Since no one would give me a job, that left me with only one option. I opened Mom's spreadsheet and looked at the two jobs listed there. Immediately, I ruled out going after the goren dealer. I knew nothing of that world, and I'd have to be insane to try to take on a level Four on my own. The level Three wasn't much better, but it was that or nothing.

I clicked on the job to open the details. The goblin had been active in the area for over a month, and based on several sightings, they suspected he was living in Prospect Park. Another team had already tried unsuccessfully to catch him before the job was handed off to my parents. In the job notes, I saw the words *Lookout Hill*. Mom and Dad must have thought the goblin's burrow was in that part of the park. If they were right, that would narrow my search a lot and save me days of walking through the park.

I sat back in the chair, mentally reviewing everything I knew about goblins. They lived alone in burrows they dug between the roots of large trees. Notorious thieves, they couldn't resist shiny, sparkly things, especially jewelry, and they were known to hoard the stuff.

I remembered a news story from a few years ago about a goblin burrow discovered under a massive oak tree in North Carolina that had come down in a storm. They'd found enough silver and gold to fill the back of a small pickup, everything from jewelry to flatware and serving dishes, to a silver urn, all items that had been reported stolen in the city over a ten-year period.

Goblins were so good at stealing and remaining at large because they were extremely fast and masters at blending into their surroundings. You could be staring right at one and not even know it. They weren't dangerous unless they were cornered, which meant if I somehow managed to find this one, I needed to be prepared.

Filled with a new sense of purpose, I went to the bookcase and found the two books I'd read that contained the most information on goblins. I laid them on the desk, and Finch and I spent the next hour going through them for any mention of goblins. The books were worn from use and full of little slips of paper that Mom or Dad had tucked between the pages, containing their own notes on the subject matter. Touching something of theirs made me feel closer to them, despite the physical distance between us.

When I realized I'd gleaned all I could from the books, I closed them and stood. It was barely noon, which meant I had less than six hours of daylight left. Goblins were diurnal, so the only time I could hope to see him was before sunset.

I went through the gear, and with Finch's help, I gathered the supplies I would need and placed them in my old school backpack. I donned one of my mother's lined leather jackets because it was practical and warm, and wearing it gave me the little added boost of confidence I needed. Leaving Finch with a bowl of blackberries and a promise to try to be back by dark, I set out on my first job as a bounty hunter.

I quickly found a parking spot within walking distance of the park, and I hoped that was a sign this would be a lucky day for me. Pulling on my wool cap and gloves, I grabbed my backpack and got out.

It was a cold day, so I walked at a brisk pace as I went over my plan again. It was a simple one that I'd formulated with Finch's help, and I worried I was overlooking something. Let's face it; if goblins were easy to catch, they wouldn't be a level Three, and that other team would have brought him in. Chances were I was going to fail spectacularly today, but I had to try.

Dad used to take me to Prospect Park all the time, so I knew exactly where Lookout Hill was, and I'd parked near the entrance closest to it. Despite the frigid temperature, it was a clear, sunny day, so there were a fair number of people in the park. I would have preferred to do this without an audience, but it wasn't as if people weren't used to bounty hunters doing their thing.

Before long, I was climbing the steps to Lookout Hill with my stomach fluttering in excitement. I couldn't believe I was actually doing this. Sure, when I was younger, I'd had daydreams of going on a big job with my parents, but I'd never really seen myself following in their footsteps. If they hadn't gone missing, I'd be out on my job search now and leaving this work to them.

Halfway up the steps, I came to a strip of yellow caution tape and a downed tree blocking my path. I stared at the tree for a long moment, mulling over what to do. Adjusting my backpack straps, I lifted the tape and ducked under it. There were no signs telling me to keep out, so technically I wasn't breaking any laws, right?

I'd never been up here alone, and the place had a sad, deserted feel without other people around. But the view was amazing. With the trees bare of leaves, I could see across the rooftops of Brooklyn and the lake below me. It was quiet, too. Not quiet like in the country, but the constant sounds of the city were a little muted. I could see why a goblin would want to make his home up here.

Thinking of the goblin reminded me of my purpose for being here, and I hurriedly climbed the last few steps. I stopped at the top and looked around the deserted area. There were some decent sized trees up here, big enough for a goblin to burrow beneath them. He could be in his home now, mere feet from where I stood. Hell, he could be standing in the woods watching me at this moment, and I wouldn't know it.

That last thought gave me the willies. When I heard a small movement in the trees, I nearly gave myself whiplash jerking my head in that direction. I let out a breath when I caught the glint of sunlight on a tiny pair of wings. Squinting, I made out the shape of a green, four-inch tall pixie perched on the low branch of a tree. Seemingly immune to the cold, the miniature faerie stood and stuck out its tongue at me before flying off.

I smiled to myself as I took off my backpack and unzipped it. I knew lots of stuff about pixies, such as that they lived in colonies and made their homes inside tree trunks, they lived off insects, and their bite was worse than a bee sting. But the only fact I cared about now was that they preferred to live near other tree-dwelling faeries – particularly goblins.

Reaching inside the pack, I withdrew a plastic bag full of Swarovski crystals that glittered like diamonds. I'd found them among my parents' supplies, and something told me Mom and Dad had bought them for this job. Goblins couldn't resist jewels, and it didn't matter if they were diamonds or crystals.

I opened the bag and made a small pile of crystals on the concrete walkway, noting with satisfaction how they sparkled under the bright sunlight. Walking a few yards away, I created a similar pile. I kept going like that until I had used up the whole bag.

That done, I took a pair of metal shackles from the backpack and stuffed them into my coat pocket for quick access. Then I opened a side pocket on the pack and pulled out the little leather pouch of fey dust I'd brought to Teg's with me. With nothing left for me to do, I sat on the concrete ledge near the top of the stairs and waited.

And waited.

Two hours later, I was freezing my butt off and longing for a steaming mug of hot chocolate. The only visitors I'd had were a squirrel and several pixies that made rude gestures at me from the trees. I hadn't seen a sign of the goblin, and none of my crystal piles had been disturbed.

So much for my brilliant plan. I shook my head at my audacity, thinking I could do something that an experienced bounty hunting team had failed at. All I'd succeeded in doing was making my butt numb. At least, no one was here to witness my failure.

I started to stand when something caught my eye. Or more like the absence of something. The pile of crystals farthest from me was gone.

I froze as my heart began to thud. Carefully, I opened the pouch and poured a little of the precious fey dust onto my palm.

A breeze rustled some dry leaves on the walkway to my right. I looked that way in time to see another pile of crystals disappear before my eyes.

"Pretty," rasped a gleeful disembodied voice.

I went to the closest pile of crystals, knowing the goblin would not leave any behind. The moment I reached them, something barely brushed my back, and I felt a sharp, quick tug on my hair. I spun, but it was too late. He was already gone.

Turning back, I swore softly when I saw the empty spot where the crystals had been. A thin reedy laugh floated to me on the air, and I clenched my jaw.

I ran to the next pile, determined not to fall for his tricks this time. He could have snatched up the other unguarded piles of crystals, but I knew in my gut he'd come for this one. He was toying with me.

The air shifted right in front of me. I reacted quickly, throwing the fey dust at him, but he was too fast. All I got for my efforts was a face full of powder and a sneezing fit.

"Silly human," he taunted, laughing. "No one can catch Tok."

Eyes watering, I started toward one of the three remaining piles. I was two feet away when a four-foot tall, green faerie with yellow hair and eyes and a long, hooked nose appeared beside it. The goblin flashed me a wide grin as he scooped up the crystals and poured them into a little sack. "Thanks for the pretty baubles."

"You're not welcome," I growled, earning another infuriating chuckle from him as he blinked out of sight again.

I stayed where I was and watched the rest of the crystals disappear into his sack. He didn't even bother to hide himself now. He knew as well as I that I was no threat to him.

After he'd scooped up the last crystal, Tok faced me and patted the bulging sack with a smirk on his round face. "You more fun than the last two. You come back."

I scoffed. "Sure. We'll make s'mores and sing camp songs."

His eyes narrowed with interest. "What is s'mores?"

"S'mores are –" I stared at the goblin as the seed of an idea took root in my mind. I dismissed it immediately. No way. It would never work.

But...what if it did? What did I have to lose at this point?

"What is s'mores?" Tok repeated. His expression changed to one of annoyance, and he slowly walked toward me. "Why you not speak?"

I smiled. "Forget the s'mores. I have something you'll like even more."

"More baubles?" he asked eagerly.

"Better."

His look said I was clearly out of my mind because nothing was better than the sparkly contents of his sack.

I grinned like someone bursting to tell a big secret. "You want to know what it is?"

"Yes, tell me," he demanded.

"Okay, here goes." I inhaled deeply.

And I began to sing.

5

For a few seconds, Tok watched me with a puzzled expression, and I began to feel like an idiot. But as the lyrics to Finch's favorite song filled the air around us, the goblin's eyes took on a dazed look, and his face went slack. He stood there in a trance, his sack of crystals hanging limply from his hand.

I stared at him in disbelief. *It worked. It actually worked.*

Tok blinked, and I realized my words were trailing off. I took up the song again, singing loudly enough for anyone within a half-mile radius to hear. The moment I saw the goblin fall back into the trance, I leaped into action.

Still singing, I raced to him, yanking the shackles from my pocket as I went. Carefully, I locked them around his thin wrists, making sure they were snug but not too tight. After checking my work twice to make sure the restraints were secure, I took two steps back and let the song die on my lips.

It took about five seconds for him to come out of the trance and for outrage to replace the blank look in his eyes.

"Trickster!" he screeched. "Wicked human."

He backed up a step, his brow creased in confusion. Then his eyes widened in horror, and he stared down at the shackles around his wrists. Panicking, he wrenched and twisted the shackles, but his efforts were futile. They were Agency-issue Fae restraints, infused with enough pure iron to sap a faerie of their magic and strength without harming them.

"Take them off," he shouted.

"I can't. I'm sorry." I pushed away the guilt pricking me. I hated the sight of any creature in a cage or in restraints, but if I was going to follow through with this and become a bounty hunter, I had to be as tough as I'd told Tennin I could be.

Tok let out an ear-piercing shriek that made all the birds in the nearby trees take flight. When that didn't elicit a reaction from me, he stomped his feet and began to screech like he was being tortured.

I let his tantrum go on for a minute, until my ears couldn't take the abuse anymore. When he showed no signs of stopping, I did the only thing I knew would silence him.

After a verse, I stopped and watched the goblin awake from his trance. He began to rant and scream, and I took up the song again. We went back and forth like this for a good ten minutes before he gave up and stood there, glaring daggers at me.

"Horrid human," he spat.

"Hey, I'm not the one who has been stealing from innocent people." I pointed at the sack he still held. "How many jewels does one person need anyway?"

He clutched the sack to his chest. "These mine!"

"I don't want them. But you're coming with me."

Fear flashed in his eyes. "Where?"

How did I explain the whole bounty hunting process to a goblin? I would take him to the bond agent, where he'd be held until the Agency collected him. They would then tag him and turn him over to faeries to return him to his own realm. The tag was actually a special tattoo that couldn't be removed without the right technology, and it somehow prevented the wearer from leaving the faerie realm.

"We're going to the authorities, and you'll be sent back to your own world," I told him.

"But this my home." His voice grew louder. "I want stay here."

"Maybe they'll let you stay. I don't know," I lied. Goblins couldn't change their nature, and if the Agency let Tok go, he'd be back to his thieving ways in no time.

I approached him cautiously. He couldn't run or overpower me while he was wearing the shackles, but that didn't mean he couldn't bite. When I reached him, I wrapped my fingers around his thin arm and said, "Let's go."

If I thought he would come peacefully, I was sorely mistaken. The moment I picked up my backpack and we started to descend the steps, he began to bemoan the loss of his home and all his treasures. I felt bad for him, but there was nothing I could do about it. A few times when his voice rose to a near screech, I resorted to threatening him with song. He stomped down the steps sullenly, giving me a brief reprieve from the noise before he started up again.

We reached the base of the hill, and I steered him in the direction of the exit. I tugged my cap down and tried to ignore the stares we received as we walked through the park. Faeries were a common sight, but it wasn't every day that you saw a goblin. A goblin walking beside a human was even stranger. More than one person pulled out a phone and took pictures of us.

"Great," I muttered under my breath. I had no desire to be all over social media, but there was nothing I could do about that now. I maintained an impassive expression as if this was something I did every day, and I marched on.

Tok kicked up another fuss when we stopped at the Jeep. Like most woodland faeries, he'd never ridden in an automobile, and the sight of the big metal box on wheels frightened him. When I opened the rear hatch and lifted the tarp hiding the cage that took up the entire rear of the vehicle, he went into full freak-out. The cage bars contained enough pure iron to keep even a Court faerie from breaking free, which was why my parents always took the Jeep when they planned to do a capture.

"Alright, alright, no cage," I told him after I'd calmed him down with song.

I had to sing two more verses just to get him in the front of the SUV, enduring even more strange looks from pedestrians. I caught sight of one guy across the street recording us on his camera, and I groaned. Pictures were bad enough. I hoped he was too far away for his phone to pick up my singing.

Of course, as soon as I started around the front of the vehicle to the driver's side, Tok tried to open his door and escape. It was only my threat to sing all the way to the Plaza that made him stay in his seat.

"You cruel human," he whined when I slid behind the wheel.

I snapped my seat belt. "I told you the Jeep won't hurt you."

"It hurt when you sing."

"Oh, come on. It's not that bad." I scowled at him. I was no virtuoso, but I'd never been called a horrible singer.

He nodded. "Awful sound."

"If it's so bad, why do you look so blissed out when I sing?"

His mouth turned down. "Can't stop it. But it torture."

"Right." I started the engine and focused on the street. "Just remember that if you get it into your head to try to run again."

I might as well have been speaking to the dashboard. The first time I had to come to a stop in traffic, Tok unbuckled his seat belt and dived for the door. Thanks to my fast reflexes, I was able to grab him before he was able to open the door. I spent the rest of the drive singing every song I knew to keep him from trying to escape again. By the time I pulled up near the Plaza, I was hoarse, and I couldn't wait to be free of the cantankerous goblin.

"Stay," I ordered him as I opened my door and got out. I closed the door and turned to see the last person I wanted to run into today.

"Jesse, what are you doing here again?" Trey called as he sauntered up the street toward me.

I sighed, but it wasn't like he wouldn't find out soon enough. I walked around to the passenger side of the Jeep. "I'm here on business."

Trey laughed condescendingly. "Really? You in the bounty hunter business now?"

"As a matter of fact..." I opened the door and helped Tok out of the vehicle. Grasping his arm with one hand, I shut the door with the other, revealing the goblin to Trey for the first time.

Trey's eyes bugged out, and he nearly tripped over his feet. I have to say the sight of his mouth gaping like a fish out of water made every minute I'd spent in Tok's company worthwhile.

"That's...a..." he stammered.

"Tok, this is Trey," I said to the goblin. "Don't mind him. He always looks like that." Keeping a firm grip on my captive, I ushered him toward the Plaza and past Trey, who still hadn't recovered his ability to speak.

We reached the steps to the building, and Tok balked, fighting like crazy to get away from me. Trapping him in a tight embrace, I softly sang a few lines against his ear until he calmed.

"Stop that," he growled when he could talk again.

"Behave, or I'll sing until your ears fall off," I warned in a low voice.

The look of horror on his face was almost comical, and it took me several seconds to realize he'd taken my threat literally. I opened my mouth to correct him but changed my mind. It wouldn't hurt to let him believe that a little longer if it made him stop giving me trouble.

I tugged him up the steps. "Come on before Trey catches up to us."

Tok walked quietly beside me, clutching the sack of crystals like it was a lifeline. At the top, he recoiled again when I reached for the door, and I tightened my hold on him. I hadn't made it this far just to let him get away from me now.

"Jesse," Trey called from the street. "What the hell are you...?"

I yanked the door open and entered the building before Trey could finish his question. The lobby was even busier than it had been on my first visit, but you could have heard a pin drop when I walked in with Tok.

A dozen heads turned in our direction, shock etched on their faces. That soon gave way to disbelief and suspicion as they took in the restraints on the goblin's wrists. I didn't need to hear their thoughts to know what was going through their minds. I'd be incredulous, too, if I were in their shoes.

Bruce was the first to speak. He left the small group he'd been talking to and hurried over, stopping a few feet from us. His gaze kept flitting between Tok and me as if he was still trying to believe what he was seeing.

"Jesse, what is this?" he asked in a hushed voice. "What on earth are you doing with a...?" He stared at Tok again as words failed him.

While I had been freezing my butt off waiting for Tok to appear, I'd thought about what I would say when we got here. I knew there were going to be questions and opposition to my plans, but I wasn't going to let anyone stop me from doing whatever it took to find my parents.

I squared my shoulders, channeling my mother, who was the picture of self-assurance. "I'm taking care of the business while Mom and Dad are gone."

"You can't be serious. You don't know anything about hunting."

I tilted my head at the goblin by my side. "I caught him."

The other bounty hunters had drifted closer to hear our exchange. One of them let out a disparaging snort, earning a few chuckles from his companions. Someone else said, "Sure you did."

Tok shifted nervously. I gave his arm a comforting squeeze before I met the gaze of the young man who had spoken. "You think he put those restraints on himself?"

The man scoffed loudly. "No, I'm thinking you're working with someone else who is trying to pull one over on us. Like that TV show that plays pranks on people."

A few people nodded, and some even looked around for the hidden cameras.

"You believe what you want, but if you look hard enough, I'm sure you'll find pictures and video online to back me up. There were enough people taking pictures of us at the park."

"What park?" Bruce asked over the murmurs around us.

"Prospect Park. I just came from there."

"Prospect Park," echoed Trey, coming up behind me. "That was our job."

"It *was* your job, and then it came to us," I said to him over my shoulder.

Mom's notes hadn't said what team had the job before them, but I wasn't all that surprised to learn it had been Trey's. I liked Bruce, and I respected him, but his son was definitely not a chip off the old block. No doubt Tok had run circles around them, just as he had with me before I'd figured out how to get the better of him.

A man who had at least ten years on my father stepped forward. He had salt-and-pepper hair and a scar on the left side of his face that went from his cheek to his hairline. His hard stare made me want to back up a step, but I held my ground. If I showed weakness now, they would never accept me as one of them.

"You're a girl," the man said with a sneer. "No way you were able to catch a goblin on your own."

"Ambrose, are you saying women can't hunt?" demanded a female voice as a blonde woman in her mid-forties pushed through to the front of the group. She was lean and muscled and looked like she could hold her own against anyone here.

Ambrose scowled. "Stop trying to pick a fight with me, Kim. I'm talking about the girl."

I opened my mouth to retort that the girl was right here, but Bruce intervened.

"Jesse, did you really capture this goblin on your own?" he asked kindly.

"Yes."

He rubbed his jaw, looking like he still didn't know what to believe. "How?"

Tok tensed beside me, but I had no intention of sharing our secret with them. "Does it matter? He's here, and the job is done."

"It matters because he's a level Three," said Kim, flashing me a conspiratorial smile. "And it's inconceivable to all these big, strong men that one of us itty bitty gals could bag one."

"Damn it, Kim," Ambrose growled. "You're such a pain in the ass."

She punched him in the arm. "That's why you love me, big brother."

"Jesse," Bruce said, drawing my attention back to him. "Why would you finish one of your parents' jobs on your own?"

"I told you I'm taking care of the business."

"But you're not a bounty hunter," Trey said in that superior tone that grated on my nerves. "You can't just decide to be one. You need a license...and a partner."

I faced him, prepared for this argument. "Actually, I can. Mom and Dad have a family license that covers me, and I brought in my first capture, which puts me on the books. I'm just as much a bounty hunter as you are."

Kim hooted. "She's right."

"But you have no partner," Trey protested. "You can't do this alone."

"I didn't say I don't have a partner," I said evasively. "Now if you'll excuse me, I need to hand this guy off to the bond agent."

I took a step forward, but no one moved out of my way. Tok let out a low growl, and I looked down to see him baring his teeth at everyone. He wasn't much of a threat while in the restraints, but he was fierce enough to make people clear a path for us.

No one tried to stop us as we walked to the elevator, although there was plenty of talk. As the elevator doors opened, I heard someone say, "Look here. There's a video."

The doors slid shut, and Tok hit his breaking point when he realized he was trapped in a metal box. My assurances that it was perfectly safe fell on deaf ears, and I had to resort to singing to keep him from clawing the doors open. What I hadn't counted on was him losing his grip on the sack of crystals.

The elevator doors opened on the fourth floor to the sight of me on my hands and knees, gathering up the sparkling stones, with a goblin bellowing at me from the corner. And who should be standing there, waiting to catch the elevator, but Levi Solomon?

"What the hell?" the bond agent wheezed, making me fear for a moment that the shock might send him into cardiac arrest.

"Sorry." I scrambled to collect the last few crystals.

"Miss James, is that you? With...a *goblin*?"

Before I could answer him, Tok yelled, "Make her stop."

I lifted my head to glare at the goblin. "If you hadn't freaked out, this wouldn't have happened."

Tok answered me by leaping out of the elevator and hiding behind Levi's considerable girth. "Save me from horrid human," he begged Levi. "I go home to Faerie now."

I sat back on my heels and held out the sack of crystals. "Don't you want these?"

Tok peeked around Levi. "Is another trick," he accused before disappearing behind the man again.

I stood and stepped out of the elevator to face a speechless Levi. This wasn't exactly how I'd hoped to present myself to him when I came in and asked for more jobs.

"What is the meaning of this?" Levi asked when he regained his voice.

"You gave my parents a job to catch a goblin near Prospect Park." I pointed at the goblin hiding behind him. "That's him. I'm here to turn him in and collect my compensation."

"Compensation?" Levi echoed dumbly.

"Yes. You do pay bounty hunters when they finish a job?"

"Of course," he snapped. "But you aren't a bounty hunter."

I heaved a sigh, not wanting to go through this again. "If you check, you'll find I'm covered under my parents' license, and as you can see, I'm capable of getting the job done."

His beady eyes narrowed on me. "Is this some kind of trick? I'm a busy man, and I don't take lightly to being toyed with."

"Trickery! Yes!" piped in a voice from behind him.

Levi's lips pressed together in disapproval, and I threw up my hands. "I just caught him and brought him here against his will. Are you seriously going to take his word over mine?"

"Do you seriously expect me to believe you apprehended a goblin?" he shot back. "I don't care who your parents are. No one is that good on their first job."

I inhaled deeply to control my frustration. It hadn't really mattered if the bounty hunters in the lobby believed me. The people I really had to convince were the bond agents because they were the ones who gave the jobs to the hunters. If Levi didn't believe me, my career as a bounty hunter would be short-lived.

"If we can go to your office, I'll explain it to you," I said in a conciliatory tone.

He stared at me for a moment longer before he nodded. "Fine. You get one chance, but only because I respect your parents. If I think you're lying to me, I'll see that you don't set foot in this building again."

He ambled toward his door, leaving Tok and me facing each other. The goblin looked like he was debating if he should try to make a run for it.

"Don't even think about it." I snagged the chain between his cuffs and forced him to accompany me into Levi's office. Once we were inside, I stood in front of the desk and waited for Levi to take his seat.

"Alright, Miss James. You have five minutes."

Less than five minutes later, the bond agent stared at me with a mix of awe and suspicion. "That is a rare ability. I'll need a demonstration to believe it."

"I figured as much." I turned to Tok, who was watching me warily. "Last time, I promise."

Before the goblin could protest, I sang a few bars of a song. His jaw went slack, and his eyes took on that dreamy look I knew well. I stopped singing, but this time I was prepared for his rant. I held up a handful of glittering crystals, and he stopped yelling immediately. Then I thrust the sack into his hands, and he hugged it to his chest.

I looked at Levi again to see a calculating gleam had replaced the suspicion in his eyes.

"Impressive." He clasped his meaty hands on the desk. "That is a valuable weapon for a bounty hunter to possess."

"It doesn't work on every lower faerie," I reminded him.

Tok grumbled resentfully beside me.

"But it will work on some," Levi said more to himself. "You might be onto something here."

"What do you mean?"

He turned his shrewd gaze back on me. "You don't look like a bounty hunter. You look like a harmless teenage girl, but you obviously inherited your parents' cunning and resourcefulness. And you have a secret weapon."

I held up a hand. "A weapon I can't rely on."

"True, true, but it will come in handy at times." He drummed his fingers on the desk. "Okay, Miss James, you've convinced me. I'm inclined to offer you another job on several conditions."

"Really?" I couldn't suppress the little squeal that slipped from me. So much for being professional.

Levi scowled. "With *conditions*. This will be a probationary period, and you will only do level One and Two jobs until I say otherwise."

I started to protest, but he cut me off. "You got lucky this time, but Threes and Fours are too much for a new hunter to handle."

"What if there's a bulletin, or I'm in a situation where I come across a Three or Four and I can bring them in?"

He scoffed. "Go right ahead, but make sure you're not stepping on another hunter's toes. They don't take lightly to someone grabbing their bounty."

"But that happens all the time." I'd heard enough stories from my parents and their friends about hunters stealing captures from each other.

"It happens, but they still get upset when it does. Just remember that."

"I will. When do I get my next job?"

Levi laughed, and it turned into a cough. "I can see you take after your mother in more than looks." He turned to his computer and clicked around a bit. "Here is a level One that just came in. You think you can handle a peri? If not, we'll have to wait a few days for something else."

"No problem," I said in a rush.

A peri was a faerie about the size of a pixie that loved to wreak havoc. They weren't dangerous to humans, but they were one of the most destructive pests to come out of Faerie. If you left one of them alone in a room for a day, they would scorch anything that could burn. Their magic normally wasn't strong enough to start actual fires, but every now and then, one of them got lucky.

Pleased, Levi printed the job and handed the sheet of paper to me. "Everything you need to know is on that. Head over to Agency HQ today to register and get your ID done. You'll need that before you take on new jobs."

I folded the paper and tucked it into a pocket. "What about my friend here?"

Levi opened a drawer on his desk and pulled out a pair of shackles that looked like mine, except his were black. Holding them out to me, he said, "Put these on him, and then you can remove yours."

"That's it?"

"That's it for you. He'll go in one of my detainment cells until someone from the Agency comes to collect him in a few hours. He's lucky you brought him in when you did. Most captures come in after the daily pickup and have to stay here overnight."

I took the shackles and locked them around Tok's thin wrists. I didn't ask Levi how long the goblin would be in the Agency's custody before he was sent back to Faerie. I could see how anxious Tok had become at the sight of the other set of shackles, and I didn't want to upset him more.

Once my shackles had been removed, I said an awkward goodbye to Tok before Levi led him through the door at the back of the office. There wasn't much you could say to a goblin who hated you for forcing him from his home and treasure hoard.

Levi returned after a few minutes and wrote out a check for the job. I stared at the amount, finding it hard to believe I'd earned five thousand dollars in one afternoon. It was more than I'd earned in two months at the Magic Bean.

"You made the check out to me." I pointed out his mistake.

"You do the job, you earn the payout," he answered. "There's more where that came from if you can prove you're not a one-trick pony."

I stuck the check in my back pocket. "I'm not."

His mouth curved into some semblance of a smile. "Good. I look forward to seeing you back here in a few days with that peri."

I knew a dismissal when I heard one. Picking up my shackles, I said goodbye and left his office. I nearly ran into Trey and Bruce, who were standing on the other side of Levi's door.

"I take it everything went okay with Levi?" Bruce asked, reaching for the door before I could close it.

I smiled. "Couldn't have gone better."

"Good." He started to enter the office and stopped to look back at his son, who hadn't moved from his spot. "You coming?"

"I'll be there in a minute," Trey told him.

Bruce gave me what could only be an apologetic look and went inside. At least, he wasn't completely blind to the fact that his son was a moron.

Trey turned to me. "Did Levi actually believe you caught that goblin?"

I scowled at him. "I *did* catch him."

"How?" He crossed his arms.

"Sorry, trade secret. That's between me, Levi, and the goblin."

"Come on, Jesse. You honestly expect anyone to believe you snared a level Three on your first job?"

I lifted a shoulder. "Levi believes me. In fact, he gave me another job to do."

Trey's jaw went slack. "You have got to be kidding."

"Why? I have a valid license."

He shook his head. "Levi shouldn't give you a job just because of who your parents are."

It took considerable effort not to let him get a rise out of me with that insult. I cocked an eyebrow at him. "And you got your first job based on your own merits or because of your father?"

"That's not the same thing," he blustered. "I'm older than you, and I trained for six months with Dad before I got my license."

"But without your dad, you wouldn't have gotten a job as easily," I said pointedly. "I'm not denying my last name probably had something to do with Levi's decision. But I also proved myself to him, and he's willing to take a chance on me."

Trey surprised me by switching gears. "Fine. But don't go off on your own. Work with Dad and me."

My annoyance lessened at the concern in his voice. "I'll think about it." I already knew I wouldn't join their team, but letting Trey think I might would appease him for now. I'd go work with surly Ambrose before I'd test my sanity working with Trey.

"Okay, then." He smiled, letting his arms drop to his sides.

I pointed a thumb in the direction of the elevator. "Well, I have to be going."

"Call me," he said.

Not likely. I offered up a small smile and turned to the elevator. "Happy hunting."

6

"Ow," I yelped when a thick hardcover book glanced off the side of my head and landed with a thump on the floor. I glared up at the tiny, brown, stick-like faerie that grinned back from the top shelf of the bookcase. "That hurt!"

The peri snickered and disappeared from sight. Rubbing my injured head, I bent to pick up the heavy copy of *Moby Dick* that bore several scorch marks on the front cover. He couldn't have found a smaller book to clobber me with?

"That thing is a menace," cried the middle-aged man with a tragic comb-over, who rushed at me. The proprietor of Howell's Used Books snatched the tome from me and ran his hand over the damaged cover. Hugging the book to his chest, he said, "Don't just stand there. Do something."

I looked up at the spot where the peri had been and let my gaze sweep over the cramped space between the rows of bookcases. Mr. Howell had filled every inch of his small store with merchandise, and while I'd normally be happy at the sight of so many books, it was only going to be a hindrance to me now.

The man huffed impatiently. "Are you sure you know what you're doing?"

"I need to assess the situation before I do anything." I studied the layout of the store and mulled over possible ways to trap the peri.

"Well, while you're *assessing*, that thing is going to burn everything I own," he snapped.

I turned to him and asked the question that had been bugging me since I got here. "Don't you have a fire ward?"

Mr. Howell sniffed and drew back. "I did, but it expired, and with sales down from the recession, I can't afford to get a new one yet."

"I don't think you can afford not to have one with all these books." I went back to studying my surroundings, but not before I caught the indignant look he shot me.

He could glare all he wanted, but we both knew I was right. Fire wards were one of the best things to come out of Faerie. You paid a Court faerie a fee to come and ward the place, and the cost depended on the size of the building and the strength of the ward. Most apartment and office buildings in the city had them, including ours, and I'd heard it would soon be required by law.

I walked down one of the narrow rows, listening intently for movement on the shelves. Up ahead, I heard a faint shuffling. *Aha.*

"How exactly do you plan to catch this thing?" Mr. Howell asked loudly, following me.

I put a finger to my lips. "Maybe you should go up front while I do this," I whispered.

I moved away in the direction of the peri without waiting for a reply. My feet made no sound as I crept toward the spot where I suspected the peri was hiding. The rustle of pages made me smile. *Got you.*

Something smacked against the floor behind me, making me jump. I spun to find the shop owner bending to retrieve the copy of *Moby Dick* he'd dropped.

"Sir, please go –" I broke off when another fat book came flying off a shelf to nail the man in the back of the head.

Mr. Howell yelped and fell over, swearing. I went to help him up and saw the peri had thrown a *George R.R. Martin* book this time. How was that little wretch even strong enough to pick up these heavy books?

"Am I bleeding? I think I'm bleeding," Mr. Howell wailed, poking at the back of his skull.

"You're okay," I assured him.

The corners of his mouth pulled down. "I might have a concussion, no thanks to you. I'm going to call the Agency and ask for someone who knows what they're doing."

A tic started at the corner of my eye, but I resisted the desire to tell this annoying, ungrateful man what I really thought. I nodded and said, "As you wish, sir."

"Where are you going?" he demanded when I turned to leave.

"If you want another hunter, there is nothing for me to do here," I said over my shoulder.

His voice grew shrill. "You can't leave me alone here with that monster."

I almost laughed. The peri was hardly a monster. A nuisance, yes, but it posed no real threat to him. I was sorely tempted to leave him to deal with it alone. Maybe that would give him a new appreciation for others – like me – who tried to help him.

Then I thought about going back to Levi and telling him I hadn't been able to complete the first job he'd given me. He'd never take me seriously if I couldn't even finish a level One, no matter the reason. Part of being a bounty hunter was handling difficult people like Mr. Howell, and if I couldn't do that, I didn't deserve the title.

Taking a deep breath, I turned to face the man again. "I'll stay on one condition. You go to the front of the store and leave me alone to do my job."

He opened his mouth to argue, but I cut him off. "It's that, or I'm out of here."

With one last glare at me, he walked off in a huff.

Finally. I let out a long sigh of relief and smiled. One problem solved; one to go.

My good mood lasted for approximately four seconds. That was how long it took for the peri to fling another book at me. The heavy volume brushed the back of my head, and a second later, the smell of singed hair reached my nose.

"Son of a..." I reached up and patted my hair, thankful it wasn't on fire.

"What's going on?" Mr. Howell yelled. "Did you get him?"

Was he serious? He'd left me less than half a minute ago.

"Not yet," I called back.

Movement overhead caught my eye, and I looked up in time to see the peri leap over my head to the opposite bookcase. I unclipped the holster on my hip and pulled out the weapon I'd brought with me for this job. Holding it before me, I crept to the next aisle. But there was no sign of the little faerie.

A small thump had me tiptoeing to the far side of the store to peek around the last row of shelves. Something moved on a small table that held a display of the Harry Potter series, and I gasped when I saw the peri's hands hovering over one of the books. You can clobber me with books all you want, but you do *not* mess with Harry Potter.

I stepped into view with my weapon pointed at the faerie. "Back away from Harry," I said slowly.

The peri froze, his gaze on the gun in my hands. He looked from the gun to me as if sizing me up as a real threat. One of his hands lowered until it almost touched the cover of the book.

My finger tightened on the trigger. "Go ahead. Make my day." I fought back a silly grin. I'd always wanted to say that.

He smirked, and a wisp of smoke rose from the book cover.

I pulled the trigger. A stream of water hit him square in the face, sending him ass over teakettle. He got to his feet, sputtering, and tried to flee, only to fall on his butt again. He shook water from his hair and shot me an accusing look.

"It's just water. It won't hurt you," I said, walking toward him. I didn't feel the need to tell him a pinch of iron dust added to water made it like kryptonite to his kind. I was pretty sure he'd already figured out this was no ordinary water.

I holstered my water gun and shrugged off my backpack. Unzipping it, I pulled out a mason jar with half an inch of water in the bottom. Scooping up the indignant peri, I deposited him gently inside the jar, and then I screwed on a different lid that had holes punched in it. It wasn't the most sophisticated equipment, but it worked in a pinch.

The peri banged his tiny fists against the sides of the bottle, squeaking in outrage. Not that I blamed him. I wouldn't want to be trapped in a glass jar either. Hopefully, it wouldn't take too long for the Agency to tag him and send him back to Faerie.

I picked up my backpack and walked to the front of the store where Mr. Howell sat behind the counter. He eyed the mason jar nervously as I approached.

"All done." I carefully placed the jar in my pack, wrapping it in a wool scarf.

He scowled petulantly. "What about the damage to my merchandise?"

"You can take that up with the Agency," I said, though I already knew what they'd tell him. Property damage during a capture was not the responsibility of the Agency unless it was excessive and unwarranted. They would tell him he could have prevented the damage by having a fire ward.

I gave him a parting smile because I was nothing if not professional. "Have a nice day, sir."

He grumbled something that definitely wasn't a thank you – not that I was expecting one from him. If this peri wasn't worth a thousand dollars, I'd be sorely tempted to release him back into the store with my blessing.

I stepped outside and sucked in a lungful of cold air. Even mingled with the unpleasant odors of the street, it was better than the cloying, musty smell of the bookshop. I looked down at my clothes and made a face. Mr. Howell wasn't overly big on housekeeping either, judging by the dust on my hands and coat.

I was rooting in my backpack for my keys when I was struck by the uneasy feeling that someone was watching me. I scanned the street and buildings but saw no one looking in my direction. It wasn't the first time I'd had this feeling in the last few days, but then, I had been jumpy since Mom and Dad disappeared.

I patted my coat pocket to make sure I had the small stun gun Dad had given me when I'd first started using the subway. I'd never had occasion to use it, but I felt safer having it on me now. And I needed some kind of protection if I was going to be out in the city, especially at night.

Fishing my keys out of my pack, I started for the Jeep. I don't know what drew my eyes to the window of the pawn shop next to the bookstore, or why I walked over for a closer look at the display labeled *Faerie Talismans*. My heart sped up, and a single word played in my mind when my gaze fell on an intricately braided leather bracelet that was the twin to the one on my wrist. *Mom.*

When I was twelve, Mom had a set of bracelets made for her, my father, and me. Dad's bracelet was wider than ours, but all three had an identical braiding pattern designed by Mom. The bracelets were more than jewelry. Hidden in the braiding were dried filaments of muryan, a fibrous plant that grew only in faerie. If used properly, muryan was a powerful talisman against faerie glamours.

Mom had made me promise to never go out without my bracelet, and I knew she would not have removed her own outside of our apartment. The thought of how it could have come off her wrist and ended up in this pawn shop made my stomach knot painfully.

The bell above the door jingled when I entered the shop. A skinny man in his thirties with a pony tail and wearing a Black Sabbath T-shirt watched me from behind the glass counter.

"Buying or selling?" he asked when I approached him.

I gripped the edge of the counter. "Neither. I want to know where you got that leather bracelet in the window display."

His eyes darted from me to the window and back again. "What bracelet?"

"The one that looks exactly like this." I yanked up my coat sleeve to show him mine.

"If you already have one, what do you need another for?"

"I didn't say I needed it. I asked where it came from."

He frowned. "You have any idea how many people come in here in a week? I can't remember them all."

"That's why you have records." I pointed to a pad of forms on a shelf behind him. "You give a pawn ticket to everyone who sells to you, right?"

He crossed his arms. "Yeah, but I can't just show that to anyone who wants to see it. People got a right to their privacy. Only the proper authorities can see my records."

"I'm a bounty hunter for the Agency. That gives me the authority to see them." My knowledge in this area was a bit fuzzy, but I was sure I'd read that somewhere in the thick manual.

The man howled with laughter. "A bounty hunter. Good one!"

Annoyed, but not surprised by his reaction, I plucked my shiny, new bounty hunter ID from my back pocket and held it up. His laughter stopped as he leaned forward to squint at the card.

His eyebrows shot up. "No shit. You're really a bounty hunter?"

"Yes." I returned the card to my pocket. "Now can you tell me who sold you that bracelet?"

"Not so fast. Is this personal or related to Agency business? I keep my business on the up-and-up, and I need to know I'm not breaking any laws."

My chest tightened. "Both. That bracelet belongs to a bounty hunter who went missing five days ago. My mother. You can tell me what you know, or we can wait for someone from the Agency to come out. Either way, I'm not leaving here until I know where you got her bracelet."

He put up his hands. "Okay, okay, no need to get carried away. I don't mind cooperating, but let's keep them out of it. The last thing I need is to have a bunch of agents poking around and scaring off my customers."

He opened a door behind the counter and entered what looked like an office. I clenched my hands together as I listened to him rifling through the contents of a filing cabinet. This was the first real lead to my parents since they'd disappeared, but my gut twisted at the possibility of where it would take me.

I heard a filing cabinet drawer sliding shut, and then the man was back, holding a paper. He laid the form on the counter and pointed to the name on it. "Carl Porter. He comes in every now and then. Nice guy, quiet."

I studied the name and address, noting he didn't live far from here. I could pay him a visit before I took the peri to Levi.

As if the tiny faerie had read my mind, he started to squeak angrily.

"You got a rat in there or something?" the pawn shop owner asked warily.

"Peri," I said as I took a picture of Carl's address with my phone. "I caught him in the bookshop next door."

The man's lip curled. "You should have let the little bugger burn the place down. I bet Howell didn't even thank you."

I smiled because I *had* thought about letting the peri loose in the store again. "I get paid whether he's grateful or not."

"I guess that makes it easier. Anything else I can help you with?"

I pointed a thumb at the window display. "I want my mother's bracelet."

He looked like he was about to argue and thought better of it. With a sigh, he went to get the bracelet for me. Something told me that if not for his dislike of having agents in his store, he wouldn't be as willing to part with an item he'd paid for. Legally, he could hold onto it because I had no proof it had been taken from my mother. If she'd lost it, which I knew in every fiber of my being was not the case, then neither he nor Carl had broken any laws.

"Here you go." He gave me the bracelet, and I turned it over in my hands to examine it. The tie was broken, and someone, probably Carl, had sewn on a new one.

"Everything good?" the man asked.

"Yes." I swallowed around the tightness in my throat, needing to get out of there before my emotions got the better of me. "By the way, I hope you have a good fire ward on this place because Mr. Howell doesn't have one."

"I knew it! Cheap bastard." The man shook his head.

I opened the door. "Thank you for your help."

Outside the pawn shop, I ignored the lingering feeling of being watched and set off for the Jeep. As I walked, I typed Carl Porter's address into my GPS app to find the fastest route there. With any luck I'd find him at home. If not, I planned to wait there until he arrived because this was too important to put off until tomorrow.

Mr. Porter lived on the second floor of an apartment building that had seen better days. I knocked on his door and shifted from one foot to the other for a minute before I knocked again.

I was resigning myself to waiting for him in the Jeep when I heard the dead bolt move. The door opened as far as the chain lock would allow to reveal dark skin and a single brown eye.

"Hello. Do I know you?" asked an older male voice.

"Mr. Porter, hi. My name is Jesse James, and I wanted to ask you about this bracelet you sold to King's Pawn Shop." I held up my mother's bracelet.

His jaw flexed nervously. "How did you find me?"

"I got your address from the pawn shop." I produced my bounty hunter ID and showed it to him.

"I-I didn't steal it. I found it."

I gave him my most disarming smile. "No one is accusing you of anything. I only want to know where you found the bracelet because it's related to an important job I'm working on. You don't even have to let me in. We can talk right here."

He gave me a one-eyed stare for a moment before he nodded. Then he stepped back and unhooked the chain.

———

"Are you sure you've never seen either of them here?"

The immaculately groomed receptionist behind the front desk at the Ralston looked down his nose at me. "We cater to Fae royalty and celebrities, not exactly the kind of people a bounty hunter would be interested in."

"Will you just look at the picture again?" I held up my phone, which had a recent photo of my parents on the screen.

He lowered his eyes to look at the phone for no more than a second. "As I said, I don't recognize either of them, and I would have noticed them had they come in. They wouldn't exactly blend in here."

I bit back my retort and looked around the opulent marble and glass lobby of the hotel. In a corner of the lounge area, a female Court faerie in a stunning red evening gown stood with a blond man in a tux. On the other side of the room was a faerie couple who were similarly attired.

At a thousand dollars a night, the Ralston wasn't a place I'd ever visit if it wasn't for my current circumstances. Their clientele came from the upper crust of society, and no one I knew moved in those circles. The only reason I was here now was because of the bracelet in my pocket.

Carl Porter had been eager to tell me all he knew, once I'd convinced him he wasn't in any trouble. The middle-aged man worked in maintenance at the Ralston, where he said he'd found the bracelet in one of the ballrooms the morning after my parents went missing. When I asked about the condition of the bracelet, he'd told me it had been damaged when he found it.

I couldn't tell the receptionist about the bracelet or how I'd found it because I'd promised Mr. Porter I would not mention him. I didn't want to repay him by getting him fired from the job he'd worked at for over twenty years.

"Is there anything else I can help you with?" the receptionist asked haughtily. You'd think he was a guest here instead of an employee with all the attitude he was throwing around.

"What about other employees who might have been working that night?"

"I already told you –"

"I know what you said, but just because you didn't see them doesn't mean no one else did. You could have been busy with something and missed them."

I leaned toward him over the counter. "This is really important, and I'm not asking for much. Help a girl out, will you?"

He pressed his lips together and finally nodded. "Take a seat, and I will see what I can do."

"Thank you."

I did as he requested and sat on one of the stiff embroidered chairs closest to the front desk. He picked up a headset and spoke quietly into it. Then he went back to whatever he'd been doing when I arrived and pretended I wasn't there.

I was getting fidgety by the time a freckle-faced young man in a bellhop uniform approached me ten minutes later. He stopped in front of my chair. "I'm Alan. Bryce said you wanted to ask me about some people who might have been here last week."

I stood so we were at the same eye level. "Thanks for taking a minute to talk to me." As I spoke, I opened the photo of my parents on my phone and showed it to him. "Do you remember either of these people being here last Thursday night?"

Alan took the phone and studied the photo. "Oh, yeah, I remember them. They got on the elevator when I was bringing some luggage up to one of the rooms."

My stomach fluttered. "Did they say anything to you?"

He thought for a moment. "Don't think so. I got off on four, and that was the last I saw of them."

"Can you remember what time that was?" I asked as he handed the phone back to me.

"Around eleven, I think, because I'd just come back from my break." He smiled apologetically. "I wish I knew more."

"So do I, but I'm grateful for your help."

He tilted his head, listening to the small headset he wore. "I have to get back to work. Sorry I couldn't be of more help."

He hurried off to grab a luggage cart and then headed for the elevators, leaving me wondering where to go from here. The fact that my parents had been here that night could be totally unrelated to their disappearance, but my gut was telling me otherwise.

The problem was that I couldn't just search the hotel for them. The Ralston was known for its discretion and security, and they were not going to let me snoop around, invading the privacy of their high-profile guests.

A feeling of powerlessness washed over me. What good was being a bounty hunter if I couldn't use it to find my own parents? I would report what I knew to the Agency, but they hadn't exactly done much so far to instill any confidence in me. They didn't seem to be too concerned about two missing bounty hunters.

The dinging of the elevator pulled my attention in that direction as the doors slid open and a couple walked out. The man wore a tux, and the woman was decked out in a shimmering pale blue gown. Her ash-blonde hair was styled in an elegant updo, and she wore a diamond and sapphire choker that had to cost a fortune. She looked familiar, and it took me a few seconds to place her. She was Victoria Hart, Hollywood darling and star of numerous movies over the last two years. According to Violet, Victoria was on the arm of a different faerie each week and had even been linked to one of the royals.

That made me look at her escort, whom I'd only given a cursory glance, and my stomach did a little flip when I met the cold, assessing stare of Lukas Rand. Our gazes locked, and for a moment, I felt like a moth hypnotized by a deadly flame. Unlike the moth, I could sense the danger and break free from its pull.

Lukas and Victoria made a striking couple as they walked in my direction, the picture of wealth and elegance. I didn't suffer from poor self-esteem, but it was impossible not to feel a little dowdy here in this grand hotel and in the presence of such beauty.

"I hope I didn't make us late," the actress simpered coquettishly, running a hand up and down his arm. "But I had to take that call from my agent. I hope you understand."

Lukas smiled at her. "We have plenty of time."

I turned my back on them and strode to the exit. There was nothing else I could do here tonight. My time would be better spent preparing for the new job Levi had given me when I dropped off the peri this afternoon. And I needed to get home to Finch, who had been alone for far too long.

The doors slid open, and a blast of cold, damp air hit me, along with the flash of a camera. I scowled at the small pack of paparazzi. There was always someone famous staying at the Ralston, so I wasn't surprised to see them there.

"She's no one," a short, bald pap called.

"Thanks," I muttered as I passed them.

A fog had rolled in while I was in the hotel, shrouding Manhattan in thick mist and distorting the lights and sounds. I could barely see ten feet in front of me as I headed to the Jeep, which I'd had to park a block away.

I was so wrapped up in thinking about my parents that I didn't register the footsteps behind me at first. I looked over my shoulder, but whoever was back there was hidden by the swirling fog. It was very likely we were just walking in the same direction, but the memory of all those times I'd felt like I was being watched had me walking faster.

My heart began to pound when I heard the footsteps keeping pace with mine, and I broke into a run. It was hard to judge distance in this fog, but I should be almost to the Jeep. If I could just get in and lock the doors –

"Oomph!" I cried when I barreled into a male elf walking toward me.

He steadied me and took a step back.

"I'm so sorry," I panted.

"No harm done." He smiled, but it did nothing to ease my anxiety. If anything, it made me want to put more distance between us.

I moved to go around him, and his hand snaked out to latch onto my arm. "Why the hurry?"

"Let me go." I tried to wrench my arm from his grip, but elves were a lot stronger than they looked. Balling my free hand into a fist, I punched him hard in the face.

"Bitch!" He grabbed his bleeding nose but didn't loosen his hold on me.

"You'll get worse than that if you don't get your hands off me." I stomped on his instep and followed that with a punch to the side of his throat. His grip slackened as he gasped for air.

"You had one job," said a male voice as a second elf emerged from the fog in the direction of the hotel. "Why didn't you just glamour her?"

The elf beside me spit blood and glared at the newcomer. "I tried, but it didn't work," he griped in a nasally voice.

"She must be wearing one of those talismans," mused his friend as he drew near. "At least, you managed not to lose her."

I faced off against the elf who must have followed me from the hotel. "I have no money or jewelry, so you're wasting your time."

His chuckle made the hair on the back of my neck stand up. "Don't want your money, little girl," he drawled as he took a step toward me.

7

M y heart thudded against my ribs. "Do you know what the punishment is for attacking a human?" I asked as my hand inched toward my pocket.

"I don't see any agents or bounty hunters around here. Do you?" my pursuer taunted, stalking me.

"Yes," I said the second he was within striking distance. His entire body seized when I hit him with the stun gun, and he began to spasm when I kept the prongs pressed to his chest. Stun guns worked on faeries, but you had to give them a bit more juice for it to be effective.

His legs gave out, and he crumpled to the sidewalk. I turned to give the first elf the same treatment, but he released me and fled into the fog.

The elf on the ground tried to roll to his hands and knees, but his body wasn't cooperating. I bent down and gave him another good jolt until he collapsed facedown. Better safe than sorry.

I patted my pockets, cursing myself for not carrying a pair of Fae shackles on me. That wouldn't happen again.

"What is this?" asked a new voice.

I let out a tiny scream and jerked up to face the tall figure standing a few feet away. Expecting another elf assailant, I was shocked to see Lukas Rand standing there.

I put a hand over my racing heart. "Jesus! Didn't anyone ever tell you it's rude to creep up on people?"

Ignoring my question, he pointed to the prone elf at my feet. "What happened here?"

"He and his friend jumped me. The other one got away, but this one wasn't so lucky."

Lukas's brows drew together. "Why did they attack you?"

"I was a little too busy fighting them off to ask," I quipped dryly. I took in his expensive tux that looked so out of place on the foggy street. "What are you doing here? Did you lose your date?"

He crossed his arms. "My date is waiting for me at the hotel. What I'd like to know is why you were at the Ralston."

A tiny shiver went through me at the hard edge that had crept into his voice. "Why do you care?"

"I make it my business to know what's going on around me," he replied coldly.

I matched his stance. "Not when it's my personal business."

The fog shifted, and two more faeries appeared on either side of Lukas. I recognized Conlan and Faolin, the latter looking even more hostile, if that was possible.

"Lukas, you left without telling us," Faolin growled.

Lukas didn't take his gaze from me. "Something came up."

Conlan grinned. "Jesse James, I didn't expect to see you again so soon. And what's this? You starting fights again?"

The elf groaned and tried to push up off the ground. I put my foot on his back to hold him down. "Stay."

I looked up to see the three faeries watching me. Lukas raised an eyebrow, Faolin glowered, and Conlan laughed. All three reactions grated on my already frayed nerves.

"What?" I snapped.

Conlan held up his hands. "Don't mind me. I'm just enjoying the show."

"What do you intend to do with the elf?" Lukas asked.

"I'm going to turn him over to the Agency and let them deal with him."

Upon hearing this, my attacker fought to rise. I let out an aggravated sigh and gave him another jolt from my stun gun. At this rate, the thing would be out of juice soon.

"If you don't mind, I need to get this guy shackled before he wakes up again."

"You just happen to have Fae shackles on you?" Faolin looked seconds away from lunging at me. "How convenient."

I looked from him to Lukas to Conlan to see the three of them were watching me suspiciously now. Even Conlan had lost his smile and seemed more alert.

"Yes. All bounty hunters have them," I informed the nosy trio. "And I'd call it decidedly *inconvenient* since I left mine in the Jeep."

Lukas tilted his head to one side. "*You're* a bounty hunter?"

"I'm so sick of people asking me that," I muttered between gritted teeth as I reached into my back pocket for my ID card.

Faolin jumped in front of Lukas, snarling like a rabid dog and forcing me back a few steps. If I hadn't been so annoyed, I might have had the sense to be scared.

"Whoa. Chill, *Cujo*." I whipped out the card and held it before me like a shield. "It's not my best photo, but I don't think it will kill you."

Lukas stepped around Faolin and took the card from me. He studied it for a moment before handing it to Faolin, who turned it over in his hands, looking for what, I had no idea.

"So, bounty hunting is what brought you to the Ralston tonight?" Lukas asked in a voice that had lost a little of its bite.

"No." I dragged out the word for emphasis. "As I said, it was personal business."

He narrowed his eyes, clearly unsatisfied with my answer. Too bad. I didn't owe him or his friends any explanation about my activities.

Faolin sneered. "And you just happened to run into us."

"Hey, you guys followed me, in case you've forgotten." I snatched my card from him. "Now if you don't mind, I have places to be."

Faolin looked at Lukas. "What do you want to do?"

Lukas's dark gaze burned into mine before moving away. "Let her go."

It was on the tip of my tongue to say "How kind of you," but I bit back the retort. Now that the adrenaline rush from the attack was wearing off, I remembered these faeries were dangerous, possibly criminals, and not people I should be messing with. Compared to them, the elves that had attacked me seemed as harmless as Finch.

I bent to help the elf to his feet, but Conlan nudged me aside. Picking up the half-unconscious faerie with ease, Conlan tossed him over his shoulder and turned to me. "Lead the way."

I wasn't too proud to accept help, so I showed him where the Jeep was parked nearby. I'd started keeping a duffle bag of hunting gear in the back, and it proved to be a smart decision now. After I shackled the elf's wrists, Conlan put him in the cage. A small shudder went through the big faerie when his hand accidentally brushed the metal.

"You always drive around with an iron cage in your Jeep?" Conlan asked as I padlocked the cage door.

"It's part of the job." I didn't bother explaining this was my father's Jeep, and he and Mom mainly used it for work. For everything else, we used her car.

I closed the rear hatch. When I was done, I turned to find him watching me inquisitively. "What?"

"You're different than most human females I meet."

I scoffed softly. "You need to work on your pickup lines."

Conlan chuckled. "I mean there is a lot more to you than I first thought. I'm still trying to figure you out."

"Good luck with that. Half the time, *I* can't figure me out."

That got a hearty laugh out of him, and I smiled in return. I couldn't figure him out either. He seemed too easygoing to be a part of Lukas Rand's circle, but something told me he could be as dangerous as the rest of that group. I needed to remember that.

I climbed into the Jeep, waved goodbye to him, and drove away. Within seconds, he was swallowed up by the fog.

Traffic was heavier with the dense fog, and it seemed to take hours to get to the Plaza. The drive was made worse by my prisoner, who woke up after ten minutes and railed at me nonstop. I tried singing, but of course, that didn't work on him. The elf hurled insults and threats at me until I was ready to stop and gag him. I would have stunned him again, but I'd drained the stun gun's battery already.

The moment we entered the Plaza, the elf shut up, cowed by the half dozen armed bounty hunters in the lobby. I was getting used to the curious looks by now, and I ignored them as I towed the elf to the elevator.

Levi was gone for the night, so I turned the faerie over to another bond agency. Neither of us would earn a fee for the elf's arrest, but the bond agency was legally required to process the arrest. He grumbled the whole time I was filling out the stack of paperwork, and I was glad to get out of there and away from the two of them.

It was after midnight when I finally let myself into the apartment, and all I wanted to do was collapse on my bed. I might not even stop to kick off my boots.

I expected Finch to be asleep, so I was surprised to find him sitting on the back of the couch waiting for me. I felt a familiar pang of guilt about leaving him on his own all day. He was pretty independent and could feed himself, but the last week had been even harder on him than on me. At least, I could go out and search for our parents.

"Hey, buddy, sorry I was gone so long." I hung up my jacket. "You holding down the fort?"

He whistled shrilly and signed, *Someone tried to open the door.*

Alarm shot through me. "What? When?"

Not long ago. But they couldn't come in.

I turned to stare at the door. I'd lived here my whole life, and not once had anyone tried to break in or cause any trouble in the building. The entire borough had heard of my parents, and no one was stupid enough to mess with them.

We had either been visited by an incompetent burglar...or a faerie had tried to come in uninvited.

I headed for the office. "Come on. Let's see who our visitor was."

I sat at the computer and logged in. We had security cameras on each floor and in the stairwell. My parents took the safety of their family and residents seriously. In addition to the cameras, the whole building was covered with fire wards. Because of Mom and Dad's work, our apartment was also protected by a powerful anti-faerie ward. Any faerie who wanted entry had to be granted access using a secret incantation that was known only to us.

I brought up the camera feeds and checked the activity log for the last hour. The cameras had built-in motion detectors that logged every time something moved in front of them. I watched Gorn arriving home at eleven thirty, and a few minutes later, the front door opened again. Two tall people, males judging by their size, entered the small lobby. Both wore long coats with hoods pulled up to obscure their faces, and they kept their heads down, deliberately avoiding the cameras.

The two males headed straight for the stairs and reappeared on our floor. They looked at Maurice's door as if uncertain about which apartment they wanted. Then they approached our door, all the while carefully keeping their faces hidden.

The video went fuzzy for a good thirty seconds. When it cleared, it showed the backs of the two strangers as they hurried down the stairs. It didn't take a genius to know they had tried magic to open the door. Only Fae magic could affect technology that way.

Finch whistled, and I looked at him. *Faeries,* he signed.

I nodded and sat back in the chair, watching the mysterious faeries leave the building without once revealing their identities. Whoever they were, they knew what they were doing, which ruled out a random break-in.

A chill went through me. Why would faeries try to break into our apartment? I wasn't naïve enough to think my parents didn't have any enemies among the Fae, considering their line of work, but most of their jobs dealt with lower faeries. Those two who had come here tonight were definitely Court faeries.

What had they been looking for? It was too much of a coincidence that I was attacked by elves on the same night two faeries tried to break into my place. Tennin had said the goren dealer was an elf. Could my attackers have been working for him? And why would they come after me?

What didn't make sense was the Court faeries. As far as I knew, they didn't work with lower faeries, and they certainly wouldn't do the dirty work for one.

I massaged my temples as a headache started to form. Exhaustion and stress pressed down on me, and I would have given anything for one of Mom's hugs or Dad's warm laughter. I'd never realized how much I'd taken the little things for granted until I no longer had them.

Finch walked across the desk to sit on the mouse. *Are you sad?*

I summoned a smile I didn't feel. "I'm just tired. I'll feel better in the morning after I get some sleep."

Are you going out tomorrow? he asked.

"Yes. We have another job to do."

Will you look for Mom and Dad?

"I'll never stop looking for them," I promised him. I thought about the discoveries I'd made today, from finding my mother's bracelet to talking to the porter at the Ralston. It had to be enough to warrant the Agency sending someone over to the hotel to investigate. "I think it's time I paid a visit to the Agency."

"State your business," said one of the four security guards stationed in the lobby of the building that housed the headquarters of the Fae Enforcement Agency.

"I'm here to speak to an agent about a case." I passed him my ID card, and he inserted it into a scanner.

He nodded and returned the card to me. "Level seventeen."

"Thanks." I pocketed the card and headed for the elevators. To get to them, I had to pass through the body scanner, an experience I did not remember fondly from the day I'd come to get my new card. The two granite posts were embedded with a Fae stone called lurite that created a powerful ward for detecting weapons. Not even bounty hunters were permitted to bring weapons into the Agency.

I grimaced when my entire body suffered from an intense pins and needles sensation. It only lasted a few seconds, but it was enough to make me shudder after I'd cleared the scanner. If the scanner detected a weapon, it held the person until one of the security guards freed them. I couldn't imagine enduring it for that long, which was why I'd double-checked to make sure I was carrying no weapons before I'd entered the building.

I took the elevator to the seventeenth floor where I had to sign in with the receptionist there. She gave me a visitor badge and directed me to sit in the crowded waiting area. You'd think bounty hunters would get preferential treatment because we worked for the Agency, but no, we had to wait like everyone else.

An hour passed before someone called my name. I glanced up from my phone to see a thirty-something man with close-cropped brown hair looking around the room expectantly.

"Here." I stood and walked over to him, noting the ID badge clipped to his breast pocket that read *Special Agent Daniel Curry.*

"Follow me, please," he said with an impatient air, as if I'd been the one to keep him waiting and not the other way around.

He led the way to a small office, and I took in his crisp black suit and athletic build. The Agency required their agents to dress professionally and to stay in top physical condition. If I'd joined them, this would have been my life in a few years. The thought held even less appeal now than it had when they'd tried to recruit me.

"You are here to inquire about the case involving the missing bounty hunters?" Agent Curry asked once we were seated.

"My parents," I said, not appreciating his disdainful tone.

"And you are a bounty hunter as well?"

"Yes."

"I see." His mouth turned down in the beginning of a sneer as he opened a file folder and read from the top page. "Patrick and Caroline James, last seen on November twenty-six. Reported missing by bond agent Levi Solomon."

"Yes."

He shot me a disapproving look for interrupting him before going back to scanning the page. Closing the folder, he clasped his hands together on top of it. "This case has been transferred to our special crimes division."

"Special crimes? Why?"

"Recent evidence suggests your parents were involved in illegal activity." He gave me an accusing stare. "The Agency does not take lightly to bounty hunters breaking the law."

"My parents would never break the law," I declared, letting my anger get the best of me. "What kind of illegal activity are you talking about?"

He pressed his lips together. "Drug trafficking. Goren to be exact."

I relaxed a little, knowing this was all a big misunderstanding. "The job they were working on was to find a goren dealer. You can ask Levi Solomon, and he'll tell you."

"We've interviewed Mr. Solomon," the agent said sharply. "He echoed your sentiments, but the evidence doesn't support your opinion."

My indignation flared again. "It's not an opinion. And what evidence are you talking about?"

Agent Curry didn't answer immediately and seemed to be deciding how much to tell me. I was preparing for an argument when he spoke.

"Your mother's vehicle was found in the Bronx outside the residence of a drug den that was raided by the NYPD two days ago. They impounded the car, which is how we located it in their system." He opened the folder again and sifted through the pages until he found what he was looking for. "When the car was searched, they found a large sum of money and vials of goren with a street value of fifty thousand dollars."

I shook my head in denial. "They were hunting a goren dealer. He must have put that stuff in her car to set them up."

"Or they were in business with the dealer and something went wrong."

"No," I shot back vehemently. "If you knew them, you'd never say that. Talk to the other bounty hunters. Everyone likes and respects my parents."

The agent tapped his fingers on the desk. "We will interview their peers during the investigation, but it would not be the first time people have been fooled by someone they know."

I ground my teeth in frustration. This man had already decided my parents were guilty, and he wasn't looking to clear them.

"If you're so sure my parents are drug dealers, why haven't you or the police come to our home yet with a search warrant?"

Agent Curry shifted unhappily in his seat. "We have protocols to follow. Rest assured, that will happen soon."

His tone was accusing, but I caught a flicker of uncertainty in his expression. He might be ready to condemn my parents, but whomever he reported to wasn't convinced.

I pulled my mother's bracelet from my pocket and laid it on the desk. "This is my mother's. An employee at the Ralston found it there the morning after she and my father disappeared. I went there and spoke to a bellboy, who said my parents were there that night."

He reached across the desk to pick up the leather bracelet. "How do you know this is hers?"

I pulled up my sleeve to show him my identical bracelet. "My mother had these custom-made for us. My father has one, too. It's a protection against Fae glamours, and she would never take it off. The ties on hers are broken, and I think it came off in a struggle."

Agent Curry studied the bracelet. "This just proves she was at the hotel that night. It doesn't mean she didn't leave there and meet up with the drug dealer."

"But you will check it out, won't you?" My jaw hurt from clenching it to keep from shouting at him.

He tossed the bracelet back onto the desk as if he were discarding a piece of trash. "We'll look into it, but I assure you, if there had been any kind of disturbance at the Ralston, we would have heard about it by now." He glanced at his watch. "I'm due for a meeting in a few minutes. If there is nothing else, we need to wrap this up."

I snatched up the bracelet and stood. He'd made it quite clear finding my parents was not an Agency priority. If I ever wanted to see them again, I'd have to find them myself.

We walked back to the reception area in silence. I hit the elevator button, and Agent Curry headed back toward his office. The elevator doors opened, and I stormed inside.

"Miss James."

I turned to find the agent just outside the doors. "Yes?"

"I understand you are worried about your parents, but this falls under Agency jurisdiction now."

"Meaning what?"

"Meaning do not interfere in an ongoing Agency investigation."

"Ongoing?" I echoed scornfully. "You've already written them off."

The doors closed on his scowling face, and I hoped it was the last time I'd ever have to see it. If he thought I was going to sit at home twiddling my thumbs while the Agency did nothing, he was out of his mind.

I called Levi as soon as I left the building, and he confirmed what Agent Curry had said. The Agency had taken over the search for my parents, and bounty hunters were being told to stay out of it.

My anger had turned to anxiety by the time I made it to the Jeep. If the Agency wasn't taking my parents' disappearance seriously, I really was on my own. The enormity of that revelation felt like a heavy yoke across my shoulders, and I didn't know if I was strong enough to carry it alone.

As I started the Jeep, I received a text from Violet. **Coffee? My treat.**

God yes! I wrote back. **Where n when?**

Oliver's. 20 min?

Oliver's was a hip coffee house in Brooklyn that had survived the bean shortage. They'd had to hike up their prices, but they catered mostly to young professionals who didn't care as long as they got their coffee.

I calculated how long it would take me to get there from here. **Make it 40 and I'm there.**

Her reply came seconds later. **See you soon.**

I was just entering downtown Brooklyn when the traffic slowed to a crawl. I craned my neck to see a bunch of flashing red and blue lights up ahead amid a sea of people. I leaned forward to peer up at the buildings, expecting a fire, but I could see no sign of one. Whatever was going on, I was stuck here until it was over.

Groaning, I picked up my phone to let Violet know I wasn't going to make our coffee date. The phone vibrated in my hand, and I looked down to see an incoming message. I almost rear-ended the car in front of me when the words **LEVEL 3 BULLETIN** flashed across the screen.

Sometimes, a situation arose that couldn't wait for it to go through the process of being assigned to a hunter, like when that hobgoblin had gone crazy in Manhattan a few years ago. When that happened, the Agency sent out a bulletin to the phone of every licensed bounty hunter in the city, and the first one to make the capture earned the bounty.

I clicked the alert and quickly scanned the message. I had to read it again to make sure I was seeing it correctly. A bunnek was on the loose in the Hatten Building, and there had been attacks on several people. The police and fire department were on site, but their job was to get the people out of the building and tend to the injured. They were leaving the capture of the bunnek to the bounty hunters.

A bunnek in New York? The Fae Enforcement Agency had a list of Fae creatures that were restricted from entering our world, and bunneks were near the top of that list. In Faerie they were harmless animals, but in our world, they turned into monsters with the temperament of a wild boar with a ravenous appetite. I shuddered, thinking it was probably just as well that I was stuck in a traffic jam.

I looked up at the buildings again, trying to figure out the cause of the commotion, and that's when I saw it – a giant ornate H at the top of the building closest to the emergency vehicles. As in H for the Hatten building.

Sinking back in my seat, I stared at the message on my phone. I was authorized to go after the job, and by a stroke of luck, I had arrived here just as the bulletin had gone out. Unless there were other hunters nearby, I would be the first one on the scene.

I let out a long breath. Was I really thinking about going after that thing? I had a ton of gear in the back and a head full of knowledge, but facing a bunnek in real life was nothing like reading about it in a book.

A bulletin update appeared on the screen. **Threat elevated to level Four. Multiple human fatalities expected.**

I chewed my lower lip. I wasn't obligated to respond to the bulletin, but people could die. Could I live with myself if I didn't try to help them?

I eyed the entrance to a parking garage a few feet away. Unfortunately, the car in front of me wasn't going anywhere. I looked around to make sure no police were close by, and then I drove over the curb and into the garage.

Pulling into a parking spot, I reviewed all I knew about bunneks. After doing a quick inventory of my gear, I hefted the heavy bag onto my shoulder and set off at a fast walk.

I had to push my way through the people crowding the police barriers. A uniformed police officer intercepted me when I climbed over a barrier, but he let me pass when I showed him my ID.

The scene when I neared the building was one of utter chaos. Police officers yelled to each other over the noise of the crowd and the sounds of crying. EMTs from two ambulances were busy treating the wounded, and I sucked in a breath at the sight of the blood coating one man's white shirt.

"I'm out of my freaking mind," I said under my breath as I entered the building.

In the lobby, I found four officers with their guns drawn and looking too trigger-happy for my comfort. I had to flash my ID again before they'd let me by. They filled me in on the situation and told me the bunnek was confined to the top floor, which housed a law firm. At least twenty people were still up there, barricaded in a conference room.

"Don't you have a partner?" asked a portly, gray-haired officer when I headed for the door to the stairs.

"He'll be along soon," I lied because the older man would try to stop me from going upstairs if he knew I was alone. Hopefully, other hunters would arrive soon, and I wouldn't be up there alone for long.

I adjusted the duffle bag strap on my shoulder and started up the twenty flights of stairs to the top floor. By the tenth floor, I was wishing I'd spent more time at the gym with my parents, and by the twentieth, I was vowing I'd start endurance training tomorrow... or as soon as I recovered from this.

I was sweating when I reached the top floor landing. I set the duffle bag down quietly and bent over with my hands on my knees. The elevator would have been a lot easier, but the noise would have attracted the bunnek. I wanted to be prepared before I faced off against this one.

Removing my jacket, I hung it on the stair rail and rummaged through the bag. I pulled out a small bottle and made a face as I sprayed myself with a nauseatingly sweet fragrance that was made from a variety of Faerie flowers. I'd found it when I went through the supplies at home, and it was supposed to mask a human's scent from faeries. I was about to find out how well it worked.

Once I was doused in the perfume, I strapped on a custom weapons harness and armed myself with whatever I could use to snare a bunnek. In addition to shackles, I grabbed some strong rope and a net with tiny iron weights sewn into it. The net made one side of the harness sag slightly, but I couldn't go after the bunnek without it.

I was almost ready when I heard someone running lightly up the stairs. Glancing down, I spotted a figure four floors below, and I exhaled in relief. I waited for the person to reach me, and I didn't know whether to laugh or groan when Trey came into view. Of all the people to show up first, it had to be him.

His face registered his shock when he saw me at the top of the stairs. "Jesse, what the hell are you doing here?" he asked in a loud whisper.

"Same thing you are," I answered, annoyed to see he didn't look nearly as winded or sweaty as I'd been after my climb. I was definitely hitting the gym tomorrow.

He set his gear bag beside mine and put his hands on his hips. "Listen, I get that you're trying to prove yourself or something, but you're in over your head with this one. It's not worth getting hurt or killed over."

"And how many bunneks have you hunted?"

Trey flushed. "None, but I've worked with Dad on other level Three jobs."

"Is Bruce here?"

"No. He and Mom are over in Jersey for the day." Trey unzipped his bag and began loading up on gear. "I was working on a job nearby when the bulletin went out. I'd say we have less than twenty minutes before anyone else gets here, and I plan to have that bunnek bagged by then."

"Does he know you came here alone?" I asked, though I already knew the answer. Bruce would have ordered Trey not to come here without him.

Trey scowled. "I don't have to check in with him on everything I do. And you came alone."

"Yes, but I was hoping others would show up and we could work together."

He pulled a net similar to mine from his bag. "I'm not trying to be mean, but you aren't ready for this. Stay out here, and let me handle it."

"I know as much about bunneks as you do, probably more." There was no probably about it. Trey hadn't liked to study in school, and I was betting he'd never taken the time to read his father's reference books.

He laughed quietly and shook his head. "Jesse, being book smart will only get you so far. You need real street smarts to make it in this business." He adjusted his harness and took a step toward me, only to stop and wrinkle his nose. "What is that smell? Are you wearing perfume?"

I rolled my eyes at him. "It's scent blocker, and you better put some on if you don't want that bunnek taking a bite out of you."

Trey looked uncertainly down at his bag and back to me. "I don't have any with me."

Of course not. I fished the bottle from my bag and sprayed him liberally. He might be the most annoying person in my life, but I didn't want him to get hurt.

He put a hand over his mouth to smother a cough. "Thanks."

"No problem." I tossed the bottle into my bag as a distant scream came from somewhere beyond the door.

Unless more bounty hunters had arrived and taken the set of stairs on the other end of the building, we were the only hope those people had.

Trey grasped the door handle. "We'd better get going before other hunters show up and take the bunnek from us."

"Wait," I whispered harshly. I pushed past him and put my ear to the door, listening for movement on the other side. Hearing nothing, I pushed down on the handle and eased the door open an inch. When nothing charged at me, I opened it wide enough to slip quietly inside.

I found myself in a corner of the reception area. From here, I could see overturned chairs and papers strewn across the floor. Streaks of red drew my gaze to the white marble reception desk, and I shuddered when I realized it was blood. There was more blood smeared on a wall, and a trail of blood on the tile floor that went all the way to the elevator.

It was official. I had lost my damn mind.

8

"S hit," Trey whispered from behind me, reminding me he was there.
I put a finger to my lips to shush him and then tapped my ear, indi-
cating we needed to listen. He nodded, and we cocked our heads, trying to
locate the bunnek. From somewhere in the depths of the large office space
came a faint rustling sound, but I couldn't tell where it was coming from. It
could be the bunnek or one of the people trapped up here.

Trey heard it, too, and he started to walk past me. I grabbed his arm to
halt him, and he gave me a questioning look.

"I'm serious, Trey. We should work together on this one." The sight of all
that blood made me sure we were in over our heads. I had no problem splitting the bounty, and we'd both be credited with bringing in the bunnek, if
that was what he cared about.

"Okay," he readily agreed. "But I get seventy-five percent of the purse
because I have more experience. Plus, you took that goblin that should have
been ours."

I scowled at him. "That job was mine fair and square. I didn't take it from
you."

"It would have come back to us because your parents didn't finish it," he
said in a low voice.

"Do you really want to argue about this now?" I hissed. "Are we equal
partners or not?"

He shook his head and started to say something, but a crash somewhere
in the office made us jump.

"Fine. Good luck, then," I told him before I left to quietly make my way deeper into the office. As I rounded a cubicle, I looked behind me and saw Trey was gone.

For a moment, I stood there torn by indecision as my conscience argued that I should go after him. The sound of glass breaking and a woman's scream decided my course of action for me. The best way to keep Trey from getting himself eaten was to catch the bunnek. I just hoped I wasn't about to serve myself up instead.

The law firm was laid out in a large rectangle with offices and conference rooms along the perimeter. The interior of the space was full of cubicles, a lunchroom, and a printer room. I was grateful for the tall cubicle walls, and for the Chucks I'd worn today, as I ran quietly toward the noise.

I stopped and peeked around a corner. A thrill of excitement went through me, along with a healthy dose of terror, when I got my first look at a bunnek outside the pages of a book.

Standing at almost five feet tall, the bunnek resembled a blond, winged chimpanzee from behind – a very angry chimpanzee that was trying to climb through the broken window of a conference room.

The people in the room were using chairs to barricade the window as the bunnek snarled and swiped at them. One man cried out in pain when a claw raked his forearm, and the scent of blood seemed to excite the creature more.

I had to do something. The window was made up of three separate panes, and if the rest broke, there'd be no way the people inside could hold out against the bunnek.

As soon as the thought passed through my mind, I heard the crack of another window breaking. I did the only thing I could think of. I put my fingers to my lips and let out a sharp whistle.

The bunnek's head swung in my direction, and my legs went a little rubbery when I stared into its milky white eyes. It growled, and my gaze lowered to the blood staining the fur around its mouth and across its chest.

I gulped.

The bunnek roared.

I ran.

As soon as I rounded the corner, I searched frantically for a place to hide. I had been an even bigger idiot than Trey, thinking I could catch that thing on my own. I'd be lucky if I lived long enough for the real bounty hunters to arrive and save my pathetic ass.

A whooshing sound came from behind me, and it took me a moment to realize it was the flap of wings.

I ran into the first cubicle I came to and dived under the desk. In the next instant, I heard the bunnek fly over me, growling savagely. I froze, not daring to breathe as it circled and came back around, trying to sniff me out. Not going to lie. I almost wet my pants when it hovered above me for a good ten seconds, and I was afraid to move for a whole minute after it flew away.

I crawled out from under the desk and crouched to listen. Hearing nothing, I tiptoed from the cubicle – and almost screamed when I found myself less than ten feet from the bunnek. It was facing away from me, so I backed up silently to make my escape.

My foot struck something, and I flailed my arms as I tripped backward over a potted plant. The bunnek roared as I scrambled to my feet and bolted.

I heard it take to the air again, and I ran in a zigzag pattern to evade it. At one point, I swear it got so close that I could feel its hot breath on the back of my neck.

There was no sign of Trey as I raced through the place like the hounds of hell were on my heels. He must have found a good spot to hide. For the first time in my life, I wished I was with him.

I thought I was a goner when I ran left instead of right and got cornered in the printer room. Spotting a door at the back, I yanked it open to find a supply closet. I ran inside and closed the door, panting hard.

The bunnek slammed into the door, making it rattle in the hinges. It wouldn't hold for long. I looked around desperately for something to prop against the door, but all the shelves were bolted to the walls.

The door shuddered under another blow just as an idea came to me. I climbed to the top of the nearest shelving rack and pushed up on the ceiling tile. It lifted easily, and I shoved it aside to climb through onto one of the support beams. I put the tile back into place and crawled along the beam in the dark until I hit a wall.

I eased up a corner of a tile and peered down into a large office. Listening intently, I heard the bunnek crashing around farther away. From the noise, it sounded like it was thrashing the printers.

The crashing stopped abruptly, and I held my breath. If I stayed perfectly still, it wouldn't find me. I just had to stay right where I was until backup arrived.

A chorus of screams cut through the air, raising gooseflesh on my arms. I'd forgotten about the people trapped in the conference room.

Before I could change my mind, I dropped down into the office below. I slipped out of the room and looked around, trying to figure out how to save those people without getting myself killed.

Maybe I could lure it away from the conference room and trap it somewhere. Only this time, I needed to be better prepared and have an escape route.

I glanced down at the gear I had on me, and a plan began to form. It was risky and more than a little crazy, but it might work if I timed it right.

More screams filled the air, spurring me into action. I made my way to the employee lunchroom I'd passed earlier and opened the refrigerator. It wasn't quite noon yet, so the fridge was full of packed lunches. I emptied the fridge as quickly and quietly as I could and made a pile of food on the floor. Once I got its attention, the bunnek's nose would lead it right to the food.

After all the food was laid out, I prepared the second part of my plan. My hands shook a little as I repositioned a table and some of the chairs, and my body felt like a wire pulled too tightly. There was so much adrenaline coursing through me that I was sure I wouldn't be able to touch caffeine for a week.

I looked around to make sure everything was as ready as it could be. Taking a few deep breaths for courage, I stepped outside the lunchroom and yelled at the top of my lungs. "Dinner time."

The second I heard the bunnek take flight, I raced back into the room and scurried up the tower of furniture I'd made in the corner. I was up in the ceiling and positioned above the pile of food by the time the bunnek came roaring into the room.

The beast tore into the food, completely oblivious to my presence. I eased the tile above it to one side and took out my bag of precious fey power. Deciding this was not the time to be frugal, I dumped the contents of the bag on the bunnek's head and waited.

And waited.

It took a minute for the powder to have any effect on the bunnek, and it wasn't exactly the result I'd hoped for. The creature's movements slowed a little, but it went right on shoving food into its mouth as if nothing had changed.

On to plan B. I pulled the net free from my harness and spread it out. *Here goes everything.*

I released the net. It covered the bunnek, the edges of it hitting the floor with a soft thump. This time, the bunnek took notice, and it thrashed around, only managing to get more tangled in the netting. Before long, the iron did its job, draining the creature of its strength until it lay panting heavily on the floor.

I let out a silent whoop. I'd trapped the bunnek and stopped it from hurting anyone else. I didn't need to do anything else but stay up here and wait.

But... I pursed my lips as I stared down at the bunnek. Why should I let someone else step in and reap the rewards of my hard work? I was the one who had put my life on the line. I should be the one to claim this capture.

I climbed down from the ceiling and turned around to find Trey standing over the bunnek. The creature glared and growled, but it was helpless under all that iron.

"What are you doing?" I demanded when Trey pulled out a length of rope.

He didn't look up as he began to bind the bunnek with the rope. "I'm securing our capture."

"The hell you are." I stood over him. "You didn't want to be partners, remember? And you hid away while I was out here trying not to get eaten."

"I wasn't hiding. I was biding my time, waiting for the right time to strike."

"Meaning you waited until I did all the work," I retorted. "You don't get to jump in now and take credit for this one."

He lifted the now subdued creature to its feet. "You owe me for that goblin job, and besides, no one is going to believe you caught a bunnek on your own."

"I *did* catch it on my own," I said through clenched teeth. "And like I told you, that goblin job was rightfully mine. I don't owe you anything."

"I disagree." He smiled smugly. "Now, let's get this fellow downstairs before someone comes to steal him from us."

I shook my head in disgust and followed him out of the lunchroom. "This is low, even for you, Trey."

"No, it's just the way things are done. If you don't learn to play the game, you won't survive long in this business."

It was a short walk to the stairwell to grab our duffle bags and then continue on to the elevators. I shot daggers at Trey while we waited for the car to arrive.

He let out an exaggerated sigh. "Stop glaring at me. I told you that you need street smarts, not book smarts, to make it as a hunter. Think of this as on-the-job training."

"Pretty expensive lesson, don't you think?"

The elevator doors slid open, and we walked in. Trey hit the button for the first floor and turned to me. "It's not like I'm taking all the bounty for myself. We'll split it, fifty-fifty."

"Wow. How generous of you?" I dropped my bag and leaned against the wall, suddenly tired.

Trey said something else, but I'd stopped listening to him. On a scale of one to ten, this day sucked an eleven. First, Agent Curry had accused my parents of being low-life drug dealers, and now Trey was stealing half the credit for my capture that I'd nearly gotten eaten for. On top of all of that, I'd missed out on having coffee with Violet.

We had descended several floors when I noticed the bunnek's chest heaving as if its breathing was labored. One look at the creature's wide eyes and panting mouth told me it was freaking out. Most faeries hated being inside a metal box, even one that wasn't made of pure iron, but the bunnek looked like it was on the verge of a total meltdown.

Something niggled at me, and I focused on the memory that was trying to surface. Words on a page began to form. It had to do with bunneks...

Oh, no. The bunnek was drooling now, and its eyes were rolling around in its head.

I fell to my knees and started digging frantically through my duffle bag. *Please, let me have packed it in here.*

My fingers closed around a nylon strap. I yanked it from the bag so hard the small gas mask attached to it almost whacked me in the face.

"What are you doing?" Trey asked as I fitted the mask over my mouth and nose.

A low rumbling filled the elevator. It grew louder and ended in what sounded like a small explosion that echoed off the metal walls.

Trey slapped his hands over his mouth and nose, trying futilely to block out the noxious fumes that must be filling every inch of the enclosed space. He sagged against the walls until his legs gave out, and he sank to the floor, gagging.

I could have shared my mask with him, but I didn't. The gas might be fouler than a skunk's spray, but it wouldn't harm Trey. It would, however, teach him a very valuable lesson.

"Bunneks pass gas when they're frightened, and nothing scares them more than enclosed spaces. You'd know that if you'd read a book every now and then." Leaning down, I smiled sweetly at him even though he couldn't see it through the mask. "Think of this as on-the-job training."

He tried to speak, but it ended in a fit of coughing.

I hefted my duffle bag on my shoulder and picked up the end of the rope Trey had dropped. The elevator stopped on the ground floor, and the doors slid open to reveal half a dozen police officers and two bounty hunters I recognized from the Plaza. Their expressions of surprise turned to grimaces, and they backed up when they got a whiff of the smell that flowed from the car.

"I guess being book smart isn't such a bad thing after all," I said so only

Trey could hear me. Then I walked out of the elevator with *my* capture in tow.

"Are you sure you should be doing this?" Tennin asked as he slid a slip of paper across his desk toward me. "Don't get me wrong. I'm seriously impressed by how far you've come since our first meeting, but tracking down a goren dealer is not your average job. There's a reason it was given to your parents and not some other bounty hunter."

I picked up the paper and read the name and address written on it. "I'm not sure of anything anymore, but it's all I have to go on. The Agency has already made up their mind that my parents are working with the dealer, and the only way I can clear their names is to find him."

Tennin leaned back in his chair. "I admire your tenacity, but be careful of whose toes you step on in your search. The Agency doesn't take lightly to anyone getting in their way or making them look bad."

"I'll keep that in mind." The last thing I wanted was trouble with the Agency, but if that's what it took to find my parents, then I'd risk it.

"I have to say I'm curious to see where you go from here. You are definitely Caroline's daughter."

"Thanks." I tucked the paper into a pocket for safekeeping. "How does a Fae paparazzo become a confidential informant to a bounty hunter?"

The faerie snickered. "That's between me and your parents. Let's just say I was a little too eager to prove myself when I started in this business, and I landed in a tight spot one night. If not for your father, I wouldn't be here now."

"I can see why you'd keep your arrangement a secret. Other faeries probably wouldn't like you helping out the bounty hunters."

Tennin nodded. "Most of the faeries I associate with don't care, but there are some others who would not be happy."

"Your secret is safe with me." I looked over his head at the new photos that had been added to his wall since my last visit. "Your pictures of Prince Rhys caused quite a stir."

His chest puffed out a little. "That they did. You've been following the story?"

"Hard not to. The pictures are everywhere. Is it true the network is suing you over them?"

"They're throwing their weight around, but my lawyer says they don't have a case." He grinned slyly. "If I go a month without someone taking offense, I'm not doing my job right."

My gaze traveled over the collage of photos on the walls. Some were of human celebrities, but most of the pictures had royals in them. "Do the royals ever get angry at you for following them around and taking their pictures?"

"Are you kidding? They love being in the spotlight. If they didn't, they would stay in Faerie."

"I guess that's true." There were royals we'd only heard about, who never left Faerie. The Seelie queen and Unseelie king were two of those. And since technology didn't work in Faerie, there wasn't a single photo of them or any other royal who chose to stay in their realm. Hence the feeding frenzy over Tennin's pictures of the new prince.

I'd never cared much about celebrity gossip, but I'd always been interested in the Faerie realm. Faeries were closemouthed about some things, such as the inner workings of their courts. I'd read all I could find on the subject, so I knew the realm was divided into two regions – Seelie, known as Light Fae, and Unseelie, known as Dark Fae – each with their own court.

Each court was ruled by a single monarch, and the monarch's life mate was called their consort. The current Seelie monarch was Queen Anwyn, and the Unseelie monarch was King Oseron.

Since Court faeries were immortal, a monarch could rule indefinitely – unless they stepped down or were killed. It was said that Oseron had been king for over a thousand years, while Anwyn was a young queen with less than two hundred years on the throne.

There wasn't much information available about Faerie politics, except that the two courts were constantly jostling for power. The faeries of the two courts might get along here, but back in their realm, they would be considered enemies. I suspected that was why so many of them chose to live here.

I studied a picture of the new Seelie prince. "Can I ask what court you're from?"

My question surprised Tennin. "I'm Unseelie. Most humans don't know or care much about our politics. You do?"

"I know a little." I voiced another question I'd always wondered about. "Can you tell if another faerie is Seelie or Unseelie?"

Tennin quirked an eyebrow in amusement. "You're full of questions tonight."

"I have an unquenchable thirst for knowledge."

He laughed. "Yes, we can. And before you ask, we normally only fraternize with others from our court, except for public events where everyone puts on a smile and pretends to be civil."

I thought about the other Court faeries I'd met recently. "What about Orend Teg and Lukas Rand? Are they Seelie or Unseelie?"

Tennin's easy smile fell away. "How do you know Lukas Rand?"

I was taken aback by his sharp tone. "I don't. He and his friends were at Teg's the night I went there. I got the impression he was someone important."

"You could say that. He's not someone you want to mess with."

"Is he dangerous?"

"Yes. And his men are even more lethal. They'll think nothing of killing anyone they believe is a threat to him."

My stomach gave a nervous flutter. "Are they criminals?"

"No, but that doesn't make them any less dangerous," Tennin said soberly. "Let's just say Lukas Rand is very powerful in our realm."

"So, he's Unseelie?"

"Yes. And that's all I will say about him. Heed my advice, and stay far away from him and his men."

"It's not like I went looking for him. He isn't someone I'd ever choose to be around. He's too...intense for my liking."

"Good. If you see him or his men again, remember what I said and walk the other way."

"I will." I shivered at his words, though his unwillingness to discuss Lukas only made me more curious about the other faerie. But not curious enough to ignore Tennin's warning to stay away from him. All I cared about was finding my parents, and unless Lukas Rand could somehow help me with that, I didn't have the time or the energy for him.

Tennin was heading out for the night, so I thanked him for his help and left. He lived in a nice area, but I was wary after my run-in with the two elves. I kept one hand on the fully-charged stun gun in my pocket as I walked to the Jeep one street over.

My phone buzzed, and I stopped to check it. It was a text from Violet asking if I wanted to do coffee in the morning. **Definitely. My place at 9?** I texted back.

She replied immediately. **See you then.**

Smiling, I stuck my phone back in my pocket and resumed walking.

"You again," said a voice so cold it chilled me to the bone.

I jumped as Faolin stepped out of the doorway of the building I was passing. The faerie's face was hard as he closed the distance between us, and a knot of fear formed in my stomach. My first thought was to flee, but there was no way I could outrun him.

"What do you want?" I asked with false bravado, but the slight quiver in my voice betrayed me.

He stopped in front of me, and his scowl was even scarier up close. "I will ask the questions. Who do you work for, and what is your interest in Lukas?"

"I don't work for anyone, and I have no interest in him." Could Faolin have somehow overheard me talking to Tennin?

"Try again, and I want the truth this time."

"That was the truth." Anger replaced some of my fear. Did this guy have a problem with me specifically, or was he this paranoid with everyone?

"Is that so?" He moved until he was in my space. "Why is it that before last week, I'd never laid eyes on you, and now you're suddenly everywhere we go?"

I stood my ground, despite the instinct to back away. "I could say the same thing about you."

His lip curled angrily. "Really? You expect me to believe that you being in *this* neighborhood is a coincidence?"

"I was visiting someone. And what's so special about this neighborhood?"

"Who were you visiting?" he demanded, ignoring my question.

"I'm not telling you that."

He leaned menacingly close to me. "Because you're lying. I'm giving you one more chance to come clean with me."

My mouth went dry at the threat in his voice. "I'm not lying."

"Have it your way." His hand closed around my wrist in a bruising grip, and he set off down the street, pulling me along beside him.

"Let me go!" Panic filled me, and I struggled helplessly to yank free from his hold. I tried to reach for my stun gun, but it was on the opposite side from my free hand and I couldn't get to it.

Humans and faeries passed us on the sidewalk, and every one of them gave us a wide berth. Not one person tried to intervene, even though I was clearly being dragged off against my will. What the hell was wrong with people?

We reached a building that looked like it used to be a retail space at one time. Instead of entering the front door, Faolin led me around to the back where several SUVs were parked. A brick fence that had to be at least ten feet tall separated the private parking lot from a garden, if the trees and vegetation peeking above the wall were any indication.

Security cameras and motion lights were mounted on the building and wall, and there was an electronic key pad on the door. The building owner was serious about security, and I had a strong suspicion I knew who that was.

Tennin's warning came back to me as Faolin pulled me toward the door. He switched his hold to my other arm so he could enter the code, and my hand went immediately to the stun gun in my pocket. I was debating whether or not I was brave enough to use the weapon on him when his voice startled me from my thoughts. I looked up into his cold, knowing eyes.

"Don't even think it." His gaze dropped to where my hand was hidden in my pocket. "Your toy will not work on me like it did on the elf, except to piss me off."

I let my hand fall to my side. He hadn't physically hurt me so far, but I didn't doubt he would if I provoked him.

He unlocked the heavy steel door, and it swung inward, revealing a small foyer. More cameras watched us from the corners of the room, and to our right was a second door with another keypad.

Faolin led me none too gently into the foyer, and I fought to control my breathing as a sense of impending doom hit me. I felt like a sacrifice being brought to the monster's lair, and my imagination went wild about what was waiting for me inside.

9

The inner door swung open before we reached it, and I saw one of the other faeries who had been at Teg's with Lukas Rand. His eyes were lit with curiosity as he watched us approach, but he said nothing. He merely stepped back to allow us entry.

Faolin pushed me through the door. I wasn't sure what I had expected, but it was not the large, inviting living area. I saw a massive gas fireplace, brick walls, brown leather couches, and a large window overlooking a patio and the garden I'd suspected was behind the wall. An island separated the kitchen from the rest of the room, which had a distinctly masculine feel to it, and a flight of stairs led to the second floor.

My mind couldn't process having so much space. You could probably fit our entire apartment in just this room.

Faolin shoved me down on one of the couches, reminding me this was not a social call. "Stay," he commanded, towering over me. He looked past me at the other faerie. "Where is Lukas?"

"I'm right here."

Lukas Rand descended the stairs. He wore jeans and a gray Henley with the sleeves pulled up to display his muscled forearms. Even casually dressed, he carried the same air of dangerous authority he had the other times I'd seen him.

"What's going on?" Lukas walked over to stand beside Faolin, and I had to fight the urge to squirm under their scrutiny.

"Caught her hanging around during my walkabout," Faolin told him.

Indignation surged in me again. "I wasn't hanging around. I was walking to my car and minding my own business when you stopped me and dragged me here."

Ignoring my outburst, Faolin looked at Lukas. "She claims she was visiting someone, but she refuses to say who."

"Because it's none of your business." I tried to stand but Faolin put a hand on my shoulder and shoved me back to the couch. I smacked his hand away. "Will you stop manhandling me?"

Lukas crossed his arms over his chest, the action pulling his shirt taut over his shoulders and making him look even bigger. His unsmiling eyes met mine. "Seeing you twice in a week could be labeled a coincidence, three times is pushing it, but four is one too many to ignore."

I frowned at him. "Four times? This is only the second time I've seen you since that night at Teg's, and not by choice I might add." I shot an accusing glare at Faolin, who answered with a sneer.

"And that day in Manhattan before Teg's?" Lukas asked pointedly as if I had a clue what he was talking about.

"I never saw you in Manhattan. Before this week, I barely even left Brooklyn except to..." I trailed off as I thought about the day I'd crossed the bridge looking for a job, the day I'd hidden the elf boy who had turned around and stolen my train money. That had also been the last day I'd seen my parents. Had it really only been a week ago?

Then I remembered the faerie watching me before he'd gotten into a car and left. "That was you on the other side of the street." How had I not recognized him at Teg's? He wasn't exactly forgettable.

"So, you admit you were there," Faolin said as if I'd just confessed to some heinous crime.

"I have no reason to deny it. Last time I checked, there was no law against me going to Manhattan."

Lukas eyed me suspiciously. "For a person who rarely leaves Brooklyn, you have a habit of popping up wherever we are."

I huffed angrily. "I said I didn't leave Brooklyn before this week, but things have changed. And trust me when I say I'm starting to wish I'd never laid eyes on you."

"What changed?" Lukas asked.

My chest squeezed. "It's personal, and I'd rather not discuss it with you."

"You seem to be under the illusion you have a choice," Faolin cut in. "We have ways of making you talk."

I felt the blood drain from my face as a lump of ice formed in my belly. His expression told me he could and would carry out that threat, and he'd probably enjoy it.

A door opened, and several sets of footsteps sounded behind me. A moment later, Conlan and the other two faeries came to join Lukas and Faolin. I shrank back against the couch at the sight of the five large males looming over me.

"Goddess, what have you done to her?" Conlan demanded. "She looks ready to faint."

Faolin didn't take his eyes from mine. "We've done nothing...yet."

Conlan shot him a dirty look and sat on his haunches so we were at the same eye level. "You okay, Jesse?"

I shook my head, afraid to talk and show them how shaken up I was. I'd been less scared of the bunnek yesterday than I was of Faolin. I remembered Tennin's warning to steer clear of Lukas and his men, and I swallowed convulsively.

Conlan's smile was kind. "No one's going to harm you. I promise."

He stood and faced Lukas. I couldn't see either of their faces, but the edge in Conlan's voice told me he was no longer smiling.

"What is this, Lukas? We don't harm innocents."

Faolin laughed harshly. "She might have fooled you, but not me. She's up to something, and I mean to find out what it is."

"Not everyone is a threat to us."

"That is for me to decide," Faolin said.

Conlan's voice grew harder. "You can question her all you want, but I won't allow you to harm her. That is not who we are."

"Have you forgotten what is at stake here?" Faolin growled. "Would you risk his life for some female?"

His life? Who were they talking about?

"He will always come first," Conlan shot back. "But you know he would not approve of this if he were here."

"Enough," Lukas barked in a tone that brooked no argument, but did little to ease the tension in the air. He stepped around Conlan to look down at me for a long uncomfortable moment before he said, "Come with me."

I didn't move. "Where are we going?"

Annoyance flashed in his eyes, and I knew he wasn't used to being challenged. "Somewhere we can talk alone, unless you'd rather stay here and talk to Faolin."

That got me on my feet. I skirted around an angry, protesting Faolin, giving him a wide berth, and followed Lukas through a door I hadn't noticed. I almost had to run to keep up with his long strides as he led me down a short hallway to an open door.

As soon as I saw where we were, some of my apprehension left me. It was a library with a large polished desk in one corner and two upholstered chairs near the cold fireplace. The room had a manly feel to it from the navy-blue drapes on the window to the dark hardwood floor.

Instead of sitting at the desk, Lukas walked over to the chairs and motioned for me to sit. I did, and he took the other one. It was my first time alone with him, and his presence seemed to fill every inch of the room. He was still formidable, but it was his raw masculinity that I found most disquieting.

He wasted no time with small talk, and the first words out of his mouth took me by surprise. "I apologize for the way you've been treated in my home," he said with the stiffness of someone not used to issuing such statements. "We have good reason to be suspicious of strangers, but we should have handled this better."

I let out a breath. "Thank you. Does this mean you're letting me go?"

"That depends on you. I have no wish to harm you, but I won't risk the lives of my men either. You're going to have to answer some questions to prove I'm not making a mistake by letting you leave."

I tensed. "What kind of questions?"

He tilted his head slightly, his gaze locked with mine. "Let's start with what brought you to my neighborhood tonight, and we'll take it from there."

"I didn't even know you lived here."

"That doesn't answer my question. Who were you visiting?"

I clasped my hands in my lap. "I can't tell you."

The corners of his mouth turned down. "Then you should make yourself comfortable because we will be here a while."

"It's not that I don't want to tell you," I blurted. "Trust me; I don't want to be here anymore than you want me here."

Lukas was unmoved. "You're not making a great case for your freedom."

I couldn't betray Tennin's confidence, especially to people he feared. But if I didn't tell Lukas something, he wasn't going to let me go.

"You know I'm a bounty hunter," I said, and he nodded. "The person I came to see is a confidential informant who helps out on certain jobs. That's why I can't tell you his name. I gave him my word, and I won't break it."

I expected him to push me on it, but he switched gears. "You said something changed in your life recently. What was that?"

"I told you that's personal."

His stare was unrelenting. "You have to give me something."

I bit the inside of my cheek so hard I tasted copper. The last thing I wanted to do was discuss my parents with him. For all I knew, he could hate them because they'd put away some friend of his, and he'd hold that against me. But I couldn't see any other way out of this.

My shoulders slumped in defeat. "A week ago, my parents went missing. The last day I saw them was the same day you saw me in Manhattan, and I've been looking for them ever since. That's why I was at Teg's. And I was at the Ralston the other night because I found out they were there the night they disappeared."

I hated the way my voice cracked, making me feel small and weak. No matter how many times I talked about their disappearance, it didn't get any easier.

Lukas studied me for a long moment, his expression telling me nothing of what he was thinking. Finally, he asked, "What do your parents do?"

"They're bounty hunters."

His brow furrowed as if something had just occurred to him. "James… Patrick and Caroline James?"

My pulse leaped. "You know them?"

"No, but I've heard of them. They're well-known in New York."

I lifted my chin proudly. "Because they're the best in the business. That's why it makes no sense for them to disappear the way they did."

"And how did they disappear?"

Feeling a little more at ease with him, I told him about the job they'd been working on and how they'd gone out that night to see their informant. I described the disturbing call from my mother, and I was emphatic about them never going off without telling me.

He rubbed his jaw. "This is the first I've heard of their disappearance. Why aren't the other hunters looking for them?"

"Because they were told not to," I said bitterly. "The Agency is running everything, but they've decided my parents are working with that goren dealer. Anyone who knows my parents will tell you that's insane."

Lukas rested his elbows on his knees. "So, you're searching for them on your own?"

"If I don't, who will?" I asked defensively.

Something resembling admiration flashed in his eyes. "How long have you been a bounty hunter?"

I squirmed self-consciously. "Less than a week."

He didn't try to hide his surprise. "You just decided to become a hunter?"

"No one would tell me anything. People in this business don't open up to outsiders, even if you're the daughter of hunters. The only way I could get them to take me seriously was to become one of them."

"Did it work?"

I shook my head. "Not yet. But being a bounty hunter gives me freedom I didn't have before. Now I'm going to do what I should have done from the start. I'm going to track down the goren dealer my parents were after."

"The world goren dealers operate in is nothing like what you know," Lukas said grimly. "It's treacherous and inhabited by the worst of society. You'll be lucky if you come out of it alive."

I shivered as a chill went through me. "I know, but I have to try. They're my parents, and I'm all they have."

He sat back in his chair, and I stared at my clenched hands. For a long moment, neither of us spoke, and I could only hope I'd convinced him to let me go. He no longer seemed angry, so that was a good sign, right?

He stood abruptly, and I lifted my head to watch him walk out of the room. I was debating whether or not to follow him when he returned. My stomach lurched sickeningly when Faolin entered the room behind him, looking no less contemptuous than he'd been when we got to the building. Then Conlan came in, and some of my dread eased when I saw his reassuring smile.

Lukas sat on the corner of the desk. "Faolin is the head of my security. Tell him what you told me. He's going to check out your story, and once he's satisfied you're telling the truth, you'll be free to leave."

One look at Faolin told me he wasn't happy with this arrangement. What if he wasn't satisfied even after I told him everything? What would they do with me?

I nodded at Lukas, avoiding Faolin's icy gaze as long as possible. "Okay."

I repeated my story, and a few times, Faolin interrupted me to ask questions. His tone and the types of questions he asked made it clear he was trying to trip me up and show I was lying. But that didn't happen because I was one hundred percent honest with him.

The only time I refused to answer a question was when he demanded the name of the informant I'd visited tonight. Not even his glares and unspoken threats could make me give up Tennin to him.

I did show them the paper Tennin had given me with the name and address of someone who might know where I could find the goren dealer. Faolin took a picture of the information with his phone and said he'd check it out.

I filled them in on what I knew about the goren job and that the dealer was an elf. I also relayed my suspicion that the elves who attacked me near the Ralston might be working for the dealer.

When I told them about the two faeries who had tried to break into my apartment, my interrogators exchanged indecipherable looks between them.

"How do you know they were faeries?" Faolin demanded in his drill-sergeant tone.

"I don't for sure, but they caused the cameras to go out while they were at the door, and they couldn't get past our ward."

Faolin's stare grew even harder. "Why do you have an anti-Fae ward on your apartment? Do you have something to hide?"

I huffed out a breath. "All bounty hunters have them. The job doesn't exactly make us popular with certain people."

"Do you still have the security footage?" Lukas asked.

"Yes, but they kept their faces hidden the whole time."

Conlan spoke up. "Doesn't matter. We'll be able to tell if they were faeries."

Faolin continued to fire questions at me. The interrogation lasted over two hours, and I felt emotionally drained when it was finally over. He turned on his heel and left the room without a backward glance at me.

"Faolin can be a bit extreme, but he's thorough," Lukas said when I slumped in my chair.

"A *bit* extreme?" I gave him a weak scowl, earning a small smile from him that did funny things to my stomach. I looked away, irritated he could affect me even while he was holding me here against my will.

"You did well. Not many people can hold their own against Faolin." Conlan came over and offered me a hand.

I allowed him to pull me to my feet and lead me back to the main living area. He settled me on one of the comfortable couches and went to the kitchen to grab a bottle of water for me. There was no sign of Faolin or the other two, and I sat in uncomfortable silence, wondering how much longer they were going to keep me here. I needed to get home to Finch.

Lukas strode back into the room, holding his phone. "I need to take care of a few things. Conlan, help our guest settle in while we wait on Faolin."

"Settle in?" I echoed.

"You'll stay here tonight while Faolin checks into your story."

I shot to my feet. "I can't stay here. I have to go home."

"You can go home tomorrow," he said with a note of finality that set my teeth on edge. I wasn't one of his men to boss around.

I took a few angry steps toward him and froze when something growled, low and menacingly, behind me. Fear gripped me as a huge, black cat stalked past me so close that its thick fur brushed against my hand.

The feline stopped six feet away and turned to face me. Its tufted ears, bushy ruff, and bobtail made it resemble a lynx, but its size and the amethyst eyes staring back at me told me the creature was not of this world. I couldn't remember ever reading about it, so I had no idea what it was or what it would do.

As if it could hear my thoughts, it bared its teeth at me and let out another growl. I backed up until my legs hit the couch.

"Hey there, nice kitty," I squeaked as my heart drummed against my ribs.

The creature watched me like a cat waiting to pounce on a mouse. I started to feel lightheaded until I realized I was holding my breath. I let it out in a slow whoosh that made the creature's nose twitch.

"Kaia, sit," Lukas commanded, and the creature abruptly sat on its haunches. Its eyes stayed locked on me, and sweat broke out on my upper lip.

Lukas walked over to scratch the large head, and the creature's loud purr filled the room.

"She won't hurt you without my command," he said to me. If that was supposed to make me feel better, it failed miserably.

I found my voice. "What is she?"

"She's a lamal, a domesticated feline from Faerie."

"T-that's your version of a house cat?" I stared at the cat rubbing her head against him.

Lukas smiled. "Lamals live in the wild, but some – like Kaia – are bred in captivity."

"I've never heard of them," I said hoarsely, wishing I had that water Conlan had been getting for me when Kaia put in her appearance.

As if on cue, Conlan came over and handed me a bottle of mineral water. His friendly smile helped unravel the knot of fear in my gut, and not for the first time, I wondered how he'd ended up with Lukas and Faolin, who were so serious and intense. Iian and Kerr didn't seem to be as angry as Faolin, but they weren't exactly friendly either.

"Thanks," I whispered as I opened the bottle and took a long drink.

"There is a lot about Faerie you don't know," Lukas said, bringing my attention back to him. Something in his tone told me I was better off not knowing everything.

I looked at Kaia, and the moment our eyes met, she hissed at me. Lukas said something to her in Fae, and she stared up at him adoringly.

"I don't think she likes me," I said in a weak attempt at humor.

"She doesn't, but it's not personal," Lukas replied. "She's never met a human before, and she sees you as a threat to me."

"Lovely." I sank wearily down to the couch I'd been sitting on earlier.

Lukas's brows drew together as he studied me. "If you're tired, you can retire for the night. Conlan will see you to a room."

I thought about Finch alone in our apartment, and my chest squeezed. "I need to go home."

"Not tonight," he said firmly.

"You don't understand," I protested. "My little brother is there alone, and he'll be frightened if I stay out overnight."

"You never mentioned a younger sibling." His eyes narrowed in suspicion.

"Do you tell strangers about your family?" I challenged.

His frown faded. "How old is your brother?"

"He's ten."

"You left a child alone at night?" Lukas asked sharply.

I bristled defensively until I realized he had no way of knowing my brother wasn't like other children. "Finch is a sprite. He can mostly take care of himself, but he's been upset since our parents disappeared. If I don't go home, he'll think something happened to me, too."

"You own a sprite, and you call him your brother?" asked a new voice as one of the other faeries walked in from the foyer.

"He's not a pet." I almost spat the words, offended on Finch's behalf. "When he was a baby, my parents rescued him from traffickers and brought him home to live with us."

My tone must have been too aggressive because Kaia started growling again. I watched the big feline as Lukas stroked her head until she relaxed, and I made sure my voice sounded non-threatening when I spoke again. "Now do you see why I can't stay here?"

Lukas's jaw hardened again, and my heart sank. He didn't have to speak for me to know what his answer would be. I'd never hated someone before, but in that moment, I think I hated him.

"Do you have one of those answering machines at home?" Conlan asked suddenly, forcing my gaze away from his friend.

"Why?" I asked warily.

He smiled. "Because if you do, you can call and leave a message, and your sprite will hear it."

"My brother," I corrected. "And yes, we do." We had a phone in the kitchen, and Finch would definitely hear it if I called him. He couldn't answer, but it might ease his mind to know I was okay.

"When you're done, Conlan will get you anything you need," Lukas said dismissively. He turned away and started back toward the library. "Kaia, come."

I waited until they were out of sight to take out my phone. Turning away from Conlan, I dialed my home number and heard it ring three times before the machine picked up. Hearing my father's voice telling me to leave a message made my eyes sting a little.

"Hey, Finch, it's me," I said in a steady voice. "I know I told you I wouldn't stay out too late, but something's come up and I won't be home until tomorrow. I'll buy you a whole bucket of blackberries to make it up to you, okay? I love you."

I hung up and took a deep breath before I spun to face Conlan, who was watching me curiously. I raised my eyebrows in question, but he only smiled and held out his hand. It took me a few seconds to realize he was asking for my phone.

"You'll get it back tomorrow," he said after I relinquished it. "Come on. I'll show you where to sleep."

Suddenly bone-weary, I gave a small nod. Conlan led me up the stairs to the second floor, and I silently marveled at the work and money that must have been required to turn a commercial building into this beautiful home.

We turned right at the top of the stairs and walked to a closed door at the end of the hall. Conlan opened the door and ushered me inside a large bedroom. In the center of the room was a king bed with a black wooden headboard and a dark red coverlet. I didn't see any personal items to indicate whose room this was, but it clearly belonged to one of the males.

"This is not a guest room," I said, my voice higher than normal.

"We don't have any guest rooms. Don't worry. No one will bother you here." Conlan crossed the room and opened several drawers in a tall dresser until he found what he was looking for. Pulling out a white shirt, he came over to hand it to me. "You can sleep in this."

I took the large shirt that was made of material so soft it had to come from Faerie. I had to resist the urge to press it to my face. "Thank you."

"You're welcome. Get some sleep."

"Conlan," I called as he reached the door.

He turned and gave me an inquisitive look, and I debated for a moment whether or not to voice my question. My curiosity won out.

"Is he always like that? So..." I cast about for the right word to use to describe Lukas.

"Obstinate?" Conlan suggested with a quirk of his lips, and I nodded.

He seemed to think about how to answer. "Lukas has a lot of responsibility and people who depend on him. He's harsh when he needs to be, but he's also a man of honor."

He left, closing the door quietly behind him. I waited for the click of a lock, but all I heard was his footsteps. I didn't bother to try the door. With the five of them and Kaia, I wouldn't get far if I tried to escape.

Resigned, I took off my coat and tossed it on a chair. I went into the bathroom and splashed water on my face, wishing I had a toothbrush. Did faeries even need to brush their teeth? It was something I'd never considered before.

I undressed in the bathroom and donned the shirt, which was miles too big for me. It felt heavenly against my skin, and it smelled amazing. I was too tired to care that it belonged to one of the faeries holding me here against my will.

Pulling back the covers on the bed, I crawled in, feeling tiny and out of place in this huge bed and unfamiliar room. I stared at the ceiling for long minutes, willing my racing mind to calm and my body to relax. The sooner I slept, the sooner tomorrow would come, and I could leave this place.

The sound of a door opening woke me sometime later, and I had to stop myself from leaping out of the bed. I lay still, feigning sleep, and listened to the two faeries speaking in low voices near the door.

"You put her in my room?" Lukas asked in an accusing tone.

"Where did you expect her to sleep?" Conlan replied dryly. "You insisted she stay, so it's only fair you give her your bed."

"Sometimes I think you forget you work for me."

Conlan chuckled. "I'd never forget that, my friend."

They were silent for a moment, and I thought they'd left until Conlan said, "I think she's telling the truth."

After a brief pause, Lukas said, "I do, too."

I was so overcome by relief I almost missed Conlan's whispered, "She's a gutsy little thing, but she's going to get herself killed if she goes after that goren dealer alone."

Lukas said something that sounded like, "I know," making my stomach twist with dread.

I waited for them to say something else, but all I heard was the soft click of the door as it closed. I lay awake for hours, thinking about my parents and trying not to imagine the horrible things that could have happened to them. In my heart, I knew they were still alive, but that didn't mean they hadn't been harmed in some way.

The thought of my strong parents helpless and hurt filled me with renewed anguish and determination. Conlan and Lukas thought I'd fail in my quest, but they weren't the first people to underestimate me, and they probably wouldn't be the last. I'd just have to prove them wrong, too.

10

I blinked my eyes open and stared at my ceiling in confusion. Why did it look so high? Where was the crack in the plaster that Dad had been meaning to fix? And why was it so darn bright in here?

I shot up in bed with a gasp and stared at the unfamiliar room. Last night came back in a torrent of memories, sending me scrambling from the sheets tangled around me. In my haste, I tumbled off the bed and landed on the floor in an undignified heap.

"Ow." I massaged my elbow as I got to my feet. Spotting my clothes where I'd left them neatly stacked on a chair, I dressed quickly, afraid someone might walk in on me.

In the bathroom, I combed my fingers through my messy hair and found a hair tie in my pocket to wrangle it into a ponytail. My mouth tasted disgusting from not brushing last night, and my breath would probably knock out anyone who got too close. Served them right for forcing me to stay here without so much as a toothbrush.

Once I was as presentable as I was going to be, I grabbed my coat and cracked the door to peek out. The hallway was empty, but that didn't mean Kaia wasn't lurking nearby, ready to pounce.

I gnawed on my lip as I debated whether to leave the room or stay and wait for someone to come get me. Five minutes later, when there was no sign of anyone, I decided to risk it. I couldn't wait around here all day. I needed to get home to Finch.

Feeling like a burglar, I crept quietly down the hall and descended the stairs. The main room was empty, making me wonder where everyone had gone. I couldn't see them leaving me here alone, especially not Faolin.

The thought of the angry faerie sent a shiver through me. He was the last person I wanted to run into. If I never had the pleasure of his company again, it would be too soon.

I was almost at the door when I remembered Conlan had taken my phone from me last night. Shoot. I walked around the room looking for it, but it was nowhere in sight.

"Gah!" I yelled when I turned and almost ran into Lukas, who looked even bigger in the light of day. I slapped a hand over my heart. "What is it with you creeping up on me?"

His eyebrows arched. "We're in my home, and you appear to be the one doing the creeping. What are you looking for?"

"My phone," I said crossly. "Conlan said I could have it back before I left."

"Then I'm sure he will return it to you." Lukas walked into the kitchen. "There are breakfast pastries if you're hungry."

I stayed where I was, my eyes darting nervously around the room for his pet.

"Kaia is outside in the garden," he said.

I followed his gaze to a spot on the other side of the window, and sure enough, there was a dark, furry shape rolling around in the grass. How I'd missed her when I'd come downstairs, I had no idea.

"Aren't you worried she'll jump over the fence and take off?" I asked, watching as the lamal rolled agilely to her feet and took off after a bird.

"No. Now have a seat."

I turned to face him. "I'd rather just get my phone and be on my way."

"In due course," he replied in that unyielding tone I was starting to recognize.

"Fine." I walked over and sat on one of the tall stools at the island. Lukas slid a plate of sweet and savory pastries toward me, and I gingerly picked one up.

"If I wanted to do you harm, I wouldn't need to use food," he said when I held it without taking a bite.

I moved the pastry toward my mouth and stopped. "This is not Fae food, is it?"

Back in elementary school, a boy in my class had brought in some Fae fruit he'd found in his older brother's room. My parents had warned me against eating Fae food, so I'd refused it when he offered me some. Seven other kids, including the boy, weren't so lucky, and it had taken two days for them to come down from the high the food had given them.

Lukas laughed softly, and the sound traveled straight to my belly, setting off a swarm of butterflies there. Annoyed by my traitorous body's reaction to him, I glowered at the pastry in my hand. He didn't need to poison me when he was capable of rendering me stupid with just a laugh.

"Are you always this distrustful?" he asked.

"Do you always give your *guests* breakfast?" I retorted, using air quotes.

He leaned back against the opposite counter. "As you are my first and only guest, I'd have to say yes. And to answer your first question. No, it's not Fae food. It came from the bakery down the street."

"Oh." I held the pastry to my nose and sniffed it before taking a small bite. Warm apple and cinnamon filled my mouth, and I chewed happily.

He pointed at a cup with the bakery's name on it that I hadn't noticed. "There is coffee if you want it."

"God, yes." I picked up the cup and took a long whiff of the aromatic brew. "Mmm. I haven't had coffee in forever. This makes me almost willing to forgive you for last night."

That earned another smile from him, and I averted my gaze before my stomach could start doing crazy flips again. His pleasant expression made it too easy to forget we were not friends and that he had forced me to stay here against my will.

"Almost," I reiterated.

"Speaking of last night." He crossed his arms, making the muscles in his shoulders more prominent. "Faolin confirmed your story about your parents' disappearance. You'll be free to go after we discuss a few things."

"That's because it wasn't a story," I said tightly. "What things?"

"First, we want to see the security footage you have of the faeries who came to your apartment."

I wiped crumbs from my mouth. "I'm surprised Faolin didn't already go to my place and take it." Lukas's head of security wasn't exactly the type to ask permission.

Amusement flickered in Lukas's eyes. "He couldn't get past your ward."

"That's because my parents take our security very seriously." I couldn't keep the smug smile off my face as I imagined Faolin's reaction when he couldn't enter the apartment. "Do you think those faeries are working for the goren dealer?"

"No," Lukas said without hesitation. "Court faeries would never work for an elf."

I frowned. "So, who are they, and what do they want?"

His face grew serious. "That is what I'd like to know."

"I'm confused. Why do you even care about someone breaking into my place?" Just because he was suddenly being all hospitable and giving me breakfast, I was under no illusion he was concerned about my welfare.

He pushed away from the counter and came over to rest his hands on the breakfast bar. "The name your informant gave you led us to a person of interest in something we've been working on for the last six months. I don't believe in coincidences, and I think your parents' disappearance might be related."

My breath caught. "How?"

"I don't know yet, but if there is a connection, I'll find it. And if your parents are alive, I'll find them, too. You don't need to do anything but give us information when we ask for it."

My chest squeezed, and my body felt light as if a giant burden had been lifted from me. Ever since my parents had gone missing, I'd felt alone and adrift in a world I was struggling to navigate. I'd never been on my own before, and I knew I was in over my head here. I also knew Lukas wasn't offering to help out of the goodness of his heart, but if he could find my parents, I didn't care what his reasons were.

I cleared my throat. "Thank you. I'll take any help you can give me, but I can't sit back and do nothing. No offense, but I hardly know you, and this is my parents' lives we're talking about. You'd feel the same way if it were your family."

His voice hardened. "You're right. I would do anything to protect my family. Your devotion to yours is admirable, and you're smart to not trust strangers. But you're not experienced enough to track down a goren dealer on your own."

"I know," I admitted.

He nodded as if that settled everything. "This is what we're going to do. We will go after the dealer, and you'll tell us if you learn anything new. I'll keep you updated on our progress."

"But –"

"No buts. Don't mistake my offer for kindness. This is as important to me as it is to you, and I won't have you impeding my search. If it's necessary, I will force you to stay here while we work, but I honestly don't want to have you underfoot."

My stomach lurched. I couldn't stay here and leave Finch alone. And I'd go crazy if I was stuck here with all these scowling males, especially Faolin.

I nodded. "I'll leave the goren dealer to you, but I'm still going to look for my parents."

"I'll allow that unless you get in the way of my search."

"Gee, thanks."

The door opened, and Faolin entered, followed by Conlan. Faolin, as expected, scowled at me as if my very existence was an affront. I thought about him trying unsuccessfully to get past our ward, and I couldn't stop the small smirk that curved my lips. His eyes narrowed even more. I was crazy to provoke him, but I'd earned the right after what he'd put me through.

"You're looking well this morning, Jesse," Conlan said with his usual smile. "I trust you found the room comfortable." He shot a sly glance at Lukas.

"The bed was okay." I scrunched up my nose. "But that shirt I slept in had a funny smell. You might want to change your laundry detergent." I didn't look at Lukas, but Conlan's grin told me my barb had hit its intended mark.

Sliding off the stool. I held out my hand. "Can I have my phone back? I'd really like to go home."

Conlan pulled my phone from his pocket and came over to hand it to me. "As promised."

"Faolin will follow you home to get a copy of your security footage," Lukas announced from behind me.

I spun to face him. "I don't think so."

His nostrils flared. "Did you forget our agreement already?"

"Our agreement was that I give you information and let you go after the goren dealer. It does not include allowing *him* into my home." I pointed over my shoulder at Faolin, as if there was any confusion about to whom I was referring.

Faolin strode angrily into my line of vision. "I'm the head of security here, and I will decide –"

"You're in charge here, not at my home." I drew the line at certain things, and this was one of them. Poor Finch would be traumatized after a few minutes in Faolin's company. Our apartment had been his safe haven since the day he'd joined our family, and I wouldn't let this bad-tempered faerie take that from him.

I met Lukas's hard stare. "I'm grateful you're going to help look for my parents, and I'll give you anything you need if it will help us find them. But my brother's been through too much already, and I'm trying really hard to keep our home life stable for him."

Lukas crossed his arms. "What do you suggest then?"

I thought for a moment. "Conlan can come instead." Out of all of them, he was the only one I trusted not to scare Finch out of his wits.

At first, I thought Lukas was going to refuse, but then he gave a curt nod. I could see he wasn't happy about me setting the terms, but he seemed willing to let it go. I decided to get out of there before he changed his mind.

I looked at Conlan. "Is that okay with you?"

"Whatever you want, beautiful," he said in a flirty way that made me roll my eyes.

"Does that really work on women, or are you being over-the-top for my benefit?"

Conlan's cocky smile slipped a little, and Lukas made a sound that was suspiciously like a laugh.

I hadn't meant to insult him, and I rushed to explain. "That came out wrong. I meant –"

"I know what you meant." He shook his head and gave me a good-natured smile. "I'm not sure if my poor ego can survive you, Jesse James."

"Right," I drawled. It was a universally known truth that Court faeries enjoyed a healthy self-esteem. His ego was in no danger from me.

He held out an arm toward the door. "After you."

I started forward, eager to be out of there, but I stopped and looked at Lukas. "Um... how should I contact you if I find something you might need to know?"

"Conlan put our contact numbers in your phone this morning and took your number," he said.

"Of course, you did." I clutched my phone, wondering what else they'd done with it. Had they gone through my photos and texts? My contacts? I tried to remember what could be on there. Thankfully, I hadn't added Tennin's number to my phone. I had put his address into my GPS app, but that only showed the street number, not the apartment number.

I exhaled in relief when Conlan and I exited the building. Conlan walked me to the Jeep and told me he would follow me in one of their vehicles. Faolin would have insisted we drive together, not trusting me out of his sight for a second. Those two were like night and day.

I made it to my building a minute ahead of Conlan. I was walking up the street when a silver Mercedes SUV approached with him behind the wheel. He waved, and I returned the gesture before I went to wait for him at the front entrance of the building. Not long after, he jogged toward me.

As soon as he reached me, I asked something I'd always wondered about. "If you guys can use portals to travel, why do you need cars?"

Amusement lit his eyes. "Portals require a lot of magic, and we'd drain ourselves quickly if we created one every time we wanted to go somewhere. We'll use one for cross-city travel from time to time, but only out of the deepest necessity."

Faeries weren't all powerful and able to appear and disappear in the blink of an eye like they did in old books. But they all had some degree of magic, from the tiny pixies to the elegant Court Fae. Court faeries had the most magic, with royals being the strongest. The bluer the blood, the stronger the magic, which explained why they were the ruling class in their realm.

I wanted to ask Conlan more questions, such as what it was like passing between the realms, but I kept them to myself. He wasn't here on a social call, and I needed to get upstairs and show Finch I was okay."

We entered the building where Mrs. Russo was waiting for me. She studied Conlan with sharp eyes before looking at me. "Any word on your parents, Jesse?"

"Not yet, but we're working on it."

Two days after Mom and Dad went missing, the old woman had called to ask why my father hadn't been down to fix her pipes. I'd had to let her and the other tenants know about my parents, and I'd assured them nothing would change in the building. I prayed I was right and that nothing broke. Dad handled the repairs here, and I had no clue about most of that stuff.

She swung her shrewd gaze back to Conlan. "And who might you be? I don't remember seeing you here before."

I smiled at her parental tone, touched she was trying to watch out for me while my parents were gone. "Mrs. Russo, this is Conlan. He's helping me look for Mom and Dad."

"Is that so?" She eyed him up and down. "I don't know how your parents would feel about you having young men upstairs, but as long as he keeps his hands to himself, I suppose it's okay." She patted my arm and whispered, "I have an extra taser if you want it."

I swallowed back a laugh. "Thanks, but I'm good."

Mrs. Russo wasn't the only person waiting for me. When I reached the third floor, I found Violet sitting at the top of the stairs. She jumped to her feet the second she saw me.

"Finally! I've been waiting here for..."

She trailed off as her gaze landed on Conlan behind me. Recognition filled her eyes, followed by shock. She knew I had no romantic interest in faeries. I could see the wheels turning in her mind as she tried to make sense of seeing Conlan and me together.

"Violet, you remember Conlan," I said as I drew level with her.

She recovered her voice. "How could I forget?"

"Jesse's ravishing blue-haired friend." Conlan moved past me to take her hand. Lifting it to his lips, he pressed a light kiss to the back of it. "You are the unforgettable one."

Violet giggled, swept away by his faerie charm. When he released her hand, she cradled it against her chest and batted her eyelashes at him. What on earth had he done to my self-assured – and very gay – best friend?

Behind Conlan, I made a face at her to let her know she was acting weird, even for her, and she gave me a sheepish look.

"Did we have plans?" I asked her.

Her brow furrowed. "Coffee, remember? I texted you yesterday, and you said to be here at nine."

"Oh, that's right." I shot Conlan a condemning look, which he ignored. "Sorry, crazy night."

"I bet." Violet gave me her "you've got some explaining to do" look. "I can come back later if you need some time."

"No, stay." I went to my door and inserted my key in the lock. "Can you keep Conlan company while I check on Finch and deactivate the ward?"

"Sure."

I opened the door and entered the apartment, which looked tiny now compared to the building Conlan shared with his friends. "Finch, I'm home."

I barely made it to the living room when Finch appeared on the back of the couch and dived at me. I caught him easily and gently held his trembling body against my chest.

"It's okay, Finch. I'm here."

He let out a series of whistles that told me how upset he was, and it was another five minutes before he released his grip on my shirt and leaned back to look up at me.

Where were you? he signed. *Why didn't you come home?*

My heart sank. "You didn't hear the message I left last night?"

Yes. But you never stay out all night, and I was worried.

"I'm sorry. If I could have come home, I would have." I set him down on the couch. "I have great news. Someone is going to help us look for Mom and Dad."

His big eyes lit up. *Hunters?*

"Not quite. Faeries."

His eyes grew round, and I smiled.

"I'll explain it all later. One of them is outside with Violet, waiting to come in. He's going to look at the video of those two faeries who tried to break in."

Finch leaped off the couch and ran to his tree house. I waited until he was hidden from sight before I walked back to the door to recite the words that would allow Conlan through the ward. I'd never used the incantation before, and I hoped I did it correctly since there were no visual signs it had worked.

I opened the door and waved for Violet and Conlan to enter. "Come on in."

Violet entered first, followed by Conlan. I let out a breath when he was able to pass through the ward.

I watched the faerie's gaze sweep over my apartment, and I imagined how it must look to someone used to wealth and luxury. Not that I was ashamed of my home. I loved this apartment and the life I had here with my family.

"We have to go to the office to watch the security feed," I told him. "This way."

I led him to the office with Violet following. She stayed quiet, but I could tell she was bursting with questions.

I logged into the computer and brought up the clip I'd saved. The first faerie had barely appeared on the monitor when Conlan hissed a Fae word I didn't understand. What I did understand was the tightening of his mouth and the intense way he was studying the two faeries.

"Do you know them?" I asked breathlessly.

"No. They're from Seelie." He pointed at the computer. "Can you make a copy of that for me?"

"Yes." I dug around in the desk drawer until I found an empty flash drive. Mom had a dozen of them for some reason. As I inserted the drive to copy the file, Conlan took out his phone and made a call.

"You were right," he said to the other person.

"Right about what?" I asked him.

Conlan kept talking into the phone. "What do you want to do?"

He listened for a minute, making sounds of agreement. "The ward is powerful. I tested it. I'll take care of that. Okay. See you soon." He ended the call and looked at me. "Lukas wants to add some extra security here, just a new ward that will alert us if there is trouble."

"Jesse, who are those guys on the video," Violet asked, sounding a little scared. "Did they try to break in here?"

"I'll explain it later." I ejected the flash drive and handed it to Conlan. "How will the new ward work? Will it cancel out the one we have now?"

"I'll add it on top of the existing ward, and it will notify us if anyone tries to break in."

"Will it notify me, too?"

Conlan shook his head. "No, but Lukas will let you know if we get an alert."

"Okay. Do it." I wasn't going to turn down extra security. I'd do anything to keep Finch safe.

We left the office, and Violet and I watched as Conlan walked around the apartment, murmuring in Fae. Every time he stopped at a window or door it would light up briefly, and he would nod in satisfaction.

It took less than ten minutes for him to ward the entire apartment. When he was done, he turned to me. "My number is in your phone. Call me if you need anything, day or night."

"I will. Thanks."

I walked him to the door. He smiled at me, but his eyes were troubled. "Be careful when you go out, Jesse. Pay attention to your surroundings, especially at night. This city can be a dangerous place for a young woman, bounty hunter or not."

"Oh, my heart!" Violet cried the moment the door closed behind Conlan. She grabbed my hand and dragged me to the couch. "Tell me *everything*, and don't leave out one juicy detail."

It took a while to bring her up to speed on everything that had happened since our visit to Teg's. She already knew about the bounty hunting, but I hadn't told her about the developments in the search for my parents. Her eyes grew wider with each mention of Lukas Rand and his men, and at one point, I had to reach over and put a finger under her chin to close her mouth.

"Shut up! You slept in his bed?"

"You would focus in on that one detail."

"Because it's a very important detail. You stayed the night in a house with not one, but *five* male Court faeries. Do you know how many women would kill to be where you were last night? Not me, obviously, but thousands, no, millions of them."

"I was a prisoner, not a guest. Lukas is only tolerating me because he thinks we can help each other. And Faolin would probably kill me and hide my body if Lukas let him. That guy is seriously demented. Conlan is the only one who is nice to me."

Violet slumped. "That does put a damper on things."

"You think?"

She toyed with the ends of her hair. "But they did offer to help you find your parents."

"That's the only thing that makes last night worthwhile." I looked at Finch, who was sitting in his doorway listening to us. "Lukas and his men are powerful, and they know a lot of people. If anyone can find Mom and Dad, it's them."

"Great!" Violet picked up her phone and started typing into it. "I wonder if we can find anything about Lukas Rand."

I leaned in to see her phone as she searched a popular site for Fae gossip. "I thought only royals made the gossip sites."

"Mostly, but you saw Lukas with Victoria Hart. If he's hanging with celebrities, he's someone." Her fingers flew over the screen. "Aha!"

She opened an article about a black-tie charity event at the Prince George Ballroom, and the lead photo was of Lukas and the sultry actress arriving at the gala.

"Yummy," Violet breathed.

I poked her in the ribs. "Did you switch teams when I wasn't looking?"

She snorted indelicately. "I'm looking at his date. Although, he's hot, too."

"He's got the whole sexy, brooding Alpha male thing going on," I admitted. "But you know those guys are only ideal in books. In real life, they're stubborn, overbearing, and unfriendly." *And dangerous*, I thought, but I didn't want to voice that with Finch in the room.

Violet pretended to swoon. "He's certainly nothing like the boys we knew in school. Let's face it. If it had been Lukas Rand trying to feel you up at Vijay Patel's party instead of Felix Madden, you wouldn't have spent most of our junior year being called the nutcracker."

"Shut up." Heat flooded my cheeks, and I threw a pillow at her. "You are never going to let me forget that, are you?"

"No one's going to forget that, my friend. It was in the yearbook, remember?"

I wish I could say she was joking. She wasn't. And being the best friend that she was, she took great delight in bringing it up whenever she could.

She went back to her search. "I see him mentioned at a few celebrity events, but other than that, nothing."

"I'm not surprised. He doesn't seem like someone who likes the limelight." I stood and went to the kitchen. "You want something to drink?"

"Whatever you're having," she called, not taking her eyes off her phone.

I poured two glasses of soda. As I picked them up to carry them to the living room, my phone rang. I froze, and the glasses slipped from my hands to smash on the tile floor.

Violet's shouts freed me from my stupor. I jumped over the mess and raced to where my phone lay on the coffee table, playing *Bad to the Bone*.

The song ended just as I snatched up the phone. There was a notification for a missed call, and I stared at the name.

Mom.

11

My hands shook as I hit the button to call her number. It went straight to voice mail. *No!*

"Jesse, what's wrong? Who was that?" Violet asked.

"My mom."

"What?" Violet jumped up and came over to look at my phone. "Oh, my God! What do we do?"

"I-I don't know. It's going to voice mail again."

"If her GPS is on, you can track the phone," Violet said.

I stared at her. Track the phone. I could track the phone. "God, I'm so stupid."

I took off for the office. Why hadn't I thought to do that when they went missing? My parents always kept their GPS on, and even if the phone was turned off, it would show the GPS location of the last call. I'd thought Mom had butt-dialed me, but what if she had been letting me know how to find them – and I'd failed her?

The computer already had an app installed for tracking all the phones in a household, and Mom had put each of our numbers in there. I clicked on hers and hit the "Find" button, and a few seconds later, a map appeared with a phone icon on it. I clicked the icon, and it displayed a message telling me the phone appeared to be off but that this was the location of the last call, three minutes ago.

My heart pounded as I read the Bronx address. My mother could be there right now, waiting for me to come find her. I would not fail her a second time.

I entered the address into the GPS app on my phone and turned to Violet. "I have to check this out. Will you come with me?"

"You don't even have to ask." She looked at the shelves of gear in anticipation. "Are we going to load up on weapons first?"

I rummaged through one of the bins and handed her a taser, the kind that shoots out the prongs. "Here, take this. And keep the safety on unless you have to use it."

I was afraid to let her handle any of the bigger weapons. The most dangerous thing I'd ever seen her wield was a hammer in the school theater, and she'd nearly brained the drama teacher while working on a prop.

"Roger that." She pointed the taser at an imaginary target and pretended to shoot. "What about radios? Do we need those?"

"No, because we are not splitting up," I said firmly as we went back to the living room to grab our coats. I saw the mess of glass and soda in the kitchen, but there was no time to clean it up. Every second counted.

"Finch, I'll be back soon. I promise," I called as I sped out the door. Guilt weighed down on me for leaving him alone again so soon, but he'd heard the call and knew what it meant.

"Are you sure you want to come with me?" I asked Violet as we climbed into the Jeep. "It could be dangerous."

She snapped her seat belt and grinned at me. "Are you kidding? This is all so cloak and dagger. I can't believe you get to do this every day."

I pulled out into traffic. "It's not exactly like this. A lot of it is boring stuff. Well, except when something is trying to eat you."

"Ha!" She waited for me to laugh with her, and when I didn't, she murmured, "Holy crap."

My GPS took us to a two-story, red brick house in a nice neighborhood. I parked across the street and looked for signs that someone was home. There were no cars in the driveway, but it looked like there was a detached garage behind the house.

"What do we do now?" Violet whispered.

"I'm thinking." I gave her a sideways look. "Why are you whispering?"

She blushed. "Sorry. Caught up in the moment."

I went back to studying the house. It looked well-kept, although the grass was ready for a trim. I could imagine a doctor or a lawyer living here, definitely someone with money. Which led to the question of why my parents would be here.

My gaze landed on two objects lying on the front step, and it took me a moment to realize they were rolled newspapers. The owner must be away and forgot to suspend the paper delivery.

Pawn

"I don't think anyone is home. I'm going to look around," I said.

Violet reached for her door. "Not without me."

We got out and crossed the quiet street. It was late morning, so most people had to be at work and school. I went up to the front door and checked the newspapers, and sure enough they were for yesterday and today.

Taking a deep breath, I rang the doorbell. I could hear the chimes inside the house, and I listened for footsteps that never came. I pressed the button again and waited. Nothing.

Leaving the step, I walked around to the fenced backyard that housed a stone patio, a postage-stamp sized patch of grass, and a detached two-car garage with what looked like an apartment above it.

I went to the garage and cupped my eyes to peer through a window in one of the doors. When my eyes adjusted, I could make out what looked like a car under a cover in one bay. The other bay was empty.

There was a set of stairs on the side of the garage, leading to the apartment above it. I climbed the stairs and knocked firmly on the door just in case. When no one answered, I tried the door, not surprised to find it locked.

I chewed on my lip, not sure what to do. I'd been in such a mad rush after that call that I hadn't really thought about what I'd do when I got here. I couldn't leave without knowing if my parents were here, but I wouldn't know for sure unless I could get inside the house.

Violet joined me at the top of the steps. "What now?"

I heaved a sigh. "I'm going to try to get into the house. You go back to the car. I don't want you getting into trouble if something goes wrong."

"No way. You said we wouldn't split up," she protested. "How are you going to get in?"

"I don't know. I have a pick set in my bag in the Jeep, but I'm not that good at it." I had been practicing with the locks at home, but so far, I'd only managed to unlock a few padlocks. Nothing close to a dead bolt.

"No problem. I can do it."

I stared at her. "Since when can you pick locks?"

She shrugged. "Remember last spring when I was auditioning for a role in that movie about the gang of teen cat burglars? I thought it might help me get into character more if I could actually pick a lock. Turns out I'm a natural."

"Wow. I can't believe you didn't get the part."

She sniffed indignantly. "I know. I'd make an awesome burglar."

"Police. Hands in the air," boomed a deep voice from behind us.

Violet and I raised our hands above our heads and turned slowly. A pit opened in my stomach when I saw two uniformed officers below with their guns drawn.

"Yikes," Violet squeaked. "Please, tell me you can flash your bounty hunter ID and get us out of this. I'm too cute to go to prison."

***

"She's doing it again," Violet whispered fearfully in my ear.

I shifted on the hard bench and followed her gaze to the blonde, who stared back at us from the other side of the crowded holding cell. The woman had to be around forty, and her thick makeup and skimpy clothes made it clear what her profession was. The makeup couldn't hide the ravaged face of someone who hadn't had an easy life.

Violet pressed into my side. "What's taking so long? We're probably going to get shanked before they spring us."

I smothered a laugh, happy to find any humor in our situation. After being arrested for trespassing, we'd spent the last four hours in this cell that stank of sweat, cheap perfume, alcohol, and vomit. It turned out that the neighbor whose house we'd parked in front of had been at home, and he was vigilant about reporting suspicious people on their street.

I'd shown the police my ID and tried to explain about tracing my mother's phone to the house, but they hadn't wanted to hear it. We were lucky they had arrived before we'd picked the locks, or they would have us for breaking and entering, too.

"I don't think people get shanked in holding," I said in a low voice.

A very tattooed and pierced woman near us, who looked like she was coming off an all-night bender, spoke up. "Oh, it happens. I knew a girl who got cut up good."

Violet whimpered, and I patted her knee. "Just think. If you ever need to audition for the part of a criminal, you can use this to really get into character."

She perked up. "Ooh, that's true."

A female police officer approached the cell and stuck a key in the lock. "James and Lee."

"That's us!" Violet sprang up and practically dragged me out of the cell.

We accompanied the officer to the clerk's office to get our belongings, and then she led us to the reception area of the precinct where our savior waited for us. My one call had been to Conlan because he was the only person I could think of to ask for help.

I came up short when I entered the reception area and saw Lukas, not Conlan, waiting for us. What on earth was he doing here?

"I called Conlan," I said dumbly when I reached him.

"Conlan is occupied elsewhere," he replied brusquely. "Let's go."

He turned away and strode to the exit without looking to see if we were following. Violet and I had to almost run to keep up with him. Outside, Iian waited for Lukas. The four of us walked to a silver SUV with Kerr behind the wheel. Lukas took the front passenger seat, while Violet and I got into the back with Iian.

"It's been less than eight hours since I last saw you, and in that time, you managed to land in jail for trespassing," Lukas said as Kerr drove us away from the police station.

Finally, someone who would take me seriously. "Like I told Conlan, I got a call from my mother, and I traced her phone to a house in the Bronx. We went to check it out and got arrested."

Lukas turned his head to look at me. "What did your mother say?"

"I didn't talk to her. The call ended before I could pick up."

His eyes burned into mine. "So, you and your friend decided to go off on your own with no idea what you could be walking into."

"I..."

"Did it not occur to you that someone could have been using your mother's phone to lure you into a trap?"

My shoulders slumped. "I was so shocked by the call that I wasn't thinking straight."

"That must also be the reason why you didn't call us before you ran off half-cocked," he said pointedly. "Did we not agree I would handle this?"

"You said you would go after the goren dealer. I didn't think you wanted me to call you about anything else."

He looked out the windshield with an audible sigh. "Let me rephrase what I said this morning since I wasn't clear enough then. Anything that concerns your parents is of interest to me. The next time you get a lead on them, you call me immediately. Is that understood?"

"Yes." I pressed my lips together. How was it possible for someone to give me butterflies in one encounter and make me feel like a scolded child in the next?

"Good."

I leaned forward. "What about the call I got from my mother? Her phone didn't just end up at some random house. We have to go back and search for it."

"Faolin and Conlan are there now. They found no sign of your parents or

KAREN LYNCH

your mother's phone, but Faolin said it looks like someone was in the house earlier today."

"I was so close." Despair washed over me. What if my parents had been there while I was outside? If only that neighbor hadn't called the police.

Lukas's voice cut through my heavy thoughts. "The person in the house could have been there lying in wait for you. Remember that. As for your little adventure, the charge has been dropped."

"Thank God," Violet whispered, speaking for the first time since we left the station.

Relief swept through me. "Are you taking us to my Jeep?"

"Conlan will return your vehicle to you. You're fortunate the police were slow to impound it." He held out a hand. I slipped the car key off my key ring and gave it to him.

Lukas went back to staring out the window, apparently done with the conversation. No one spoke for the remainder of the drive, and I had never been so happy to see my street.

Kerr pulled up to my building, and Violet scrambled out like her seat was on fire. I followed her and turned to look at Lukas, who had lowered his window.

"Thank you for helping us out today," I told him.

"Yeah, you came just in time," Violet piped in. "Another hour and I would have been carving a shiv from a bar of soap."

Lukas shot me a questioning look, and I shook my head. "She's an actress. Drama is her middle name."

The corners of his mouth twitched, and I waited for the smile that didn't come.

"Try to stay out of trouble for at least a day," he ordered in a less severe tone. "I have more important things to do than bail you out of jail."

"I'll do my best."

He signaled to Kerr, and they drove off without another word. I waited until they had disappeared from sight before I turned to go inside.

Violet grabbed my arm. "Is he always like that? I think he scared me more than the thought of spending the night in jail."

"That was nothing. And Faolin's worse."

"Then I really don't want to meet Faolin." She shuddered. "I'm going to head home. I need a shower after four hours in that cell."

I made a face. "Me too. Thanks for coming with me today."

"What are best friends for if not to get arrested together?" She sobered. "I'm sorry we didn't find your parents."

I summoned a smile. "Not this time, but I will."

Violet pulled me in for a quick hug. "If anyone can find them, it's you."

I shivered and pulled up the collar of my jacket, but it was little protection from the frigid December wind that stung my face. I was going to be frozen through by the time I reached the Jeep, which I'd had to park two blocks away.

A minute later, when icy drops of rain began to pelt me, I discovered it could be a lot worse. I gasped as the sky opened up and dumped its contents on my head, and I looked around frantically for shelter. The sign for a diner beckoned me like a beacon, and I ran to it.

A bell jingled when I opened the door and entered the diner, which felt like a sauna compared to outside. My glasses fogged, and I removed them so I could see the hostess who greeted me.

"Table for one?" she asked, taking a laminated menu from the hostess stand.

I pushed dripping-wet hair out of my face. "Yes, please."

The diner was small with four booths along the windows and tables against the wall. The hostess led me to one of the booths where I grabbed a handful of napkins to dry my face and glasses. I was still drying off when a waitress came over to take my order.

"Do you have soup?" I asked her without looking at the menu.

"Today's soup is chicken noodle," she said. "It's really good."

"Perfect. I'll have that with lots of crackers and a small Coke."

She left, and I pulled out my phone to check for messages. Disappointment pricked me when I saw there were none. It had been three days since I'd gotten that call from my mother's phone, and except for one call from Lukas to tell me they'd found nothing in the house, it had been radio silence. The house, he'd informed me, belonged to a lawyer named Cecil Hunt, who was on vacation in Hawaii. Faolin had checked into the lawyer, and he looked clean. In other words, a dead end.

My chest squeezed, and I fought back the hopelessness that tried to well up in me. The more time that passed, the odds of finding my parents got smaller. I would never give up on them, but it was getting harder to stay positive.

I had been doing my best to keep busy, and I found that bounty hunting was a good way to do that. I'd brought in a Two yesterday, much to Levi's delight, and he'd already given me two more jobs. I no longer got funny looks from the other hunters whenever I visited the Plaza, and I was starting to feel like I'd been accepted by them. Bringing in a bunnek on my own had pretty much taken care of that.

The waitress brought a steaming bowl of soup, and I almost moaned at the first mouthful. It was homemade and hearty, and perfect for such a cold, miserable day. I hadn't had a good home cooked meal since Mom and Dad disappeared. It hit me now how much I missed that.

A fresh wave of melancholy threatened, and I shook it off. Reaching for my jacket I'd tossed on the seat beside me, I pulled out my ear buds and stuck them in my ears. I selected my favorite playlist on my phone and listened to music while I enjoyed my delicious soup and watched the rain lashing the window.

I looked up as two men in their twenties walked by to sit at the corner booth behind me. Something about the furtive looks they gave me as they passed made me turn off my music. With everything that had happened in the last two weeks, it wouldn't hurt to be extra vigilant.

It wasn't until after I'd stopped the music that I discovered the men weren't alone. Someone had been sitting at the booth behind me before I came in. I immediately felt foolish. Unless the men could see the future and knew I'd duck in here out of a sudden rainstorm at this exact time, it was highly unlikely they were here because of me.

I was about to turn on my music again when someone said, "Everything's in place. Vaerik won't know what hit him."

"Jesus, Dale, keep your voice down," another man whisper-yelled.

Someone else spoke, but all I could discern was the murmur of a male voice.

Dale's friend answered him in a low voice, but I could still make out his words. "Don't worry. Our guy is ex-military, and he never misses."

Icy tendrils twisted my gut. Were they actually talking about killing someone? I held my breath and listened. It was another few minutes before I picked out the words: *gala* and *after the speech*.

Not long after that, I heard the men getting out of the booth. I grabbed my phone and hit play before the first man walked past my booth. I bobbed my head to the music and pretended to be too wrapped up in my phone to pay them any attention.

Through the window, I watched them emerge into the rain, and it was impossible not to notice the tall, blond male who accompanied the two men. Even through the heavy rain, it was easy to see he was a faerie.

The two men pulled up their collars, but the faerie seemed unfazed by the weather. There was a ruthlessness in his expression that made me want to hide under my table until he was gone. I wasn't the only one who saw it. A female elf, who had been about to cross the street to the diner, did an about-face and fled like the devil was on her heels.

I waved the waitress over and ordered a coffee. Then I grabbed my phone and locked myself in the single restroom. Even if I'd misunderstood what I'd heard, I needed to tell someone. If I didn't and someone died because of it, I'd never forgive myself.

The men had mentioned someone named Vaerik as the intended target, and that was a Fae name. I had no idea if he was Seelie or Unseelie, but I knew someone who might.

Conlan answered on the third ring. "Jesse, you didn't go and get yourself arrested again, did you?"

"Ha-ha. I'm not in trouble, but I might know of someone who is, and I didn't know who else to call."

"And the first person you thought of was me. I'm flattered."

I stared at my image in the mirror, wincing at the state of my hair. "Actually, I called you because I think the person in trouble is a faerie."

"Ah. And who is this lucky faerie that the lovely Jesse James feels compelled to protect?" he asked, and I could hear the smile in his voice.

"His name is Vaerik, and he –"

"What did you say?" Conlan's voice went deadly quiet.

"V-Vaerik," I stammered, taken aback by this side of him.

Sounds on his end told me he had started walking. "Where did you hear that name?"

"At a diner in Queens." I told him where I was and what I'd overheard. "One of them was a faerie."

"Stay there," he ordered. "Faolin and I are coming to you."

I groaned. "Does he need to come?"

Conlan's tone softened. "I understand why you dislike him, but you're going to have to talk to him about this. I'll be there to make sure he behaves."

"Fine, but whoever this Vaerik is, he'd better be grateful for what I have to suffer for him."

A chuckle came from the other end. "I'll make sure he knows how much you suffered."

We ended the call, and I went back to my booth where a steaming cup of coffee waited. I summoned the waitress and ordered a piece of apple pie with ice cream. I might as well treat myself while I waited.

I had barely touched my pie when Conlan and Faolin entered the diner and headed straight for me. A stony-faced Faolin sat across from me, while Conlan stood guard outside the booth.

"Did you take a portal here?" I asked them. It was the only way they could have gotten here so quickly, and it told me how important this was.

"Yes," Faolin snapped. "Tell me everything you heard and saw. Leave nothing out. Speak in a whisper. I will hear it."

This might save someone's life, I reminded myself as I recounted the story again. And again. By the third retelling, I wasn't sure if Faolin was super fastidious or if he just enjoyed making me repeat myself.

"How did you come to be at this particular diner?" he asked with his usual dose of suspicion.

"I was at the Plaza dropping off a capture, and I got caught in the rain on the way to my Jeep. I saw the diner and came in to get out of the rain."

His expression didn't change. "Why do you care about the life of a faerie you don't know?"

I scowled at him. "Because I'm a good person. What other reason would I have?"

"Most humans expect rewards in exchange for information."

"I am not most people," I bit out. "I thought I would do a good deed and stop someone from getting killed. I don't want anything from you or this Vaerik."

His lip curled. "You expect us to believe you have no idea who Vaerik is, yet we were the first people you called?"

I let out a puff of air to control my anger. I would not be surprised to know steam was coming out of my ears. "I didn't call *you*. I called Conlan because he told me to contact him if I needed anything. And I don't know any other faeries. If you'd rather I not call the next time I hear something like this, just say the word."

"You did the right thing," Conlan said softly without taking his eyes off the room. "Vaerik will be grateful."

"I'm glad I could help."

Faolin slid out of the booth. "There is a camera over the door. I'm going to see if they caught the men on video."

"What if they won't let him see the video?" I asked Conlan after Faolin left.

"Faolin can be very persuasive," he said. Then he added, "He'll use a glamour, not force."

I frowned. "Glamours are just a different kind of force. And they are against the law."

"Faolin is in service to the Unseelie crown, so he is permitted certain freedoms."

I wasn't sure how I felt about Faolin having any freedoms, let alone the right to use glamours. "Are you in service to the crown, too? And Lukas?"

He nodded. "All of us are."

"I assume Vaerik is Unseelie, too?"

Conlan met my eyes like he was gauging my reaction. "Vaerik is an Unseelie prince."

"Oh." Now it all made sense why they were acting this way. Faeries were very protective of their royals, and they'd just learned of a possible assassination plot on one of their own.

I wondered what they would have done if Vaerik had been Seelie. Would they have passed the information along to the other Court? I almost voiced the question to Conlan, but decided I didn't want to know.

Faolin returned, his expression darker, if that was possible. "I have the video. Let's go," he said to Conlan.

"Oh no, there's no need to thank me. I'm happy to help out," I mocked as he turned away without an acknowledging glance in my direction. *Don't poke the bear*, my inner voice said, but I ignored it.

He stopped walking and half turned to glare at me. Then he gave me the barest head tilt and left.

"What was that?" I asked Conlan, who seemed fascinated by our interaction.

"I believe my friend just thanked you." He gave me a devilish smile and followed Faolin. "Well played, Jesse James. Well played, indeed."

12

"Alright, everyone, quiet down." Levi Solomon's voice carried through the crowded Plaza lobby, and the murmurs around me quickly subsided. There had to be at least fifty bounty hunters packed in here, all dying to know why we'd been summoned. The only time someone called an assembly was for a job that required multiple teams, and those didn't happen often.

"I know you're all busy people, so I'll get right to it," Levi said. "In the last three days, there have been eight drownings in the East River near the Bronx. Those are the ones we know about."

A ripple of excitement went through the crowd, and my stomach quivered nervously. There were several Fae creatures that could harm a human in the water, but only one that would cause the powers that be to call us all together like this.

"This morning, an eyewitness reported a kayaker being pulled under by something she couldn't identify," Levi continued. "At the same time, another attack was witnessed half a mile away. The Agency believes it's a pair of kelpies, and they've made the kelpies' capture a top priority."

The room erupted as people fired questions at the bond agent.

"Are they treating this as one job or two?"

"Is the bounty doubled for a pair?"

"Do we have to split the bounty?"

Levi held up his hands for silence, and it took a minute for everyone to settle down again.

"Here's how it's going to work. Harbor Patrol is providing us with boats, and six hunters will be assigned to each one. Each kelpie carries its own bounty, and that will be shared by the hunters on the boat that makes the capture. However, because of the urgency, the bounty for each kelpie has been increased to thirty thousand dollars."

I leaned against the wall as everyone began to talk at once. Thirty thousand dollars was a lot of money, even split six ways, but this wasn't going to be as cut and dry as Levi made it sound. Kelpies were a level Four for a reason. They were powerful, fast, and vicious. And kelpie sightings were rare, which made it likely that very few people in this room had experience with them. As far as I knew, not even my parents had hunted one.

Joining the hunt wasn't mandatory, and as much as I'd like to see a real live kelpie, I was prepared to sit this one out. I didn't have a partner, and I doubted anyone would want to take a newbie like me on their team.

Around me, hunters had already begun to form teams, and I felt a bit like an outsider watching these people who had known each other for years. Bruce and Trey talked to Ambrose and Kim, the tough brother and sister team, and they were soon joined by Phil Griffin. Except for Trey, they had years of hunting experience between them. If any team could catch a kelpie, it was probably them.

Pushing away from the wall. I headed for the exit. I'd almost made it to the door when I heard someone calling my name, and I turned to see Kim weaving through the crowd toward me.

"You're not thinking of missing out on all the fun, are you?" she asked when she caught up to me.

I cocked an eyebrow at her. "Why? You offering me a spot on your team?"

"Yeah."

My mouth fell open. "Why?"

Kim laughed. "Because there is far too much testosterone on my crew, and I need someone to keep me from tossing Bruce's offspring overboard."

"I don't think your crew agrees with you." I looked over at them to find all four men watching us. Ambrose and Phil didn't look happy, Bruce looked concerned, and Trey flushed when he met my eyes. I hadn't told anyone about that day in the elevator with the bunnek, but two other bounty hunters had seen enough to guess some of what had happened and to tell everyone else.

"Don't mind them. You single-handedly captured a bunnek less than two weeks on the job, and I hear you're pretty smart, too. That's the kind of person I want watching my ass out there." She waved a hand at her team. "What do you say?"

I didn't take long to come to a decision. Aside from Trey, they were a solid team. And I might never get another opportunity to see a kelpie up close.

"I'm in."

That was how, an hour later, I found myself aboard one of the seven Harbor Patrol boats that were slowly circling the river between Queens and the Bronx. The overcast sky threatened rain, and the wind had picked up, making the water choppy.

In the middle of the ring of boats, two very brave souls paddled around in kayaks. The men, experienced Harbor Patrol divers, were wearing full wetsuits and breathing apparatuses, and were armed with dart guns. Their job was to act as bait, wait for a kelpie to attack, and then shoot it with a special tranquilizer. The goal was to capture the creature, not harm it, and there was enough iron in the dart to slow down a kelpie long enough for us to move in.

The light was starting to fade when a shout went up from one of the boats. "Kelpie!"

I watched in a mix of horror and awe as a large, black horse-like creature erupted from the water. The kelpie screamed and lunged at a man in one of the kayaks.

The man twisted and pointed his gun at the kelpie. I couldn't hear the shot, but the creature's enraged scream told us the dart had struck him.

The kelpie landed on the bow of the kayak, sending the man flying from his seat. Before he'd hit the water, we were already racing toward them.

I kept my eyes on the kelpie, which was thrashing wildly. Was the iron not working on him? Beside me, Bruce and Ambrose held a large net between them, while Kim and Phil held another.

We reached the kayak a few seconds before another boat, and Bruce and Ambrose wasted no time in throwing their net. But at the last second, the floundering kelpie rolled off the kayak and into the water. All I could hear was the thuds of the net's iron weights hitting the kayak, followed by a colorful string of curses from Ambrose.

Something hit the deck beside me and I looked down to see a tranquilizer dart. I would bet my entire share of the bounty that this dart had come from an enraged kelpie.

Shouts filled the air as a net flew from the second boat and landed just shy of the creature. The kelpie's black eyes were so wide I could see the whites, and it was snorting wildly and foaming at the mouth.

My heart constricted with compassion for the magnificent beast, and I had to remind myself the kelpie was a danger to humans and had already killed some. It wasn't like we were going to harm it. It would be tagged and sent back to Faerie, where it could live out its life and never hurt another human.

I jumped aside as Kim and Phil moved into position with their net. A third boat had joined us, and I could see them readying to throw one of their nets. It was getting very crowded and noisy as people yelled and the three crews jostled to be the one to make the capture. Bagging a kelpie meant more than a payout. It would give the hunters bragging rights and look pretty impressive on the books.

Nets flew from two of the other boats at the same time. Weights clashed as the nets collided and tangled in the air before falling into the river and sinking. Angry shouts volleyed between the boats as Kim and Phil took aim and made their throw.

As the net hit its target, the kelpie roared and flailed desperately. Cheers went up around me, but I could only feel sadness as I watched the kelpie become helplessly ensnared in the net.

Our boat maneuvered closer. Ambrose and Bruce prepared to throw a second net. The rest of us stood ready to help secure the nets and pull in our catch.

The water between us and the kelpie exploded upward and over us as the second kelpie made its appearance. This one was pure white and a little smaller than the first one, but its scream of rage nearly pierced my eardrums.

The kelpie leaped straight at us, its lips pulled back and its hooves creating sparks when they struck the rail of the boat. One of the hooves struck flesh, and Bruce yelled in pain as he stumbled backward.

For one second, the kelpie's silver eyes met mine before she disappeared below the waves again.

"She's nursing," I shouted at my crew, who ignored me as they scrambled to get the net ready.

"Jesse, move back," Trey ordered as he helped his father to his feet.

I raised my voice to be heard above the shouts. "Stop! These nets won't hold her."

"Out of the way." Ambrose shoved me aside. "I told you she'd be useless," he yelled to his sister.

Kim shot me a disappointed look like I'd let her down. That was going to be the least of her worries if I didn't get these people to listen to me.

I pushed forward again. "Didn't you see her eyes? She's a nursing female."

"Yeah. So what?" Phil asked as he and Ambrose braced themselves against the rail with the net between them.

I stared at him in disbelief. Did none of these people ever read? Female kelpies' eyes turned silver when they were nursing, which meant this was a mated pair with a foal nearby. And kelpie mares were never more dangerous than when they were protecting their young.

The female kelpie burst from the river again. Her powerful jaws latched onto the net ensnaring her mate, and she shredded the strong fibers with a shake of her head. Before anyone could react, the pair slipped beneath the surface.

"Goddamnit!" Ambrose bellowed, slamming his fist into a post. His furious gaze turned on me as if I were somehow to blame.

I glared back at him, holding my ground. He was looking for a scapegoat, but it wouldn't be me. I'd tried to warn them, and no one would listen.

Someone shouted from the nearest boat. I looked past Ambrose in time to see the male kelpie drag one of the hunters into the water. Chaos erupted as the man's scream was cut off by the water closing over his head. Everyone on our boat ran to the rail.

"Back up," I yelled to my crew, sensing the approaching danger. They ignored me.

Water washed over us. One second, Trey stood there leaning over the rail, and in the next, he was gone.

"Trey!" Bruce shouted in horror, limping to the rail. "Oh, God."

I didn't think. My mind went on autopilot as I stripped off my jacket and kicked off my boots. Before anyone could stop me, I dived off the rail.

The river was so cold my body went into shock at the first impact, and I almost sucked in a mouthful of water. I managed to keep my wits about me as I swam straight down. Kelpies dragged their victims down just far enough for the person to run out of air and drown. If I had any hope of saving Trey, I had to follow.

I was a strong swimmer, and within seconds, I saw something white below me. I pushed through the water, ignoring my body's demand for oxygen.

Something brushed against my fingers. The kelpie's mane. I grabbed for it and pulled myself toward the creature. Through the gloom, I could see Trey struggling to break free of her hold on his arm.

I pulled back my free hand and punched the kelpie in the face. It wasn't enough to harm her, but it startled her into releasing Trey. She whirled toward the new threat, but her mane was wrapped around my hand, so I moved with her.

She screamed, twisting and turning agilely in the water. When that didn't loosen me, she sped through the water. It was too dark beneath the surface to see where we were going, but soon that didn't matter. My lungs burned, and I began to see white spots in my vision. I was going to die down here.

I gripped the flowing white mane with my free hand, and my fingers touched something hard and smooth about half the size of my pinkie. I didn't know what it was, but instinct told me it was important. I grabbed it and yanked as hard as my failing strength would allow.

The kelpie stopped dead in the water. I wasted no time releasing her mane and kicking for the surface. My chest hurt, my vision was going dark, and my limbs felt like lead.

I broke the surface, gasping for air. Water filled my nose and mouth, and I coughed violently. Freezing air burned my lungs, but it felt glorious because I was alive.

I looked around for the boats, but I couldn't even see their lights in the choppy water. The kelpie couldn't have taken me that far from them.

My eyes adjusted to the dark, and I could make out a large, shadowy shape ahead of me. Land. I had no idea where I was, but I needed to get out of the water before the kelpie decided to come after me again.

I swam slowly, my energy sapped and my limbs almost numb from the cold. It felt like a lifetime passed before my feet were able to touch the bottom, and I crawled onto a small stretch of sandy beach.

I lay face down in the sand panting for a few minutes before I pushed up onto my hands and knees. It was a supreme effort to stand, but I needed to assess my situation. Fighting off lightheadedness, I squinted at the blurry lights and mourned the loss of my glasses that were somewhere at the bottom of the East River.

I tried to make out the lights. Was that the Bronx? If so, then where the heck was I?

I racked my muddled brain until the answer came to me. I was on North Brother Island.

North Brother Island was an abandoned island that used to house a hospital early in the last century. Now, it was nothing more than a wild bird sanctuary. There had been some talk a few years ago about the Agency using it as a holding facility, but that had fallen through. The island was strictly off-limits to the public, and no one ever came out here. Good for the birds. Not so good for me.

A gust of wind hit me just as I felt a few fat raindrops. I shivered violently, and my teeth chattered so hard they hurt. Someone was bound to come looking for me, but that could take hours, maybe all night. It was already below freezing, and I was soaking wet. If I didn't find shelter soon, I'd die of exposure before rescue came.

There were buildings on the island, but they were little more than ruins. I had no flashlight, and I'd probably fall through a rotting floor or down some shaft. That didn't leave me with many options, but I'd read enough to know a little about surviving in the wilderness. I couldn't start a fire, but I could make a shelter, of sorts.

I stumbled in the dark without even the moon to light the way. I'd almost made it to the trees when a weak ninny floated to me on the wind. It had to be the kelpie foal crying for its mother. Great. I'd escaped the mare, only to end up on the same island as her young. If I was lucky, I'd freeze to death before she tore me apart.

I entered the trees where a thick carpet of dry leaves and pine needles crunched beneath my feet. I bent to pile up the leaves into a nest and realized I was clutching something in my numb right hand. I pried my fingers apart, but it was too dark to see anything. I didn't need to see the oblong stone to know it had come from the kelpie's mane. Whatever it was, it had saved me, so I held onto it for dear life.

I managed to make a pile of leaves and debris without letting go of the stone. Then I lay down and burrowed inside my crude shelter. It protected me from the wind, but it was impossible to get warm in my wet clothes. I curled into a ball, shivering. It was going to be a long, cold night, and I prayed I would still be alive at the end of it.

Sleep pulled at me, no matter how hard I tried to stay awake. I was too exhausted to keep my eyes open. Several times, I thought I heard a motor, but then it was gone and I wasn't sure if I'd dreamed it or not.

I thought I must be hallucinating when something soft and warm lay down beside me. It neighed plaintively, the sound of a child crying for its mother, before it laid its head down. I curled against its back with my numb hands tucked between us and tried not to think of what would happen if its mother came back and found me with her foal. For whatever reason, the foal had sought me out, and I wasn't going to refuse this gift that might just save my life.

"Thank you, little one," I murmured as blessed heat began to seep into my chilled body. I closed my eyes and slept.

Something jostled me awake at dawn. I opened my eyes as the foal stood and left our warm nest. Movement nearby drew my eye, and my breath caught when I saw the white kelpie standing a dozen feet away.

The mare watched me until her foal reached her side. I barely dared to breathe, waiting for the attack that never came. She sniffed and nudged her foal with her muzzle as if checking that her child was okay. Then she walked away into the trees with the foal trailing after her.

I sat up, grimacing as my body protested from the night spent on the hard ground in wet clothes. My jeans and top were still damp and stunk of salt water and decayed leaves, and it felt like half the forest floor was stuck to my hair. But I had survived the night, and that was all that mattered.

My legs wobbled when I stood, and I had to brace my hand against a tree to stay on my feet. Through the trees, I saw the beach and water, and I could hear the distant sounds of the city waking up. It was a comforting sound that made me feel less alone despite my situation.

Pushing away from the tree, I took a step toward the beach. I cried out as sharp pain shot through the soles of my feet. I lifted one foot to inspect it, and I was shocked to see the bottom of my sock caked with dirt and dried blood. I must have cut my feet last night, and they had been too numb to feel the pain.

I eased myself to the ground again and carefully removed my socks to check the damage. There were a few cuts on each foot, but thankfully, I couldn't find anything embedded in my feet. This island might have been deserted a long time ago, but that didn't mean there weren't old nails or glass fragments lying around. The last thing I needed was an infection on top of everything else.

I made a face as I donned my filthy socks again. They weren't much, but they were better than going barefoot. With any luck, I wouldn't be here much longer.

The sound of a boat had me pushing up off the ground and hobbling toward the beach. I couldn't see the boat, so it must be on the other side of the island. Lightness filled my chest. They had to be searching for me. If I stayed out here in the open, someone would find me.

A minute later, I heard the sound of an approaching helicopter. I yelled and waved my hands when a white and blue chopper appeared over the tops of the trees. At first, I didn't think they'd spotted me, until they came around and hovered above me. My throat tightened as the emotion I'd held back threatened to overwhelm me.

I managed to get my emotions under control by the time a speedboat came into view. I did a double take and nearly tripped over my feet when the boat got close enough for me to see its occupants. Kerr stood behind the wheel, and beside him were Lukas and Iian.

The helicopter moved away as Kerr took the boat as close to the beach as he could. Lukas and Iian jumped out, and I could only gape as they sloshed through the water toward me.

"I can't decide if you have incredibly bad or incredibly good luck," Lukas teased when he reached me.

"What? Why...are you here?" I croaked, reeling more from the identity of my rescuers than from being rescued.

Lukas gave me a smile that would have turned my insides to goo under different circumstances. "Prince Vaerik owes you a debt of gratitude, and he always repays his debts."

"Tell him he didn't have to repay me for that, but I'm thankful he did," I said hoarsely. I took a step toward Lukas, and my legs suddenly decided they could no longer hold my weight.

Lukas caught me before I face-planted in the sand and swept me up into his arms. My brain short-circuited for a few seconds, and I wasn't sure if it was from exhaustion or from the warm, hard chest I was pressed against.

"I can walk," I protested weakly, though we both knew I was lying.

He didn't respond as he carried me to the boat. Iian jumped on board, and Lukas passed me into the other faerie's arms. I expected Iian to set me down on one of the seats, but he handed me back to Lukas once he was aboard. Lukas sat with me cradled on his lap as Kerr took us out into deeper water.

I shivered when the wind hit me, and Iian pulled off his coat to cover me with it. Murmuring my thanks, I rested my head wearily against Lukas's shoulder. I couldn't remember the last time I'd felt this safe.

Over the wind and the engine, I heard Kerr mention my name and realized he was talking into the radio. That was when I noticed the Harbor Patrol boats on the river.

"Are they looking for me?" I asked Lukas.

"Yes, but I believe they are on a recovery mission, not a rescue."

I lifted my head as shock rippled through me. "They think I'm dead?"

"They did. Kerr is letting them know we have you."

My mouth opened, but no words came out. Everyone thought I was dead. I couldn't blame them when I'd jumped in the water after a kelpie. But the idea that they were out here looking for my body sent a shudder through me. I burrowed under Iian's coat for warmth, and Lukas wrapped his arms more tightly around me.

"How did you find me?" I asked when I could speak again.

"You can thank Faolin for that. He monitors Agency communications, and he heard a report this morning about the three bounty hunters who went in the river last night and two were presumed dead. You were listed as one of the missing hunters."

Faolin was the reason I had been rescued? I wasn't sure my brain could take any more shocks today. "So, you decided to look for me even though you thought I was dead?"

"Only the body of a male hunter had been recovered, and Conlan said we shouldn't write you off so easily." Lukas chuckled. "As always, his instincts were right."

I frowned, realizing for the first time that Conlan wasn't here. "Where is Conlan?"

"He and Faolin are in the helicopter that located you."

Neither of us spoke for several minutes until he said, "Do you want to tell me how you went from being drowned by a kelpie to alive on that island?"

I recounted the events of last night. I explained how I'd gotten away from the kelpie and described the object I'd plucked from her mane. He didn't say anything until after I'd finished my story.

"Do you still have the stone?" He sounded curious.

"I..." I patted my pockets and looked up at him in dismay. "I remember holding it when I went to sleep, but it's gone. What was it?"

He was quiet for a moment. "If I were to guess, I'd say it was a goddess stone."

"I've never heard of that."

"I'm not surprised. It's a Fae legend. According to lore, the stones come from Aedhna's throne and were gifted by her to creatures that had won her favor. Kelpies are said to be among her favorite creations."

"Wow." Aedhna was the Fae deity who had created Faerie and every creature in it. The idea that I had actually held something touched by her hand gave me goose bumps. "What does it do?"

"No one knows. The stone can only be worn by one who has won the favor of Aedhna, and to my knowledge no Court faerie has ever been goddess-blessed."

"Goddess-blessed," I repeated softly. "If you want to go back and look for it, I can show you where I slept. It might still be there."

Lukas started as if my words surprised him. "That's a generous offer, but it won't be there. The stone goes with its rightful owner."

"The kelpie." I remembered how she'd watched me this morning. "There's one thing I don't understand. Why didn't she attack me when she found me with her foal?"

"I don't know," he admitted. "She might have perceived it as you comforting the foal while she was gone. Or the foal's lack of fear of you made her believe you weren't a threat."

"Or you do have incredibly good luck," said Iian. I looked up to find him smirking at me, and I realized it was the first time he'd ever spoken around me.

Talking had worn me out, and I closed my eyes to rest for a few minutes. The next thing I knew, I was being lifted into the back seat of an SUV and settled once again on Lukas's lap.

"Are you taking me home?" I asked through a yawn.

"You need to see a doctor," he said firmly. "We're taking you to the hospital."

I looked at the empty space beside him. "You don't have to keep carrying me. I can sit on my own."

"Your feet are injured, and you can't put weight on them until they've been treated by a doctor."

I slumped against him, too tired to argue.

Before I knew it, I was in the emergency room at the hospital. I expected a wait, but Lukas spoke to someone and I was seen to immediately. A chipper male nurse cleaned and dressed my feet and joked that I'd be back on them in no time. Then the doctor informed me I had to stay overnight because of my "harrowing ordeal." I needed to get home to Finch, who had to be freaking out by now, but no amount of arguing on my part could convince them to let me leave.

A nurse wheeled me to a room where I used the phone to call Violet, who took a good five minutes to calm down when she heard my voice. Like everyone else, she'd believed I had drowned in the river. Once she was talking sensibly again, I asked her to go to my apartment and check on Finch before she came to the hospital. She said not to worry, that she'd take care of everything.

I hadn't seen Lukas or his men since I was admitted into the ER, but I didn't expect them to hang around here. They'd gone above and beyond, and they could consider their prince's debt repaid and then some.

"Can I take a shower?" I asked the nurse who brought me to my room.

She took in my grimy appearance and pointed to the adjoining bathroom. "You can shower in there. Do you need help?"

"I think I can manage."

She provided me with towels and a clean gown before leaving. I dropped my filthy clothes on the bathroom floor and stepped gingerly beneath the hot spray, moaning at the sheer pleasure of it. I would have stayed in there for an hour, but my feet hurt too much and I was bone tired.

Quickly, I shampooed my tangled hair and soaped down my body before rinsing off and getting out. It felt amazing to be clean. All I needed was some food and a warm bed, and I'd be as good as new.

I towel-dried my hair, but I had no brush to get the tangles out. I tried to comb my fingers through it and had to laugh at the futile effort. Without conditioner and a good detangling comb, my hair was impossible to manage.

My laughter died when my fingertips touched something small and hard attached to a lock of hair at the back of my head. I twisted and pulled back my hair to see it in the mirror, but I already knew what it was. I stared at the smooth stone less than an inch long that was almost hidden in my thick hair. But instead of being white, it was now the exact shade of red as my hair.

13

I sniffled and reached for a tissue to blow my nose. Immediately, Violet was at my side.

"Are you too cold? Do you need another blanket," she asked like I was nearly at death's door.

"I have two blankets already. Sit down, and stop worrying. It's just a little head cold."

Violet frowned. After she'd shown up at the hospital yesterday and had nearly strangled me with her hugs, she'd appointed herself as my personal nursemaid. The nurses had to force her to leave when visiting hours were over, but she was back again first thing this morning to take me home when I was discharged.

"You nearly died," she reminded me for the umpteenth time. "I think I have the right to be a little worried about you."

Finch, who sat on the back of the couch next to my head, whistled in agreement.

"Sorry." Being sick always made me grumpy, and I'd never liked being fussed over. I was taking my bad mood out on her when all she was doing was being a good friend.

The doorbell rang, and Finch ran to his tree house as Violet went to answer the door. People had been calling or stopping by all day to hear my tale of survival and to bring me cards and food. I'd always thought you only brought food when someone died, but apparently almost dying was a food occasion, too. I had more casseroles and desserts than I could eat in a month, and I'd already sent a bunch of them down to Mrs. Russo.

Guilt washed over me when I thought of the family of Jeff Burry, the hunter who had died. They were also receiving food gifts, but instead of get-well cards, theirs were sympathy cards.

As footsteps approached, I glanced up at an unusually subdued Trey. His eyes were tired, and he was paler than normal.

"Hey, Jesse," he said with a small smile. "You look good."

I returned the smile. "Thanks. You, too."

He stood awkwardly for a moment before he seemed to remember why he'd come. He held out a white paper bag with handles on it. "Mom sent a pie, but I figured you already have more food than you can eat. I got you something else from me."

"You didn't have to bring me anything." I took the bag and peeked inside. I let out a squeal when I saw the bag of dark roast coffee beans that had to have set him back at least fifty dollars. I hugged the bag to my chest. "This is perfect! Thanks."

"It's the least I could do after you saved my ass. Dad told me how you jumped in after me." He shifted anxiously from one foot to the other. "I swear I didn't know you were the reason I got away. I never would have left you alone with that kelpie."

"I know," I said softly. "It all happened so fast, and it was hard to see down there."

He stuffed his hands in his pockets. "You could have died."

"But I didn't." I waved at the couch. "Please, sit."

He did, looking slightly more relaxed. "I can't believe you spent the night outdoors on the island. It dropped into the twenties that night."

"It wasn't my best night." I made a face. "But the next time I go out on the water, I'll be sure to have waterproof matches on me."

Trey smiled. "I heard you made a shelter out of leaves and dirt. How do you know about that stuff?"

"Books. Where else?"

He grew serious again. "That's how you knew the female kelpie was nursing, too. You read that their eyes turn silver."

"Yes."

"We should have listened to you. Jeff Burry might still be alive if we had."

"You don't know that. Anything could have happened out there." Kelpies were unpredictable creatures, which was one of the reasons they were so dangerous. Even if the female hadn't been nursing, she would have come after us for hurting her mate.

"I guess we'll never know." He rubbed his palms on his jeans. "Did you hear that they sent a team to the island to trap the kelpies? Dad said it's a lot easier on land, and the foal is too young to swim yet."

"Did they get them?" I felt bad for the kelpies, but they were too much of a threat to humans to be left alone. Besides, they'd be together and happy in some lake in Faerie.

"Yeah. It took twelve hunters, but they did it."

"That's good." I yawned so big my jaw cracked. "Sorry."

He stood. "I'll leave and let you get some rest. I just wanted to stop by and see how you're doing."

"Thanks. And thanks again for the coffee."

His smile was boyish. "You're welcome. Get better soon."

Violet showed him out and came back to flop down beside me. "Was that the same Trey Fowler we went to school with? He was downright humble."

I laughed, and it turned into a sneeze. "I'm sure he'll be back to his usual cocky self in a few days. It was sweet of him to come by, though."

"You need to save his life more often, and you'll never run out of coffee," she deadpanned, making us both crack up.

She grabbed the remote off the coffee table and turned on the TV. "What are you looking for?" I asked as she clicked through the channels.

"It's almost time for the red-carpet coverage of Prince Rhys's debut party." She stopped on a channel and put down the remote. "I'm getting some pie. You want a piece?"

"Sure." I picked up my spare glasses from the side table, bummed that I'd lost my favorite pair in the river. Turning to the TV, I watched a woman reporter talking about the huge gala that was being held in Manhattan. It was being touted as the social event of the decade, and everyone who was anyone was expected to attend.

"I don't get what the big deal is," I called to Violet. "Everyone already knows what he looks like."

She came in carrying two plates of lemon meringue pie and handed one to me. "Pictures are not the same as seeing him live. And all of Hollywood will be there. This thing is bigger than the Oscars."

She wasn't wrong about that. We watched the celebrities arrive at the event, decked out in their designer fashions. It was easy to distinguish the faerie females from the human women without even looking at their faces. Humans went for flare and jewels, while faeries preferred simple elegance. When you were that beautiful, you didn't need any adornments.

"Ooh, look, it's Lukas!" Violet pointed at the screen.

I'd seen Lukas in a tux that night at the Ralston, but he looked even hotter now, if that was possible. Watching him walk the red carpet with crowds swooning over him, it felt surreal that only yesterday, this handsome faerie had come to my rescue and carried me all the way to the hospital.

On Lukas's arm was Jocq, a gorgeous pop star, whose dark skin and black hair were stunning against her glittering, white, floor-length dress. They stopped for photos, and he smiled down at her. An unpleasant burning sensation suddenly filled my stomach when I imagined what the two of them would be doing after the gala.

I am not jealous. I don't even like Lukas that way. If it wasn't for the fact that he was helping me find my parents, I wouldn't have anything to do with him at all. Sure, I was physically attracted to him, but who wouldn't be – except maybe Violet.

I'd been physically weak and emotional when he'd found me yesterday, and it was normal to manufacture feelings under extreme circumstances. I was sure I'd read that somewhere.

I looked at the TV again and spotted another couple behind Lukas and Jocq. It was Conlan and a woman I didn't recognize. Next to them was Kerr and a model who had been on the cover of *Sports Illustrated* last summer. I wasn't surprised to see no sign of Faolin. I couldn't imagine him at one of these things, let alone coming with a date.

Violet sighed dreamily. "Someday, it's going to be me walking the red carpet with a gorgeous model like that on my arm."

"What? I always thought I'd be your guest." I made a face of mock indignation. "Some friend you are."

She shot me a sly grin. "Okay, but you have to let me pick out your dress."

"Um."

Laughter bubbled from her. "That's what I thought."

My gaze returned to the TV, but the camera was focused on someone else, and Lukas was nowhere in sight.

I ran my hand through my hair, my fingers seeking out the stone hidden in it. It was so light I couldn't tell it was there unless I touched it.

Yesterday, when I had found the stone in my hair at the hospital, I'd panicked a little and removed it. But this morning when I woke up, the stone was back in my hair. I didn't know what to do about it or if I should be worried. What did it mean? I wasn't a faerie. More than that, I hunted them – even if I didn't harm them. Why would their goddess favor me with one of her stones?

My first thought had been to tell Lukas and ask his advice. But how much did I really know about him? He was helping me search for my parents, but only because their disappearance was related to his own interests. And he'd come to rescue me because he was repaying a debt for his prince. He was powerful, and I trusted his ability to make things happen, but did I trust him on a personal level?

The red-carpet coverage seemed to go on forever, and I was yawning behind my hand by the time the last celebrity arrived. The reporter's excitement was almost palpable as she talked about the dinner and speculated on the seating arrangements. Seriously, did people really care about this stuff?

It wasn't until she mentioned Prince Rhys's much anticipated speech that pieces clicked together in my mind. I sucked in a breath as the snatches of conversation I'd overheard in the diner came back to me. Those men had talked about shooting Prince Vaerik at a gala after a speech. Lukas and his men were at this one. Were they there to protect their prince? I'd heard no mention of Vaerik though, which was strange because Fae royalty were always the center of attention. Maybe he'd backed out because of the threat.

I must have dozed off because I started when Violet gently shook me. "What time is it?" I murmured.

"Ten." She tugged on my arms. "Come on, sleepyhead. I have to go, and you'll be stiff tomorrow if you sleep on the couch."

I let her help me to my sore feet. "You can stay here tonight if you want."

"I have an audition at nine, so I need to sleep in my own bed tonight. I'll come by after and tell you about it."

"Okay. I'll provide the dessert and coffee," I said as I limped to the door with her. My feet were healing nicely, but I wouldn't be doing much for a few days. Doctor's orders.

"It's a date." She hugged me goodbye and let herself out.

I locked the dead bolt, turned off the lights, and went to bed. Being in my own bed again felt so good after a night on the ground and another in a hospital bed. I felt myself drifting off not long after my head hit the pillow.

I had no idea how long I'd been asleep when a high-pitched whistle woke me. I bolted upright in bed and peered through the darkness of my room. "Finch?"

He ran across the bed and pulled frantically on the front of my pajama top. I was reaching for the bedside lamp when I heard it, the sound of the front door opening.

Someone was in the apartment.

My first thought was that the faeries had returned, but it couldn't be them unless they had somehow managed to get past our ward.

I slid quietly out of bed, wincing when I put weight on my damaged feet. I looked at Finch, who stood in the middle of my bed. "Hide," I whispered.

I went to my bedroom door and listened for movement. Hearing nothing,

I dared a peek into the hallway before I crept down the hall to the office. I looked around the dark office for a weapon, cursing myself for leaving my stun gun in the Jeep. The creak of a floorboard in the entryway had me grabbing the first thing I saw, which was a length of thick chain. It clinked softly, and I held my breath, but no one came running into the room.

Standing at the back of the dark office, I tried to control my erratic breathing. I jumped at the sound of a chair skidding in the dining room and the hushed whispers that followed. Whomever they were, they definitely weren't faeries. Court faeries had excellent vision and could move with the stealth of a cat.

That realization bolstered my courage. There was no way I could have fought off two Court faeries, but against humans, I had a chance. And I had the home advantage. I just had to be smart and keep my wits about me.

I listened as the intruders moved through the apartment. They'd obviously removed their footwear, but this was an old building, and the occasional creak of a floorboard told me where they were.

My heart was almost bursting from my chest by the time a dark shape appeared in the office doorway. A flashlight shone in my eyes, blinding me. And then the overhead light came on, revealing the men.

The man holding the flashlight was tall and skinny, and his friend was short and stocky. They both wore dark clothes and black ski masks, telling me this wasn't some random break-in. These guys meant business.

"This will only go harder on you if you fight," the shorter man said with the smugness of someone who knew they had the upper hand.

My breathing grew ragged – but not from fear. In the last two weeks, my parents had disappeared, I'd nearly been eaten, almost drowned, and come close to dying of exposure. I'd been attacked by elves, interrogated and held hostage by one group of faeries, arrested, and had more faeries trying to break into my home. And on top of all of that, I had a cold. This was the last damn straw.

I swung the end of the chain. "You guys broke into the wrong apartment."

The tall one pulled a roll of duct tape from his pocket. "No. I'm pretty sure this is the right one."

I opened my mouth to speak when something crashed against the floor in my room.

"I thought you said she was alone," the tall man hissed at his friend. "Go see who that is, and take care of them."

Shorty ran to my room, leaving me alone with the tall one. I barely had time to worry about Finch before the man lunged at me.

I swung the end of the chain, but he dodged it, moving more nimbly than

I'd expected. He slammed into me, pushing me hard against the wall, his bony elbow hitting my left eye and making me see stars.

I shook off the daze from the blow and realized I'd dropped my chain. The man wasted no time in pinning me against the wall, with one of his hands holding both of mine above my head. His eyes gleamed with triumph as he lifted the hand holding the duct tape.

I moved my legs into a defensive position and twisted my hips sharply, rotating my entire torso. Taken off guard, he offered little resistance when I swung him around into the wall.

I followed with a strike to his throat. Our height difference made it difficult to put much force behind it, but my blow was hard enough to allow me to break free.

I backed away from him, searching for a new weapon. My gaze fell on a small mesh bag of iron weights on a shelf, and I grabbed it just as the man came at me again.

I waited until he was within reach, and then I kicked him in the shin. When he stumbled, I slammed the heavy bag against his temple with all my strength. It made a sickening crunch, and he collapsed, out cold.

I didn't check to see if I'd killed him. I could hear Shorty tearing my bedroom apart, and it wouldn't be long before he found Finch. There were all kinds of weapons in here to use against faeries, but none of them would help me now. If only I had my stun gun.

I froze. Dad kept his handgun on the top shelf of their closet. I hated guns, but I'd do anything to protect my brother.

The noise in the other room stopped just as I made a run for it. I'd barely made it five steps down the hall when I was tackled from behind. The man was short but heavy, and the air was knocked out of my lungs when he landed on top of me.

Panic filled me when I couldn't suck in a breath. The man rolled me over roughly, straddling my waist, and I was finally able to draw a breath.

"Get off me," I wheezed, trying to buck him off.

He backhanded me, and I saw stars. The next thing I knew, his beefy hands were around my throat, choking me.

They say your life flashes before your eyes at a moment like this. Not for me. I saw my father's face and heard his voice as he yelled at me to break his hold in my self-defense training.

Muscle memory took over, and I hooked my legs around my attacker's, throwing him to the side. The hallway was narrow, but there was enough room to bring my knee up into his groin before he could recover. That was all I needed to scramble free from him.

I staggered to my parents' room, dizzy from the fall and the choking, and shut the door, locking it. It wouldn't hold for long, but it might give me the time I needed.

I yanked open the closet door and reached up for the metal box that held the gun. It wasn't until I pulled it down that I remembered it was locked and the key was at the back of his sock drawer.

A body rammed against the door, and the sound of cracking wood filled the bedroom. I looked around frantically, but there were no weapons in here, except the box.

Another blow sent the door crashing inward. I jumped and almost tripped over Dad's wooden baseball bat that had fallen from the closet.

I wrapped both hands around the base of the bat and spun toward the man as he fell through the broken door. Swinging low, I struck the side of his knee with enough force to make him scream in pain as he went down. His back hadn't touched the floor when I brought the wide end of the bat down against his skull.

Wood snapped behind me. Like a cornered animal, I bellowed and whirled, striking out blindly. The bat hit flesh, and I heard my assailant let out an "oof." I could make out his shape through the curtain of hair obscuring my vision, and I swung upward, feeling the wood connect with his jaw with a satisfying crunch.

I raised the bat again, but it was yanked from my hands. Long fingers circled my wrist in a steel grip, and I struggled wildly to free myself.

"Jesse, stop. It's us," said a vaguely familiar voice. But I was in survival mode, and I lashed out with my other fist.

Strong arms wrapped around me, holding me immobile against a hard body. "Shhh, you're safe, *li'fachan*," a soothing male voice said against my ear.

The beautiful lilting sound of the Fae language broke through the craze of fear and anger, and I sagged against Lukas.

"The girl is deranged," growled an angry voice.

I lifted my head to meet Faolin's furious gaze. He was rubbing his jaw as if he had a toothache, which was ridiculous since faeries had perfect teeth.

One look at me and his scowl grew even darker. "She's been beaten."

As soon as he said the words, the pain that adrenaline had been keeping at bay came flooding in. It hurt to swallow, and there wasn't a part of my body that didn't feel bruised. One side of my face felt tight, and it was getting hard to see out of my left eye. I didn't need a mirror to imagine what I must look like.

Lukas sat me on my parents' bed and went to his haunches in front of me.

He brushed my hair aside, and a muscle ticked in his jaw when he saw my face.

"Can you tell us what happened?" he asked with controlled anger.

My voice was raspy, and it hurt when I spoke. "I was asleep. Finch woke me up. Oh, God. Finch!" I stood unsteadily, and Lukas didn't try to stop me when I ran from the room.

"Finch," I called hoarsely when I reached my room, which had been ransacked. "You can come out now."

A sob caught in my throat when silence greeted me. Then the curtain fluttered, and Finch landed soundlessly on the floor. He started toward me and stopped, staring at something over my shoulder.

"They're here to help." I crouched and held out my arms, and Finch ran into them. His tiny frame trembled as I sat on my bed and whispered soothing words to him.

Lukas walked over to stand beside the window. "What happened here, Jesse? Do you know those men?"

"I don't think so. I never even saw their faces." I told him everything from when Finch had woken me up to when he and Faolin had arrived. When I talked about the man choking me, emotion welled in my chest as the gravity of what had almost happened pressed down on me.

I looked at Lukas and frowned when I realized he was wearing the tux I'd seen him in earlier tonight. Had he come here from the gala?

"How did you know I was in trouble? And how did you guys get past our ward?"

"That was my doing," Conlan said from the doorway.

I glanced over my shoulder at him and saw that he, too, was still wearing his tux. His lips flattened when he took in my appearance, telling me I must look even worse than I thought.

"What do you mean?" I asked him.

Conlan stepped into the room, which was starting to feel cramped with the two large faeries in it. "The ward I created alerted us to the break-in. It also overrode your existing ward, which allowed us to enter the apartment."

I fixed him with an accusing stare. "You removed the old ward?"

"I didn't remove it," he assured me. "There was no way to put my ward on the apartment without attaching it to the one already there."

"You might have told me that," I griped as my anger fizzled. I wasn't happy about what he'd done, but it felt ungracious to be upset with them after they'd come running to help me.

"What will we do about those men?" I asked Lukas. "Should we call the police?"

His eyes turned cold, and I shivered even though I knew it wasn't directed at me. "Faolin will take care of them."

"What will he do to them?"

Conlan snickered. "Nothing worse than what you've already done to them."

Lukas didn't smile. "He'll question them and find out why they came after you. Then we'll decide what to do with them."

"Okay." My gaze swept the room and fell on my guitar laying in two pieces on the floor. A lump formed in my throat. That guitar had belonged to my grandfather, who had taught me to play, and it had come to me after he'd died.

Lukas's voice cut into my thoughts. "Pack a bag. You're staying with us for a few days until we can secure this apartment and find out why these men came after you."

"What?" I looked from him to Conlan. "That's not necessary."

"The two masked men in your apartment would suggest otherwise," Lukas said harshly. When I didn't respond, he said, "Do you want to pack a bag, or shall I do it for you?"

"What about Finch? I'm not leaving him."

Lukas's expression didn't change. "He'll come with you."

I wanted to argue with him, but he and I both knew I was in no shape to stay here alone. For the first time in my life, I didn't feel safe in my home, and that hurt more than all my bruises.

I set Finch on the bed and packed enough clothes and toiletries for two days, along with my laptop. Lukas carried my bag to the living room, while I changed and packed a smaller bag for Finch, containing his favorite blanket, stuffed bear, and a Tupperware container of fresh fruit.

When I was done, I went to the office where Faolin had the two men sitting with their backs to the wall, their hands and feet bound with the same duct tape they'd planned to use on me. He had removed their ski masks, and I was satisfied to see I wasn't the only one sporting some bruises.

I studied their faces, but I couldn't remember seeing either of them before. They'd lost their cockiness now that our situations were reversed, and I didn't feel an ounce of pity for them. I had a feeling Faolin would have them wetting their pants and telling him whatever he wanted to know in no time.

"How will we get to your place?" I asked Lukas when I walked into the living room with Finch tucked inside my coat. They'd gotten here too fast to have driven, which meant they'd used a portal.

He opened the door. "Kerr and Iian followed us in the SUV."

I started to walk out and yelped when he picked me up. "I can walk," I protested.

"You are in no condition to walk down three flights of stairs." He waited for Conlan to come out carrying our bags, and then he set off down the stairs.

I glared up at him. "This is the last time you're carrying me. I'm not some invalid."

A light rain was falling when we exited the building. Lukas ran to the waiting SUV where Iian stood with the back door open for us. Lukas set me down on the seat and buckled me in before he went around to the other side. I expected Conlan to join us, but he placed my bags into the cargo area and went back inside the building.

I looked at Lukas. "I didn't give him my keys. How will he lock the door?"

"They'll stay here tonight. In the morning, they'll have new locks installed for you."

"Okay." I made a mental note to have a new key made for Violet. She and Maurice were the only two people outside of our family who had keys to our apartment. I felt better knowing someone had a key in case anything happened to me.

"Conlan will handle things at your apartment. You worry about yourself tonight." Lukas studied my face until I turned away.

I'd caught a glimpse of my swollen face and wild hair in the bathroom mirror, so I knew how bad I looked. Tomorrow, it would be even worse when the bruises around my eye turned black. I hadn't seen my neck, but I knew I'd have bruising there, too. I wasn't a vain person, but no one wanted to see a reminder of being attacked when they looked in a mirror.

The rest of the drive was quiet, allowing me to replay the last hour over and over in my head. Who were those men, and why had they come after me? Did it have something to do with my parents or those faeries who had tried to break in? I didn't want to think about what would have happened to Finch and me if I hadn't been able to fight them off.

Kerr parked in the private lot behind their building, a luxury in this city. I unbuckled my seat belt, but Lukas reached over and picked me up before I could get out.

I wriggled to get free. "Put me down. I told you I'm not an invalid."

As usual, he ignored me. He followed Kerr to the door and waited for the other faerie to unlock it. Behind us, I heard Iian getting my bags from the trunk, and I sighed in resignation.

Inside, Lukas set me down on the same couch I'd sat on the last time I'd been here. He left me to go to the kitchen, and I unzipped the top of my coat to check on Finch, who was fast asleep. Poor little guy. He'd been through so much lately, and now he'd been forced to leave his home. It was temporary, but change was hard on him, and I wasn't sure how he'd handle being in a strange place.

Lukas returned with a hand towel full of ice. I reached for the towel, but he surprised me by crouching and holding the ice gently against my swollen eye.

"Are you hurting anywhere else?" he asked with a tenderness I'd never seen from him, not even when he had rescued me from the island.

"My throat hurts," I admitted. "I have a feeling I'll find some more bruises tomorrow, but nothing's broken."

He brushed my hair aside with his free hand and examined my neck. Fury flashed in his eyes, and I couldn't stop the tremble that went through me.

He moved the ice away from my face. "Are you cold?"

"No. The ice feels good." I took the towel from him, and he gave it up without an argument.

His hands dropped to rest on my knees. I didn't know if he was even aware of the contact, but my body practically buzzed from the heat of his hands on my legs and the warmth in his normally cool gaze.

"You fought well tonight. Few women can fend off two male attackers, let alone incapacitate them."

"My parents made me take self-defense lessons, and my father was a tough teacher." I smiled sadly, wondering if I'd ever get to tell him his training had saved my life. "I think I might need to up my game, though. Maybe take up martial arts."

His eyes gleamed with amusement. "People rarely surprise me, but you've managed to do it several times in the few weeks I've known you."

"Just keeping you on your toes," I retorted lightly, earning a chuckle from him.

His phone rang, and he stood to answer it. I felt the loss of his touch more than I wanted to acknowledge. My thoughts and emotions were all jumbled after the last few days, and I couldn't trust these new feelings I was having for him.

"Any news?" Lukas asked, walking toward the kitchen.

Exhaustion hit me, reminding me it was the middle of the night and I was still recovering from my night on the island. I rested my eyes while I waited for someone to show me where I was to sleep. But Iian and Kerr were nowhere to be seen, and Lukas was talking to Conlan by the sound of it.

Maybe I was supposed to sleep here since they had no guest rooms. At this point, I didn't care as long as I could sleep. Kicking off my boots, I checked on Finch again and stretched out my sore body with my head on the arm rest. The couch was comfortable, and sleep pulled at me as soon as I closed my eyes.

I awoke as Lukas laid me in his bed. I moved to sit up, but fell back on the bed with a small groan. My body felt like it had been trampled by a herd of kelpies.

Lukas's brow creased. "Are you in pain?"

"Nothing I wasn't expecting."

"I can use a glamour to help you stop feeling the pain," he offered.

"No," I blurted fearfully, looking down to make sure I was still wearing my bracelet. "I don't want to be glamoured. Promise me you won't ever do that to me."

Lukas didn't strike me as someone who gave his word lightly, but he nodded. "I promise. Now go back to sleep. I have work to do, and you need to rest."

I realized then that my coat was gone. "Where's Finch?"

"He's hiding under the bed." Lukas pulled the covers up to my chin before going to the door and flipping off the light. All I could see of him was his silhouette from the dim light of the hallway. "Sleep well."

The moment the door shut behind Lukas, Finch jumped on the bed and curled up in the crook of my arm.

"You okay, buddy?" I asked him and got a soft whistle in reply.

I smiled in the dark. "I'm so proud of you. You were so brave, making that noise to trick the men. I don't know what I would have done without you."

He whistled again and snuggled closer.

"Goodnight, Finch," I whispered, closing my eyes.

My last thought before succumbing to sleep was that Lukas had left a beautiful pop star to come to me. That should not have made me as happy as it did.

14

M ale laughter greeted me when I slowly descended the stairs the next morning. I found Kerr and Iian in the living room, and they quieted when I made an appearance. I stood awkwardly at the foot of the stairs, feeling out of place and unsure of what to do around these two who rarely spoke to me.

Kerr's gaze swept over me. "You look much improved."

"Thanks. I feel a lot better." I'd looked a fright last night, but a few hours of sleep and a hot shower had done wonders. I'd even managed to braid my unruly hair without much difficulty. My body still ached and I had quite the shiner, but I no longer looked like the lone survivor of a horror movie.

Iian got up and went to the kitchen. He set a plate of pastries and a large coffee on the island and waved me over. "Lukas said you would be hungry and you like these."

I sat on one of the stools and went straight for the coffee that bore the same bakery logo as from my first time here. "This is great. Thanks."

I had taken two bites from a cheese Danish when I noticed I was the only one eating. "Aren't you going to have some?"

"No, these are for you," he said.

I looked down at the plate piled high with an assortment of pastries and burst out laughing. "I can't eat all of these."

Kerr came to stand beside Iian. "Eat what you can. Humans need sustenance to heal."

I looked at the two big faeries, whom I'd seen tossing ogres and trolls around at Teg's like they were toys. It was hard to reconcile those fierce males with the earnest faces in front of me.

I didn't have the heart to tell them that pastries weren't exactly good fuel for the body. Faeries ate for pleasure and never had to worry about their health. I wasn't sure they would understand the concept of healthy eating if I tried to explain it to them.

"Is Lukas here?" I asked between sips of the delicious coffee. I wouldn't have minded if they'd brought a few cups of this instead of all the pastries.

"No," Kerr said.

I assumed Lukas was with Conlan and Faolin, and I wondered if they were at my apartment. I looked from Iian to Kerr. "Let me guess. You two got stuck with babysitting duty. I guess it could be worse. I could have had Faolin scowling at me all day."

The two faeries laughed like they shared a private joke.

"What's so funny?" I asked them.

"You." Kerr grinned. "Faolin will think twice about provoking you after last night."

I gave an exaggerated eye roll. "Right. I'm sure he's really impressed I could fight off a couple of human men. He can probably take down half a dozen at once."

"More like a dozen," Iian said jovially. "Which is why none of us will let him forget this anytime soon."

I frowned at them. "What am I missing here? Let me in on the joke."

Kerr could barely hold back his laughter. "It's no joke when someone lands a blow on Faolin. There is a reason he is head of security."

Iian cut in. "But when a little human girl gets in two strikes with a wooden bat, we think that is hilarious."

"What are you talking about?" I thought back to the moment when Lukas had shown up as I was fighting off the man in my parents' room. I ran through that scene in my head and realized the second man hadn't been in the bedroom. He'd still been unconscious in the office. But I'd hit him with the bat. Hadn't I?

Everything had happened so fast that the memories were a little muddled, but I clearly remembered hitting him right before Lukas had taken the bat from me. Faolin had been there, and he'd called me deranged and...

I slapped a hand over my mouth as I remembered Faolin glaring at me and rubbing his jaw like he had a toothache. *Oh, no.*

I wrung my head in my hands. "He's going to kill me."

Kerr and Iian threw back their heads and laughed again, and I stared at them in disbelief. "How is this funny? He already hated me. After this, I'll be lucky if he doesn't murder me in my sleep."

Kerr smirked. "If Faolin wants you dead, he won't wait until you are asleep."

"Not helping," I griped.

Iian thumped Kerr on the arm. "Stop scaring her." To me, he said, "Faolin won't hurt you."

I scoffed. "Have you met the guy? He could be the poster boy for roid rage."

"What is roid rage?" Iian asked.

"Have you ever heard of steroids?"

They nodded, and their lips curled in distaste. Faeries didn't drink alcohol, smoke, or take drugs of any kind.

"Roid rage is when a man takes steroids to bulk up, and the drug sends him into a psychotic rage," I explained.

Iian considered what I'd said. "You're right. That does sound like Faolin."

"Lovely." I threw up my hands.

"Now who is scaring her?" Kerr shoved Iian and smiled at me. "Do not fear Faolin's wrath. He might not like you, but he respects fighting prowess. Gaining his respect is not easily done."

Iian nodded. "And none of us, including Faolin, would harm someone under our protection."

I was under their protection now? Talk about a one eighty from the last time I was their guest.

Kerr's eyes sparkled with laughter. "I wish I had been there to see you get the drop on Faolin. Lukas said his first thought on seeing you was that he was gazing upon one of the *Asrai*."

"What are the Asrai?"

"They were an ancient race of wild female warriors who protected the home of the Goddess many millennia ago. Some even had hair the color of fire like yours, but they were much taller than you."

I rested my arms on the counter and leaned forward, my coffee forgotten. "What happened to them?"

He shrugged. "They renounced males and refused to take mates. Eventually, they died out, and they were no more."

"That's kind of sad."

Iian smiled. "It is, but they decided their own fate, which is the sign of a true warrior."

Kerr pointed to the plate of pastries. "You need to eat more to build up your strength."

"Maybe later. I should go call my friend Violet. She's supposed to come see me today, and she'll be upset if she can't find me."

I thanked them for breakfast and returned to Lukas's bedroom, surprised to see the bed had been made and the room straightened. I'd been with Iian and Kerr the whole time I was downstairs, so who had cleaned the room?

Crossing the room, I peeked inside the crude tent I'd made in an arm chair with Finch's blanket. He looked up from the slice of apple he was eating and smiled contentedly at me. I'd worried about how all of this would affect him, but he was doing a lot better than I could have hoped for.

He put down the apple and signed to me. *Are we going home now?*

"Not yet. Lukas is going to put new locks on the door to make it safer, and we'll go home then."

Okay.

"Who tidied the room while I was gone?" I asked him.

Ven, he said as if I should know who that was.

"Who's Ven?"

He's the brownie who lives here.

"Ah." Brownies were domestic faeries that loved to do nothing but clean. All you had to do was give them food and a cubbyhole to sleep in, and you'd never have to clean your home again. They were rarely seen and intensely loyal to the residents of their home.

Can you play a song? Finch asked hopefully.

I thought sadly about my smashed guitar. "I don't have my guitar with me. But I can sing for you if you want."

Okay.

I sat on the floor and softly sang a verse from his favorite song, watching as he went into his weird trance. When I was done, he went back to eating his fruit, looking a little happier.

I picked up my phone to text Violet, who was probably still at her audition. I had to think for a minute about what to say that wouldn't make her freak out. **Had to go out. Call me when you get out of the audition. Good luck.**

Sliding off the bed, I walked to one of the tall windows that gave me a great view of the mysterious garden behind the fence. There were more trees and shrubs than flowers, but it looked peaceful and inviting. Maybe Finch and I could spend some time out there instead of staying cooped up in here all day.

A squirrel darted across the grass with something in its mouth. It stopped and froze, its nose twitching as it sniffed the air.

The shadows beneath a tree moved, and a large shape shot forward. I watched in fascinated horror as Kaia pounced on the unfortunate squirrel and ate it in one bite. As if sensing her audience, the lamal looked up at my window and licked her chops.

A shudder went through me. "So much for that idea."

I spent the next two hours alternately reading and surfing on my iPad, trying to stave off boredom. I wasn't used to being cooped up like this, without so much as a television to distract me.

When Violet called, I gave her a watered-down version of the break-in, making it sound less serious than it had been. Telling her the whole truth would only make her worry more, and there was nothing she could do about it.

"He rushed to your rescue and swept you away to his place?" she asked with a little squeal.

I made a face. "Technically, I rescued myself."

"Work with me here, Jess." She exhaled dramatically, and I grinned when I pictured her throwing her hands up in the air. "He came running when he thought you were in trouble. That's so romantic."

"I told you it's not like that. They're all being nice because I helped out their prince."

"Who cares why they're doing it? You have an opportunity here that most women only dream about."

I stared at the ceiling. "And what's that?"

She let out a suffering sigh. "You've been invited into the inner sanctum of not one but five male Court faeries. If there ever was a time for you to let loose and have a little fun, it's now. Pick one, and get to know your wild side."

"Violet!"

"What? Would you rather cash in that V-card with some fumbling boy or with a faerie who knows exactly how to take care of a woman?"

"Gah. I can't even with you. I am not having sex with one of these guys," I whisper-yelled into the phone.

Someone knocked on the bedroom door, and I nearly jumped a foot off the bed. "Yes?" I called shakily.

"Lunch is here," Iian said.

Was that laughter in his voice? Oh, God. Had he overheard me?

"Thanks," I managed to say. "I'll be down in a minute."

Tittering came from the phone. "I wish I could see your face right now."

"No, you don't. Because the next time you see me, I'm going to hold you down and sing the entire *Les Misérables* soundtrack to you."

Violet gasped. "You wouldn't."

"Oh, I would. See you soon." I smirked to myself as I hung up.

It took me a few minutes to get up the courage to face Iian. But if he had overheard what I'd said to Violet, he was too polite to let on.

Lunch was a club sandwich with a side of fruit salad from a restaurant I'd never heard of. Kerr told me it was a place they ordered from often and the food was great. I was relieved to see they'd gotten sandwiches for all of us and I wouldn't have to eat alone while they watched.

They were surprisingly good company. I learned they were cousins, not brothers, but they didn't say much more than that about themselves. We mostly talked about the break-in, and they wanted a blow-by-blow description of my fight with the two men. They were especially interested in the part where I'd hit Faolin with the bat.

We had just finished eating when the door opened, and Lukas came in. My stomach fluttered at the sight of him, and I took a drink from my water bottle to hide the flush I felt creeping up my neck. Why was he the only one who affected me this way?

Lukas joined us, laying the phone he'd been carrying on the island. His eyes moved over my bruised face. "How are you feeling today?"

"Much better," I said a little too cheerfully. "So much that I think Finch and I can go home today."

The slow smile that curved his lips did nothing to dispel the butterflies in my belly. "Nice try, li'fachan. But plan to be our guest for another night."

"What does that word mean?" I asked, recognizing it from last night.

"*Li'fachan* means 'little hunter,'" Kerr said.

"Little?" I looked down at my body. I was five seven, a few inches taller than the average height for women. I wasn't overweight, but I wasn't skinny either, and no one had called me little since I was ten.

Iian laughed. "You are small compared to our females. It is one of the reasons I like human women so much."

"Small and soft," Kerr added lustily. "And amorous."

Heat flooded my cheeks as I thought about the conversation I'd had with Violet an hour ago. It wasn't like I was a prude or anything. I'd dated a few guys, and I'd even gone to second base. But those teenage boys hadn't been anywhere near the same league as Court faeries.

Lukas said something in their language that I didn't understand, but his gruff tone made me think he wasn't happy with the direction of the conversation.

Kerr immediately changed the subject. "How goes the interrogation of the men?"

Lukas glanced briefly at me. "They say they were hired by an elf, and they were supposed to bring Jesse to a specific location where they would be paid the rest of their money."

"You think it was the goren dealer we're looking for?" Iian asked.

"That makes the most sense. He must think Jesse knows something about him."

Someone had paid men to break into my home and kidnap me. The sandwich I'd eaten soured in my stomach and threatened to come back up.

Lukas's warm hand touched the middle of my back. "No one is more adept than Faolin at getting to the truth. We will find out who is behind this."

I swallowed convulsively and hoped my face wasn't as green as it felt when I looked up at him. "What did Faolin do with the men?"

"He glamoured them to make them believe they had escaped, and he and Conlan are tailing them now. If we're lucky, they'll make contact with the person who hired them and lead us to him."

"That's good," I said weakly.

Lukas took the stool next to me. "No matter what happens, we'll keep you safe, Jesse."

"Why are you suddenly being so nice to me?" It was a valid question considering our rocky start. Offering to help find my parents didn't make him responsible for my safety. I'd told Violet it was because I'd helped their prince, but they'd more than repaid that debt.

He leaned toward me until his warm breath tickled my cheek. "Because someone needs to keep me on my toes."

A delicious tingle ran down the length of my body. If I turned my head only a few inches, our lips would meet, and I was suddenly, intensely curious about how his would taste. It took more self-control than I'd known I possessed to not give in to the impulse.

Lukas's phone rang, and I'd never been happier for an interruption. I watched out of the corner of my eye as his lips thinned, and he gave the phone a look of pure annoyance. He swiped the screen to ignore the call and looked at me.

"I have business to see to, so I'll be out most of the afternoon. One of us will be here at all times, so you won't be alone."

"Okay," I said because what else could I say.

He glanced behind him at the large window in the living room. "It's a nice day. Feel free to use the garden if you want some fresh air."

"I don't think Kaia will take kindly to a human in her domain." Remembering the way the lamal had watched me earlier, I suppressed a shudder.

Lukas smiled. "Kaia won't harm you. But if it will make you more comfortable, I'll confine her to the library for the afternoon."

I turned halfway on the stool to look at the garden that was greener and lusher than it should be for this time of year. I'd feel bad about making the lamal leave her little sanctuary, but I would go crazy cooped up in here all day with little to do.

I tugged on my lower lip. "Are you sure it's safe for me to be around her?"

He stood. "Come. I'll take you out there myself before I leave."

I picked up some of the trash from our lunch. "Let me clean this up first."

"That's not necessary."

The words were barely out of his mouth when a short faerie with green-ish-brown skin, yellow eyes, and short brown hair appeared on the other side of the island. The brownie kept his gaze averted as he began cleaning up our mess.

"Thank you, Ven." I handed him the containers I held.

His startled eyes met mine briefly as he took the trash from me. Brownies liked to keep to themselves, and they didn't normally interact with the people they were serving. Because of that and their ability to move about mostly unseen, people tended to ignore their presence, as Lukas, Iian, and Kerr seemed to be doing now.

I turned back to Lukas to find him watching me with raised eyebrows.

"You know the brownie that cleans my home?"

"Finch told me his name. Brownies do such a great job, and they are rarely thanked for it."

Iian chuckled. "Cleaning is what they do. They don't care about being thanked for it."

I slid off my stool. "Have you ever asked him that?" It was a stupid question because Court faeries rarely conversed with lower faeries, particularly the ones cleaning their toilets.

I followed Lukas to a door that had been concealed by a large tropical fern. He opened the door and motioned for me to go first.

I wasn't wearing a coat, so I braced myself for the cold. I was shocked when I took a step outside and warm air washed over my skin. It had to be over eighty degrees out here.

I gaped at Lukas. "It's so warm!"

"There's a ward shielding the entire building and garden. It keeps people out and allows us to regulate the temperature. Kaia doesn't mind the cold, but she prefers a warm climate."

He'd created a little paradise in his backyard just to keep his pet happy. Lukas Rand might be hard and overbearing at times, but he'd just revealed a side of himself that earned him a lot of points in my book.

The covered patio was furnished with a small table and a few cushioned chairs that didn't look like they were used often. I guessed when you were in the service of the Unseelie Crown, you didn't have much time to sit around and admire the flowers.

We stepped off the patio onto the grass, and it felt like we'd walked into another world. Everything was green and vibrant, and when I took a deep breath, I inhaled the perfume of gardenias, jasmine, and other flowers I couldn't identify. Birds sang in the trees, and a few colorful butterflies fluttered past. It was an oasis in a city that would soon feel the first snow of winter.

"This is amazing." I turned in a slow circle to take it all in. When I stopped, I stifled a gasp, finding myself face-to-face with the lamal I hadn't heard approach.

"Kaia, this is Jesse," Lukas said in a quiet but commanding voice. He clasped my hand in his, and before I could recover from the jolt of pleasure that shot through me, he placed our joined hands on Kaia's head. I instinctively tried to pull mine back, but Lukas held it in place.

"Let her feel you are not afraid of her," Lukas murmured.

"But I am afraid of her," I hissed out of the side of my mouth, earning a chuckle from him.

He moved my hand slowly through the thick, warm fur on the back of her head. I startled when I felt a vibration under my fingertips, and it took me a minute to realize she was purring.

Without warning, Lukas released my hand, leaving me touching the lamal. I tensed, but Kaia continued to purr and push against my hand.

"What do I do now?" I asked him.

"Nothing. She knows you're welcome here and you're no threat to me."

I looked up at what I thought was my bedroom window. I couldn't leave Finch up there alone while I was out here enjoying this little paradise. "What about Finch?"

He smiled like I'd said something funny. "Lamals don't harm sprites."

"That's a relief because I think he'll like it out here."

"I'm sure Kaia will enjoy the company." He reached out to stroke her head. "She's been alone too much lately."

I removed my hand from her. "Why didn't you leave her in Faerie with others of her kind?"

"Lamals imprint on their masters when they are kittens, and they don't do well with long separations. Kaia is happier here with me than she would be at home without me."

There was so much I didn't know about his realm, and I was dying to ask him more questions. But a knock at the window had us turning to see Iian waving Lukas's phone at him. We went back inside, and Lukas got the same displeased expression on his face when he looked at his phone and saw who had called him. Whoever it was, he did not want to talk to them.

"I should be back by dinner. Kerr will stay with you until we return," Lukas said to me. "If you need anything, he'll get it for you."

"Thanks."

He and Iian left, and I went upstairs to convince Finch to check out the garden. Sprites loved trees, but he hadn't seen a real tree since he'd come to live with us. We had tried many times over the years to get him to go outdoors, but he'd refused. He seemed to be doing well here, and I hoped that meant he was ready to take the next step.

It took an hour to coax Finch out of the bedroom. I carried him out to the patio where I was ready for another round of persuading to get him to go into the garden. But I was not prepared for what happened next.

A bird trilled. Finch lifted his head from where he'd been hiding his face against my neck and looked around, trying to locate the bird. The next thing I knew, my little brother leaped from my arms to the thick grass and took off running for the nearest tree. He scaled the trunk of the tree like he'd been doing it his whole life and began imitating the bird's call.

I knew every whistle Finch made, and I'd never heard these sounds of pure joy from him before. It made my heart fill near to bursting. The last few weeks had been confusing and difficult for him, and he deserved some happiness.

Finch climbed down from the tree and lay sprawled on his back in the grass. I laughed when he fanned his arms and legs like someone making a snow angel. He did that until a butterfly captured his attention and sent him scampering across the garden.

I let out a small scream of horror when Kaia leaped from her hiding place and landed in front of Finch. "Kaia, no!" I cried as the lamal crouched low like a cat stalking a mouse, her hind quarters wriggling in excitement.

Finch moved, but it wasn't to flee. I watched in shock as the sprite walked up to Kaia and touched her nose. Purple magic flowed from his tiny hand and wafted around the lamal's head like a fine mist before it dissipated. The next thing I knew, Kaia was rolling around playfully in the grass.

I didn't realize Kerr was beside me until he spoke. "Sprites are one of the weakest species in Faerie, but their magic can tame the wildest forest beast."

"I had no idea," I said as I willed my heart rate back to its normal pace.

"The forests in Faerie hold many dangers, yet the gentle sprites thrive there because Aedhna gave them the power to protect themselves from the strongest predators."

I turned my head to look at him. "The more I hear about your goddess, the more I like her."

Kerr smiled. "I believe she would like you too, Jesse James."

I thought about what he'd said later while I sat on one of the patio chairs trying to read. My fingers sought out the small stone hidden in my hair, and I wondered again what it meant. I wished I could ask Kerr, but I wasn't ready to share my secret. What if it upset the faeries to know a human was in possession of a goddess stone – if indeed this was one? Would they turn against me, or worse, stop helping me search for my parents? Until I knew more about the stone, it was better to keep its existence to myself.

I was in for another pleasant surprise when I went to the kitchen for something to drink and spotted a shiny chrome espresso machine in a corner of the counter. I squeaked in delight and went to check out the expensive machine. How on earth had this beauty escaped my notice? A quick search of the cabinets and fridge revealed several brands of espresso beans and everything needed to make an assortment of espresso drinks.

"Kerr?" I called to the faerie who was nowhere in sight.

He appeared from the hallway that led to the library. "Do you need something?"

"Is it okay if I use the espresso machine?"

"Help yourself to anything in the kitchen," he said.

I grinned so wide I was sure I showed all my teeth. "Want me to make you something?"

"No, thanks. I never touch the stuff." He made a face and turned back to the library.

"Okay, but it's your loss because I make a killer cappuccino."

I whipped up a drink and took it out to the patio, where I spend the rest of the afternoon, reading, napping, and watching Finch having the time of his life. It was the best day we'd had since before our parents went missing.

It wasn't until after I'd been out there for hours that I realized I'd left my phone in the bedroom. What if Violet was trying to reach me? Or what if I got another call from Mom's phone?

Leaving Finch to his fun, I went inside and climbed the stairs to the second floor. There was another flight of stairs to the third floor, but I hadn't gone up there to see what it was like. It was probably more bedrooms since I doubted any of the males living here would want to share a room. I had wondered briefly where Lukas was sleeping while I was here, and I'd decided that was a detail I didn't need to know.

I opened the door and entered the bedroom – but came up short at the sight of the nearly-naked male walking from the bathroom. Lukas's hair was wet, and droplets of water clung to his broad chest and chiseled abs. The white towel hanging precariously low on his hips looked one slip away from falling to the floor.

"Gah!" I whirled to face away from him. "I'm so sorry. I had no idea you were here."

"You were so engrossed in your book that I didn't want to interrupt you," he said casually, but I detected amusement in his voice.

Something landed on the hardwood floor, and my stomach pitched wildly when I realized it was the towel. I feared my face would catch on fire from the heat building in my cheeks.

I heard a drawer opening. "Kerr said you have been making good use of the garden. I'm glad you're enjoying it."

"Um, thanks. It's great." I stared at the open door, but my stupid legs refused to move.

"I hope you are finding the sleeping accommodations more to your liking this time," Lukas said in a teasing tone.

My lips twitched as I thought back to my first time here when I'd said his shirt had smelled funny. "Yes, but I did bring my own clothes to sleep in."

He chuckled so softly I almost missed it. I heard the closet door open and the whisper of fabric, and I tried to focus on anything but thoughts of all that naked glistening skin. It didn't work.

"I'll go so you can dress," I said in a rush.

"Didn't you come up here for something?" he asked before I could make my escape.

"Not this," I almost said. I licked at the beads of moisture on my upper lip. "My...phone."

He moved so quietly I almost jumped out of my skin when he came up behind me. He stood close enough for me to feel the heat of his body without touching it and to smell his intoxicating male scent.

One of his hands appeared in front of me holding my phone, and I swallowed when I saw his bare arm. I stared at it for several seconds until I remembered I was supposed to take the phone from him. My breath hitched when his fingers grazed mine, and I almost dropped the phone.

"Thanks," I said in a husky voice that didn't sound like it belonged to me.

"You're welcome." He withdrew his hand but didn't move away. "Anything else I can do for you, Jesse?"

"I'm good."

I fled the room as fast as I could, with Lukas's soft laughter following me.

15

I waved to Gorn as I passed him in the lobby of our building and started up the stairs to my apartment. I'd just returned from my first job since the kelpie incident a week ago, and it felt good to be back to work.

Today, I'd caught my second peri, and it had been a breeze compared to the other jobs I had done. When I'd turned over my capture, I told Levi I wanted more Twos. To my surprise, he'd agreed.

The murmur of male voices above me slowed my steps and put all my senses on alert. I hugged the wall and peeked around the corner to see who or what was waiting for me.

Two men in dark suits stood outside my apartment door talking in low voices. One of them held a small device in his hand. I couldn't get a good look at it, but he appeared to be scanning my door with it.

I didn't need to see their faces to figure out they were from the Agency. All male agents had a similar build and the same signature look to make them more recognizable to the public. It was when an agent didn't wear their normal attire that you really needed to worry.

Why were agents at my home? I hadn't heard a peep from the Agency since my unpleasant visit with Agent Curry almost two weeks ago. Were they here with news about my parents? My stomach twisted at the possible reasons why they would visit me in person.

"Can I help you?" I asked, making my presence known. It wasn't smart to sneak up on armed agents.

The two men turned in unison to face me, and my heart sank even more when I saw one of them was Agent Curry. He didn't look happy to see me either.

The other agent gave me a businesslike smile. "Jesse James?"

"Yes."

He held out a hand. "I'm Agent Ryan. I believe you've met Agent Curry.

I took his hand. "Are you here about my parents? Did you find something?"

"We're here to search your apartment," Curry said tersely. "Please, unlock the door."

I clenched my keys in my fist. "What are you searching for?"

Curry's eyes hardened even more. "We don't share details of ongoing investigations with civilians."

"Then I'd like to see the search warrant, please." Even the Agency needed probable cause to search a private residence.

"We don't require a search warrant for a special crimes investigation," Agent Curry informed me.

I didn't need to see the frown his partner shot him to know that statement was BS. If Agent Curry was counting on my ignorance of the law, he was out of luck. One of my senior year electives had been Fae Law Enforcement, and I didn't have a four-point grade average for nothing.

"You need a warrant signed by your regional head and a district court judge to enter the home of a bounty hunter without consent," I told him, ninety-nine-point-nine percent certain I was right. A small nod from Agent Ryan confirmed it.

Agent Curry's lips formed a thin line. "A warrant isn't necessary if the homeowner grants us permission to enter the premises."

"I won't do that unless you can tell me exactly what you're looking for and how it will help my parents."

He glared at me. "Are you refusing to cooperate with an ongoing investigation? Do you have something to hide, Miss James?"

"Are you implying I'm under investigation?" I demanded.

Agent Ryan spoke for the first time since introducing himself. "No."

"But your parents are," Agent Curry said. "And if you impede our investigation in any way, I'll see you arrested for obstruction."

"I've done nothing illegal, and I'm pretty sure you know that," I said calmly because getting angry would only play into his hands. He was looking for a reason to put me in handcuffs. "If you come back with a search warrant, I'll cooperate in any way I can."

Agent Curry started to say something, but his partner cut him off. "Thank you for your time, Miss James."

I stood back to let them pass, but Agent Curry wasn't going to leave without getting in the last word. He got in my face as close as he could without touching me. "Your parents are dirty, and I'm going to prove it. You'll be seeing me."

I waited until they were out of sight to unlock the door with trembling hands. Once inside, I sagged against the door as my mind raced. I wasn't easily intimidated, but having two agents show up at your door demanding entry was enough to freak anyone out. Especially when one of them was set on proving your parents were guilty of a crime they didn't commit.

Finch whistled, drawing my attention to him standing on the back of the couch. *What's wrong,* he signed.

I pushed away from the door and smiled at him. "Just Agency business. Nothing for you to worry about."

I went to the kitchen to start dinner, just for something to keep my hands busy while I figured out what to do about Agent Curry. He wasn't going to give up. If he managed to get the proper search warrant, he'd be back and he'd tear this place apart looking for evidence to prove he was right. He wouldn't find anything, but he could confiscate our computers and files for an indefinite time, and where would that leave me? I'd back up the drives tonight, but I'd have to buy a new computer if ours were taken. One more thing to worry about.

My phone rang as I was taking a foil-wrapped potato from the oven. I tensed, my first thought that it was the Agency calling. I let out the breath I was holding when I saw Violet's name on the screen.

"How was the first day back to work?" she asked when I answered.

I leaned against the counter. "It was great until I came home and found two agents wanting to search the place without a warrant."

"What?" she shrieked.

Someone spoke in the background, and Violet repeated what I'd said. A few seconds later, a new voice came on the line.

"Tell me what happened," said Mrs. Lee in her courtroom voice that immediately made me feel better. I relayed my conversation with the two agents, as well as my visit to the Agency two weeks ago.

"I'll contact Ben Stewart and see what I can find out," she said when I finished. "He's the head of the Agency's special crimes division for New York."

"What should I do if the agents come back?"

"If they return with the proper search warrant, you have to allow them entry. Call me if that happens, and I'll get there as soon as I can. If I'm in court, one of my associates will come."

"Okay." I wasn't happy about the prospect of letting Agent Curry into the apartment, but it took a weight off to know I wasn't alone in this.

"You have enough to worry about, Jesse," she said in her mom voice. "Let me handle this."

My eyes misted. "Thanks, Mrs. Lee."

"Anytime, dear."

She handed the phone back to Violet, and we chatted until my meal was ready. I hung up with a promise to come over for dinner in a few days.

Finch whistled as I was cutting up some fruit for him. "Dinner's almost ready," I called.

He whistled again, louder this time, and I stuck my head out of the kitchen to see what he wanted. He pointed at the TV, which was showing the evening news, and on the screen were photos of two men I instantly recognized. They were the men who had broken in here and attacked me.

I ran over to turn up the volume in time to hear the news anchor say that the bodies of Charles Dixon and Kevin Dunn were found in an apartment in the Bronx, along with the body of a male elf. Drugs found at the scene had authorities believing this was a goren deal gone wrong.

I stared at the TV after the anchor moved to the next story. Those men were dead. I didn't know how to feel about that. I wanted them to pay for what they'd done, but with jail time, not their lives.

Could the dead elf be the goren dealer we were looking for? And was this related to the two agents paying me a visit today? The timing was too close to be a coincidence.

I went back to the kitchen and picked up my phone. Scrolling through my contacts, I found Lukas's number and dialed it for the first time.

After that embarrassing scene in his bedroom, I'd gone out of my way to avoid Lukas for the rest of my stay. The amused looks he'd shot me the few times we were in the same room told me he had enjoyed my discomfort. It hadn't helped that I was sleeping in his bed. Every time I looked at the door to the bathroom, I grew flushed when I remembered seeing him standing there in that towel.

"Jesse, I was expecting a call from you," Lukas said when he answered.

"Did Faolin kill those two men?" I blurted.

Lukas was silent for a beat. "No. And he's already working to figure out who got to them under our surveillance." An edge in his voice told me he wasn't happy about it, and I could only imagine how pissed off Faolin was.

"Do you think the elf who was killed with them was the goren dealer?" I held my breath, praying he'd say no. The dealer was the last link to my parents and the only reason Lukas had offered to help me find them.

"It looks that way."

My heart was a stone in my chest as I waited for him to tell me I was on my own again. I wouldn't stop looking for my parents, but it would be a lot harder without him.

As if he could read my mind, he said, "This doesn't change anything. Our search doesn't end with the goren dealer."

"Okay." I took a breath. "What happens now?"

"Now we hunt down whoever killed those men while you stay out of trouble."

I was about to make a retort when he said, "Unless you want to be my guest again. I did enjoy your last visit."

I scowled as my cheeks grew warm because I knew exactly what he was referring to. Arrogant faerie.

His laugh was low and sexy. "Talk to you soon, Jesse."

I clutched the small bouquet of flowers in my gloved hand as I wound through headstones, searching for a small white one. Even though I came to the cemetery once a year with Mom and Dad, I had trouble remembering the exact location of Caleb's grave. This place looked and felt a lot different without them.

A shiver went through me that had nothing to do with the cold, and I picked up my pace. The cemetery didn't usually creep me out, but today it made me think too much of death.

I hadn't wanted to come here today. But every year Mom brought flowers to Caleb's grave on his birthday, so I couldn't not come. When she got home, I wanted her to know that no matter what, my brother wouldn't be forgotten.

An angel atop a white marble headstone caught my eye, and I hurried toward it. I crouched beside the tiny grave and placed the flowers in the small vase at the base of the headstone.

"Happy birthday, Caleb."

I never knew what to feel when I visited his grave. How do you grieve someone you'd never known? The sadness that filled me when I looked at his headstone was for the life I could have had if Caleb had lived. Was that selfish? My life had been a happy one, but I often wondered how it would have been if my brother hadn't died. What would he have been like? Would he and I be close? Would he be away at college now or following in our parents' footsteps? I had so many questions I'd never know the answers to.

"I wish you were here. I could really use my older brother right now." The words on the headstone blurred. "What if I can't find them, Caleb? I'm so afraid we'll never be a family again."

My voice broke. Saying those words aloud for the first time threatened to open a floodgate of emotions. Part of me wanted to curl up on the ground and cry until there were no more tears. But I couldn't do that. It would weaken me, and I had to stay strong for our family.

I cleared my throat and blinked away the moisture in my eyes. "Wherever Mom and Dad are, I know they wish they could be here with you today."

Standing, I laid a hand on the top of the headstone. "Bye, Caleb."

I tugged my wool cap down over my ears and headed back to the Jeep. A few other people stood near graves, but other than that, the place had a desolate air to it.

Beside a large tree, a female elf stood huddled inside a long coat, holding the hand of a little elf child. They looked out of place here, and I wondered if they were waiting on someone. Faeries didn't bury their dead, at least not in this world.

My gaze met hers, and for a moment, it looked like she was going to say something to me. But then she abruptly walked off with her child in tow.

"Miss James," called a male voice as I reached the Jeep.

I turned to see a man in a long dark coat striding toward me, and I clenched my teeth when I recognized Agent Curry. His partner was nowhere in sight.

"Are you following me?" I demanded.

He stopped a few feet from me, anger radiating from him. "You might have used your connections to get the Agency to back off, but you won't get rid of me so easily."

"What are you talking about? I don't have any connections like that." As soon as the words were out, I thought about Violet's mother. Mrs. Lee was a big attorney, but she didn't have that kind of clout with the Agency. Did she?

Agent Curry crossed his arms. "Your lawyer just happened to have a meeting with my department head this morning, and an hour later, I was told to focus my efforts elsewhere."

Wow. Mrs. Lee had said she would make a call for me. I hadn't expected her to actually pay a visit to the Agency. Of course, it would be no use trying to tell him that. Nothing I did or said would sway his opinion of me.

"We have two dead men and a dead elf in the morgue, and it looks like the elf is the goren dealer you claimed your parents were hunting. What do you know about that?"

I put my hands on my hips. "My parents *were* hunting a goren dealer. And why would I know anything about some bodies in the morgue?"

"It's very coincidental that the very dealer they were supposedly hunting was just murdered," he said pointedly.

"Agent Curry, maybe if you were as dedicated to finding my parents as you are to condemning them, you'd actually get somewhere on this investigation." My heart pounded as anger burned through me. At this point, I didn't know if he carried some personal grudge against my parents or if he really believed what he was saying. Either way, he was harassing me, and the more he did that, the less time he spent looking for them.

If looks could kill, his would have made me a corpse. "Are you trying to tell me how to do my job now?"

I opened the door to the Jeep. "No. I'm asking you to please find my parents. Then you can interrogate them all you want."

"For someone who only cares about finding her parents, you seem to be in a hurry to leave."

"You're not the only one with a job to do." I got in but didn't close the door. "You're welcome to follow me, but I'm sure you have better things to do than watching me deal with a problem troll."

He didn't say anything, and I took that as my signal to leave. "Have a nice day," I said before I shut the door and drove away.

"Ouch!" I winced as I dabbed antiseptic ointment onto a shallow four-inch cut on my thigh, thankful that trolls were terrible fighters.

The job had been to bring in a troll who was threatening residents of a seniors' apartment building and demanding money from them. I was able to get him in the shackles, but he hadn't gone down without a fight.

I should have checked him for weapons, a mistake I wouldn't make again. He'd pulled a knife on me and managed to slice my leg before I disarmed him. It wasn't more than a deep scratch, but holy crap, it stung.

Finch whistled on the other side of the bathroom door.

"I'm okay. I'll be out in a few minutes."

I applied a few steri-strips to the cut and pulled on a pair of leggings. By the time I opened the bathroom door, the cut was no longer stinging.

"All good." I smiled at Finch, who watched me with worried eyes. "It was just a scratch."

Finch didn't look convinced, so I did a little jog on the spot to show him I was okay. "See. You know some troll isn't going to get the best of me."

That got a smile from him, and he ran ahead of me to the living room. I'd missed dinner, but I was too tired to think about food. What I really needed was sleep, but I wanted to spend some time with Finch first because he'd been alone here all day. We settled on the couch with a soft blanket and watched TV until I could no longer keep my eyes open.

I awoke late the next morning, tired, aching all over, and nursing a headache that wouldn't go away, even after two cups of coffee. I prayed I wasn't getting the flu. I didn't have time to be sick. At least, my cut was healing nicely, and it didn't even sting after I applied more ointment.

I spent the day napping on the couch. I had no appetite, which was just as well because I didn't have the energy to cook. Thankfully, Finch was able to feed himself from the bowl of fruit on the table.

By late afternoon, I was alternating between sweating and shivering under my blanket and cursing the fates for giving me the flu. Violet texted to see if I wanted company, but I warned her to stay away. She was leaving in three days for a trip to China with her parents, and the last thing she needed was to get sick.

I dragged my ass off the couch around dinner time to try to eat something, but all I managed to get down was half a sandwich. I spent the next ten minutes retching in the bathroom and feeling sorry for myself.

Dizziness hit me when I stood, and I had to grab the edge of the vanity to stay on my feet. The face looking back at me from the mirror was ashen with purple shadows under tired eyes and a pinched mouth. Even my hair looked dull and lifeless. I couldn't remember ever being this sick with the flu.

Holding on to the vanity with one hand, I brushed my teeth with the other. I felt sticky from sweating earlier, but I didn't have the energy to shower. That would have to wait until tomorrow.

The hallway tilted like a funhouse room as I walked slowly to my bedroom. I used up what little energy I had left to change out of my sweaty clothes into sleep shorts and a T-shirt. I fell into my bed and barely managed to pull up the covers before I passed out.

Finch's loud whistling woke me. I rolled to the edge of the bed and looked down at him standing on the floor beside my phone, which he must have dragged in from the living room.

"Thanks, buddy," I mumbled, reaching down to pick up the phone. Suddenly, there were two Finches and two phones, and I had to grab a few times before my fingers closed around the phone.

I had a missed call from Violet and a text from her asking if I was okay. I tried to text her back, but my thumbs wouldn't work properly and I ended up with a screen full of gibberish.

I decided to call her, but I dropped the phone twice and had to dig for it in the sheets. It felt like I was moving in slow motion, and there were dark spots floating in front of my eyes. What kind of flu was this?

I brought up my recent calls and hit dial. Violet's voice came from a long way off, and it sounded strange through the ringing in my ears.

"Vi, I think I'm dying," I slurred in a poor attempt at a joke.

She said something, but the ringing had gotten too loud to make it out. The phone slipped from my hands as the dark spots in my vision came together, and I sank into oblivion.

16

Cool hands touched my face. "Jesse, can you hear me?"

"Mmmm." I turned my head to the side to press my flushed cheek into one of the hands.

"She's burning up," said the voice.

A second voice spoke. "I see nothing suspicious. Do you think she's been poisoned?"

The hands disappeared, and warm breath grazed my lips. Someone breathed in deeply, and then the warmth was gone.

"I detect something, but it's too faint to identify." The hand returned to my forehead. "We have to bring her fever down."

The hand was replaced by a cold, wet cloth. It was a small relief from the fire blazing inside me.

"Humans are prone to infections when they are hurt," said the second voice. "Does she have any injuries?"

"Not that I can see."

Those hands ran over my arms. Cold air touched my skin as the bedcovers were pulled down.

"There. It looks like a knife wound, but it doesn't appear to be infected."

"Damn troll," I mumbled.

Someone patted my cheek. "Jesse, did a troll do this to you?"

I smiled, or I think I did. "Yes. But I got him."

"*Kolosh*," the two voices said in unison.

There seemed to be a conversation going on between the voices, but I couldn't make out what they were saying.

"You're going to be okay. Faolin has gone to get the antidote," said the male voice that was starting to sound familiar.

"Faolin's so nice," I murmured sleepily.

The man chuckled. "Now I know you've been poisoned. Come on. Let's sit you up."

"Sleep," I protested weakly as he picked me up.

"No sleep. You have to stay awake."

I lifted my heavy eyelids and saw a masculine throat and the outline of a jaw. Lukas?

He set me down on the sofa chair in the living room. Only it didn't look like my living room. A kaleidoscope of colors filled my vision, and the room was twisted out of shape. Across from me, where Finch's tree house should be, a wall of vines undulated like snakes.

Whoa. This was the craziest dream I'd ever had.

Dream Lukas disappeared and reappeared holding a facecloth. He placed the cold cloth against my cheek and began moving it over my heated face.

I sighed and closed my eyes again. "That feels nice."

He tapped my cheek. "Stay awake, Jesse."

I groaned in frustration and forced my eyes open. Dream Lukas was just as bossy as real Lukas.

"How is she?" asked the other voice. Faolin. Why was *he* here? This was my dream, damn it, and I should be able to choose who was in it.

"Same," Lukas said.

He stood, and suddenly Faolin was there crouching in front of me. Having him so close made me press back into the cushion.

Faolin held what looked like a small red leaf to my mouth. "Eat this."

I pressed my lips together and shook my head. I wasn't stupid enough to eat something he gave me.

"It will make you feel better," he said brusquely, touching the leaf to my lips. "Eat it."

I stared him down mulishly, which was a feat considering how hard it was to focus.

Faolin scowled. "Shall I get your sprite to eat some to prove it is safe?"

"You leave my bro-"

He pushed the leaf into my mouth. His other hand pressed up on my jaw, preventing me from spitting it out. I had no choice but to chew it up. It was almost tasteless, but I thought I detected the faint scent of citrus.

He waited until I swallowed the leaf to release me. "You'll live."

"Don't sound so happy."

If I had any doubts this was a dream, they were put to rest when the corners of his mouth lifted in a mocking smile. Wow. It transformed his entire face, and I almost didn't recognize him.

"You're cute when you're not all grumpy," I told him because I could say that to dream Faolin. Real Faolin would never smile like that.

A bark of laughter came from behind me, and Faolin's smile vanished like it had never been. He stood and walked around me, out of my sight. I could hear him and Lukas talking in low voices, but I was too tired to try to listen in. All I wanted to do was sleep.

"No, you don't." Lukas shook me gently until I opened my eyes. "You can't sleep yet."

"But I'm tired," I whined.

"I know, but you have to be awake for the antidote to work."

I let my head fall back to squint at the ceiling. It was the only thing in the room that wasn't spinning. "This dream sucks."

Hours passed, or maybe days, with me struggling to keep my eyes open and someone prodding me awake when I failed. Sometimes it was Lukas, and other times, Faolin. They gave me water to drink, and it felt so good to my dry throat. But when I asked for more, they said too much would make me sick.

Pink was tingeing the sky outside the window when heat blossomed in my chest. It spread rapidly to the rest of my body, growing hotter and hotter until it felt like I was going to combust. I cried out and tried to stand, but hands on my shoulders held me down in the chair.

"That's it, *li'fachan*. The worst is over."

As quickly as it started, the fire inside me burned out, leaving me as weak as a rag doll in sweat-soaked clothes. The room no longer swam before my eyes, but everything still had a dreamlike quality. Was I awake or still dreaming?

I shifted in the chair and grimaced at the feel of the wet fabric against my skin. I had to get out of these clothes. Grabbing the bottom of my T-shirt, I tried to pull it off, but it clung to me.

"What is she doing?" Faolin asked.

"Stripping, by the look of it."

That made me giggle. Me stripping? Now Violet was another matter. That girl was an exhibitionist if I ever saw one. They must be talking about her.

"Violet," I called. "Can you help me? My clothes are all wet, and I think I need to pee."

"I'll let you handle this one," Faolin said. Was that a note of laughter in his voice? Yep. I was definitely still dreaming.

Lukas scooped me up and carried me to the bathroom, where he deposited me in front of the toilet. He left me there, and after I'd done my business, he returned carrying a small bundle of clothes.

"Turn around," he ordered and I complied, presenting him my back. He grabbed the bottom of my wet top and pulled it off over my head. It landed on the bathroom floor with a wet plop that made me think of that day in his bedroom. Only this time, I was the one naked from the waist up. My stomach fluttered, but for some reason I wasn't embarrassed at all.

"Hands up," he said gruffly.

I grinned at the shower curtain. "Are you arresting me?"

"No, but I'm starting to think you're more dangerous than you look." He lifted my arms in the air and slipped a dry T-shirt over them. I let my arms drop and tugged the shirt down.

Lukas thrust a pair of dry shorts into my hands. "I'll turn around so you can change your bottoms."

I nearly fell over trying to get out of the wet shorts. "The last time I was in a bathroom with a boy, he tried to cop a feel."

"Why did you go to the bathroom with a boy?"

I made a sound of disgust. "I didn't go to the bathroom with him. I was at a party, and he followed me in."

"Did he hurt you?" Lukas's voice had an edge to it that wasn't there before.

"No. But I might have overreacted a little. I blame it on my dad. He's the one who drilled all those self-defense lessons into me."

Lukas chuckled. "What did you do?"

I donned the clean shorts he'd handed me. "Let's just say poor Felix walked funny for a week."

"Sounds like he deserved it."

"He did. But after that, no boy at school would come near me, except Trey Fowler." I made a face, but Lukas couldn't see it because his back was to me.

Lukas was quiet for a moment. "Trey is your boyfriend?"

"God, no. I'm not desperate." Changing my clothes had worn me out, so I braced a hand against the wall. "I'm done."

I wasn't surprised when he swept me up in his arms again and carried me to my bedroom. It must be a Fae thing, this need to carry women around. I thought about him carrying other women this way and felt an unpleasant tug at my stomach.

Instead of placing me in my bed, he sat me on the chair in the corner. "Stay there."

He left and returned with a warm facecloth. Kneeling in front of me, he used the cloth to clean my face and neck.

This didn't feel like the way you treated someone to whom you owed a debt. It felt like something more, but my mind was still too muddled to figure it out.

"Are we friends?" I asked when he finished wiping my face.

He rested his hands on the arms of the chair, his eyes dark and unfathomable. "Do you want us to be friends, Jesse?"

"Yes...but don't tell Violet."

"You don't want her to know we are friends?"

I swatted at the air. "It's not that. Violet thinks I should hook up with you because...well, you know."

"Know what?" He looked like he was fighting a smile.

"That faeries are better lovers," I said as if he didn't know. "I keep telling her it's not like that, but you don't know my best friend. It's a good thing I didn't tell her I thought about kissing you. She'd never let it go."

Heat flared in his eyes. "You thought about kissing me?"

"I was curious about what it would be like."

"And you're not curious anymore?" His voice had gone low and husky, and the air between us seemed to crackle with electricity.

My gaze fell to his mouth, and I swallowed. I'd just told him I wanted us to be friends, but friends did not have the thoughts going through my head. One side of me said what I was feeling was just a natural human reaction to a Court faerie, and I had nothing to be ashamed of. The other side argued that acting on my desire was a bad idea because there could never be anything between Lukas and me.

And above it all, I heard Violet's voice in my head, yelling at me to stop overthinking everything and just be impulsive for once.

Reaching out, I grasped the front of his shirt and tugged him toward me. My other hand slipped behind his neck, and I leaned forward until I could brush my mouth against his. The first taste of him made heat pool low in my belly and left me wanting more. I swiped my tongue across the seam of his lips, and that was all the coaxing he needed.

Lukas's fingers threaded through my hair as he took possession of my lips and showed me why I was in way over my head with him. His kiss was slow and sensual yet demanding, and all I could do was cling to him, lost in sensation. No one had ever kissed me like this, and I knew that no kiss after this would compare.

I wanted to protest when he broke the kiss, but I was a little lightheaded and incapable of speech. He rested his forehead against mine, his breaths uneven and his hands still tangled in my hair. One of his hands moved down to tenderly stroke the back of my neck, and I almost melted into him.

"I was right," he said roughly. "You are very dangerous, Jesse James."

Disappointment filled me. "Is that why you stopped?"

He pulled away to look into my eyes. "I stopped because you are not yourself. I've done some questionable things in my life, but taking advantage of a female is not one of them."

"But I like the way you kiss me. Will you do it again when I *am* myself?"

Lukas's laugh sounded pained. "No, *mi'calaech*. But not because I don't want to."

His words took the sting out of the rejection. I leaned back and closed my eyes, feeling sleepy and content.

"Let's get you to bed so you can sleep this off." He picked me up and laid me in my bed.

"Thanks for taking care of me." I curled up on my side. "You never answered my question."

Lukas pulled the covers over me. "What question is that?"

"Are we friends?"

His knuckle grazed my cheek. "Yes. Now go to sleep."

A loud banging pulled me from a heavy sleep, and I shot upright in bed. I stared around my room in confusion, until a wave of dizziness forced me to lie down again.

I put an arm over my eyes to block out the light from the window as I tried to recall how I'd gotten this way. I remembered having the flu, but beyond that, all I got was a jumble of foggy images and snatches of conversation that made absolutely no sense.

The sound of a pan clanging against the kitchen floor had me rolling out of bed and walking to the door on unsteady legs. I made my way to the kitchen and stopped at the sight of Violet standing at my stove, making scrambled eggs.

She turned halfway and wrinkled her nose as she looked me up and down. "You look like death warmed over."

"I feel like it." I sat at the table because I was feeling dizzy again. "What time is it?"

"Almost four." She put the eggs on a plate along with some bacon and buttered toast. When she set the food in front of me, my stomach growled painfully, making me wonder when I'd last eaten.

Violet brought me a glass of orange juice. "Eat."

I dug into the eggs and almost finished them before I asked, "When did you get here?"

She looked up from washing dishes. "Around two. You didn't text me back last night, so I figured you were asleep. I tried calling this morning, but you didn't answer. You were out cold when I got here. That must have been some flu."

I laid down my fork and rubbed my temples. "Last night is a blur. I think I had a fever because all I can remember is bits and pieces of crazy dreams."

"Are you sure they were dreams?"

I looked up at her through my hands. "I dreamed Faolin was feeding me."

Violet snorted. "The angry one? You must have been tripping."

"Yeah." I ate a piece of bacon. "I'm going to feel terrible if you catch this flu."

She waved a dish towel in the air. "I'll be fine, but I feel bad leaving you here alone and sick at Christmas."

"I won't be alone. I have Finch, and I'm already over the worst of it." I frowned as another dream fragment came to me, and I could hear Lukas saying, *"That's it, li'fachan. The worst is over."*

I shook it off and finished my meal. Having a full stomach made me feel better, and there was no dizziness when I stood to carry my dishes to the sink.

Violet took my plate and glass from me. "I got this. You go shower." She scrunched up her nose. "Trust me; you need one."

Laughing, I left her to finish cleaning the kitchen. On my way to my bedroom, I stopped to check on Finch, who was surprisingly absent. "Finch, you in there?" I called to his tree house.

He appeared in the doorway. *Are you better?*

"Good as new. Why are you hiding in there?"

In case they come back, he signed.

I walked over to him. "Who?"

The faeries.

I tried to make sense of what he was saying. Was he referring to the two Seelie faeries who had tried to break in here weeks ago?

"Don't worry. Even if they come back, they won't be able to get in. Our ward will keep them out."

Finch shook his head. *They came last night. They gave you medicine.*

"What?" My voice rose an octave as I replayed a part of my dream. "Faolin was really here?"

And Lukas, Finch said. *They stayed all night.*

I sank down on the couch with a hand to my chest. It wasn't a dream. Lukas and Faolin really had been here, and Faolin had given me medicine.

But how had they known I was sick, and why would they care about me having the flu? It wasn't like that was life-threatening.

Another memory floated free of the fog in my head, one of Lukas wiping my face with a washcloth. It was followed by one of him pulling the covers over me in bed. I tried to focus on those images, but they kept slipping away the harder I tried to remember them.

"Did the faeries frighten you?" I asked Finch.

He nodded. *But they didn't hurt me.*

"I'm sorry you were scared."

I'm glad they came, he said. *You were really sick, and they helped you.*

Violet came into the living room. "What are you two talking about?"

"Finch just informed me I was not tripping on crazy dreams after all." I brought her up to speed on our conversation.

"Holy Shih Tzu!" She jumped up and down. "He must really like you. What are you going to do about it?"

"Nothing."

Her face fell. "Why not?"

"All I want right now is to find Mom and Dad. I don't have time for anything else."

"But you have thought about it," she pressed.

If she only knew how much I'd thought about Lukas while I was staying at his place. "Yes, but we're just too different."

Violet scoffed. "He's not an alien, Jess. You are compatible in all the ways that matter."

"Not all the ways. He's immortal, and I have an expiration date, which means it could never go anywhere. Other people are okay with a faerie fling, but I don't think I would be."

She tilted her head to one side to study me. "No, you wouldn't."

I pushed up off the couch. "On that note, I'm going to get my shower."

I returned to the living room thirty minutes later to find Violet and Finch sitting on the couch together. They were completely engrossed in some reality TV show where people competed for a date with a faerie.

"That stuff will rot your brain," I teased as I sat on the couch with my legs tucked under me.

She slanted a look at me. "You sound like my mom."

"Your mother is a brilliant woman, so I'll take that as a compliment."

"Oh!" Violet tossed the remote on the couch. "I can't believe I forgot to tell you this. Mom told me about this lawyer who owns a warehouse that got broken into yesterday. Get this. His name is Cecil Hunt."

My mouth fell open. "The same Cecil Hunt who owned that house we almost broke into?"

"Yep. What are the odds?" She smirked. "At least we both have alibis for this one."

I shook my head in disbelief. "I can't believe your mom knows him, out of all the lawyers in this city."

"I don't think she knows him well. They're both representing clients in the same trial, and he asked the judge for a recess yesterday because of the break-in."

"Wow." I shifted until I was facing her. "Does your mom know you were arrested for trespassing at his house?"

Violet gave me a hard stare. "Are you kidding? She would murder me if she ever found out."

"Then it's probably a good thing Lukas made those charges go away," I joked.

"No kidding." She shuddered dramatically. "I'd rather spend a whole night in that horrible jail than face Mom's wrath."

"She's not that bad."

"Um, are you forgetting this is the same woman who made a police officer cry on the stand last year?"

I laughed. "Who could forget that? I'm glad to have her on my side."

Violet grinned. "She is a total badass, isn't she? She took care of your Agency problem."

"Yes. Though, I don't think I've seen the last of Agent Curry." I pursed my lips. "I honestly can't tell if he's corrupt, inept, or just seriously misguided, but he definitely has it out for my family."

"If he harasses you again, you call Mom, and she'll take care of it."

"I will." I didn't point out that in two days' time, she and her parents would be on another continent for two weeks. All I could do was hope nothing bad happened that required an attorney.

Violet cast a sly smirk at me. "Or you could call Lukas. I bet he'd take care of *all* your needs."

"You have a one-track mind." I tried to scowl at her, but she waggled her eyes at me, making us both dissolve into girlish giggles.

On the outside, I was laughing, but in my belly, butterflies took flight at the thought of being intimate with Lukas. Not that it was going to happen, but for the first time, I almost wished it would.

17

I hung the last stocking on the mantle. "How does it look?"

Finch whistled and gave me a thumbs-up when I looked at him. I hadn't planned to decorate for Christmas because it felt wrong putting up a tree without Mom and Dad. But when Finch had pointed out that we needed our stockings for Santa, I couldn't say no.

I stepped back to look at my work, and my throat tightened at the sight of Mom's and Dad's stockings hung in their usual spots. I'd been doing my best to keep our spirits up today for Finch's sake, but sometimes it was hard to fight the sadness pressing down on me. I'd never had a Christmas without my parents, and I missed them so much it was a physical ache.

Sleet swished against the windows, and the lights flickered. It had snowed all morning, coating everything in a pretty blanket of white. But around noon, the snow had turned to freezing rain, and the news reports were now predicting heavy icing and widespread power outages.

We had lanterns, a gas stove and fireplace, and plenty of fruit and canned foods so we'd be okay. I should check on Mrs. Russo, though. She lived alone, and she had no relatives in the city to help her out.

The lights flickered again and went out. It was only mid-afternoon, but the room was thrown into semi-darkness. I picked up the flashlight I'd placed on the coffee table and went to light one of the kerosene lanterns I'd brought up from our storage unit in the basement.

"Finch, I'm going to run down and see if Mrs. Russo is okay." Grabbing my flashlight and a spare lantern, I headed down to the first floor.

After one knock, Mrs. Russo answered her door, wearing a long, orange, wooly cardigan that looked older than my mother. It clashed violently with her bright red hair, which was piled in its usual messy updo. Behind her, the soft glow of candles lit her apartment, and I could see her friend Mrs. Henry, who lived one street over, sitting on the couch.

The old woman looked delighted to see me. "Jesse, we were just talking about you. Do you have plenty of candles up there? Nora and I have enough to last us through Armageddon if you need some."

"I'm good. I came to see if you needed anything."

"We've lived through much worse storms than this." She motioned for me to enter. "I just put on a pot of tea, and Nora brought cookies. Come in, and have some with us."

For the next hour, the two women regaled me with tales of working on Broadway when they were young. Neither of them had been a star, but they'd met and worked with a lot of big names at the time. I'd heard a lot of Mrs. Russo's stories before, but I didn't let on because she loved to relive her past.

It was dark outside when I left Mrs. Russo's apartment. I peered out through the window in the main door at the vehicles already coated in a layer of ice. The sleet had turned to a heavy rain, but it was supposed to freeze overnight. The streets were going to be a mess tomorrow, and I was glad I had nowhere to be for once.

Finch was sitting on the window ledge looking out when I got back to the apartment. He loved storms, and he could sit there for hours watching the rain. I left him to it and went to fill up some large water containers because we had lost our water before during a bad storm. After that, I filled the bathtub with water for flushing the toilet just in case. It never hurt to be prepared.

I was thinking about what I could heat up for dinner when a knock came at the door. Wary of unannounced visitors, I quietly approached the door. I checked the peephole, but it was too dark in the hallway to make out the person standing there.

"Who is it?" I called.

"Trey."

I opened the door and stared at him. He was drenched from head to toe and shivering. "What happened to you?" I asked as I moved aside to let him in.

"Some asshole in a truck splashed me," he said through chattering teeth as he pulled off his wet coat and hung it on the back of a chair.

I couldn't stop the laugh that burst from me. "What are you doing out in this weather?"

He kicked off his boots. "I called when the power went out, but you didn't answer. So, I came over to see if you were okay."

Touched by the gesture, I said, "I was downstairs at Mrs. Russo's, and I forgot to take my phone with me."

I pointed him toward the bathroom and went to grab some of Dad's clothes for him to change into. I laid the clothes on my parents' bed and returned to the kitchen to make coffee in Mom's old stovetop percolator.

"Coffee smells great," Trey said from behind me.

"It's the stuff you gave me." Taking two large mugs from the cabinet, I turned toward him. I yelped and almost dropped the mugs when I caught sight of him standing there in nothing but a towel.

"Trey, what the hell?" I yelled at him.

He leaned one shoulder against the wall and crossed his muscled arms over his chest. He was in good shape, and it was obvious he worked out, but I couldn't help comparing him to Lukas. Trey was a good-looking guy with a great body, but he didn't make my insides quiver or my heart race the way Lukas had done that day in his bedroom.

"Like what you see?" he asked with a smug smirk. Ah, there was the old Trey.

I set the mugs on the counter. "No. Now go put on some clothes."

Laughing, he straightened and started to turn away when the towel around his waist suddenly loosened and fell to the floor.

"Oh, my God." I averted my gaze but not before I got an eyeful of parts of Trey Fowler that I could happily have gone my whole life without seeing.

"Impressive, huh?" he drawled as he bent to retrieve the towel.

"Yeah. There really is something smaller than your IQ."

His brow furrowed, and I nearly laughed at his look of confusion. The fact that he had to think about it said more than words could.

I removed the coffee percolator from the burner just as there was a loud knock at the door. "What now?" I pictured Mrs. Russo standing outside, and I glared at Trey as I passed him. "Would you please go put on some damn clothes?"

I didn't bother with the peephole. "Who is it?"

"Me," said a male voice that sent a small thrill through me despite my annoyance.

"Perfect," I muttered as I unlocked the door and opened it to Lukas and the ever-dour Faolin.

"I called you. Why didn't you answer your phone?" Lukas demanded. His gaze swept over me as if he expected to find me bleeding out.

"Hello to you, too," I said with false cheer. Then I registered that he'd said he had tried to call me. I hadn't spoken to him in days. Why would he call and come out in this weather to see me unless there was a new development? "Do you have news?" I asked quietly.

His eyes lost their angry glint. "No."

"Then why are you here?"

The look he gave me was part exasperation and part amusement. "The power is out in half the city, and you're here alone."

"Maybe not as alone as we believed." Faolin cocked an eyebrow as he looked past me into the apartment.

I glanced over my shoulder and narrowed my eyes on Trey, who had donned the jeans I'd set out for him, but was still shirtless and barefoot. My face heated because I knew exactly how this must look to Lukas and Faolin.

"Are we interrupting something?" Lukas asked, no longer sounding amused.

Trey crossed his arms. "Yes."

I made a face. "In your dreams, Trey. And put your shirt on!"

A frown marred Lukas's handsome face. "Trey Fowler? The boy you went to school with."

"How do you know that?" I shot Lukas a suspicious look as I tried to remember if I'd ever mentioned Trey or my friends from school to him. I didn't think I'd spoken about anyone but Violet.

Trey pulled on the shirt I'd loaned him and came up behind me. "Jesse, are you going to introduce me to your friends?"

I invited the faeries inside and made the introductions. "Trey and his father are bounty hunters, too," I said to Lukas, not sure why I felt the need to clarify that.

"And we go way back," Trey added in a tone that implied there was more than work between us. "How do you know Jesse?"

"Lukas and Faolin have been helping me look for Mom and Dad," I told him.

"I thought the Agency was searching for them."

I was unable to keep the anger from my voice. "The Agency doesn't seem to care much about a pair of missing bounty hunters. So, I'm doing my own search."

Trey's forehead wrinkled in concern. "I don't think that's a good idea. What if you get hurt out there alone?"

"She's not alone," Lukas stated crisply, and I tried not to think about how much I liked hearing that from him.

Trey's gaze shifted to Lukas. "And what's in this for you?"

"That is between Jesse and me."

"Is that so?" Trey took a step toward the faeries, displaying as much sense as someone sticking their hand into the lion's cage at the zoo. How he'd survived this long was a mystery to me.

I turned to Trey, placing myself between him and Lukas. "It was really sweet of you to come by to check on me, but as you can see, I have everything I need here." The words had no sooner left my lips than the lights flickered on. "See. The power is back. But you should probably get home before the roads freeze."

He cast another wary look at Lukas and Faolin. "You want me to leave you alone here with two strange faeries?"

"They're not strangers to me." It was on the tip of my tongue to say Lukas was a friend. I didn't know where that thought came from, but it felt right. If I was being honest with myself, the only time I felt completely safe these days was when I was with him.

"But what would your parents say about this?" Trey pushed.

"My parents would trust my judgement, and they'd know I would do anything to bring them home." I laid a hand on his arm. "I appreciate your concern, but I know what I'm doing."

"Okay." He pulled on his boots, and I grabbed one of my father's leather jackets from the closet for him. It was freezing outside, and I couldn't let him walk home in his wet coat.

"Thanks." He donned the jacket, which was a size too big for him, and picked up his own coat. "Call me if you need *anything*."

"I will." I walked him to the door. "Merry Christmas, Trey."

He smiled. "Merry Christmas."

I shut the door behind him and faced Lukas and Faolin, who stood near the kitchen, watching me. Now that we were alone, I felt awkward. This was the first time I'd seen them since Finch had told me they'd taken care of me when I was sick. Faolin, of all people, had given me medicine. I needed to thank them, but I wasn't sure how to bring it up.

"This storm is going to get worse," Lukas said. "The power will go out again soon, and it's not likely to return for a day or two."

"We have lanterns and heat. We'll be okay." I didn't like the thought of being without power that long, but it wouldn't be the first time we lost it.

"And when your phone battery dies, you'll be cut off here with no way to contact anyone if you need help. Or for anyone to contact you," he added.

I pressed my lips together. He had a point. I had been meaning to buy one of those mobile phone chargers, but I'd never gotten around to it. What if someone tried to call me about Mom and Dad, and they couldn't reach me?

"You won't have power either," I said.

Faolin cut in impatiently. "Our building has a backup power source."

"Of course, you do." I'd read about the Fae crystals that could power an entire building. Hospitals and key government buildings had them, but they weren't available to the general public. I wasn't at all surprised to learn Lukas had them. He wasn't the type to be inconvenienced by a storm.

Lukas assumed that authoritative stance I knew well. "You and your sprite would be better off with us."

"Are you guys going to try to make me go if I don't want to?"

Faolin scoffed, and Lukas's eyes lit with amusement. "If I thought you were in danger, I would *try*."

Arrogant asses. "I appreciate you coming over, but you don't need to worry about us. This isn't our first storm." I walked past them into the kitchen. The least I could do was offer them something to drink. "I was making coffee when you got here. Would either of you like some?"

"No, thank you," they said together.

Okay then. Abandoning the percolator, I turned to face them. "I want to thank you for taking care of me when I was sick. I don't remember much of that night, but Finch told me what you did. How did you guys know I had the flu?"

They exchanged a look before Lukas said, "You didn't have the flu, Jesse. You were sick from kolosh poisoning."

I stared at him. "What are you talking about?" Kolosh was the sap of a faerie tree that was toxic to humans. I was pretty sure I'd remember if I had touched one.

"You fought a troll, and he cut you," Faolin said. "Trolls in this realm sometimes coat their blades in kolosh."

"How did I not know this?" I said more to myself than to them. I couldn't remember ever reading about trolls using poison on their weapons.... I stared at Lukas. "Wait. How do you know about the troll?"

"You told us when we asked how you got the cut on your leg," Lukas said.

"That still doesn't explain why you were here in the first place."

Faolin's mouth turned down. "You called Lukas and told him you were dying."

I let out a startled laugh. "I...I did what?"

Lukas smiled wryly. "And considering some of the misfortunes that have befallen you since we met, it wasn't outside the realm of possibility."

"I can't believe I did that." I put a hand to my cheek. "God, *why* would I do that?"

"It was the kolosh," Lukas explained. "It causes fever and delirium."

"And memory loss, apparently." I winced. "Did I say or do anything else crazy that night?"

An odd expression passed over Lukas's face, but it was gone so fast I was sure I'd imagined it. I was about to ask him about it when he chuckled and said, "Aside from telling Faolin he's cute?"

I glanced at Faolin, whose sour look told me all I needed to know. Heat crept up my neck. "I don't think I want to hear anything else."

"Good. Go pack enough for two nights," Lukas said.

"I'm not –"

I broke off when the lights went out again. The lantern was still lit, and it gave off enough light to see Lukas's I-told-you-so expression.

"Smug is not a flattering look on you." I picked up my flashlight and went to tell Finch we were going to be spending Christmas with Lukas.

I stuffed the last present in Finch's bulging stocking and laid it in front of the fireplace in Lukas's living room. I'd had to wait hours for Finch to settle down and go to sleep in our room before I could slip away to fill his stocking. I was determined at least one of us was going to find some joy this Christmas.

Straightening, I looked around the empty room. The building was quiet except for the rain against the windows. It felt strange and a little spooky being all alone here, and I hugged myself even though the room was warm.

Not long after we'd gotten here, Kerr and Iian had shown up with food from a Mediterranean restaurant I hadn't heard of. All six of us had sat or stood around the island eating our meal, while Finch played with Kaia out in the garden.

It had surprised me how comfortable I was with them, including Faolin. He barely acknowledged me, but when he did, he was courteous. And I had to admit this was a lot better than eating canned ravioli by candlelight at home.

Our meal had been cut short when Lukas received a phone call and stepped away to take it. When he returned, there was no trace of the warmth I'd seen earlier. He was once again the cold and commanding faerie I'd met at Teg's. He'd barked something in Faerie, and the others had jumped into action as if he'd cracked a whip.

In less than thirty seconds, they were out the door, leaving me wondering what the hell had just happened. Other than the knowledge that they worked for the Unseelie crown, I really had no idea what Lukas and his men did. Part of me didn't want to know.

That had been hours ago, and there was still no sign of them. I wandered around the first floor, looking for something to occupy me. I was curious about what the rest of the building looked like, but I wouldn't invade their privacy.

I ended up at the large window overlooking the garden that appeared strangely dry despite the heavy rain. Curious, I opened the door and stepped outside onto the pleasantly warm patio. On the other side of the high fence I could hear rain falling, but in here it was dry. I walked to the edge of the stone patio and looked up at the dark sky. It was dizzying to stand there watching the rain fall and evaporate ten feet above me.

Curling up on one of the patio chairs, I pulled my phone from my pocket and checked for messages. There was a recent text from Violet, and I grinned when I read her complaints about her grandmother dragging her from bed at the ungodly hour of 7:00 a.m. to go to the market. China was twelve hours ahead of us, which meant it was almost ten in the morning there now.

I texted her back and picked up where I'd left off in the book I was reading. A few minutes later, I was startled when the door opened and Kerr stuck his head out.

"She's out here," he called over his shoulder.

He went back inside, and Lukas came out, looking almost as surly as when he'd left. "Why aren't you in bed?"

I raised my eyebrows at his curt tone. "I wasn't aware I had a bedtime."

He continued to scowl at me for a few more seconds before he looked away and raked a hand through his hair. "We came back, and you weren't in my room when I went to check on you. My first thought was that you were out in the storm."

I tried to understand what had brought this on. "Why would I be out in this weather? The only thing that would get me to leave Finch and go out in the storm is my parents."

He didn't answer, and I sucked in a breath. "That call you got during dinner, was that about my parents?"

"No. I hoped it might lead us to them, but it was a dead end."

"Why didn't you tell me?" I asked accusingly. "I had a right to know."

Lukas shook his head impassively. "The caller didn't mention your parents. They said they had information about something we've been searching for. I had no idea if the information was real or if it was connected to your parents."

Realizing I was clenching my poor phone, I stopped. "I take it you didn't find what you're looking for either." Based on his current mood, I was guessing he hadn't.

"No." His anger and frustration were almost palpable as he took the chair next to me. Whatever he was looking for, it was very important to him. Or maybe it was important to the Unseelie crown.

"Is it something I can help you with? I've been told I'm pretty smart on most days."

The planes of his face softened, and he gave me a small smile that made my heart flutter. "I know. I read Faolin's background check on you."

"And what did it tell you?" I knew Faolin had dug up what he could on me and my family the night he'd brought me here. I had never asked Lukas what he'd found.

"It said you recently finished school with top academic honors, were aggressively recruited by the Agency but you turned them down, and you have been accepted into several top colleges." His eyes searched mine. "What it didn't tell me was why you're not in college, with an academic record like that. Did you want to follow in your parents' footsteps?"

I smiled wistfully. "No. My dream is to go to college, but it's expensive and my parents can't afford to pay for it. I'm hoping to earn the money by bounty hunting, but I can't go anywhere until I find my parents. And I can't leave Finch."

"You've taken on a lot of responsibility for someone your age."

I shrugged. "It's my family. I'd do anything for them."

His eyes warmed. "I can see that, and I respect it. I'd do anything for my family and friends as well."

"You've never mentioned your family. Do you have brothers and sisters?" I asked casually, trying not to show how curious I was about him. He and his men didn't talk about their personal lives, and I suspected they didn't share those details with many people.

He stared out at the garden. "I have one brother and one sister. They're younger than I am and live at Court with our parents."

"Do they ever leave Faerie?"

"No, they prefer to stay in our realm."

I studied his handsome profile. "Do you get to see them often?"

"Only when I am summoned home on Court business." He smiled. "My work here keeps me very busy."

"What will you do when you find what you're looking for? Will you go back to Faerie?" The thought of him leaving this realm for good made my heart constrict.

For a few seconds, it looked like he carried the weight of the world on his broad shoulders. "I have many responsibilities in Faerie, so I will have to spend more time there. But I have little patience for all the pomp and politics of court, which means I'll spend time here as well."

I looked up at the rain. "I don't know how you do it."

"Do what?"

"Court, the celebrities and galas, all of it. Do you ever wish you could just be a normal person and get away from it all?"

"Court life is normal to me. As for the rest, I attend as few celebrity events as possible." I could feel his eyes on me when he said, "Do you ever wish for a different life?"

"No," I answered without hesitation. "I love my life, and when my parents come home, I'll have everything I want."

"Except for college."

I turned my head to look at him. "College isn't going anywhere. I'll get there eventually." I'd already earned over fifteen thousand dollars from bounty hunting in less than a month. At this rate, I could make enough money in a year to cover my expenses. It sure beat saving up tips from my old barista job.

"I have no doubt you will." Lukas smiled, drawing my gaze to his mouth.

I was suddenly hit with the odd feeling that I knew how those firm lips felt against mine. The remembered taste of his mouth made mine water and sent warmth unfurling in my stomach. I swallowed and lifted my eyes to meet his. For a heartbeat, I thought I saw desire smoldering in his midnight blue depths. He blinked, and it was gone.

Confused and disoriented, I lifted my face toward the stormy sky again. What the hell was wrong with me? There was no possible way I had kissed Lukas and forgotten it.

"You look like you're in another world," Lukas said. "Are you thinking about your parents?"

"Yes," I lied, grateful he had no idea what was really going through my mind. I picked up my phone and stood. "I should go to bed. Finch will wake me up early tomorrow."

Lukas stood as well. "I'll walk you up."

I nodded, unable to come up with a reason for him not to accompany me to my room. At the bedroom door, he looked like he wanted to say something, but he only smiled and wished me a good night before he walked away.

I was lost in thought as I got ready for bed. Slipping beneath the soft sheets, I lay on my side and closed my eyes. I was close to drifting off when I dreamed of me reaching out to grab Lukas by the shirt and pulling him toward me until our lips met.

I jerked awake; my skin flushed from the vivid dream. I'd been attracted to Lukas for weeks, but I couldn't remember having a single dream about him until now. Where was this coming from?

Finch whistled softly, and I sat up to see him standing on the chair he was using as his bed. I'd left a lamp on so we could communicate if he needed to.

"Why are you up?" I asked him.

I heard a noise, he signed excitedly. *Did Santa come?*

"Not yet. You know he only comes when everyone is asleep."

Finch dived into his makeshift tent, and I fell back to the bed, grinning. Banishing all thoughts of the dream kiss, I focused instead on picturing my brother's happy face when he opened his presents tomorrow. I fell asleep with a smile on my face.

The storm blew itself out overnight, leaving the city coated in a thick layer of ice. It took another day for the power to return to my neighborhood, so Finch and I spent Christmas Day at Lukas's. I didn't know what was more fun: watching Finch tearing through the presents in his stocking or watching the faces of the five faeries that had never seen a sprite who believed in Santa Claus.

It was noon when Conlan brought us home the day after Christmas. I slipped several times on the icy front steps, and as soon as I dropped Finch off at the apartment, I went to the basement and got the bag of salt to spread on the steps. It felt strange doing something Dad had always done, and I told myself that next year, this would be his job again.

After I'd taken care of the steps and looked in on Mrs. Russo, I decided I should check on the Jeep. Two years ago, a truck had skidded on ice and slammed into Mom's car, causing a lot of damage. It would be just my luck for something like that to happen to my only vehicle.

Aside from being coated in ice, the Jeep looked okay. I would have started it up to melt the ice, but the doors were frozen shut.

I started to walk back to the building when something caught my eye on the windshield. Leaning in, I saw what looked like a folded piece of paper tucked under the wiper, which was buried beneath a sheet of ice.

My heart thudded as I rushed back to the building to find a window scraper. I told myself it was probably a flyer, but no one would have been out delivering flyers in that storm.

I carefully scraped the ice away from the windshield until I was able to extricate the paper, which had been placed inside a sandwich bag to keep it dry. Pulling off my gloves, I unfolded the paper and stared at the three words written on it in neat handwriting.

They are alive.

18

"That's it for all the cameras except the one over the front exit." Conlan tapped the mouse to bring up the activity log for the camera that showed us a view of the outside steps. Thank goodness Dad had positioned the camera so it didn't pick up sidewalk traffic, or we would have been here all day.

We had been able to narrow the timeline down to a twenty-four-hour period, from when I'd last used the Jeep to when the storm had iced the vehicles. Very few people had come or gone from the building during that time, which meant there wasn't much to look at.

"There." I pointed at the monitor where it showed someone arriving at the bottom of the steps. They were mostly out of the camera range, but we could see their arm as they stood there.

A minute went by. The person climbed the first two steps, allowing us to see that they were of average height and bundled in a heavy coat with the hood pulled up. It was snowing too hard to make out much more than that. I looked at the time stamp on the video where it said 10:24 a.m. on December twenty-fourth.

The person stopped on the third step and looked from the door to the street several times, like they were debating whether or not to enter the building. Finally, they turned and walked down the steps and out of sight.

Conlan replayed the video several times. "It's either a woman or a small man. Definitely not a Court faerie. You're sure you don't recognize them?"

"No, I don't."

The apartment door opened, and footsteps approached. We looked up as Lukas and Faolin entered the office.

"Any luck?" Conlan asked them.

"We could find no outside cameras on the buildings near the vehicle." Faolin scowled at me as if I'd deliberately chosen a bad spot to park.

Lukas walked toward us. "Did you find anything in here?"

We showed him and Faolin the video of the person on the steps, and they agreed with Conlan's assessment.

I picked up the paper that was lying on the desk, and hope swelled in me, as it had every time I'd read the words on it. "My parents are alive."

"Jesse, I want you to find your parents, but this note might have been meant to lure you into a trap," Lukas said.

I shook my head. "If that were true, wouldn't they have left an address or a phone number? And no one has bothered me since those men broke in."

He crossed his arms. "That doesn't mean they aren't watching and waiting for the right opportunity."

"Yeah, them and the Agency," I joked dryly. At their questioning looks, I said, "I'm pretty sure I have at least one agent keeping tabs on me."

Faolin eyed me suspiciously. "Why would the Agency be watching one of its bounty hunters?"

"Because they have nothing better to do." I told them about my interactions with Agent Curry and his conviction that my parents were working with the goren dealer. "His boss told him to leave me alone, but he's not the type to give up easily."

Lukas was not appeased. "Even so, I don't like this, and the timing could not be worse."

"What do you mean?"

"We've been summoned to Court, and we will be away for at least two days. I want you to stay at my building until we return." I started to object, but he cut me off. "Conlan is staying behind to manage things in my absence, so you won't be alone there."

I looked at Conlan, who grinned. "A sleepover. Fun."

Lukas shot him a dark look, which Conlan ignored, as usual. When Lukas turned away from him, Conlan winked at me. He was incorrigible and, while it would be fun to hang out with him, I had no intention of hiding away if someone was trying to reach out to me about my parents. Not to mention, I did have a job to do.

"I appreciate the offer, but I'm staying here. I have jobs to finish, or they'll be assigned to another hunter, and I can't afford that. You have no idea how impossible it is to find a decent job in this economy."

"If you need money –"

"No." I shook my head vigorously. "You've been more than generous to me, but I'm not a charity case. I don't want your money."

His jaw clenched. "It's not charity. It's to keep you safe."

"Giving someone money to help them out in any way *is* charity. I do have some pride."

"And refusing help because of your pride is unreasonable," he argued. "It's only money."

I drew in a breath, trying to think of how to explain it in a way he would understand. Money meant little to him, so I had to find something that did matter.

"Let's say you somehow lose your magic and you can no longer create portals or do any of the things your magic lets you do now. But Faolin still has lots of magic, so he generously offers to do all of that for you. How would that make you feel?"

His lips parted slightly as understanding dawned in his eyes.

I continued before he could speak. "I earned my scholarship and my admission into college, and I'm going to earn the rest of the money I need for school. Bounty hunting wasn't my first choice for a job, but it turns out I'm actually good at it. And I'm more equipped than most people to take care of myself."

"Having seen what you did to those two men, I would have to agree," Conlan piped in, earning a grateful look from me and another scowl from Lukas.

As much as Lukas wanted to keep me safe, the truth was that I'd been taking care of myself since my parents disappeared. He'd stepped in when I was hurt and sick, but I'd fought off those men, just like I had fended off the elves who had tried to attack me on the street. I wasn't naïve enough to think I could take on any opponent, but I could hold my own as well as the next person.

Faolin spoke up. "Lukas, we have to go. The king is expecting us."

Lukas nodded, but he didn't seem too happy to be going home. He looked at me. "You will call Conlan if you are contacted again, or if you feel unsafe."

"Yes." I decided it wasn't worth the argument to mention that he didn't get to order me around.

"Good." He walked to the door of the office and stopped. "When we return, we will redouble our search efforts. If your parents are alive, we will find them."

Emotion clogged my throat at the conviction in his voice, and I knew he would keep that promise. Just as I knew that, despite my best efforts, I was falling for this beautiful, enigmatic, and overbearing faerie, who would only break my heart when all of this was over.

"Those are thirty dollars each."

Looking up from a rack of banti dreamcatchers I was pretending to examine, I smiled at the middle-aged woman behind the flea market display table. "Do they really protect you from banti dreams?"

She lifted a shoulder. "I've had one on my headboard for years, and I've never had a banti dream."

Just to be polite, I made an appreciative sound and studied the dreamcatchers. They were similar to the decorative Native American version, but these had a tiny iron pendant at the center. If these dreamcatchers could actually stop a banti, they'd be worth a lot more than thirty dollars.

A banti was a small faerie that looked like a miniature goblin. But where goblins liked to steal your jewelry, banti got their kicks from creeping into your bedroom at night and giving you nightmares. They never did physical harm, which was why they were only a level Two, but they could definitely mess with your head.

Someone bumped me from behind, reminding me I wasn't here to shop. I walked slowly along the row of tables, pretending to look at the merchandise while casting covert glances around the large indoor flea market. You'd think people would be sick of shopping a few days after Christmas, but this place was a hive of activity. And that made it the perfect spot for the thief – or thieves – I was hunting.

This morning, Levi had called me in about a new job. There had been multiple police reports in recent weeks of shoppers being robbed at this popular flea market in Queens. The victims all had a similar story. They'd lost a chunk of time and had discovered that any money or valuables on them were gone. It was clearly a faerie at work, but three different bounty hunters had staked out the place to no avail. They believed the perpetrator could recognize hunters and knew to steer clear of them.

Levi had decided to try a new tactic – send in someone who didn't look like a hunter, namely me. I wasn't sure whether to be flattered or insulted by his assessment of me, but the use of glamours on humans made this a level Four job. I wanted that ten-thousand-dollar bounty even more than I wanted to get my second Four on the books. Lukas's offer of money two days ago had only strengthened my resolve to earn enough for college.

A troll couple talking nearby caught my eye. I inched closer until I could hear them arguing over a lamp she wanted to buy. Moving on, I focused on three elf teenagers loitering by the wall. The two boys and a girl looked close to my age, and they appeared to be scoping out the place. Or they could be three bored kids hanging out like Violet and I used to do not that long ago.

Channeling my not-much-younger self, I strolled toward them. Even if they weren't the ones I was looking for, being seen with them would help my cover.

A male elf bumped into my shoulder as he walked past, and he murmured an apology. I glanced at him and came up short when our eyes met. It had been foggy that night outside the Ralston, but I hadn't forgotten the faces of the two elves who had attacked me. This was the one who had gotten away.

His eyes widened in recognition a second before he bolted. Spinning on my heel, I took off after him. My cover be damned, I wasn't letting this guy escape a second time.

He was fast and agile, but weaving through the people and tables slowed him down enough for me to stay on his heels. He shoved a few people aside, and I called a "Sorry" to them, but I didn't slow to help anyone. I wasn't letting this guy out of my sight.

My quarry reached the end of the tables and sprinted toward the back exit. I was about to lose him when a little girl ran in front of him, slowing him down. I leaped and tackled him around the waist, taking him to the floor.

We wrestled on the floor as he tried to free himself. A sharp tingle went through my body when he used his magic on me, and I lessened my hold for a second. It was all he needed to pull free and jump to his feet.

"Oh, no you don't," I said through gritted teeth as I grabbed his ankle and yanked his leg out from under him.

The elf flailed and hit the floor again. This time I was on him before he knew what was happening.

I flipped him to his stomach and straddled his legs, wrenching one of his arms behind his back. He tried to buck me off, and I pushed on his arm until he howled in pain.

"Help!" he yelled. "Someone get this crazy human off me."

At the sound of running feet, I looked up as two female trolls and a male elf approached us. The trolls stopped and looked on curiously, but the elf kept coming. Reaching into my back pocket, I pulled out the ID I always carried there and flashed it at him. "This is Agency business."

He stopped a few feet from us, his nervous gaze flitting between my card and the elf beneath me. Finally, he nodded and hurried away.

"Nice try," I said to my captive as I pulled a pair of Fae shackles from my coat pocket and put them on him.

Standing, I helped him to his feet and walked him past curious onlookers toward the main exit.

The elf didn't speak again until we emerged into the weak afternoon sunlight. "Where are you taking me?"

I led him around the corner of the building to the parking lot. "I'm turning you in. But first, you're going to tell me why you and your buddy tried to jump me."

"I have no idea what you're talking about," he protested unconvincingly. "I've never seen you before."

"Is that so? Then why did you run when you saw me?"

"Because you're a bounty hunter, and you make money off arresting innocent people like me."

I tugged him toward the Jeep. "And how did you know I was a bounty hunter if you never saw me before?"

"I..." he stammered, knowing he'd caught himself in a lie.

We reached the Jeep, and I opened the rear door. His already pale skin blanched when he saw the cage, and he tried to twist out of my grip.

"Please, don't put me in that thing," he begged.

"I'm sorry, but I have no choice." I steeled myself against the pity I felt for him. I'd be afraid to go in a cage too, especially one that could rob me of my energy. But it was the only way to safely transport him.

I pushed him toward the cage, and he began to struggle more violently when he got close enough to sense the iron.

"No!" he shrieked on the verge of a full meltdown and drawing the attention of some people in the parking lot. As soon as they saw the shackles on him, they went about their business. Only Agents and bounty hunters carried Fae shackles, and no one messed with Agency business.

I sighed in aggravation. "If you don't go willingly, I'll have to use my stun gun on you. Either way, you are going in the cage."

"Wait!" He stared at me with wild eyes. "I know where your parents are."

The world came to a screeching halt. "What?"

"Your parents, Jesse James. I can take you to them if you let me go," he said with more confidence.

My mind raced. He would probably say and do anything to get me to let him go, but he knew my name and the fact that my parents were missing.

I pushed him roughly against the Jeep. "Where are they? Are they okay?"

"They're alive...for now."

Roaring filled my ears. "If you've hurt them, so help me..."

"I never laid a finger on them."

"Where are they?" I asked through clenched teeth.

"Not until we have a deal." He straightened his shoulders, and I caught a sly gleam in his eyes.

"I promise I'll release you if you take me to them," I vowed. I produced the key to the shackles and dangled them before him as an incentive. I wasn't lying. I would let him go free if it meant getting my parents back.

He held up his bound hands. "Then take these off, and let's go."

"Not so fast." I pocketed the key again and pulled a second pair of shackles from my gear bag.

"What are you doing?" Fear crept back into his voice.

"You don't want to go into the cage, and I don't want to have to hold onto you so you don't run away." I hooked one end through the pair on his wrists and secured the other to the cage.

"I thought I was taking you to your parents."

I took out my phone. My gut told me he was telling the truth, at least about knowing where my parents were. But I wasn't stupid enough to go up alone against people who could kidnap my mother and father and hold them captive this long.

"Who are you calling?"

"Reinforcements. I'm not going anywhere with you alone." I dialed Lukas's number. He'd said he would only be in Faerie for two days, which meant there was a chance he was back.

It felt like a heavy rock rested upon my chest when the call went to voice mail. I left him a message before I hung up and called Conlan. He'd know the best way to handle this.

The phone rang four times before the call also went to voice mail. My heart sank, and it hit me how much I'd come to rely on them and to expect them to be there when I needed them. I hadn't meant for it to happen, but somewhere along the way I'd started thinking of them as friends.

I went through my contacts again. Lukas and Conlan weren't the only people I could call for help. I dialed Bruce's number and let out the breath I was holding when he answered.

"Bruce, I need help," I said in a rush. "I'm with an elf who says he knows where Mom and Dad are."

"Slow down, Jesse," Bruce replied calmly. "Now, tell me what's going on."

I told him where I was and filled him in.

"You were smart to call for backup. We're less than fifteen minutes from you, and I'm going to contact some of the other hunters and get a group together. Stay where you are, and wait for us."

"I will." I almost said "please, hurry," but I didn't have to tell Bruce how important this was.

I hung up and looked at the elf. "My friends are on the way. When they get here, we'll go to my parents."

He swallowed nervously. "Bounty hunters?"

"Yes." I paced back and forth, too anxious to stand still. "Don't worry. I keep my word. As soon as you take us there, I'll let you go."

"And the other hunters? What if they don't want to release me?" He pulled against the shackles, testing the sturdiness of the cage. I didn't bother telling him to save his strength.

"Unless there is a bounty on your head, they'll have no reason to hold you."

That wasn't necessarily true. If Bruce or one of the others wanted to bring the elf in for questioning about his part in the kidnapping of two bounty hunters, they were within their right to do so. I wasn't going to tell him that and risk him clamming up on me.

Neither of us spoke for several minutes, and I couldn't stand the silence. I shot him a sideways look. "What's your name?"

"Why?" he asked warily.

"You know mine. Seems only fair that I know yours."

"Kardas," he said a little too quickly, making me suspect he was lying. He could have called himself Elvis for all I cared, as long as he led me to my mother and father.

I stopped pacing to face him. "Why did you kidnap my parents?"

"I didn't." He met my gaze without blinking. "I swear on my life. I wasn't even supposed to know where they were. I found out by accident."

I glared at him. "Then why did you and your friend try to jump me?"

His eyes darted around, and he lowered his voice. "We were hired to take you to someone. Don't ask me who because I value my life too much to say."

"Was it the same person who has my parents?"

"No."

His answer surprised me. Who else would want to kidnap me other than the people who had my parents?

"Did that person hire those two men to break into my apartment, too?" I asked him.

Kardas frowned. "I don't know anything about that. I was hired for one job, and that's it."

My phone rang, making both of us jump. I looked down to see it was Trey. I never thought I'd be happy to hear his voice on my phone.

"Dad and I are seven minutes away," he said. "We've been able to reach nine other hunters so far, so you have a whole posse headed toward you."

I bowed my head as relief coursed through me. "Thank God."

"Hang in there, Jesse," Bruce said, letting me know I was on speaker. His phone rang, and I heard him ask, "Who did you get?"

Trey's phone beeped, and he said, "It's Kim. I need to answer."

"Go ahead." I started pacing again while I waited. Kardas watched me guardedly, probably wondering about his fate when all of this was over. I was too worried about my parents to offer him more assurances.

Tires peeled, and I peered around the side of the Jeep as an old blue Chevy Impala tore into the parking lot. People shouted and jumped out of the way as the car sped toward us.

I was wondering which of the other hunters had gotten to us so fast when the car screeched to a stop a few feet away.

Two men I didn't recognize jumped out. I was about to ask who they were when the back door opened and a male elf appeared.

In the time it took for it to click that these were not my backup, the bigger man roughly grabbed my wrist, sending my phone flying from my grasp.

His arms went around me from behind, and he started dragging me toward the car. From somewhere in the parking lot, I heard shouts.

I didn't even think as one of my legs hooked around his, forcing him to stop walking. I swung my opposite hand down hard and nailed him between the legs. He grunted, and it took two more chops to get him to release me.

I broke away and was reaching for my stun gun when the other man's fist plowed into my jaw. My head snapped back, and stars floated in my vision. I landed hard on my hip, and pain shot through my head when it hit the pavement.

One of the men leaned over me, and I punched him in the throat, but there was no force behind it. For my efforts, I received a stinging slap that made my ears ring and caused my head to knock excruciatingly against the pavement again. His face swam in and out of focus as he lifted me and slung me over his shoulder.

"Wait," Kardas shouted. "The keys."

Hands rooted in my pockets, and I heard the jingle of the shackle keys as they were thrown to someone. My stun gun hit the pavement along with my car keys and a small switchblade.

I was tossed into the sedan's trunk, and my wrists and feet were quickly bound in front of me with industrial strength plastic ties. I heard a ripping sound and duct tape was placed over my mouth. The man worked with a practiced ease that sent a fresh chill through me.

The trunk came down, leaving me in darkness. Doors slammed, and the car was moving before my eyes had even adjusted to the dark interior. My eyes sought out the emergency release before I realized that this car had probably been around since before the Great Rift, and it had no release.

The car took a sharp right turn, and I moaned as nausea rose up in my throat. The dizziness and pain in my head pointed to a concussion, and I struggled to keep from passing out. I tried to keep a mental list of every turn we took, but I had trouble focusing and lost track after the first ten minutes.

It felt like no more than thirty minutes had passed when the car stopped and the engine shut off. Dread twisted my stomach as I listened to the murmur of voices and waited for someone to open the trunk.

My heart raced as I imagined what was waiting for me out there. It couldn't be good. Would I ever get to see my parents again? And what would happen to Finch if I didn't come home? My chest hurt when I thought about my brother alone and frightened.

The trunk popped, and I braced myself. A hand appeared and lifted the lid to reveal the two men, who glared at me as if me being in their trunk was a big inconvenience to them.

I caught a glimpse of a ceiling that told me we had to be in a garage. Before I could see more, one of the men leaned in and pulled a dark hood over my head. The two of them lifted me none too gently from the trunk and set me on my unsteady feet. One held me up while the other cut the tie from my ankles.

A door opened. The man holding my arm pulled me toward the door, and I tripped. He yanked me up hard, nearly tearing my arm from its socket, and I cried out against the tape over my mouth.

"Is that necessary, Barry?" asked a female voice.

"Yes." My captor shook me. "Bitch punched me in the nuts."

"And I bet you deserved it," she retorted. "You and Glen take her to the basement. Then go up and see Rogin. He's waiting for you."

Barry pulled me through the door and down a short flight of stairs. At the bottom, cold hit me along with a damp, musty odor. We didn't walk far before I heard the scrape of a metal cage door opening. I balked, and they snickered.

"Not so tough now, are you?" taunted Barry as he shoved me inside.

I stumbled and fell to my hands and knees on the cold concrete floor as the cage door clanged shut with an ominous click. It was followed by the men's receding footsteps as they left me alone in the basement.

I grunted in pain as I pushed up off my bruised knees. Once I was back on my feet, I reached up with my bound hands to pull off the hood and rip the tape from my mouth.

I took in my surroundings. I was in a cage at one end of the open basement, and a single light bulb on this side of the space cast just enough light to see a dozen feet in front of me.

I grasped the cage bars. "Mom? Dad? Are you there?"

Someone moaned softly, but not from the other side of the basement. I spun and gasped when I realized I wasn't alone in the cage. At the back corner, a tall man stood with thick iron chains wrapped around him from his bare shoulders to his feet.

My first thought was that it was my father, until I saw the bent head and the mop of matted blond hair that hung to his chest. I approached him slowly and stopped when I was two feet away.

"Can you hear me?" I asked softly.

He didn't speak or move. I waited another minute, and then I reached out and put my hands under his chin to lift his head. My shocked eyes took in the finely chiseled cheekbones and perfect brow. His pallor was gray and he looked almost frail, but there was no mistaking a Court faerie when you saw one.

His eyelids flickered and slowly opened to reveal emerald green eyes that seemed strangely familiar, although I was certain I had never seen him before. We stared at each other in silence until his tongue darted out to wet his cracked lips.

"I was right," he whispered in a voice that sounded hoarse from disuse.

"About what?"

"Angels do have fiery hair." A cough racked his body, making his chains clink. "Have you come at last to take me into the arms of the Goddess?"

My chest squeezed at his words. I saw no fear in his eyes, only acceptance and peace. I wished with all my heart that I could ease his pain, but I was as much a prisoner here as he was.

I cupped his face tenderly. "I'm no angel, and the Goddess hasn't sent for you yet."

A ghost of a smile touched his lips. "Are you sure you aren't an angel? You have the hands of one."

"And you remind me of someone I know." I smiled when I thought of Conlan's flirting, but I quickly sobered when I remembered I'd probably never see him or any of the others again. Not unless I could figure out how to get us out of here.

"What is your name, my-angel-who-is-not-an-angel?" my companion rasped.

I sat on the floor with my back against the cage. "Jesse."

"I am Faris."

"Nice to meet you, but I wish it were under different circumstances." I untied my boot laces, glad I'd worn my combat boots today instead of a pair without laces. With some difficulty, I slipped one lace through the plastic tie and knotted it with the other lace. I lifted my feet and used them to saw the laces across the tie until it broke.

Faris coughed. "Very creative."

"Just something I picked up from *YouTube*." I retied my laces and went to study the chains wrapped around him. They were tight enough to prevent movement, but not too tight to cut off circulation. I couldn't find the ends until I peeked behind him and saw he was chained to the cage with large iron padlocks.

"I might be able to get these open if I had something to use as a pick." I checked my pockets and came up empty.

"It's okay. I'm just glad for your company."

I moved back to look him in the face. "But you're covered in iron."

"Don't fret, my angel," Faris said weakly. "I've been like this so long I barely feel it anymore."

"How long?" My stomach lurched. Iron in small doses didn't harm faeries, but prolonged contact would eventually saturate their bodies and kill them. How long it took depended on the strength of the faerie and the purity of the iron.

His head lolled again. "I don't know. Months, I think."

"Months?" I stared at him, aghast. "Why would they do this to you?"

He croaked a laugh. "This is what comes from angering someone who likes to watch you die a slow death. I don't think either of us expected me to live this long."

I couldn't conceive that level of malice. I knew there were evil people in the world, but to torture someone for months on end just to watch them suffer... A shudder went through me. I was now in the hands of that person. Would they kill me quickly or draw out my death in some horrible way, too?

Needing to focus on anything besides my death, I looked around the cage and spotted a small jug and a cup on the floor outside. I stretched my arm through the bars, and I pulled them to me. The jug wouldn't fit between the bars, so I filled the cup with water and brought it to Faris. Gently, I lifted his head and put the cup to his lips. He sipped the water at first, and then he drank thirstily. I refilled the cup twice until he'd had enough.

"Thank you, my angel," he said as I went to fill the cup for myself.

"Please, call me Jesse." I took a long drink of the water.

"As you wish." He rested his head against the bars, looking slightly better after drinking the water. "Tell me, Jesse, how did you end up in this place?"

"My parents are bounty hunters, and they were working on a job when they went missing over a month ago. I've been looking for them, and I guess I pissed off the wrong person." I sucked in a shaky breath. "Someone told me they're alive, but I have no idea if that's true. Have...you seen a human couple here?"

"I haven't seen them, but the female elf brings food to someone on the other side of the basement."

My heart gave an excited flutter, and I called out again, louder this time. "Mom? Can you hear me?"

I held my breath and listened but heard nothing, not even the slightest movement. I rested my head against the bars and tried not to feel the despair threatening to crush me.

After a while, I began to shiver inside my jacket, and I noticed the basement had gotten colder. There were no windows, but I'd been here long enough for darkness to have fallen. It was going to be a miserable night without heat and nothing to sit on but the bare concrete floor.

"Are you cold?" I asked Faris. "We can take turns sharing my coat." The most I could do was drape it over his shoulders, but that was better than nothing.

"You are very kind, Jesse, but I don't feel the cold."

I studied his face. "Are you only saying that to be noble?"

He closed his eyes. "I wasn't lying when I said I could barely feel the iron anymore. The poison is starting to shut down my body, and I feel little pain. It won't be much longer. A week maybe."

I wasn't expecting the anguish that welled inside me. Going to him, I laid my hand against his cheek. "Don't give up. I'll figure out a way to get us out of here."

"Thank you." He leaned into my palm and sighed. "I thought I would leave this world without ever again feeling the warmth of another's touch."

We stayed like that until he fell asleep. When his head drooped forward, I sat on the floor beside him to wait for whatever came next.

I didn't remember dozing off, but I awoke with my head resting against Faris's chain-covered leg. I had no idea how much time had passed, but based on how cold and stiff I was, it had been hours.

I stood quietly, as to not wake Faris, whose only respite from this place was in sleep. I couldn't imagine the extent of his suffering, a faerie covered in iron for months, and I vowed silently to find a way to help him.

Something on the floor outside the cage caught my eye, and I walked over for a closer look. My stomach growled loudly when I saw a chunk of bread and an apple on a paper napkin, and a new jug of water. It wasn't much, but it was food and it looked edible.

Picking up the meager fare, I broke the bread into halves and ate one, washing it down with water. I ate half the apple, too. It wasn't filling but enough to ease the gnawing hunger for now.

I was pacing the cage to stay warm when Faris said, "You're still here. I hoped you were a dream."

"You don't like my company?" I asked in an attempt at humor.

He smiled sadly. "Not if it means you are trapped in this place with me."

"If you forget the whole prisoner thing, there are worse places to be." I picked up his half of the meal. "Someone brought food. I hope you don't mind me feeding you."

"I will endure," he quipped and dissolved into a fit of coughing.

I filled a cup with water and gave him a drink before I began feeding him bits of bread. He'd barely eaten half of it before he said he was done.

"You finish it," he said when I pressed him to eat more. "They brought it for you, not me."

I wrapped the uneaten portion in the napkin and put it in my coat pocket for him to eat later. It was too cold to stand still, so I went back to pacing.

"Where have you been that is worse than this place?" Faris asked.

"A few weeks ago, I spent the night on North Brother Island, after almost drowning. Oh, and there was a kelpie." I told him about that night, leaving out certain parts, such as who had found me the next morning. I had no idea who else might be listening, and I didn't want to put Lukas in danger after all he'd done for me. "For my trouble, I got a cold and someone else got the bounty."

"Aedhna was watching over you that night," he said softly.

"Maybe." I thought about the stone hidden beneath my hair, the one I'd removed at least half a dozen times until I'd given up. If it was a goddess stone and I was goddess-blessed, as Lukas had called it, then I must be doing something wrong. I could really use some divine intervention right now.

"Tell me more of your hunting stories."

"Okay, but I don't have that many." I told him how I'd started as a hunter and about the jobs I'd done so far. After I'd related all my hunting tales, he asked about my family and my life. I spent hours talking, but when I asked about his family, he got very quiet. I didn't press him because I could see it upset him.

"You should try to sleep," he said when I yawned for the third time.

I rubbed my freezing hands together. "It's too cold to lie down." The least they could have done was give us blankets, but what did I expect from people who would torture a faerie like this.

I was falling asleep on my feet when a sharp voice demanded, "What is this?"

I started, not having heard anyone enter the room, and blinked at the male elf standing outside the cage. His hair was pulled back in a ponytail, and he wore black dress pants and a dark green silk shirt. His mouth was pressed into a severe line as his cold eyes looked at me like I was dirt beneath his expensive loafers.

He spun and walked to the foot of the stairs to yell for Barry and Glen. Within a minute, the two men hurried into the basement.

"Can you two get anything right?" the elf shouted. He pointed at Faris. "How many times have I said no one is allowed near him? Get her out of there."

Barry pulled a key from his pocket and unlocked the cage door. His eyes went from my free hands to the plastic tie on the floor, but he said nothing as he grabbed my wrist in a bruising grip and dragged me from the cage.

He pulled me past the irate elf and toward the darker part of the basement. We passed several smaller empty cages until we came to one at the end that was the same size as Faris's cage. This one was shrouded in darkness, showing me nothing of what was waiting inside for me.

Barry opened the door and threw me inside with vicious glee, but I was able to catch myself before I hit the floor this time. There was no lock on this cage, so Glen wrapped a length of chain around the bars and secured it with a padlock.

As soon as they left me, I pressed my face to the bars and strained to see what was happening to Faris down at the other end. All I could make out were some moving shadows.

"I hope you enjoyed your little visitor," the elf taunted Faris.

I could hear the smile in Faris's voice when he said, "You mean my angel."

Barry laughed. "He's lost his mind. Had to happen sooner or later."

The elf didn't laugh with him. "Let's go," he barked. "We have a lot to do for tomorrow."

They tramped up the stairs, and silence fell over the basement again. If I'd thought it was bad before, it was ten times worse being alone in the dark. I was half afraid to see what was in the cell with me this time.

"Angel?" Faris called hoarsely.

"I'm here." I didn't bother to correct him. He could call me whatever he wanted if it made him happy.

He had another fit of coughing, and I gripped the bars, feeling helpless. I couldn't even give him water.

"Are you okay?" he managed to croak after the coughing had passed.

"Yes," I lied. "If you've been in one cage, you've been in them all."

He chuckled. "You have a spirit to match that hair."

"I get it from my mom. I wish you could meet –"

I froze.

There was something in the cell with me.

I turned slowly and pressed my back against the bars as I squinted into the deeper shadows at the back of the cage. It wasn't as dark now that my eyes had adjusted, but I still had trouble making out the shape on the floor.

Then I heard it again, a barely audible moan. And a single whispered word. "Jesse."

My heart threatened to burst from my chest as I fell to my knees beside the man, who lay hidden beneath a dirty wool blanket. I pulled back the blanket, and a lump formed in my throat when I saw him. His face was thinner and covered in a scraggy beard, but I'd know him anywhere.

"Dad." I shook him, but he just stared blankly at the ceiling. I threw myself across his chest, clinging to him like I was five years old again. "Daddy."

19

I hugged my father tightly, and for the first time in my life, he didn't wrap his strong, protective arms around me. I felt the loss like a punch in the gut, but at the same time I was overcome with joy to be holding him again. I pressed my face against his chest, feeling his strong, steady heartbeat. He'd lost weight, and he smelled like he hadn't bathed in a month, but he was alive.

I rose up to my knees and ran my hand from his forehead to his jaw. He didn't react to my touch at all, and he kept staring at the ceiling with an odd little smile on his face.

"Dad, it's Jesse. Can you hear me?" I shook him gently, trying to rouse him. "Where's Mom?"

He didn't answer, and I looked past him to a pile of dirty blankets in the corner of the cage. I crawled over him and grasped one of the foul-smelling blankets. "Please, God."

My knees almost gave out when I pulled back the blanket. My mother lay on her side, wearing the same creepy smile and staring right through me. Like Dad, she was filthy and thinner, but a quick check told me she was alive.

I sat on the cold floor and pulled her head onto my lap, covering her body with the ratty blankets. Stroking her dirty hair, I whispered, "I'm here, Mom."

I had no idea how long I sat there like that before I realized Faris was calling to me.

"Angel...Jesse, speak to me."

I lifted my head. "I'm here. I found my mom and dad. They're alive, but there's something wrong with them. It's like they're in some kind of trance."

"It's called rapture," said a soft female voice.

I stiffened as a slender woman came into view on the other side of the bars. She walked over to the far wall and flipped a switch, and a light bulb came on overhead.

I blinked at the sudden brightness and stared at the female elf. She wore a simple green dress and ballet flats, and her long platinum hair was pulled back into a thick braid.

I gently slid out from beneath my mother and stood. "What's rapture? Is it a glamour?"

"It's a state that humans enter when they take goren," she explained as she walked toward the cage.

"My parents would never take drugs," I declared vehemently. I stared at the elf as she drew closer. "Hey, I've seen you before...at the cemetery. You had a little girl with you."

She nodded and put a finger to her lips. "Please, keep your voice down. They don't know I'm here."

I moved closer to her and lowered my voice. "Who are you, and why would you do this to my parents?"

Her eyes were pools of emotion, mostly regret. "My name is Raisa, and I did this to save your parents. You must believe me. I never intended them harm."

I waved an angry hand at my parents who lay in filth. "Look at them," I bit out. "How is this saving them?"

Raisa gripped the bars of the cage. "I did what I could. If you let me explain, you will understand."

I couldn't think of any way that giving someone goren would save their lives, but I nodded. My life and my parents' lives were in the hands of this person, and I needed to know what I was up against.

"I met your parents a year ago. I was waiting for a bus one night when some men attacked me. The Goddess was watching over me that night because your parents came along and stopped the men before they could do serious harm." She held out her arm and showed me a two-inch scar on her bicep. Only a cut from an iron blade would leave a scar like that on a faerie.

"I thought I'd never see Caroline and Patrick James again." Raisa inhaled deeply. "Over a month ago, a twist of fate brought them back into my life. I believe Aedhna sent them to me so I can repay the debt I owe them."

"What happened?" I knew from the incident with Prince Vaerik that faeries took debt seriously, especially when someone saved their lives.

Raisa looked around nervously and whispered, "I don't know the whole of it, only that your parents did something to anger the Seelie royal guard."

I sucked in a breath. The royal guard of each court protected the monarch and their heirs, and they were the most lethal of all the faeries. My parents would know better than to cross them.

"The Guard didn't want to dirty their hands by killing two well-known bounty hunters, so they called someone else to do it," she said.

"You?"

She shook her head. "My brother, Rogin. For the right price, there isn't much he won't do. But I intercepted the call and had your parents brought here to our home. I gave them goren from Rogin's supply and hid them from him. He rarely comes to this house, and he has no idea they are down here."

"But why didn't you just let them go?"

Raisa's eyes clouded with fear. "I couldn't. The Guard would know we hadn't killed them, and all of our lives would have been forfeited. You do not betray the queen's guard and live to speak of it. But I could not let your parents be killed either, so I did the only thing I could think of to keep them alive."

My animosity toward her lessened when I saw she was truly afraid, and she had taken the only option available to her. But it was a strange twist of fate that the sister of the goren dealer my parents had been hunting was the one to save their lives.

"How long were you planning to keep them here like this?"

"For weeks, I have been trying to find a way to contact you." She wrung her hands. "It has not been easy to get away, and the few times I could, you were not alone."

"Is that why you followed me to the cemetery that day?"

She hugged her middle. "Yes. But the agent approached you, and I left. Weeks ago, I followed you to a diner in Queens. I was about to go inside when one of the royal guards came out with two men. I was so frightened I ran away."

I thought about the day I'd overheard those men and the faerie plotting to kill Prince Vaerik. Had Faolin known the faerie was a Seelie royal guard when he looked at the security tape? That might explain why he'd looked even more pissed when he'd come back to the booth.

"I saw you that day." It gutted me to know how close I'd come to finding my parents, but I couldn't dwell on that now. "Did you also put a note on my Jeep?"

"Yes. I saw how sad you were at the cemetery, and I only wanted to give you hope. I'm sorry I was too afraid to go to your apartment. If I had, you would not be here now."

I frowned at her. "There's one thing I don't get. Why would you send people after me if you were trying to help me?"

She took a step back, shaking her head. "That was Rogin, not me. He was paid by the queen's guard to silence you because you were asking questions. He has no idea your parents are still alive. If he did, he would have killed them already. I was afraid he had found them when he was down here earlier to check on his prisoner."

I rubbed my temples where a headache had formed, and I was reminded I probably had a concussion on top of everything else.

"Where does Faris come into all of this?" I asked her quietly so he couldn't hear me.

She pressed her lips together and turned her head to look toward his cage. "All I know is that he also crossed the queen's guard, but they chose to give him a slow death." She shuddered. "Queen Anwyn has no mercy for her enemies."

A chill went through me. "But how did he end up here?"

"My brother," she said in disgust. "As I said, Rogin will do anything for money, and the guard pays him well for certain services. He was keeping the faerie at a warehouse owned by his business partner, but he had to move the faerie when there was a break-in at the property."

Her words triggered a memory of Violet telling me about a break-in at a lawyer's property. "His partner is Cecil Hunt?"

"Yes."

Pieces began to click into place. "You called me from his house on my mother's phone."

She nodded guiltily. "That was the first time I tried to reach you. I knew Cecil was away, and I thought it would be the perfect place to talk. I was inside the house when you and your friend were arrested, and I felt terrible about it."

"At least, I know it wasn't someone luring me into a trap."

"Raisa," called a faint male voice from upstairs.

She jumped as if she'd been shocked. "I have to go," she whispered urgently. "He can't find me down here."

I grabbed her hand, which was still on a cage bar. "Will you help us?"

"I'll try." She pulled her hand from mine and flipped off the light as she ran soundlessly from the basement.

I went back to my parents, but as much as I wanted to hold them, I couldn't just sit here. I started to explore the cage for anything I could use as a weapon. It would have been a lot easier with a light, but I knew why Raisa had left me in darkness. She didn't want anyone who came downstairs to see I wasn't alone in my cage.

Crawling around on the grimy floor was not pleasant, and I let out a disgusted "eww" when I touched dried rat droppings. But I pushed on and was rewarded when my searching fingers found a small piece of hard steel wire the length of my hand.

It didn't take long to break the wire in half and bend one of the pieces into an L-shape. It took two frustrating hours of reaching my arms through the bars and working blind to pick the padlock on the cage door. When I got home, I was going to learn to pick locks like a cat burglar and always carry a pick on me.

I had to be careful not to make too much noise as I unwrapped the chain and set it on the floor. The door squeaked loudly when I eased it open, and I froze, expecting someone to come running down the stairs.

The first thing I did when I was out of the cage was check on Faris. The faerie had been quiet for far too long, and I was afraid he'd succumbed to his illness. His head was hanging low, and he didn't react when I called to him. I studied the lock on his cage and decided it was too risky to try to pick it. The best thing I could do for him and my parents was to escape this house and come back with help.

I returned to my parents and covered them with the blankets again. Making the decision to leave them after I'd just found them was the hardest thing I'd ever done. My eyes stung as I wrapped the chain around the bars and padlocked it.

"I'll be back soon, I promise," I said under my breath.

I surveyed the long, narrow basement. Faris's cage was near the stairs at one end, and my parents' cage was at the other. In the middle, there was a single window that had been boarded up with a piece of plywood. I could fit through it if I could pry the plywood off, but a search of the basement turned up nothing I could use. Aside from the cages, there wasn't much else down here.

I went to the foot of the stairs and peered up at the dark landing. There was no other option. I had to go up there if I was going to get out of here.

I crept slowly up the stairs, stopping on each one to listen. At the top, I was faced with a door on either side of me. If my memory served, we had turned right before we descended the stairs, which meant the door to my left led to the garage.

I pressed my ear to the second door and picked up muted voices. Well, that made my decision easy. Door number one it was.

I put my hand on the knob, letting out a breath when it turned easily under my hand. I eased the door open and slipped through, shutting it quietly behind me. I found myself in the garage with the same sedan that had brought me here.

Careful not to knock into anything, I went to the garage door, which had three small windows overlooking a well-lit residential street. The dark windows of the two houses I could see told me it was probably well after midnight when most people were asleep.

I was reaching for the handle at the base of the door when I heard voices from inside the house. Someone was coming.

Panicked, I ran to the back of the garage and squeezed in behind a stack of boxes. I barely had time to pull my feet in when the door to the house opened.

"Hasn't he ever heard of sleep?" Barry grumbled. "Goddamn elves."

Glen chuckled. "We'll sleep when this job is done and we're a lot richer."

Car doors opened and closed, and the engine started. I flinched when the headlights came on, shining like a spotlight on my hiding place. Curling into a tight ball, I prayed they couldn't see me. I was only getting one chance to escape this place.

The garage door rose, and my entire body coiled tight with tension as I waited for them to back out. When I could tell the car was out of the garage, I peeked around the boxes to see it slowly backing down the short driveway.

The garage door motor started again, and the door began to descend. I was trapped as long as the headlights were still on the house. What was taking them so long to turn onto the street?

After what felt like forever, the headlights swung away from the garage. I scrambled out from behind the boxes and ran to the door. Dropping to my stomach, I rolled beneath the door with only seconds to spare.

I lay there for a moment, staring at the night sky in stunned disbelief. I was free.

Sitting up, I looked around. There was a light on over the front door, but it only reached the middle of the driveway. I got to my feet and moved toward the lawn on the darkened side of the driveway. As soon as my boots hit the grass, I ran.

My foot had barely touched the sidewalk when someone slammed into me from behind. I went down hard, hitting my chin off the pavement as the air was punched from my lungs. Gasping desperately for air, I didn't fight when I was rolled onto my back to face my attacker.

Kardas grinned down at me. "I think someone is having a bad day." He leaned closer. "And it's going to get worse."

He pulled back. The last thing I saw was his fist coming at me before everything went black.

I sputtered awake when cold water hit me in the face. It took me a moment to recover from the shock and to realize I was back in the basement, but in a much smaller cage. My coat and boots were gone, and I was propped against the back wall of the cage. To add insult to injury, my hands and feet were bound with what looked like my own shackles.

"You might be more trouble than you're worth," drawled Rogin, who stood outside the cage. Next to him a sneering Kardas held an empty bucket.

My lip curled. "Excuse me if I don't apologize."

Rogin's smile was more of a leer. "I was going to dispose of you, but being a businessman, I see the financial value of things. With that red hair, you could have fetched me a tidy price with the right buyer, but I found a much better use for you."

I glared at him, determined not to show him an ounce of fear. "And what would that be?"

"You'll find out soon enough. And just to make sure you are more cooperative; I took the liberty of removing this." He held up a hand, and my heart dropped like a stone when I saw my leather bracelet dangling from his fingers. "Now, I think you should get on your knees and tell me how sorry you are for being such a pain in my ass."

"You're out of your mind," I spat.

His brows drew together in confusion. "On your knees. Now."

I lifted my chin. "Screw you."

He punched the bars and whirled on Kardas. "You missed something. She's still wearing a talisman."

"That's all the jewelry she was wearing," Kardas argued. "You want me to strip her?"

My stomach rolled, and I pulled my knees up to my chest. "Don't come near me."

A phone chimed, and Rogin pulled his from his pants pocket. "I don't have time to spare. We'll just have to make do without the glamour." He tossed me a scathing look. "Sleep well, Miss James. Tomorrow is a big day."

My body seemed to fold in on itself when he spun and left the basement with Kardas trailing after him. I hugged my knees as I began to shiver violently. I didn't know if it was from the cold or fear, but I couldn't stop.

"F-Faris, can you h-hear me?" I called through chattering teeth.

Silence greeted me. I hadn't realized how much I needed to hear his calming voice until I was denied it. I hoped he was okay, but it wasn't looking good for either of us. All I could do was pray that Raisa was somehow able to save my parents.

A wave of helplessness and despair crashed down on me, and I curled up in a ball on the floor. "Mom, Dad, I'm sorry."

Feet pounding down the stairs woke me from a restless sleep. I sat up and watched Kardas, Barry, and Glen arrive carrying towels, blankets, water, and a bundle of clothes, which they took into Faris's cage.

Glen looked at Kardas. "Is he dead?"

"Not yet, but it won't be long," Kardas replied callously as he pulled a syringe from his pocket.

I crawled to the side of my cage closest to them. "What are you doing to him?" I demanded through parched lips. I was so thirsty, but no one had brought me water, and the jug was out of reach.

"None of your business," Barry retorted as he unlocked the chains encasing Faris. He held the faerie while Glen removed the chain. Kardas kept a safe distance from them until they laid Faris's naked body on the blankets.

There was a sense of urgency around them as they quickly cleaned Faris with the towels and dressed him in the clothes.

"Hurry up," Kardas whisper-yelled at Glen, who was taking too long to put shoes on Faris's feet. "I don't want to be here when he arrives."

Barry gathered the dirty towels. "Have you ever met him?"

"No, and I don't want to. I'd prefer to live a very long life." Kardas visibly shuddered. "Rogin has lost his mind, playing both sides like this. If the queen's guard finds out, he's dead."

Glen stood. "Done."

The three of them left the cage and hurried upstairs. I looked at Faris, who was almost unrecognizable in clean clothes with the grime washed from his face. They'd even tied his matted hair back in a ponytail.

"Faris," I called.

He didn't move or answer me, not that I expected him to. He hadn't spoken since just before Raisa had come to visit me last night, and I worried it was too late for him. They had removed the iron, but the damage had already been done to his body.

A commotion upstairs drew my attention away from the unconscious faerie. One of the doors at the top of the stairs opened, and I could hear Rogin talking.

"I wanted no part of it, but you don't say no to the queen's guard when they order you to do something," he professed so earnestly that I almost believed him. "I didn't know he was one of yours until she confessed the truth yesterday, but I had no way to reach you."

"Take me to him," commanded a hard, male voice, and it suddenly felt like every bit of air had been sucked from the room.

"Of course. Right this way."

My eyes were glued to the stairs when the elf came into view, but it was the two blond faeries close at his heels that had me clutching my cage bars for support. Kerr and Iian were armed with swords, and their expressions were nothing short of lethal.

Behind them came a stone-faced Lukas, and my heart nearly burst with joy when I saw him. Conlan and Faolin took up the rear, also armed and looking ready to slice the head off the first thing that moved. If I didn't know them, the sight of this fearsome group of faeries would have had me cowering in a corner.

I wanted to jump up and shout at the top of my lungs. All I managed was a weak croak. "Lukas."

I couldn't take my eyes off him, so I saw the moment his cold gaze landed on me...and moved past me as if I didn't exist.

Pain lanced through me before I decided Rogin must have placed some kind of glamour on the cage to make it invisible. That had to be it because Lukas would never look through me as if I were nothing.

My gaze went to Kerr, and our eyes met for the briefest of seconds before his moved away. What was going on? He'd seen me. I knew he had. Why was he acting like he hadn't?

I looked at the one person in the group who had always been nice to me from the moment we met. Conlan wouldn't ignore me. He didn't have it in him to be cruel.

Conlan didn't even glance my way. Nor did Faolin, who had eyes only for the cage next to me.

If someone had told me a month ago that my heart would be broken by a group of faeries, I would have laughed and called them insane. But as I watched the five of them walk up to Faris's cage without a single acknowledgement that I was here, it felt like pieces of my heart had shriveled up in my chest.

Faolin entered the cage. As he knelt beside the unconscious Faris, I saw warmth in his green eyes – eyes that looked exactly like Faris's. Faolin's voice was gruff when he said, "Brother, can you hear me?"

Brother?

"What happened to him?" Lukas demanded harshly.

Rogin spoke, but I was reeling too much to hear his response. Faris was Faolin's brother. He was what they had been hell-bent on finding and the reason Lukas had offered to help me search for my parents. Lukas hadn't once mentioned they were looking for a person, and I'd just assumed they were on business for the crown.

I'd spent hours talking to Faris last night, and it had never occurred to me to ask what Court he came from. If he'd said Unseelie, I would have asked if he knew Lukas and his men. Not that it would have mattered.

Conlan went to kneel on Faris's other side. "It doesn't look good."

Faolin stood, and in a second, he was in front of Rogin, grabbing him by the throat and lifting him into the air. "I am going to end you."

The elf kicked and clutched at the hand choking him, but he was no match for Faolin's strength. His face turned purple, and his eyes bulged.

"Faolin," Lukas barked.

The two of them exchanged a long look and seemed to be engaged in a silent battle of wills that ended with Faolin dropping Rogin. The elf fell to his knees coughing, and Faolin's murderous gaze clashed with mine as he returned to his brother. He lifted Faris effortlessly into his arms and carried him from the cage, sparing me another look of pure hatred before he left the basement.

Conlan followed Faolin, and as he passed my cage, his angry, wounded eyes met mine. I could feel the accusation he directed at me, but I didn't know what it meant. I didn't understand any of this.

Rogin groveled on his knees to Lukas. "It wasn't me, I swear, Prince Vaerik. It was her. I tried to help him. I called you, didn't I?"

"Vaerik?" I choked out. If I hadn't already been on my knees, my legs would have given out in that moment. Lukas was Prince Vaerik?

No. I didn't believe it. I refused to believe he'd lied to me, that every one of them had lied after I'd tipped them off about the assassination plot on Vaerik's life.

Lukas's glacial eyes met mine and held, but it was like looking at a stranger. I didn't know this person who stared at me with such contempt.

"Lukas?" I whispered hoarsely. "What's wrong?"

He walked over to stand in front of my cage. "Drop the pretense, Jesse. We found the tablet."

"What tablet?"

"The one you had hidden in the basement of your building." He fingered the hilt of the sword he wore on his hip. "You should have hidden it better and used a stronger password. Faolin was able to break yours easily."

I shook my head, confused. "I don't own a tablet."

He crossed his arms. "And I suppose you didn't take the pictures we found on it. Pictures of me taken over the last two months, along with a spreadsheet tracking places I've been. I'm actually impressed because we had no idea you were following me that long, waiting for your perfect opportunity."

"Opportunity for what?" I was struggling to keep up with him, my mind stuck on this mysterious tablet he thought belonged to me.

"You can stop with the innocent act," he growled. "I read the notes in your spreadsheet about the best ways to get close to me. You forgot to add the one where you told us about the little plot to kill me at the gala. That was a stroke of genius. You even fooled Faolin with that one."

"Stop," I yelled. "I don't know where that tablet came from, but it's not mine. You have to believe me."

His mouth twisted into an ugly sneer. "Give it up. I won't fall for your innocent wiles again. You'll be lucky if I don't allow Faolin to kill you for what you've done."

I recoiled from the malice in his voice. "I haven't done anything. Why won't you believe me?"

"The evidence of your guilt speaks for itself. And this is the most damning piece." He reached inside his coat and withdrew a photograph, which he held up for me to see. It was a photo of Faris that had been taken recently, based on his sickly pallor.

I shook my head. "I didn't take that picture. I never laid eyes on Faris until yesterday."

"Yet you know his name."

Anger built in me, smothering the fear. "I know his name because I spent half of last night in his cell talking to him."

"Lies," Rogin spat. "He's been unconscious for days, thanks to her."

I lunged at the bars and grabbed them with my shackled hands. "He's lying! Faris told me they had him wrapped in iron for months. I swear on my life that he was awake yesterday."

"You mean you had him in iron, don't you?" Rogin asked in his oily voice. "The reason you're in that cage is that I found out what you were doing and put a stop to it."

"Ask Faris. He'll tell you," I told Lukas.

"How convenient," Rogin jeered. "Ask the one who will never wake up. You are even more calculating than I gave you credit for."

I turned imploring eyes on Lukas, who only stared back impassively. I wanted to beg him to believe me, but I could see in his hard expression that he'd already decided I was guilty. Nothing I said or did was going to change his mind.

I opened my mouth to tell him about my parents, who lay twenty feet away from us, but fear for them kept me silent. I didn't know this ruthless person before me, and I couldn't trust him with their safety. What if he believed they were guilty along with me and he left them to Rogin's mercy? Rogin would have them killed before the day was out.

"You have something to say, Jesse?" Lukas asked with a callousness that pierced me. But if he expected me to cower to him, he didn't know me at all.

I locked my gaze with his. "So, you came back from Faerie and decided out of the blue to search my basement, where you just happened to find this evidence against me?"

"We got a phone call from your friend here after you tried to double-cross him."

"And you believed him?" I shouted. "You took the word of this low-life drug dealer over me? How could you? What have I ever done to make you so willing to believe me capable of such a horrible thing?"

Lukas opened his mouth, but he'd had his say. It was my turn.

"I trusted you. I let you into my home with my brother, and I even thought we were friends. Stupid me." Tears burned the back of my throat, but I'd die before I let him see me fall apart. He didn't deserve a single one of my tears.

I drew myself up as far as the cramped cage would allow. "I don't know why I'm so surprised. You made it clear from the beginning that you were only helping me because it suited your purpose. Well, congratulations, *Your Highness*. You got exactly what you wanted."

For the first time since he'd arrived, doubt flickered in his eyes.

Kerr and Iian came to stand beside him, and their gazes swept over me. It must be okay to acknowledge my existence now that their prince had. Just thinking the word made my stomach twist. They were the liars here, not me. My fault lay in being too naïve to see they were using me. That was a mistake I'd never make again.

"What do you want to do?" Kerr asked uncertainly. "Are we taking her with us?"

"Yes." Lukas answered at the same time that I said, "No."

The three of them stared at me. Even Rogin looked surprised by my response. But I wasn't going to exchange one prison for another, especially not when my parents were here. Raisa had promised to help them, and I'd do whatever I could to make that happen.

Iian frowned. "You want to stay down here in this filthy cage?"

I let out a bitter laugh. "What I want is to be at home with my family, and my *real* friends, and to forget I ever laid eyes on any of you. But we don't always get what we want, do we?" I cut my gaze back to Lukas. "I think we're done here. Tell Faris I hope he gets better soon, but he'll have to forgive me if I don't send flowers."

"Jesse..." Kerr said, but I was already turning away.

The shackles clinked against the concrete floor as I crawled to the back of the cage and sat with my arms around my knees. I rested my forehead on my knees and waited for them to leave. I stayed like that until I heard four sets of footsteps ascending the stairs.

I looked around the empty basement, feeling more alone and beaten down than I'd ever been in my eighteen years. Nausea rose in my throat, and my chest felt like someone had kicked it repeatedly, but even though Lukas's betrayal cut deeply, he hadn't broken me. He might be a faerie prince, but I was the daughter of Caroline and Patrick James, and it would take a lot more than him to break me.

The hours passed in agonizing slowness. I heard activity upstairs in the house, but no one bothered me. Unfortunately, that meant they didn't bring me water or food either. I could go without food, but I couldn't remember ever being this thirsty.

Eventually, the house grew quiet and a new fear set in. Had they left us here to die? It was a terrifying thought, and my only solace was that my parents were too out of it to feel anything.

I wasn't sure how much time had gone by when I heard a loud crash from upstairs. It sounded like a dozen pairs of feet were tramping around up there. A door opened, and the light came on over the landing. I tensed and watched the stairs. The last time someone had come down them, I'd thought I was being saved. I didn't have high hopes this time.

Two men in dark suits descended the stairs, and I knew immediately these weren't Rogin's goons. They stopped abruptly when they saw me, and I lifted my shackled hands in greeting.

"Agent Curry, I never thought I'd say this, but I'm so happy to see you."

20

"Here you go, honey," said the young nurse as she set a plastic glass of water on the bedside table for me. "The doctor will be in soon."

"Thanks." I picked up the glass and sipped the water, even though I wasn't thirsty anymore. They'd given me fluids and plenty of water to drink since I was brought in a few hours ago. I just needed something to do with my hands while I lay in this bed, waiting for news about my parents.

I stared at the fat snowflakes drifting down outside my window without really seeing them. The last four hours had been a crazy blur of activity from the moment the Agency had raided Rogin's house. My parents and I had been whisked off to the hospital in ambulances, where we had been admitted immediately into emergency. I was sure someone had pulled strings when I was treated and moved to a private room within an hour of my arrival.

I hadn't seen my mother and father since they were rolled in on gurneys, and no one could tell me anything about them. My worst fear was that we'd gotten to them too late. They'd been given goren daily to keep them subdued, and I had no idea what the long-term effects of that would be.

When I wasn't thinking about my parents' health, I was fretting over Finch being alone at the apartment. I had to get them to release me today so I could go home and tell him about Mom and Dad. I prayed there would be good news to tell him.

The one thing I refused to think about was Lukas and his men, and their betrayal. It shouldn't hurt as much as it did, but the pain in my heart was all too real.

I did allow myself to think about Faris, who was the real victim in all of this, and I sent up a prayer to his goddess for his recovery. *Aedhna, I don't know how this works or if you can hear the prayers of a human, but please, take care of Faris. He's been through hell, and he could use some happiness.*

Reaching to adjust my pillows, I winced at the pain in my back, another reminder of my night in shackles in a cage. *Oh, and if you feel like doling out some divine justice today, I have a list of names you can start with.*

"Miss James?"

I looked toward the door to see an Indian doctor in a white coat enter my room. He appeared to be in his forties with graying hair and wire-rimmed glasses. My stomach lurched at the sight of the folder in his hands because I knew he was here to talk about my parents.

He walked over and held out a hand. "I'm Dr. Reddy. How are you doing?"

"I'm good, or I will be when I know what's happening with my parents."

Dr. Reddy smiled. "I've been overseeing your parents' care since they were brought in. They're malnourished and dehydrated, but none of the scans showed any internal injuries. We've started them on fluids and a strong cocktail of drugs to help with the goren withdrawal. They have a long road ahead of them, but I see no reason why they won't make a full recovery."

I put a hand to my mouth as emotions crowded my chest. "When will they wake up?"

"Not for several weeks. It's different for everyone." He must have seen my dismay because he said, "Goren is not like human opioids, meaning it doesn't just affect the receptors in the brain. It saturates organs at the cellular level, making the body physically unable to function without it. The detox drugs flush the body over time, but the initial withdrawal is very painful. Keeping your parents sedated now is the humane thing to do."

I nodded to let him know I understood. As much as I wanted to talk to my parents, I couldn't bear the thought of them in pain. "Will they be able to come home when they wake up?"

"No. They'll be confused and disoriented from the drugs, like a patient coming out of surgery, and that will last two or three days. After that, they will be transferred to a treatment facility in Long Island for detox, which can take up to six months. But it's one of the best facilities in the country for goren detox."

"Six months?" Heaviness settled over me. "Dr. Reddy, I don't think we can afford that."

He smiled, and he had kind eyes. "Your parents opted into the Agency's medical insurance for your family, which provides one hundred percent coverage. You don't have to worry about the costs."

I sagged against my pillows as my body relaxed for the first time since his arrival. "Can I go see them?"

"Tomorrow. They're in the ICU right now, where we can closely monitor them overnight. If they respond well to the drugs, they'll be moved to a ward tomorrow."

I didn't ask him what would happen if they didn't respond well to the drugs. I would focus on the positive and worry about the rest when I had to. My parents were safe and getting the treatment they needed. That was all that mattered.

"When can I go home?" I needed to get home to Finch. I couldn't wait to see his face when I told him the good news.

"Tomorrow."

I sat up straighter. "I can't stay here overnight. My little brother has been home alone since yesterday." Had it really only been a day since I'd been taken from the flea market? It felt like I'd been down in that basement for a week, maybe because of how much my life had changed in the last twenty-four hours.

Dr. Reddy's brows furrowed. "Your brother?"

Before he could get it into his head to call child protective services, I explained Finch was a sprite. If the doctor thought it was strange that I called Finch my brother, he didn't mention it.

He pursed his lips. "It's standard procedure to keep you overnight, but that is just a precaution. I'll check your chart, and if it looks good, I'll see about getting you discharged today."

He left, and I went back to staring out the window. My reverie was interrupted by a knock at the door, and I looked up as Agent Curry walked into the room. Despite the fact that he'd rescued me, he still wasn't on my list of favorite people. His sour expression said he knew that.

"Miss James, you look better than the last time I saw you."

"Thanks. I feel better. Shackles aren't a good look for me."

My attempt to lighten the mood was completely ignored. I was starting to suspect he didn't know how to smile.

"I came by to ask a few questions and to inform you that your parents have been cleared of any wrongdoing." He looked like he'd swallowed a bug, and I could tell it wasn't easy for him to admit he'd been wrong.

I quirked my eyebrows at him in an I-told-you-so expression, but I didn't rub it in. The guy *had* released me from a cage, and that earned him a free pass. This time.

"I'm very happy to hear that. What convinced you of their innocence?"

He walked over to stand with his back to the window. "We found enough evidence in the house to clear them."

"What kind of evidence?"

"That's part of an ongoing investigation, and I'm not at liberty to discuss it," he said in his imperious manner.

Of course not. I toyed with the sheet across my lap. "You never did tell me how you found the house. Did you know my parents and I were there?"

He nodded. "We received an anonymous tip that three bounty hunters were being held hostage there. After your abduction yesterday, it wasn't hard to guess who the hunters were."

"You heard about my abduction?"

"A female bounty hunter was attacked in a public place in broad daylight and thrown into the trunk of a car," he said dryly. "It made the six o'clock news."

My first thought was to wonder how Lukas could have seen that and still believed I was working with Rogin. The way Faolin monitored the news, there was no way they had missed it. But then, he'd probably dismissed the abduction and my voice mail as another ploy to trick him.

My second thought was to remind myself I wasn't going to waste another second of my time or energy on any of them. It didn't matter what Lukas's reasoning had been. He'd broken my trust in an unforgiveable way. They all had, and there was no changing that.

I twisted the blanket between my fingers. "Did you catch that piece of crap goren dealer while you were there? That would really brighten my day."

Agent Curry wore that sour look again. "Rogin Havas has disappeared, along with his sister, but they won't get far unless they go back to Faerie."

"Rogin is the one you want. Raisa just got caught up in his mess. She's the one who kept my parents alive this whole time, and I wouldn't be surprised if she was the one who tipped you off to where we were."

The Agent pulled out a small notebook and a pen. "How do you know all this?"

I told him about my conversation with Raisa, and the times I'd seen her in the last month that corroborated her story.

He asked me a bunch of questions, and he was particularly interested when I mentioned Rogin's connection to the lawyer.

"She said Cecil Hunt was her brother's partner?" he asked, jotting something down in his notebook.

"Yes. Does that mean anything to you?"

"Maybe," he replied vaguely, but the air of excitement around him told me it meant more than he let on. "Did she mention her brother and Hunt dealing in Fae antiquities?"

"What kind of antiquities?" I frowned. I thought we were talking about drug dealing.

He tapped the pen against his notepad. "Black market items. Cecil Hunt is being investigated for illegal trafficking of stolen property."

I thought back to my conversation with Raisa. "No, she never mentioned it."

"Are you sure? You've been through an ordeal and you might be forgetting details."

I clasped my hands together on top of my blanket. "Agent Curry, I can safely say I won't forget a second of my time as Rogin Havas's guest."

"Knock, knock," called Trey cheerfully as he and Bruce entered the room. Their smiles faltered when they saw my other visitor.

"We can come back," Bruce said.

Agent Curry closed his notebook and tucked it in his breast pocket. "No need. I was just leaving." He looked at me. "I'll need you to come in and give a detailed statement. The sooner the better."

"I will." The last thing I wanted to do was go to the Agency and spend hours being grilled by them, but there was no getting out of it. And if my statement could help them track down Rogin, it would be worth the trouble.

So far, I hadn't told him or anyone else about Faris or Lukas, but I'd have to when I gave my official statement. Right now, it hurt too much to speak of them.

As soon as the agent left, Trey set the vase of flowers he was carrying on a table and stood back to take in my bruised face and the pretty shiner I'd be sporting for a few days.

Remorse darkened his eyes. "If we'd only gotten there a few minutes sooner."

"It's not your fault." I swung my gaze to Bruce. "Neither of you. It was just bad timing. But I'd go through it all over again to find Mom and Dad."

Bruce's expression lightened. "How are your parents?"

"Not good, but the doctor told me they'll recover." I let out a heavy breath. "They were given goren every day, so detox is going to be hard."

"I heard," he said solemnly. At my questioning look, he said, "Levi talked to someone at the Agency."

"What about you?" Trey asked. "How are you doing, aside from the bruises we can see?"

I attempted a smile. "You know me. Takes a lot more than a goren dealer to keep me down. I'm waiting on the doctor to release me so I can go home."

Bruce frowned. "They aren't keeping you overnight?"

"They were going to, but I asked to go home, and they have no reason to keep me here."

"Is someone coming to pick you up?" he asked.

"Um..." I trailed off when I remembered I didn't have my Jeep or a ride home, or even my phone. "No."

Trey played with the remote to the TV I hadn't bother to turn on. "We'll take you home. Oh, and your Jeep is at the police impound, so it might take a few days to get it."

"Great," I muttered. One more thing I'd have to deal with.

Bruce laid a hand on my shoulder. "Don't worry about that now. All you need to focus on is you and your parents. Trey or I will take you to get the Jeep and whatever else you need." He pulled a familiar set of keys from his pocket. "All your keys are here except the one for the Jeep."

I swallowed around the tightness in my throat. "Thanks."

It was another thirty minutes before a nurse came in with my discharge papers. I was eager to get home to Finch, but I hated leaving my parents. What if something happened to one of them during the night, and I wasn't here? Knowing they were in the best possible hands didn't make it any easier to walk out of the hospital.

I was shocked to find reporters from two local TV stations waiting when I walked outside with Bruce. Trey and Bruce had told me the story about my abduction and rescue was on the news today, but I wasn't expecting this. I ignored their requests for an interview and hurried to Bruce's SUV, grateful Trey had gone ahead of us to get the vehicle.

"Don't mind them," Bruce said once we were all inside the SUV. "Prince Rhys is coming to town tomorrow, and he'll be all the press cares about."

"They do love their royals." I stared blindly out the passenger window as a fresh wave of bitter hurt washed over me. If I hadn't found out Lukas was Prince Vaerik, would he ever have told me? Or would he and his men – or should I say his royal guard – have kept up the lie?

Looking back now, I could recall multiple instances where his men had been overly protective of him. I remembered Faolin jumping in front of him that night outside the Ralston when he thought I was reaching for a weapon, and how angry he'd been when he'd dragged me to Lukas's for interrogation. I couldn't forget how Conlan had reacted when I'd told him about the threat on Vaerik's life or how fast he and Faolin had gotten to the diner. A snippet of our conversation that day came back to me.

"Are you in service to the crown, too? And Lukas?"

"All of us are."

I scowled at my reflection in the window. I'd been such a fool, and it stung.

Before I knew it, we were pulling up in front of my building. I thanked Bruce and Trey for the ride home and assured them I didn't need them to come up with me.

"You call if you need *anything*," Bruce said when I opened the door to get out.

"I will. Thanks again."

They waited for me to enter the building before driving away. I hurried upstairs so Mrs. Russo wouldn't come out to intercept me. She had to have heard about what happened on the news, and she would have lots of questions I didn't feel up to answering.

Holding my vase of flowers in one hand, I unlocked the apartment door with the other. I'd barely taken two steps into the apartment when a small blue body tackled my leg.

"I'm happy to see you, too." I set the flowers on the table and picked up Finch, who was whistling and signing so fast I couldn't keep up. I put him on the table so I could remove my jacket. "Slow down, Finch."

He let out a sharp whistle and slowed his hand movements. *Where are Mom and Dad? On the television, they said Mom and Dad were at the hospital. Why didn't they come home with you?*

"Mom and Dad have to stay in the hospital for a while." I'd forgotten he liked to watch TV when he was home alone. Of course, he would have seen the news stories.

Why? he asked fearfully.

Wearily, I pulled out a chair and sat. "They're going to be okay. But they were given something that made them sick, so they have to stay in the hospital to get better." Finch didn't understand drugs, so it was no use trying to explain goren to him.

His eyes grew round. *The bad people gave them poison?*

"Kind of."

He stomped his tiny foot. *Did you get the bad guys?*

I rubbed my eyes. "No. But they're gone, and we don't have to worry about them anymore."

Good. He gave me an expectant look. *Can we go to the hospital to see Mom and Dad?*

"We'll go tomorrow. The doctor said no one can see them tonight."

His shoulders drooped, but he nodded. *Are you okay, Jesse? You look sad.*

"I'm just tired. It's been a long day." Normally, I could hide my emotions from him, but I could feel all my defenses coming down. "I'm going to shower, and then we'll have dinner."

In my room, I moved about in a daze from the mental and physical exhaustion. I showered and dried my hair on autopilot, and then I heated up a frozen meal for my dinner.

Finch signed excitedly about seeing Mom and Dad as he ate his fruit, and I tried to work up the same enthusiasm. I was overjoyed to have them back, but my happiness was marred by thoughts of the difficult journey they had ahead of them. When I'd imagined finding them, I'd never considered a scenario where I couldn't talk to them or where it would be months before they could come home.

After my meal, I decided to turn in early since I could barely keep my eyes open. I went to double-check that the door was locked, and it occurred to me that Lukas and the others could enter the apartment whenever they wanted. I doubted I'd see any of them again, but I hated the thought of anyone being able to come in here uninvited.

I heaved a sigh and headed for bed. First thing in the morning, I would call a locksmith and hire a faerie to put up a new ward to keep Prince Vaerik out of my home and out of my life.

Now I just needed to find a way to get him out of my heart.

A soft whistle pulled my attention from the crossword puzzle I was working on. I looked at Finch, who sat on Mom's pillow, stroking her hair.

Will she wake up soon? he asked.

Remember what I told you? I signed back so no one could hear me. *The doctor said Mom and Dad will be asleep for a while so they can get better.*

Finch's eyes grew sad, and he nodded. *Do you think they know we're here?*

I'm sure they do.

He returned to touching Mom's hair. He'd been like that since we'd gotten here this afternoon, going back and forth between our parents.

There were four beds in the room, but the other two were empty, which was fortunate because sprites weren't allowed in the hospital. I'd had to sneak him in and warn him to hide whenever someone entered the room. With the number of visitors in and out of here today, he'd spent most of the time hidden in a huge basket of flowers on the table between the beds.

All day, bounty hunters and friends had been dropping in to check on our parents, and the room was full of flowers and get-well cards. Even Levi

Solomon had stopped by with flowers and to tell me there'd be jobs for me when I was ready to go back to work.

I hadn't really thought about what would happen with the hunting after I found my parents. But with them unable to work for six months, maybe longer, I decided it would be best for me to keep doing it. I told myself I was doing it to keep their license from expiring, but the truth was I liked the work and I was good at it. And how else would I earn the money I needed for college?

I set aside the puzzle book I'd brought with me and stood. My bruised body ached from sitting still too long, and I rolled my head to ease a crick in my neck.

Finch watched me curiously, and I signed, *I'm going to get a coffee. I won't be long.*

I didn't bother to tell him to hide if anyone came in. It was close to the end of visiting hours, and we hadn't seen anyone besides the nurses in a while. It was also New Year's Eve, and most people were out celebrating.

The floor was almost deserted when I left the room and walked to the nurses' station, where a middle-aged nurse named Patty smiled and asked if I needed anything. Everyone working on this floor had been so supportive since I'd gotten here. They had all heard the story about my parents' and my abduction and rescue – or at least as much as the media had reported – and they were all rooting for my parents to get better. They were even letting me spend the night here with Mom and Dad.

"Is there a coffee vending machine on this floor?" I asked her. I needed a caffeine boost, and I was even willing to pay for crappy coffee.

Patty smiled warmly. "There's a machine one floor down."

"Thanks." I took the stairs to the floor below, needing to stretch my legs, and found the machine. The coffee was even worse than I'd expected, making me wish I had some of the good stuff Trey had given me. I made a face as I sipped it before I started back upstairs.

I emerged on the floor and stopped so fast I almost spilled my coffee when I spotted a tall, dark-haired man standing outside my parents' room on the other end of the hall. From this angle, he could be Lukas, and my stomach fluttered from a mix of dread and something else I didn't want to define.

The man walked away in the other direction, and my mouth went dry. He even moved like Lukas.

I hurried toward the nurses' station. "Do you know who that man was?"

Patty looked around. "What man?"

"I saw him by my parents' door, but he left."

She smiled. "There have been so many people in to visit your parents today that I've stopped noticing them. He might have been another one of their bounty hunter friends."

"You're probably right," I said, ignoring a prick of disappointment. It wasn't that I wanted to see Lukas after what he'd done. It was a normal reaction to someone I used to care about, and it would go away in time.

A chilling thought crept into my head. What if the man I'd seen was one of the Seelie guards who had tried to have my parents killed? There was nothing to stop the royal guard from coming after my parents. How could I protect Mom and Dad from someone that powerful?

My mind automatically went to Lukas, but he was no longer a safe haven for me. That had all been an illusion I let myself believe because it had given me comfort when I was alone.

Tennin. I'd ask Tennin for help. Maybe he could put a protective ward on my parents, or he could give me the name of someone else who could. Or there might even be someone listed in Mom's contacts at home. One way or another, I had to keep my parents safe until they were well enough to take care of themselves.

Finch was nowhere in sight when I entered our parents' room. The flowers in the basket moved, and he jumped onto Dad's bed.

Was there a man in here a minute ago? I signed.

No.

I set my coffee down on the table beside my crossword puzzle book just as the last person I expected came into the room.

Shock filled me, followed by a burst of joy. "Violet! What...? How...?"

My best friend ran at me and hugged me so tightly she nearly squeezed all the air from my lungs. For a little thing, she had a tight grip.

"How did you get here?" I wheezed.

She released me. "I charmed the nurses, and they let me in."

"I mean what are you doing in New York? I thought you guys were staying in China for another week."

"Right. Like I was going to stay on the other side of the world after I heard what happened." She hopped up on one of the empty beds. "I made Mom book me on the first flight I could get."

I sat beside her. "I'm so glad you're here."

My voice broke on the last word, and she leaned over to pull me into another hug. The dam holding back my emotions cracked, and for the first time since my parents had disappeared, hot tears rolled down my cheeks.

I shook from the release of all the pent-up fear and pain, while Violet held me and rubbed my back. I was hiccupping, and my eyes felt puffy when I was finally cried out.

Violet, ever prepared, pulled a tissue from her handbag and passed it to me. "Feel better?"

"Yes." I wiped my eyes and blew my nose. "I'm sorry for all the waterworks."

"Damn, girl, if anyone is entitled to cry, it's you. If I'd been in your place, I would have been a blubbering mess weeks ago."

I let out a tremulous laugh. "Or you would have learned to carve a shiv at the very least."

She grimaced at the reminder of our stay in the police holding cell. "Thank God your hot faerie friend sprung us from that place."

All my good humor fled at the mention of him. Violet saw the change in me and handed me a fresh tissue. "Okay, tell me what I don't know."

Lowering my voice, I told her everything that had happened from the moment I was taken from the flea market to now. I left nothing out, and she alternated between shocked gasps and sounds of outrage. When I described how excited I'd been to see Lukas and what had followed, she started muttering, "That asshole!" under her breath.

"That's all of it." I looked down at my lap so she couldn't see how much it hurt to relive that horrible moment.

Violet reached out and took one of my hands. "You cared about him."

I nodded mutely without looking up. I'd known it was stupid to fall for someone like him, but I'd done it anyway. And he'd broken my heart, just like I'd known he would.

"Oh, Jesse," Violet whispered.

I lifted my head to smile at her. "Live and learn, right?"

She looked contemplative for a moment. "I think that maybe he cared for you, too."

"How can you say that after what he did?"

"Hear me out. Up until yesterday, he kept running to your rescue and taking care of you when you were sick. Those are not the actions of someone who doesn't care."

"You didn't see him in that basement or hear the way he spoke to me." My stomach tightened painfully at the memory. "If you had, you wouldn't say that."

She squeezed my hand. "He thought you betrayed him. I'd be hurt, too, and pissed if I thought you lied to me."

"That's where you're wrong." I jumped off the bed and faced her. "You would never turn on me the way he did, or think I was capable of the things he accused me of. All it took was the word of a drug dealer for him to believe the worst of me. He didn't even stop to think that Rogin could have planted that tablet at my place to save his own ass."

She smiled sadly. "I didn't say he was smart. He's a prince who is used to people fawning over him. He got butthurt and lashed out at you, and I bet he already regrets it."

"I don't care if he's the king of England. He lied to me about who he was, and then he turned around and called me the liar. That hypocrite." I ground my teeth as anger replaced the pain. I didn't like feeling this way, but it was better than hurting. "Now, can we please talk about something else?"

Violet told me about her visit with her grandparents until she started to yawn, worn out from her long flight. I suggested she take a nap on one of the empty beds, and she was fast asleep in minutes. Finch had dozed off on Dad's shoulder an hour ago, leaving me alone with too many heavy thoughts.

A check of the time told me it was close to midnight, so I turned on the TV, with the volume low, to watch the ball drop.

Last New Year's Eve, I'd been there in Times Square with my parents and Violet, blissfully unaware of what was to come. A lot had changed this year, me most of all, but at the end of it, I still had the people I loved most in this world. Maybe I really was goddess-blessed.

"Five, four, three, two, one...happy New Year!"

The Times Square crowd shouted and cheered as "Auld Lang Syne" began to play. I'd always loved that song, but tonight it made me a little forlorn.

Violet snored loudly, and I laughed, shaking off my melancholy. Looking around the room at my sleeping loved ones, I felt an intense surge of gratitude to have them here with me. As much as Lukas had hurt me, I wouldn't change a thing that had led to my parents coming home. I'd do it all again for them in a heartbeat.

A flash outside caught my eye, and I walked over to the window to watch the sky light up with fireworks, a few miles away. My chest felt lighter with the promise of a brand-new year. It was a time to make a fresh start, and I was going to do exactly that.

I smiled at my reflection in the window and sucked in a breath when I saw the outline of a tall woman with long, silvery hair standing behind me. Heart pounding, I whirled around, only to find no one there. I ran to the door of the room and looked both ways, but the hallway was empty except for two nurses at the nurses' station.

Great, I'm losing my mind. I smiled sheepishly as I returned to the room. It was more likely that I was running on too little sleep.

Turning off the television, I lay down on the last free bed and closed my eyes. I thought about Faris and sent up another quick prayer to his goddess that he recovered from the horrible things that had been done to him. Regardless of my feelings toward his friends, I wished the faerie nothing but the best.

I was somewhere between REM and deep sleep when my body felt like it was cocooned in warmth, and a sense of peace settled over me. I sighed as a gentle female voice filled every crevice of my mind.

"I think you will do nicely, Jesse James."

~ The End ~

ABOUT THE AUTHOR

When she is not writing, Karen Lynch can be found reading or baking. A native of Newfoundland, Canada, she currently lives in Charlotte, North Carolina with her cats and her three adorable rescue dogs: Dax, Des, and Daisy.

Made in the USA
Coppell, TX
25 February 2021